THE NANCY DREW FILES™
COLLECTOR'S EDITION

YOUR INVITATION TO INTRIGUE

Join Nancy Drew as she follows a trail of mystery and danger into a world of unexpected twists and startling discoveries.

Straight from the Nancy Drew Files, here are the stories that have made Nancy one of America's hottest teen detectives.

She's a master at catching criminals in the act. Now you can catch *her* in action—in three sensational mysteries!

Books in The Nancy Drew Files™ Series

Available from ARCHWAY Paperbacks

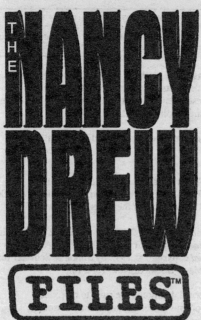

THE NANCY DREW FILES™

COLLECTOR'S EDITION

THE WRONG TRACK
NOBODY'S BUSINESS
RUNNING SCARED

CAROLYN KEENE

AN ARCHWAY PAPERBACK
Published by POCKET BOOKS
New York London Toronto Sydney Tokyo Singapore

These titles were previously published individually.

An Archway Paperback published by
POCKET BOOKS, a division of Simon & Schuster Inc.
1230 Avenue of the Americas, New York, NY 10020

The Wrong Track copyright © 1991 by Simon & Schuster Inc.
Nobody's Business copyright © 1992 by Simon & Schuster Inc.
Running Scared copyright © 1992 by Simon & Schuster Inc.
Produced by Mega-Books of New York, Inc.

ISBN: 0-671-01931-7

First Archway Paperback printing November 1998

10 9 8 7 6 5 4 3 2 1

NANCY DREW, AN ARCHWAY PAPERBACK and colophon are registered trademarks of Simon & Schuster Inc.

THE NANCY DREW FILES is a trademark of Simon & Schuster Inc.

Cover design by Jim Lebbad
Cover art by Franco Accornero

Printed in the U.S.A.

IL 6+

THE WRONG
TRACK

Chapter

One

"Wow!" Nancy Drew exclaimed, peering out the window at the snow swirling in wintry gusts. "It's really coming down!"

"That's terrific," her friend George Fayne said from where she lay sprawled on her living room floor, a bowl of popcorn at her elbow. "The trails at Tall Pines could use it," she said.

Nancy brushed her silky reddish blond hair behind her ears and pulled her royal blue sweater tight around her. "You've got skiing on the brain," Nancy joked, turning to face her friend.

"She sure does," Bess Marvin, George's cousin, agreed from the sofa. "Pass the popcorn, George."

"What about your diet?" George grinned.

Bess tossed back her long blond hair and snatched at the bowl. "It's low-cal," she insisted, popping a handful into her mouth. "No butter."

1

Nancy smiled at Bess and George. For cousins, they couldn't be less alike. Dark-haired George was tall with an athlete's slim build. She was into bicycling and skiing. Bess was short and blond, and the sports she was most into were shopping and trying to stick to the latest fad diet.

"Are you guys ready to watch this?" George asked, holding up a videocassette. She read out loud from the back of the box. "'Tall Pines—the Midwest's newest, biggest, most luxurious cross-country ski resort. State-of-the-art trails. Fully loaded exercise rooms. Spa. Sauna. Three-star restaurant and lodge—'"

"Now those last two I could go for," Bess said, reaching for the video.

George held it away from her. "'Private banquet rooms for conventions. Heated indoor pool.'"

"This place sounds like too much," Nancy said. She plopped down on the floor next to George to study the picture on the cassette box. Nestled in a deep valley of thick green pines, Tall Pines lived up to its name. The complex—which consisted mainly of cedar and glass buildings— was beautiful. "I can see why you want to work there," Nancy said to George.

George popped the cassette into the VCR and pressed Play. "I know I can teach skiing, and as soon as I memorize this video, there's no way they won't hire me!"

"What ever happened to Rob Watson's place?" Bess asked, stifling a yawn.

Bess was referring to a resort north of River

Heights where George had always gone cross-country skiing before.

"What about Watson's trails?" Nancy asked George. "Aren't they as good?"

George shrugged, her eyes glued to the TV screen as the video came on. "Sure. I guess the trails are as good, but Rob hasn't got all the extra stuff Tall Pines has."

As Nancy watched the video, she saw that George was right. She'd been to Rob's a few times, and it couldn't begin to compare to the luxury Tall Pines had to offer. Rob's was basically just a few trails and a snack bar. Nancy wondered if he was losing business to the new resort already.

She was about to ask George when the doorbell rang. George stopped the video and got up to answer the front door.

Nancy could spy a tall, brown-haired girl talking to George in the hallway. The girl seemed upset, and George was trying to calm her down. Finally she put an arm around the girl and led her into the living room.

"Nancy, Bess," George said, "this is Rebecca Montgomery. Rebecca, this is my friend Nancy Drew and my cousin Bess Marvin."

"Nice to meet you," Rebecca said, her voice unsteady. She was very pretty, with intense brown eyes and a cascade of soft brown hair. Dropping her purse from her shoulder to her hand, Rebecca perched on a nearby rocking chair.

George sat down next to Bess on the sofa.

3

"Rebecca hooked me up with the guy who's interviewing at Tall Pines."

Rebecca smiled a little, but Nancy was watching her hands as they twisted nervously in her lap. The girl was obviously upset.

"Rebecca's in trouble," George said softly, confirming Nancy's suspicions. "I told her you might be able to help."

"What kind of trouble?" Nancy asked.

"Should I tell them, or do you want to?" George asked Rebecca.

The girl swallowed a few times. "You go ahead," she said, unzipping her black and white parka. Shivering slightly, she held her hands out toward the warm blaze in the fireplace.

"Tell us what?" Bess asked, her blue eyes round with curiosity.

"Rebecca works in the office at Tall Pines." George ran her hands through her short, curly brown hair. "Or used to work there. She got fired."

Nancy saw Rebecca flinch at the word *fired*. "What happened?" Nancy asked.

"Someone stole fifty thousand dollars from the resort's safe," Rebecca moaned, "and left two thousand of it in my purse!"

"Oh, no!" Bess exclaimed softly.

"I didn't do it," Rebecca said to Nancy. "I didn't steal that money."

"Of course you didn't," George put in. She rested her elbows on her knees and squinted, deep in thought. "But somebody sure wants to make it look like you're a thief."

4

Nancy hopped up and began to pace the room, her arms crossed in front of her. Her detective instincts were on red alert, and her mind raced with questions.

"What happened, exactly?" Nancy asked politely.

Rebecca took a deep breath and plunged in. "I'm the bookkeeper at Tall Pines. It's my first job out of school. I'm lucky to have it"— Rebecca paused—"or at least I *was* lucky." Her eyes dropped to her lap. "Oh, what am I going to do?" she said suddenly, tears filling her eyes.

"Nancy'll help," Bess assured her. "She's a crack detective and will find out what happened."

Bess beamed at Nancy, and Nancy wished her friend hadn't said she'd take the case. That should be her decision to make. "Thanks for the vote of confidence," she said graciously to Bess anyway. She turned to Rebecca. "Tell us about it. Take your time."

Rebecca nodded, wiped the tears from her eyes, and went on. "The computerized payroll system wasn't working, so we had a lot of cash in the safe in Dave's office to pay the employees. Fifty thousand dollars, to be exact. The same afternoon that the money disappeared, three weeks ago, two thousand dollars of it turned up in my purse. I was so shocked when I found it, I didn't know what to do. I did report it, though—" Rebecca broke down again.

"And they accused you?" Nancy guessed.

Rebecca nodded her head slightly. "Not right

away, but Karl Reismueller—he's the owner of Tall Pines—told me this morning that the police and the insurance investigators both decided that there's enough evidence to indicate I could be involved. The serial numbers on the money I found in my purse matched the numbers on the money missing from the safe. And none of the other money has turned up!

"Reismueller said he wouldn't press charges against me," Rebecca continued, the words spilling from her now. "He doesn't want the publicity. He did say he had to fire me, and he wouldn't give me a reference, either."

"That's terrible," Bess said, biting on a fingernail. "You'll have a really hard time getting another job without a reference."

Rebecca swallowed several times. "Don't I know it," she said. "You've got to help me. If I don't work, I can't pay back my student loans."

George got up and went over to Rebecca. "Don't worry." She put a hand on the girl's shoulder. "Nancy will help, won't you, Nan?"

"You bet I will," she said, happy with her decision now. "You've got to start at the beginning and tell me everything. And I mean everything."

Late the next morning Nancy was ready to pull her blue Mustang out of her driveway with George, Bess, and Rebecca there to see her off.

"See you later!" George said with a wave. "And I've decided not to try for a job while we're there. I'll just be a guest."

Bess grinned and pulled her bright red beret down over her blond hair. "Don't forget—we've never seen you before in our lives!"

Nancy laughed and shifted the car into reverse. "Don't worry, Rebecca," she called out the window. "We'll find the real thief, and you'll have your job back in no time."

Rebecca smiled wanly. "Good luck," she called back.

Before heading off Nancy took one last look at her friends. They'd be seeing one another later, but she'd be undercover and have to pretend not to know them. Instead of Nancy Drew, teen detective, she was going to the resort as Nancy Drew, teen reporter for *Tracks,* a cross-country skiing magazine.

After hearing Rebecca's story the previous day Nancy had realized that she wouldn't get anywhere investigating without a cover. Apparently Karl Reismueller had decided Rebecca was the thief, and that was that. The police had closed their investigation, since Reismueller wasn't going to press charges.

When Nancy decided to go undercover, her father, Carson Drew, arranged a cover story with an editor of *Tracks.* Tall Pines was expecting her and would have all kinds of tours and lessons planned for her week's stay. The publicity in *Tracks* would be good for the new resort.

Bess and George were coming up later in the day, and they were going to stay at Tall Pines, too. But Nancy would have to pretend she didn't know them.

As she pulled her Mustang onto the highway that led north to Tall Pines Nancy smiled to herself. It was a great day for a drive. The roads had been plowed, and the two hours it would take to get to Tall Pines should be time enough to plan her strategy. After Rebecca's explanation the day before, Nancy was more sure than ever that the girl hadn't stolen the money. Anyone with forty-eight thousand dollars wouldn't be so worried about how to pay off student loans. But then who had taken the cash?

Nancy mentally went over the short list of names Rebecca had given her: Dave Kendall, Rebecca's boss and the manager of Tall Pines; Karl Reismueller, the owner; Ben Wrobley, a ski instructor; and Jody Ashton, a friend of Rebecca's who ran the ski shop.

According to Rebecca, Ben and Jody had been in her office the morning of the theft. They had come by to see if their pay envelopes were ready. Dave and Karl both had offices next to Rebecca's, and supposedly they were the only ones who knew the combination to the safe where the money was kept.

Still, any one of them could have taken the fifty thousand dollars and stashed two thousand dollars of it in Rebecca Montgomery's purse, especially since Rebecca had left the office at least twice that day. One time she had had to drop off a computer printout at the front desk, and the second time Dave had asked her to take an envelope over to Karl Reismueller's condo.

Nancy stopped thinking about the money and

turned on the radio. It felt great to be back on a case, even if she had to work alone. What she wouldn't give to have Ned with her, though. Ned Nickerson, her longtime boyfriend, was away at college, and she saw too little of him during the school year.

A full-blown image of Ned popped into her mind just then. She could almost feel his strong arms around her, his breath on her face, his lips . . .

The sound of a horn blaring sent Nancy's foot to the brake. She had drifted over into the far lane. Better be more careful, Nancy told herself as she steered the Mustang back. Save thinking about Ned until after you've solved the mystery.

A couple of hours later Nancy turned onto a narrow, winding country road that was far more picturesque than the highway. After less than half an hour Nancy was turning into the entrance of the resort. The private drive curved gently away from the road and was lined with tall pines, their shapes softened into white triangles by the fresh snow.

Nancy drove past the parking lot to the main lodge. "Wow!" she said to herself softly.

The resort was even more breathtaking in real life than on the video. All of the buildings were made of cedar and glass, and no two were identical. A two-story lodge dominated the complex. Nancy pulled to a stop in front of the lodge, slipped on her green parka, and slid her hands into mittens that matched the purple stripe on her green ski pants.

9

Her car was driven to the visitor parking lot by an employee as she made her way inside. "Wow again," she whispered, taking in the wide expanses of glass that flooded the area with light and gave awesome views of the surrounding pines. At the back of the room a dozen guests were sitting in twos and threes at tables around a roaring fireplace. To her left the registration desk bustled with activity. Along the same wall as the fireplace Nancy noticed a large display window filled with colorful ski clothing. A hand-lettered sign told her it was part of the Tall Pines Gift Shop.

Within a few minutes Nancy had checked in, leaving her luggage with a bellhop. The clerk at the registration desk directed her to the Tall Pines offices and said Dave Kendall was waiting for her there.

"If you go out the front, the administration building is directly across from us," the clerk explained. "You can't miss it."

Nancy thanked him. She had no trouble finding the small A-frame building across from the main lodge. She closed the door behind her and looked around. After the bustle and noise of the crowded main lodge, the offices were eerily silent. She was in the reception area, and there were two doors off a main hallway to her right. One, she knew from Rebecca's description, was Dave's office, where Rebecca had also had her desk. The other was Reismueller's.

Before Nancy could knock on either door, the one on the right flew open.

10

"I know what's going on here," a dark-haired young man with a muscular build shouted as he stormed out of the office. Nancy caught his angry expression and saw that his fists were clenched at his sides.

She heard the deep rumble of a voice responding to the young man but couldn't make out the words.

"If you think I won't tell anyone," the dark-haired young man yelled, shaking his fist, "you're wrong, Dave Kendall. Dead wrong!"

Chapter

Two

THE ANGRY YOUNG MAN strode past Nancy without seeing her. He was about to storm out the front door when an older man with brown hair came running after him.

"Come back here, Ben!" the older man yelled. "You can't go around making accusations like that."

Nancy stood still. Ben? She wondered if the dark-haired young man with the muscular build was Ben Wrobley.

"That's where you're wrong, Kendall!" the young man shouted. Without waiting for an answer he flung open the front door and strode outside, letting the door slam behind him.

For a moment there was silence. Then Nancy cleared her throat. "I'm Nancy Drew," she told the older man. "The desk clerk told me you were expecting me. I can come back later if this is a bad time."

The man smiled and extended his hand to shake Nancy's. "Come right on in, Ms. Drew. I'm Dave Kendall, general manager here at Tall Pines."

So this was Rebecca's former boss, Nancy thought. Taking a closer look, she judged Kendall to be in his midthirties, his brown hair graying at the temples. Though his voice was cordial, she could sense the anger just beneath his perfect smile.

"Let me apologize for what you just overheard," Kendall said, leading the way down the hall to his office. "That young man can get a bit overexcited."

Nancy nodded noncommittally but kept her thoughts to herself as Dave led the way into his office. The room was large and bright, with three skylights cut into the roof. The furniture consisted of two ultramodern desks, several chairs, and a row of matching filing cabinets. On top of the center filing cabinet was a huge vase of orchids. Kendall caught Nancy looking at them.

"My passion," he confessed. "I love fresh flowers." He motioned Nancy to a chair in front of his desk. "We're so glad you're here at Tall Pines. A write-up in *Tracks* is just what a new business needs." Dave leaned back in his chair. Though he appeared relaxed, Nancy felt the tension in him left over from his encounter with Ben. Nancy wondered just what kind of accusation Ben had been making, and if it involved the theft.

"It looks to me as though Tall Pines is doing pretty well," Nancy commented, remembering her cover.

"That's true. We are," Dave admitted, smiling. "But I want to make sure people come back. Resorts depend on repeat customers as well as new ones." The resort manager paused, and his tension seemed to ease as he continued talking. "I'm proud of this resort," he said with conviction. "Tall Pines isn't an average cross-country ski place."

"No, it's not," Nancy agreed. "How many guests can Tall Pines accommodate?" she asked, taking out a notebook and scanning the list of questions she'd prepared.

Kendall's smile was wide and proud. "We're an intimate place. There are one hundred condos, as well as one hundred rooms in the lodge. Skiers who come here know the trails won't be crowded. They appreciate that and pay well for the special treatment we offer. I've put together a packet of brochures for you. They should answer any of your general questions."

Nancy was about to comment when she heard the door to the lobby open and the sound of boots stomping off snow.

Dave stood up and walked to his door. "Good morning, Karl," he called to the newcomer. "Nancy Drew is here."

"Good day," said a deep voice. Nancy turned in her chair and watched a tall man stride into the room. He bowed from the waist in greeting. "I'm Karl Reismueller." As Nancy rose to shake hands with the owner of Tall Pines he took her hand in his and shook it gently.

"Welcome to Tall Pines, Ms. Drew," Karl added in a voice that bore a slight German accent. "I hope you will enjoy your stay here." He ran a hand through his blond hair, which had distinguished wings of silver at the temples.

Nancy smiled. "I'm very glad to be here, Mr. Reismueller," she said honestly.

Karl sat on the edge of the desk and faced Nancy, staring at her intently with his crystal-blue eyes. "Call me Karl, please."

"Karl," Nancy said, blushing. Reismueller really knew how to turn on the charm.

"I would have liked to have given you a tour of Tall Pines myself," Karl went on, "but I have some pressing business matters." He gestured with his right hand. "I've asked an employee, Jody Ashton, to take you around. She manages the gift shop and the ski shop and knows Tall Pines very well."

Jody was Rebecca's friend, Nancy remembered. She'd also been in the office the day of the theft. Nancy smiled to herself that she was able to spend a couple of hours with her.

Nancy thanked Karl. "From what I've seen, Tall Pines is extremely beautiful," she said.

"Once you get out on the trails you'll see the real Tall Pines," Dave told Nancy. "We'll get you fitted with some of our best skis, and you can check out the trails."

"That'll be great," Nancy said.

"Wonderful!" Karl said with a smile, glancing at his watch. "And now I'm afraid I must excuse myself. I'm expecting an important phone call," he explained. He stood up and took Nancy's hand in his once more. "I hope you'll join my wife and me for dinner this evening at the Edelweiss, which is our largest restaurant. Would eight o'clock be convenient?"

Nancy nodded, and Karl left them. Dave studied his own watch. "Let's find Jody," he said, putting on a forest-green down jacket. As he turned to pick up his gloves Nancy saw the Tall Pines logo—two pine trees—emblazoned on the back of the jacket.

Dave led the way back to the main lodge and into the gift shop that Nancy had noticed when she registered. As they entered chimes announced their arrival.

A girl with short, curly auburn hair stepped out from behind the counter. "Hi, Dave," she said, smiling at them. "And you must be Nancy Drew. Karl told me you'd be coming."

"This is Jody Ashton," Dave told Nancy. Jody had a slim, athletic build, the greenest eyes Nancy had seen, long black lashes, and high, aristocratic cheekbones. She was dressed in an oversize wool sweater with the Tall Pines emblem and a pair of matching forest green warm-up pants.

"I'd better get back to the office," Dave said. He gave Nancy a smile that didn't quite reach his eyes. "I'm sure you'll have more questions. When you do, you know where to find me."

Nancy thanked him, and Dave left. She turned to Jody, who appeared to be nervous as she blinked several times.

"I don't know what to say," Jody finally managed to get out, giving Nancy a forced smile. "I've never met a reporter before."

Nancy grinned. "I promise not to write anything incriminating about you," she joked.

Jody seemed afraid for a second and then laughed nervously. "Let me get my jacket, and I'll show you around," she said.

Nancy waited while Jody found her cap and gloves and told the girl she was working with that she'd be leaving for a while.

"This way," Jody said, pointing to a door that opened directly to the outside. She led the way back to the front of the lodge. "That's the Edelweiss," she said, gesturing to a second-story deck that jutted out above the lodge. "If you have a chance to eat there, take it. The food is out of this world."

They walked toward a large building with one solid wall of glass. Inside Nancy could spy an Olympic-size pool. "Wow!" she said.

Pushing open the front door of the building, Jody led the way into the exercise complex. "Neat, huh?" she said. "The pool's still not filled with water," she explained. "It was supposed to be open yesterday, but now they're promising it'll be ready this afternoon."

Nancy followed Jody. From inside the pool room she found herself looking out onto a forest of stately pines that stretched to the sky.

Jody was already walking around the pool to a pair of doors along one side of the wall. "The locker rooms are here," she said, leading the way. "Women's locker room," Jody pointed out, "private showers, fully stocked with all-natural bath and beauty products."

The lavender and forest green locker room, equipped with thick towels and expensive bath products, was much fancier than any locker room Nancy had ever seen. Jody smiled at her. "Our guests want luxury, and they get it. There's also a sauna and an exercise room," Jody told Nancy. "Both coed. Now if you'll follow me, I'll show you one of Tall Pines's most popular attractions."

Outside the girls made their way up a narrow path that had been shoveled in the fresh snow. A short distance from the building Nancy saw steam rising from among a grove of pine trees.

"What's that?" she asked Jody.

"Check it out," Jody said with a raised eyebrow.

Nancy laughed out loud when she discovered the source of the steam. It was an outdoor hot tub with a couple of people in it. "I'm definitely going to make time for this," she declared.

Jody laughed. "I thought you'd like it." She led Nancy down a tree-lined driveway, pointing out a one-story, modern wooden building on their right. "Some of the staff live here," she said. "A lot of employees commute, but some live too far away."

"Do you live here?" Nancy asked.

"No. I live in an apartment in Monroe with my mother. It's a little town about ten minutes away." Jody smiled, showing her pearly, even teeth, and pointed to her left. "That path leads to a frozen pond. It should be great skating, and it will even be lit at night. It's not quite done yet but will be soon."

Nancy followed Jody along a road that curved around the lodge. At the back of the curve Nancy caught sight of a cluster of A-frame buildings in a small clearing. Like the main lodge, each one had a second-story deck and wide expanses of glass.

"Awesome!" Nancy exclaimed. "These must be the condos." Jody nodded. "They're gorgeous. I can see why Mr. Reismueller is so proud of them."

"Then you've met Karl," Jody said, her striking green eyes flashing.

"He was very charming."

"Let me guess." Jody chuckled. "He played his German prince role: the accent, dinner with him and Sheila, the whole bit."

Nancy laughed and took a key from her purse. "You guessed right," she said, checking the number on the key. "I think this one's mine."

They had stopped at the third building. "Karl Reismueller is a walking gold mine," Jody went on. "He has more businesses than I can count, and they're all successful."

As they entered her condo Nancy whistled

softly. "This is fabulous!" The main living area was thickly carpeted and had a huge fireplace that dominated the back wall. A bedroom, kitchenette, and bath completed the first floor, and a sleeping loft filled the second story. There were flowers everywhere, Nancy saw, remembering Dave Kendall's weakness for them.

"No wonder Mr. Reismueller is so successful," Nancy said. "He certainly knows how to treat his guests."

"He could take some lessons on how to treat his employees," Jody said half aloud.

Nancy turned, struck by the bitterness in Jody's voice. "Oh, really?"

Jody's face flushed with embarrassment. "That's off the record," she said.

"No problem," Nancy told her, mentally storing the item away. She glanced at her luggage, which the bellman had brought in, and decided to unpack later. "I'd like to go pick out my skis."

"Sure," Jody said, leading the way back to the rear of the main lodge. "There's the school, and next to it is where we rent equipment," Jody told her. "There's a snack bar, too. The food's good but cheap. Most of the employees eat there."

Nancy took the opportunity to turn the conversation to Rebecca. "I heard you lost an employee recently. Didn't your bookkeeper leave?"

Jody stared at Nancy, her green eyes suddenly angry. "Rebecca didn't leave. She was fired. Personally, I think she probably deserved it."

"What do you mean?" Nancy asked, surprised by Jody's sudden hostility.

Before Jody could answer, a girl ran up to them. "Jody! There you are! I've been looking all over for you." She stopped next to Nancy and Jody. "Michelle's having a problem with the cash register, and she's got customers waiting."

Jody turned to Nancy. "Will you excuse me for a minute? I'll meet you at the ski shop as soon as I'm done."

As Nancy walked slowly toward the shop she tried to make sense of Jody's anger. Why was she so hostile toward Rebecca? Rebecca thought Jody was her friend. If so, Nancy would have expected her to be sympathetic toward Rebecca.

Unless Jody was the person who framed Rebecca, Nancy thought as she stomped the snow off her boots before entering the ski shop and ski school complex. The sign above her head told her that the shop was to the left and the Inge Gustafson Ski School was to the right. Jody seemed friendly enough, but Nancy had learned not to be taken in by charm. And Jody *had* acted nervous when Nancy had jokingly commented about not writing anything incriminating.

Inside, the entrance alcove seemed dark after the dazzling sunshine on the clean snow. Her eyes took a minute to adjust to the darkness.

"I'm sick and tired of this setup!" Nancy heard a masculine voice declare in the ski school to her right.

She stopped. She'd heard that voice before.

"Unless something changes soon," the man went on, "you'd better start looking for another sucker."

Nancy heard what sounded like the thump of a fist on wood. "I'm not going to put up with this much longer." There was no doubt about it. The voice belonged to the same young man who had been shouting at Dave less than an hour before.

"I've got choices," he reminded his listener. "I can always work at Rob Watson's. At least *he's* honest."

Chapter
Three

NANCY'S EYES WIDENED. Twice now she'd heard the dark-haired young man making threats about something that was going on at Tall Pines. She drew in a deep breath and stepped out of the alcove and into the ski school, resolving to find out what he knew.

When she saw that the young man was shouting at Karl Reismueller she was shocked. The two men were standing next to a black potbellied stove. The young man's face was red with anger.

Reismueller spotted Nancy first. "Come in, Nancy," he said, his voice honey smooth and charming. He gestured toward the tall, black-haired young man. "Have you met Ben Wrobley? Ben, this is Nancy Drew, a reporter from *Tracks* magazine," he added importantly. "Ben's one of our best ski instructors."

23

Ben's shoulders stiffened. He glared at Karl before reaching out to shake hands with Nancy. "Nice to meet you," he said gruffly.

Nancy's investigative instincts began to race. Ben seemed anything but pleased with Karl's compliment. There was a lot of tension between the two men, and Nancy hoped she'd get a chance to question Ben—alone—to find out why.

Ben stared at Nancy for a moment, his dark blue eyes assessing her. "So you're the reporter," he said slowly. "You'll find a lot to write about here."

"All good, I hope," Karl quipped, giving Nancy another of his charming smiles.

"Of course." Ben made no attempt to hide his sarcasm.

"I'd like to interview you for the article, if that'd be okay with you," Nancy said to Ben.

After shooting Karl an icy look Ben told Nancy, "I'd be glad to tell you everything I know." The emphasis was on "everything," and Nancy felt her heart begin to beat faster.

"Can I arrange a private lesson?" Nancy asked. "We could do the interview on skis."

Ben shrugged. "I'm booked for the rest of the day. How about tomorrow morning? Nine o'clock?"

"Nine's fine," Nancy said.

At that moment the door to the school flew open and Jody Ashton rushed inside.

"Sorry I had to leave you," Jody said breathlessly, hurrying over to Nancy. "Are you ready for the rest of the tour?"

24

"I see you're back in good hands," Karl said to Nancy, "so I'll leave you. Don't forget, dinner tonight at eight."

When the door had closed behind Karl Ben raised an eyebrow at Nancy. "Aren't you lucky? Dinner with the great man." His lips curled in disgust.

"Mr. Reismueller has been very pleasant to me," Nancy said in her most professional manner.

"I'm sure he has," Ben shot back. "After all, you're a guest."

His words echoed what Jody had said, and Nancy had to wonder if a disgruntled employee could be responsible for the theft. Someone like Ben, for instance.

"I couldn't help overhearing your argument when I came in," Nancy said to Ben, taking out her notebook. "Why would you want to work for Rob Watson? The Tall Pines trails are a thousand times better than Rob's."

Ben flushed, glancing nervously at Nancy's notebook. "I was only joking," he said, pausing. "Rob doesn't have the kind of money Karl does. He wouldn't be able to pay me what I'm worth. But there would be one good thing about working at Watson's." Ben's blue eyes were serious as he met Nancy's. "Rob's not impressed with Scandinavian names like Inge."

"What do you mean?" Nancy asked, puzzled. She wondered if Ben was referring to Inge Gustafson—the name on the sign for the ski school. The name did seem familiar to her, but she couldn't place it.

Jody shifted from one foot to the other as though she were uncomfortable with the conversation. "Ben's just blowing off steam, aren't you, Ben?" she asked, giving him a warning look and changing the subject. "Don't you have a class?"

"Yeah," Ben replied, clamping his mouth shut. He stepped over to a row of lockers along one wall, opened one, and pulled out his ski clothes. His jacket bore the familiar Tall Pines insignia.

"What's going on?" Nancy asked Jody under her breath. "Who's Inge, and why is Ben so upset about her?"

Jody became even more uncomfortable. "It's no big deal," she told Nancy. "Karl hired Inge Gustafson, a Norwegian skier, to head the ski school."

Nancy nodded, realizing now why she'd thought she remembered the name. "I've heard of Inge. She's good." She had scanned a couple of back issues of *Tracks* to prepare for her cover, and one of the stories had been on Inge. "So what's the problem?"

"There *is* no problem," Jody insisted. "Inge's just delayed in coming over, and Ben's had to take on some of her work."

Nancy heard Ben slam his locker door. The ski instructor turned to face them. "Try *all* of her work," he said, and he headed out of the school.

Jody tried to smile brightly. "Ready to get fitted?" she asked, changing the subject.

"You bet," Nancy replied. She followed the girl

back through the entrance alcove and into the ski shop. Two walls of the shop were lined with new skis, boots, and poles, and a third was reserved for the rental area. A huge glass window filled the fourth wall. Nancy spotted Ben through it. His lesson had obviously started because he was in the middle of a group of skiers. There were a couple of other ski instructors outside, too, their Tall Pines logo jackets clearly visible. Ben skied over to talk to one of them for a moment.

Jody stepped over to a low counter next to the skis where a cashier stood. She came back with a tape measure. The girl worked quickly, writing down Nancy's height and shoe size and the length of poles she'd need. When she finished Jody said, "I'll make sure everything's ready for you tomorrow morning. Sorry I can't show you around anymore, but I have to get back to work."

"No problem," Nancy told her. "I think I'd like to rest a bit before dinner, anyway. Maybe take a sauna or check out that hot tub," she added with a grin.

"Good idea!" Jody said brightly. "See you later!" With a wave, she took off.

Nancy spied Ben taking his students off onto a trail and realized there was nothing more she could do for now. She yawned, realized that she really was a little tired, and decided to head back to her condo to unpack and rest before dinner. Bess and George should be arriving soon, she thought. Maybe she could find a way to talk to them before dinner.

* * *

Later Nancy had finished unpacking and was lying on her bed on top of the luxurious down comforter when the phone rang.

"Yes?" she answered in her most professional voice. "This is Nancy Drew."

"You mean the famous reporter from *Tracks*? You're my idol!" came George's familiar voice, laughing. "How's it going, Nan?"

"Fine, just fine." Nancy twirled the cord between her fingers.

"Have you learned anything yet?" George asked eagerly.

"No, but I have met Karl, Dave, Ben, and Jody."

George whistled over the phone line. "Wow! You were busy. Do you think any of them framed Rebecca?"

"I don't know," Nancy admitted. "Jody seems to hate her, but I don't know why yet." Nancy told George about Jody's reaction when she'd asked about Rebecca's being fired. "What's really interesting, though, is that Ben Wrobley has a major grudge against Tall Pines, and he talks as though he knows something shady's going on. I wonder if it's about the money."

George was silent for a moment. "Rebecca introduced me to Ben, and I skied with him once since the theft. But I never heard him say anything about it."

"Do you know why he's so unhappy at Tall Pines?" Nancy asked. "Why he resents Inge Gustafson so much?"

"Well, he's got good reason." George paused.

"Ben's a great skier and a terrific teacher, but what does he get for it?" She answered her own question. "Nothing. Inge gets all the credit and her name on the school, but she hasn't even shown up yet. Ben's doing his job and hers."

Nancy could understand why Ben was angry. The question was, was he angry enough to steal fifty thousand dollars? And why would he frame Rebecca for the theft? What could he have against her?

"Keep an eye on Ben, George," Nancy advised. "If you run into him, see what you can find out."

"Right," George said. "Hey, why don't we all meet in the sauna? Bess said she wanted to try it out."

"Great idea!" Nancy said. "But remember, if there's anyone else there, act like you don't know me."

"Nancy who? Who's ever heard of a Nancy Drew?" George joked, and she hung up.

Nancy laughed, got up, and quickly slipped into her parka and boots. On her way out she grabbed a gym bag, which already had her bathing suit and towel in it. The snow crunched under her feet as she made her way toward the fitness building. She was climbing the steps to the back entrance of the building when she was stopped by a familiar voice.

"Going to the pool?" Nancy turned to see Dave Kendall a few feet away. "I don't think it's open yet," he added.

She shook her head. "I'm trying the sauna."

Dave's smile was earnest. "I hope you're enjoying your stay so far."

"Oh, I am," Nancy assured him. "I wanted to ask you—"

Before she could finish her question Dave interrupted. "Why don't we schedule some time to talk? I'm sure you want to get into the sauna now." He stomped the snow off his boots. "How about tomorrow afternoon? Right after lunch?"

After Nancy nodded Dave waved and walked off. That's odd, Nancy thought as she watched him retreat. It was as if Dave hadn't wanted to talk to her.

Storing the thought away, Nancy entered the sauna and exercise area. There she was greeted by a friendly attendant wearing a forest green uniform. "I hope you enjoy our facilities," the attendant said as she handed Nancy a locker key and an oversize towel.

A minute later Bess and George joined Nancy in the locker room, and Nancy and Bess changed into their bathing suits while George put on sweats. George was going to work out and join them in the sauna afterward.

"This is a great place," Nancy said as she closed the door to the sauna and sat on a wooden bench.

"It sure is," Bess agreed. She leaned back against the wall and took a deep breath of the hot, dry air. "Wonderful," she murmured.

For a few minutes the girls relaxed in silence, letting the heat of the sauna work its magic.

Finally Bess opened her eyes and looked at

Nancy. "George told me you've been busy," she said.

Nancy laughed. "I guess I have. But not busy enough. I still don't know what Ben's so angry about, or why Jody hates Rebecca."

Bess was about to speak when they both heard someone at the door. Nancy held her finger to her lips, warning Bess to be quiet. She didn't want to get caught talking about the mystery. Bess nodded. When no one entered the sauna after a minute or two, Nancy shrugged.

"So what do we do next?" Bess asked, getting back to the case.

"We have to find out more about both Ben and Jody. You and George can help with that, because you're not pretending to be reporters. Jody's careful about what she says to me." Nancy leaned back against the wall. "I'm having dinner with the Reismuellers tonight. Why don't you and George come to my condo afterward, say around ten? We can work out a plan then."

Bess nodded and stood up. "I'm starting to feel cooked," she said, pulling her towel around her. "Let's go." She walked the three steps to the door and pushed on the handle.

"Nancy, the door won't open," Bess said, pushing on the handle again, surprise showing on her face.

"Push a little harder," Nancy suggested. "It's new. Maybe it just sticks."

Bess pushed. "Nancy, it doesn't work." This time her voice betrayed her mounting panic. "It's locked."

"That's strange," said Nancy, frowning. "Sauna doors don't have locks."

She came up beside Bess and tried the handle herself. The door wouldn't budge. She tried kicking the door. Still nothing.

Bess's face was flushed. "We've got to get out of here!" she cried. "I can't take this heat."

Nancy felt her own temperature rising, and she knew they couldn't stay much longer. Her eyes scanned the walls for a thermostat to turn the heat down. Nothing.

"The controls must be on the outside," she told Bess, trying to keep her voice calm.

"Oh, Nancy!" Bess wailed. "What are we going to do?"

Nancy pressed her face against the small window in the door and peered through it to the right and left. What she saw made her heart sink. Someone had wedged a piece of wood between the door and the frame.

They were locked in!

Chapter

Four

HELP!" Bess shouted. "Somebody help!"

Nancy leaned against the door again and shoved, hoping to dislodge the wedge of wood. Nothing happened.

"We'll never get out of here!" Bess wailed.

"We'll get out, Bess," Nancy said with quiet determination. "There are lots of people around. Someone has to hear us shouting."

Bess gave Nancy a weak smile. "You're right," she said, wiping the sweat from her forehead. "I just hope that someone comes soon. I need to lose five pounds, not twenty," she joked. "Help!" she cried again, banging on the door.

At that moment Nancy heard footsteps outside the door and a loud scraping noise. Finally the door swung open.

"Thank goodness!" Bess flung herself out of the sauna and into the cooler air.

George was standing there, dressed in her sweats with a towel around her neck and a wedge-shaped piece of wood in her hand. "Why was this stuck in the door?" she asked, concern in her brown eyes.

"Someone barred the door," Nancy answered, shrugging her shoulders. She put an arm around Bess. "Maybe it was just a prank. Whoever did it must have known somebody would come along to let us out."

"I'm just glad it's over," Bess said. Nancy felt her friend start to shiver. "I'm ready to put on some clothes and grab a bite to eat. After that experience I need to rebuild my strength."

"I want to ask the attendant if she saw anything before I change," Nancy said. "And I'm going out to dinner tonight."

After Bess and George went into the locker room Nancy searched for the attendant. She found her sorting towels outside the locker room. As Nancy told her what happened the attendant became deathly white, and her eyes grew round.

"I left for only a minute. There were a lot of guests around," the girl told Nancy with a nervous shrug. "I'll keep my eyes open, though. That could have been dangerous!"

Nancy left her and went into the locker room to join Bess and George, but they had already gone. As Nancy changed she thought about the wedged door. Did the person who had done it want to trap her and Bess or someone else? Maybe it was just a prank played by someone who wanted to cause trouble at Tall Pines.

If the person was after Bess and Nancy, who knew they were going to be in the sauna? There was Jody, who had suggested it, and Dave Kendall, who saw her entering the building. Either one of them could have jammed the door. But why? It made no sense. As far as everyone at Tall Pines knew, Nancy was a reporter for *Tracks*, not a detective. Who would want to harm a reporter?

Unless . . . There was a possibility that her cover was blown and someone knew she was at Tall Pines investigating the theft. If so, Nancy could be in danger.

The air was cold with a hint of snow as Nancy headed back to her condo. It was seven-thirty; she'd barely have time to dress for dinner. She settled on a pair of black trousers and a teal blue silk blouse. A quick brush through her hair and a dash of pink lipstick and she was ready to go.

Nancy entered Edelweiss, just before eight. Crisp white linen cloths covered each table, and crystal glassware and silver flatware gleamed in the candlelight. Karl Reismueller greeted her just inside the door.

"Good evening," he said in a deep voice. "I'd like you to meet my wife, Sheila."

Sheila Reismueller was tall, thin, and stunning. She had dressed in a stylishly short rose-colored dress, and her champagne blond hair was swept up into a sophisticated French twist. Her hand was perched on her husband's arm, and Nancy thought the two of them made an elegant couple.

"I'm glad to meet you, Mrs. Reismueller,"

Nancy said. As she shook Sheila's hand Nancy noticed her perfume—roses and lilies with a hint of something spicy.

"Call me Sheila," the woman said, her blue eyes sparkling.

"And I insist you call me Karl. 'Mr. Reismueller' makes me feel a hundred years old."

The maître d' showed them to a table by the windows. When the women were seated he unfolded their napkins with a flourish.

"May I bring you an appetizer?" he asked.

Karl ordered fondue. "That's a fancy name for bread and melted cheese," he joked. "Where I'm from we always have it after a hard day's skiing."

"This is a gorgeous restaurant," Nancy said. Karl Reismueller's showmanship was obvious. Both the front and back walls of the restaurant were windowed. Several of the trails were lit, and the view was magnificent.

The waiter brought their fondue, and they set to dipping the toasted bread into the steaming pot of melted cheese. Nancy remarked on the vases of fresh roses on each table. "The flowers are wonderful," she said.

"You can thank Sheila for them," Karl said with a fond glance at his wife. "She insists that we have fresh flowers every night."

"It might seem to be an extravagance, but I just love fresh flowers," Sheila said. "That's why we named the restaurant Edelweiss."

Nancy remembered the orchids in Dave

Kendall's office and asked Sheila if she was responsible for them, too.

"No," she said, laughing lightly and fingering a large horseshoe-shaped pin on her left shoulder. Nancy assumed those were real diamonds covering the pin's surface.

"Dave deserves the compliments," Sheila said. "Indoor gardening is one of his hobbies, and, as you saw, he's awfully good at it."

"Dave's also a good manager," Karl added as the waiter cleared the fondue pot from their table. "He's responsible for whatever success we're having." Nancy noticed Bess and George taking seats at the table next to them.

Sheila turned to Nancy. "My husband is too modest," she said. "He's the genius behind this and our other businesses. Why, his printing company is the biggest in the state, and his chain of toy stores just keeps growing." She laid her hand on his arm. "Isn't that right, Karl?"

Karl frowned slightly. "Let's not bore Nancy, Sheila," he said. "Tell me, have you had a chance to ski any of the trails?"

Nancy shook her head. "I'm skiing with Ben at nine tomorrow morning, though."

"You and Sheila ought to ski together," Karl said. "She knows the trails as well as any instructor at Tall Pines."

"I'd like that," Nancy agreed.

"It'll have to be the day after tomorrow," Sheila told Karl. "I have several appointments tomorrow."

Taking a sip of water, Nancy turned to Karl. She decided it was time to get whatever information she could on the theft. "I heard about the theft you had here," she said. "I understand the police weren't able to recover most of the money."

Sheila's face grew pale. "That was the last thing we needed, more money prob—"

"We feel we know who took the money," Karl interrupted smoothly, "but have decided not to press charges. The publicity would be far too damaging. I certainly hope," he added with a rueful smile, "that nothing about that unfortunate incident will end up in the pages of *Tracks.*"

Nancy smiled and offered a quiet no. She did wonder whether Sheila had started to say "money problems." She hadn't heard of any at Tall Pines.

Before Nancy could ask any more questions, Karl moved on to the subject of Tall Pines's other attractions. As they ate their filet mignon followed by baked Alaska and coffee he amused them with anecdotes about the resort and its opening.

"Thank you for a lovely meal," Nancy said as they were leaving. "The Edelweiss will get a great write-up in our magazine."

Karl smiled, his white teeth glistening in the candlelight. "Now, that's what I like to hear!" he said. "Come, Sheila." He pulled back his wife's chair and took her arm. "This has been a long day. Come see me tomorrow, Nancy, if you like. You know where to find me."

Nancy waited for the elegant couple to leave the dining room before motioning to Bess and George, who were still sitting at the table next to hers. "See you at my condo in ten minutes," she whispered softly as she passed by them.

The three friends were in the living room of Nancy's condo, and she was just finishing telling them what she thought Sheila Reismueller was going to say before her husband had cut her off.

George had built a small fire while Nancy talked, and Bess was curled up in one of the oversize chairs.

"I don't see how it fits into the case," Nancy admitted, "but I want to check it out."

A frown crossed George's face. "We're here to clear Rebecca," she reminded Nancy.

Nancy nodded. She had a plan ready. "I want to follow up with Ben. I need to find out what kind of shady things he thinks are going on here, so I've scheduled a lesson with him tomorrow morning." She turned to Bess. "Would you cover Jody? Find out if there's any reason she needs money. And also find out why she seems to hate Rebecca so much."

Bess grinned. "No problem. I wanted to check out the ski shop anyway."

George raised a questioning eyebrow. "What should I do?"

Nancy thought for a moment. "Why don't you go over to Rob Watson's lodge tomorrow and see what you can find out there?" Nancy continued explaining. "Tall Pines is Rob's biggest rival. He may be trying to sabotage the resort."

"It's a real sacrifice, you know, leaving Tall Pines to go to Rob's," George said with a laugh.

"Let's meet here again tomorrow night," Nancy suggested as the girls were leaving.

Nancy stood in the doorway and watched them walk off toward the main lodge, where they were staying. Snow had started to fall lightly. As she went back inside she decided to check out Dave Kendall's office, where the theft had occurred.

Three whole weeks had passed, and Nancy knew she was probably wasting her time but felt a need to check it out anyway. She grabbed her ski parka and within a few minutes was at the Tall Pines administration building. Making sure no one was around, Nancy gently shoved against the front door. She was surprised that it was open.

Also surprising was the light streaming out from under Dave's office door. Someone was in there.

Nancy decided that at that time of night it was probably a cleaning crew. Then she heard someone speak and recognized the man's voice as Dave's. She was wrong—Dave was working late. As she was planning her next move the outside door to the building was flung open, and a blast of cold air rushed in. Nancy turned, wondering who was coming into the office so late.

A short, stocky man in black ski clothes stomped snow from his feet, then stopped as soon as he noticed Nancy. For an instant neither of them spoke. Nancy's eyes widened in recognition. It was Rob Watson! She'd seen his photograph in a back issue of *Tracks*, and the ruddy face, bright blue eyes, and long, curly white hair were unmistakable.

"What are you doing here?" Nancy demanded.

The man swiveled his head from Nancy to the door behind him.

"What's going on?" Nancy asked again.

Before Nancy could stop him Watson spun around and raced out the door.

Chapter

Five

WHAT WAS Rob Watson doing sneaking around Tall Pines at night? Nancy wondered, running to the door.

"What's going on?"

Nancy was stopped by Dave Kendall calling to her from the open doorway of his office. "What are you doing here?" he demanded brusquely.

Nancy ignored his question. "Rob Watson was here a minute ago, but when he saw me he ran out," she explained.

"Watson?" Dave grimaced. "What was he doing here?"

"I don't know," Nancy replied, shrugging her shoulders. "Maybe he came to check out his competition."

Rob's appearance at Tall Pines was definitely strange, and Nancy couldn't help wondering whether it was connected to the theft. She doubted Rob would have stolen the money himself but thought he could be working with a Tall Pines employee.

Kendall brushed off the question with a shake of his head. "I doubt it." Then he paused and studied her curiously. "Is there a reason *you're* here so late?" he asked Nancy.

"Actually, th-there is," Nancy stammered, searching for an excuse. The last thing she wanted was for Dave to think she was snooping around his office. She quickly explained about the accident in the sauna.

"I'm sorry that happened to you," Dave said, showing obvious concern. "I'll tell the attendant to be on guard." Nancy thought she heard Dave mumble something about "not again."

"What was that?" she asked.

Dave looked at her carefully, squinting his eyes. "I don't want this to be published—"

"Off the record," Nancy assured him.

"We have a prankster here at Tall Pines," Dave confessed. "Nothing serious, but this isn't our first incident. I was just dictating a short memo to Karl about it."

He opened his mouth as though he was going to say something more but stopped instead and took a breath. When he spoke again his words were measured. "I hope you understand that none of this is to get around," he said. "If Karl finds out I told you, he'll fire me."

Nancy nodded. Though she might need to tell Karl about the blocked sauna door, she had no reason to divulge Dave's confidence. Maybe he was right. Maybe it had just been a prank and not meant specifically for her and Bess.

Before nine the next morning Nancy met Jody at the rental office to pick up her skis, boots, and poles.

"I wish the new equipment had come in," Jody said when she handed Nancy her gear. "You'd go crazy over the new boots and bindings. They're state-of-the-art material. Really lightweight. Plus the boots go up over your ankles, which offers extra support."

"I've heard about them at *Tracks,*" Nancy fibbed. "I've been dying to try them."

"We're expecting a shipment any day," Jody told her. "With a little luck it'll arrive before you leave, and I'll make sure you get a set."

"Morning, Ben," Nancy said, spotting the instructor in the entrance alcove. "Ready for my lesson?"

Ben smiled and pushed a lock of his jet-black hair off his forehead. "You bet," he said.

Picking up her skis and poles, Nancy followed him outside to the trail head. A small crowd of guests had gathered by the trail map. Ben greeted several people by name before hooking his boots into the bindings. Nancy noticed that he had new bindings, and his boots were higher than hers.

"Ready?" Ben asked.

"Don't expect a lot," Nancy said as she slipped her hands into the pole straps. "This is my first time out this season." She looked down at her clothes. She was wearing a cherry-red outfit. "When I first learned to ski we wore jeans and parkas. Now it's neon speed suits and high-tech equipment."

Ben chuckled and led the way to what he said was one of the most popular trails. "I like to ski this one before it's crowded."

Though a light snow had fallen overnight, the tracks, which had been set the previous day, were still visible. As Ben gracefully skied into the left pair of tracks Nancy placed her skis in the right ones. "Not all our trails have two sets of tracks," Ben explained, "but it's easier to teach on them."

Nancy was a little nervous that Ben might notice she hadn't skied in a while. A reporter for a ski magazine should look pretty good on the trails. Although it took her a few glides to get used to her new equipment, Nancy was soon moving at a pretty good pace. "These skis are great!" she exclaimed, noticing that they glided farther than any she'd tried before.

They skied until they were deep in the forest. "You're good at the diagonal stride," Ben said, referring to the basic cross-country kick and glide. He tugged his zipper pull up, and Nancy noticed that hooked to it was a small thermometer. "The conditions are just about perfect. Do you want to learn to skate?"

Nancy was confused. "I thought this was a skiing lesson."

"I wasn't talking about ice skating. This is ski skating." While Nancy watched he took his left ski out of the track and pushed forward with it and his poles. A second later, he was gliding gracefully along the trail on his right ski.

"Wow!" Nancy said when Ben turned and whooshed to a stop in front of her. "That looks like fun."

"It is," he assured her. "Now watch. Your left ski is the skate ski. You push with that one and glide on the other. The trick is all in shifting your weight."

"You make it look easy."

Ben grinned. "It is—once you learn how."

As she practiced the new technique Nancy realized what a good instructor Ben was. Not only was he an expert skier, but he knew how to explain the movements. At the end of a few minutes Nancy felt confident trying to skate.

When they reached a hill Ben suggested she use a herringbone step to climb it.

"I didn't know there were hills around here," she said as she put her skis in the V position. Instead of gliding she stepped up the incline, keeping the tips of her skis far apart while the tails remained close together to prevent her from sliding backward.

"There weren't any hills until a few months ago," Ben told her. "Karl brought in bulldozers to contour slopes. He wants Tall Pines to be the perfect resort."

"But that's impossible, isn't it?" Nancy asked. This was the opening she needed. "For example, I heard you had a robbery here."

Nancy could feel Ben's eyes on her. When he

finally did reply, his voice was cold. "It's nothing for you to worry about. I know you reporters like sensationalism, but you don't have to put that in your article."

"We heard about it around the office," she pressed, ignoring his comment. "Why do you suppose that girl took the money?"

They had stopped moving and were standing side by side now. Ben's anger was apparent to Nancy. "Did you come here to ski or to ask questions about Rebecca Montgomery?"

He sounded almost hostile now, and Nancy sensed she'd touched a nerve. He certainly hadn't minded bad-mouthing the resort the day before. She didn't know why Ben wouldn't want to talk about Rebecca now, unless he knew something about the theft.

She shrugged. "News is news," she said. "For example, it might be news to our readers that I heard you talking to both Dave and Karl yesterday, and it was pretty obvious that you felt something's very wrong at Tall Pines."

Ben studied Nancy for a long time. "Nothing's wrong," he said. "Nothing a ski reporter would be interested in," he added for emphasis.

Nancy wondered whether Karl had spoken to Ben, warning him not to talk to her. "Come on, Ben," she said. "I don't believe that."

He shrugged. "It's true," he declared. "Now if you don't mind, I'd like to ski." The finality in Ben's voice told Nancy that she'd learn nothing more from him that morning.

They made their way back to the school in

silence. As they approached the end of the trail, Nancy said, "I may want another lesson. When do you teach?" What Nancy really wanted to know was Ben's schedule, and if he could have locked her and Bess in the sauna.

Ben smiled. "I'm pretty busy. We'd have to schedule a lesson early if you want to go out again." He glanced at his watch. "To tell you the truth, Nancy, I don't think you need another lesson. You're good."

Nancy laughed. "Thanks. I may need some pointers, though, because I want to try all the trails before I leave."

They skied to a stop, and Nancy released her bindings. "Are you Ben?" she heard a familiar voice ask. It was Bess, dressed in new ski clothes and carrying skis and poles over one shoulder. There was no risk of losing Bess in the woods, Nancy thought with a smile, not with her neon pink pants and green and orange jacket!

"Can you point me to a novice trail?" Bess asked Ben.

He gave her an appraising glance. "Do you have a partner? If you're a beginner, you shouldn't ski alone."

Bess shrugged. "My cousin deserted me for the day."

Turning to Nancy, Ben suggested, "Why don't you go with her? You said you wanted the practice."

"Sure," Nancy said. Skiing with Bess would give her a chance to find out if her friend had learned anything from Jody. She gave Bess a knowing look. "I'm always happy to have a ski partner. I'm Nancy Drew," she said, holding out her gloved hand.

"Bess Marvin," Bess said.

"Can you suggest a quiet trail?" Nancy turned to ask Ben.

He pulled a trail map out of his pocket. "Take Aerie," he said, showing Nancy the route. "You'll see a small hut here, and another trail branches off it." He pointed to the trail junction. "Be careful not to go on that one. You'd be able to handle it, but Cascades is too difficult for a beginner."

Nancy thanked Ben. "No problem," he said. Just then Jody came out of the shop and school entrance and pulled Ben aside. "Excuse us," Jody said, smiling at Nancy.

"Ready?" Nancy asked Bess, who had been putting her skis on with Nancy.

Bess nodded, and the two of them skied over to where the track began. Once they were safely out of sight Nancy asked Bess, "Did you have a chance to talk to Jody?"

"Not very much," she said. "There were a lot of customers when I went in so we made a date to meet for lunch." Bess reached forward with one pole and pushed off.

"You're doing well," Nancy said, skiing up next to Bess. Her eyes were on her friend, but her mind was on the mystery. She was scheduled to be at Tall Pines for only a week, so that gave her six more days to find the thief. Not a lot of time.

"Cross country's not as hard as I expected,

and the clothes are fun," Bess said, interrupting Nancy's thoughts.

When they reached the small hut Ben had mentioned Nancy stopped. "Check out the view," she said. Though it seemed that they'd climbed only a small distance, the forest ended right where they stood, and there was a drop in front of them.

"It's pretty," Bess agreed as she cautiously slid her skis backward. "I don't like the cliff, though. Let's go. It makes me feel dizzy."

Nancy looked at the trail signs: Cascade veered off to the right, Aerie to the left. The girls skied left.

"Whew!" Bess said a few minutes later. She was out of breath from climbing a small hill. "This is getting harder."

Nancy had to admit that Bess was right. For a novice trail, Aerie was very difficult. As they continued the trail grew narrower, and the second set of tracks ended. Instead of leveling out the trail continued to climb. Nancy slid her skis into the tracks behind Bess, calling out encouragement. "Just a little farther," she said, urging Bess to try the herringbone step.

When they reached the top of the incline Bess raised her poles in triumph. "I made it," she said, and her skis inched forward.

Before Bess could get her poles down and steady herself she was sliding quickly down the back side of the steep hill. Nancy gasped. The trail made a sharp right turn ahead, just before a skier would fly directly into a stream.

"Bess!" Nancy called.

It was too late. Bess was already careening down the trail, her arms and poles windmilling, headed straight for the rocky stream.

"Help!" Nancy heard Bess cry out. "Help me, Nancy! I can't stop!"

Chapter

Six

NANCY WATCHED in horror as Bess flailed her
arms, trying to get a grip in the snow with her
poles. At the rate Bess was going she would soon
land headfirst in the icy stream. Nancy's mind
raced for a solution.

"Let yourself fall, Bess!" Nancy shouted at her
friend.

Bess chose not to or couldn't make herself fall.
Instead she dragged her poles, trying to slow
herself down. She was less than fifty feet from the
stream.

Nancy knew she had to do something. Jabbing
her poles in the snow, she hurled herself forward
behind Bess.

The slope was incredibly steep, but Nancy
managed to keep her balance and gain on Bess.
Finally, when Nancy was right behind her friend,
she reached out and grabbed the back of Bess's

jacket and yanked—hard. The two girls fell, tumbling to the ground. When they came to a halt, Nancy saw the cold, rocky stream less than ten feet in front of them.

"That was close!" Bess said, breathing heavily. "If you hadn't pulled me down—" She stopped, and her eyes grew large with fear.

"Don't think about it," Nancy urged. She stood up on her skis and gave Bess a hand up. "Come on. I think we've had enough skiing for today."

Slowly Nancy and Bess made their way down the rest of the trail toward the head area. All the while Nancy tried to figure out what had happened. The trail she and Bess had ended up on was obviously not for novices. That meant that Ben had given them the wrong directions, or someone had switched the markers. Either way, she and Bess had been in danger.

"George!" Nancy heard Bess cry out when they finally made their way back to the trail head. "Oh, George, you'll never believe what just happened."

Nancy was surprised to see George at Tall Pines. She was supposed to have gone to Watson's for the day.

When Bess told her cousin what had happened, George let out a low whistle. "Sounds like more trouble for Tall Pines," she said.

Nancy nodded her agreement. Making sure that no one was around to overhear their conversation, Nancy said, "I want to check out what just happened. Do you have a trail map?"

George pulled one out of her jacket pocket and opened it up. "Here's where Aerie meets Cascade." Her fingers traced the trails back to the trail head. "I see how to get back there. Can you get back to the room by yourself, Bess?"

"Sure," Bess said. "It's time for my lunch date anyway," she said. Nancy and George waved and skied off. After a few minutes they were heading up Aerie. "What do you think happened, Nan?" George asked when they were alone.

Nancy slowed her pace. "I don't know, but I don't think it was an accident," she told George. "Especially after what happened in the sauna. Either Bess and I wandered into a trap set for somebody else, or someone's after me or Bess."

"But why?" George asked, panting slightly as they made an uphill climb.

"I'm beginning to wonder if my cover's been blown," Nancy said. "Maybe someone knows I'm a detective and wants to scare me off."

"Don't jump to conclusions," George warned. "You've always told me that's a sign of bad detective work."

Nancy laughed. "Okay. You're right. But what other reason could there be?"

"First we have to find out if the signs were switched, then who switched them. Then we'll have our reason for why the person did it," George said, pleased with herself.

Nancy was quiet as they took a slow downhill glide. At a flat part in the trail she stopped and said, "Ben knew where we were going. He could

54

have told Jody, too. I saw them talking together before Bess and I skied off."

"Ben seems to admire Rob Watson. What if they're working together to cause trouble at Tall Pines?" George asked. Then she shook her head. "What am I saying? He's too nice a guy to do anything like that."

"Hey," Nancy said, stopping short. "I nearly forgot. Did you go to Watson's this morning?"

"You bet I did," George replied. "I almost didn't recognize the place. Major construction. They're expanding the snack bar and upgrading the trails."

"It sounds like Rob's spending a lot of money," Nancy said.

"That's what I thought," George agreed. "He could have gotten a bank loan, or—"

"He could be behind the Tall Pines theft," Nancy finished. Nancy and George climbed the incline to the hut that marked the point where Aerie met Cascades. "Let's stop here," Nancy said. "I want to check something." She pulled George's trail map from her pocket to study it. It confirmed what she had guessed.

"According to the map, Aerie turns right, but the sign is pointing left." Someone had switched "Aerie" with "Cascades." Nancy carefully turned the signs so they pointed to the right trails.

"I can't believe Ben would do something like that," George said, frowning. "It must have been someone else."

Nancy didn't say anything. As George was speaking, she noticed something glinting in the snow. She bent closer, picked up the object, and whistled softly. It was a thermometer just like the one she'd seen attached to Ben's zipper. Silently she handed the tiny thermometer over to her friend.

George's expression was serious. "It does look like Ben's thermometer," she said, her voice a bit defensive. "But I'm sure there's a logical explanation. Ben wouldn't try to hurt you or anyone. Also, when would he have done it?"

Nancy put the thermometer in her pocket. "I hope you're right" was all she said.

The girls skied silently for several minutes, moving across a snow-covered meadow. The real Aerie trail skirted the edge of the man-made hill and went through a meadow rather than through the forest.

"That must be the ice-skating pond," George said as they approached a large open area. A half-finished building stood at the far end of the secluded frozen pond. Construction tape surrounded the pond to keep people out. Nancy remembered that the outdoor rink wasn't ready for guests yet.

As the girls skied past the ice two people emerged from the building being constructed. Nancy recognized the tall, slender woman in the shocking pink ski outfit as Sheila Reismueller. The man was a stranger. Seeing the furtive way that Sheila glanced around, Nancy quickly pulled George behind a bushy evergreen so Sheila wouldn't see them.

"He doesn't look like the normal Tall Pines visitor, does he?" George asked in a whisper. Instead of fashionable ski wear, the man was dressed in a black and white houndstooth suit, a black felt fedora, and an overcoat tossed casually over his shoulders. He would have looked more at home on a city street than at a ski resort.

Nancy nodded. "And Sheila looks like she doesn't want to be seen."

"I wonder what's going on," George murmured.

"Maybe he's a contractor," Nancy suggested, shaking herself. "I'm probably being paranoid because of the case." Perhaps Karl had asked Sheila to help with something, and that was why she hadn't gone to do her errands that day as she'd planned.

A few minutes later the girls resumed skiing and slid to a graceful stop at the end of the trail.

"I'm going to get some lunch," George said. "Want to join me?"

Nancy shook her head. "I have an apple to eat. Then I have an appointment to talk to Dave Kendall," she said. "Why don't you track Ben after your lunch? See what he's up to."

"No problem," George said. "He's the best instructor here. I wouldn't mind following him," she added with a smile. "Nancy, I really don't think Ben's involved, but if you want me to keep an eye on him, I will."

57

"Thanks, George," Nancy said. "If you see her, would you tell Bess to meet me at the pool at three? I want to find out if she got anything out of Jody."

"You got it," George said. With that, she skied off toward the Tall Pines ski school.

After removing her skis Nancy dropped them off at the rental counter and made her way to Dave Kendall's office. Even if he'd taken a late lunch, she thought, he should be back in his office by now.

The receptionist was away from her desk, but the door to Dave's office was open a bit, so Nancy walked to the door and started to call to him. She stopped herself as soon as she realized the man in the office was not Dave Kendall.

Intrigued, Nancy remained at the door, peering in. She watched as the man slid some papers off Dave's desk and into his backpack. A moment later he picked up the backpack and turned around, holding it in front of him.

It was Ben Wrobley!

Nancy pushed the door open and stepped inside. "Well, hello, Ben," Nancy said innocently.

"Nancy! What are you doing here?" There was no mistaking the nervous quaver in Ben's voice. It was obvious to Nancy that Ben hadn't wanted to get caught in Dave's office. What was the ski instructor up to? She was dying to ask him but knew it would totally blow her cover if she did.

"I wanted to interview Dave this afternoon," she said instead. "Is he around?"

Ben gestured toward the empty office. "Dave was called away."

"That's weird," Nancy said, making a face. "He asked me to meet with him this afternoon."

"It was an unexpected trip, he said." Ben smiled—a little too brightly, in Nancy's opinion. "Maybe he left a message for you with the receptionist." Ben must have noticed Nancy staring at his backpack because he mumbled, "Karl asked me to pick up a couple things from Dave's office for him."

Ben might be telling the truth, Nancy thought, but that didn't explain his nervousness when he had first seen her. Besides, after the scene she'd witnessed the day before in the ski shop, Nancy doubted that Karl would ask Ben to help him.

Ben took another step toward the door. "Dave won't be back for another hour," he told Nancy. It was obvious that he badly wanted to get out of Dave's office, but Nancy wasn't going to let him leave so soon. First there was something she had to check out. She moved forward quickly and pretended to stumble. Ben dropped his pack to help her steady herself. Nancy's eyes moved quickly to the front of his parka.

The thermometer that had been on Ben Wrobley's zipper pull was gone.

Chapter

Seven

"I HAVE SOMETHING of yours," Nancy said. Reaching into her pocket, she pulled out the thermometer and held it out to him.

Ben's face broke into a smile. "Thanks!" he said, taking it. "Where'd you find it?"

"Right where the Aerie and Cascades trails meet," she said, watching Ben's expression.

He shrugged, obviously unaware of the significance of what she had just said. "It must have fallen off this morning," he told her.

"Oh, really," Nancy said. "I remember that you looked at the temperature when we were out."

Ben nodded as he clipped the thermometer back onto his jacket. "True. I must have lost it afterward. My ten o'clock student canceled, so I tried to find you and Bess up by the hut where the trails meet. I guess it fell off then."

Ben's explanation sounded plausible, but Nancy still wasn't convinced. "Did you notice that the trail signs were switched?" she asked.

"What?" Ben's blue eyes widened in surprise. "That could have been dangerous."

"You bet," Nancy agreed. "The girl I was skiing with could hardly get down the trail."

Ben seemed to be outraged. "I'm going to straighten this out. We can't risk anyone getting hurt." His concern seemed genuine. Maybe George was right, and Ben wouldn't hurt anyone. But that didn't explain what he'd put into his backpack or why he'd been so secretive.

Ben zipped his jacket closed and slipped into the straps of his backpack. "Thanks for telling me about the trail signs being switched. I've got a class now, but afterward I'm going out to check *all* the signs."

With that Ben left, taking whatever papers he had stuffed into his backpack with him. Nancy was frustrated that she couldn't ask him any more questions about what he was doing in Dave's office, but the last thing she wanted was to blow her cover—especially with him. He was still a prime suspect as far as she was concerned.

Ben had given her one important fact: Dave wouldn't be back for almost an hour. That gave Nancy the chance to search his office.

Nancy scanned the office and decided that searching the files and desk drawers would be the best way to begin.

She sat down at Rebecca's desk and methodically went through each of the drawers. Nothing. Dave's desk was next. The top two drawers contained only routine business papers. Nancy started to leaf through the folders in the lower file drawer and found one labeled Rob Watson.

She pulled it out and began to read. The folder contained a confidential report about Rob's ski camp. Was this folder why Rob had come into the office building the night before?

Nancy guessed Karl had ordered the report before he built Tall Pines because he'd wanted to know what his competition was. According to the report, Rob's profits were minimal. So how could he afford the major construction George had seen?

Nancy glanced at her watch. Dave should be back in about ten minutes, and she didn't want him to find her in his office. She moved to the row of file cabinets and leafed through them quickly. Nothing unusual. There was a drawer of personnel files and one devoted to the building permits the county and state required.

Nancy was about to leaf through the personnel files when she heard a noise in the outer office. Quickly she closed the file drawer and made her way to the door. Outside she heard the receptionist singing. As casually as possible, Nancy closed the door to Dave's office and walked toward the reception area.

"I'm Nancy Drew," she told the receptionist,

a petite woman with curly black hair. "I had an appointment with Mr. Kendall and was waiting for him in his office, but he hasn't shown up."

"Mr. Kendall just called. He's still out of town," the receptionist informed her.

Nancy checked her watch. It was nearly three, and she wanted to meet Bess at the pool. "Could you please tell Mr. Kendall that I couldn't wait for him? I'll contact him myself to reschedule our appointment."

The receptionist smiled and wrote down the message. "Of course, Ms. Drew."

Ten minutes later Nancy and Bess were lying on lounge chairs by the side of the pool. Although there were a dozen people in the pool, no one was in the area Bess had chosen. They'd be able to talk without being overheard.

"Did you have lunch with Jody?" Nancy asked.

"She didn't show. I waited for fifteen minutes. Then I went to the shop. Jody told me she'd been even more swamped after I left this morning and couldn't get away." Bess's expression became serious. "Nancy, she was lying about part of that time."

Nancy raised an eyebrow. "What makes you think that?" she asked under her breath.

"A customer came in while I was there. She was complaining about the shop having been closed this morning."

"When was that?" Maybe Jody had had

the opportunity to switch the trail signs after all.

"The customer was loud and clear about the time. She told Jody three times that the shop had been closed between ten-fifteen and ten forty-five."

The timing was right. Jody would have had long enough to ski to the warming hut, switch the signs, and come back.

"I don't like the sound of that," Nancy said.

Bess sat up and smiled at a boy who'd just climbed out of the pool. "Are you going to talk to Jody?"

Nancy nodded. "I think I'll invite her to have dinner with me tonight."

"I'm so glad you could make it," Nancy said as she and Jody met at the entrance to Edelweiss. The maître d' showed them to a table for four, then pulled out their chairs.

"You don't think I'd pass up an opportunity to eat here, do you?" Jody asked. "I can't begin to afford it."

The girls opened their menus. "The Creole chicken sounds great," Jody said. "I love spicy food."

"I think I'll have the broiled salmon. Be sure to save room for dessert," she said, glancing around the room. George and Bess were seated in one corner—with Ben. On the opposite side of the room Dave was sitting with Sheila and Karl Reismueller.

"I knew Sheila would wear something white

tonight," Jody said. When Nancy appeared puzzled, Jody touched the small crystal vase filled with lilies of the valley. "Sheila has two special habits. She always wears her diamond horseshoe pin, and her dinner clothes always match the flowers."

The waiter appeared at their table. "Are you ready to order?" he asked. Nancy selected French onion soup followed by broiled salmon, while Jody chose shrimp cocktail and the Creole chicken.

"I'm starved," Jody said. "I never got a real lunch break."

Here was Nancy's opening. "I heard the shop was closed for a while this morning," she commented. "Someone said you took an early lunch." Or maybe you made a quick trip to switch some trail signs, Nancy added silently.

For a second Jody seemed surprised. "I had a family emergency," she said. "My mother locked her keys in her car, so I had to race into Monroe to rescue her. She was an hour late for work already, and I really had to help her."

"That's too bad," Nancy said, making a mental note to check Jody's alibi. She reached for her purse and pulled out her reporter's notebook. "I'd like a little background info for my article, if you don't mind."

Jody smiled, but she seemed nervous. Her unease made Nancy wonder if Jody had something to hide.

"Where did you work before Tall Pines?" Nancy asked.

"Jensen's department store during the day," Jody answered. "At night I was a short-order cook at the Arch Diner."

"Two jobs, wow! You must have been tired all the time."

Jody shrugged. "I'm saving money for college," she explained as the waiter placed a crock of steaming soup in front of Nancy and shrimp on a bed of ice in front of Jody.

Nancy took a spoonful of the soup. "This is delicious," she said, and cut through the melted cheese to taste the savory onion and beef broth below.

"Good evening, ladies," Nancy heard Karl Reismueller say in his faintly accented voice. She looked up to see him, Sheila, and Dave standing next to the table.

"I hope you're enjoying your dinner," Karl continued. He reached out to shake Nancy's hand as she and Jody rose to greet the three older people.

"It's delicious," Nancy assured him. She smiled at Sheila, and her eyes moved over the front of the dress, searching for her trademark pin. How odd, she thought. Sheila wasn't wearing the diamond horseshoe.

As Karl discussed business with Jody, Dave turned to Nancy. "Sorry I didn't make it back for our interview this afternoon. Why don't you stop by tomorrow at about eleven?"

Nancy agreed. She glanced over his shoulder

toward the back of the room and saw that George, Bess, and Ben were leaving their table.

"Ben!" Karl called as the threesome approached. "I hope you gave Nancy a good lesson this morning."

Ben's expression was wary, and Nancy guessed he was remembering their last conversation. "I tried my best," he said.

George and Bess started talking to Jody while Karl said something to Ben in a low voice.

"We never did plan our skiing for tomorrow," Sheila said to Nancy. She gestured toward the window where a group of skiers had emerged from the forested trails. "Perhaps you'd like to go this evening. Night skiing is great fun."

Though Nancy had planned to spend the rest of the evening reviewing the case with George and Bess, she quickly agreed. She could meet the girls later.

George moved to Nancy's side. "We'll go to the movies," she whispered so that no one else could hear. "Then we'll meet you at your condo when we get back—around ten, okay?"

Nancy nodded her head slightly.

"Be careful!" Dave said as Nancy felt the table jolt in front of her.

"Sorry." Ben's face flushed red—he was obviously embarrassed. "Someone bumped into me. I didn't mean to crash into the table."

Sheila turned quickly. "Is everything all right?" she asked.

Nancy noticed a small wet stain on the otherwise spotless tablecloth. "Something spilled," she said. Then she saw that the flower vase was lying on its side. "The flowers tipped over."

"I'll have the waiter bring more water," Sheila said. Dave straightened the vase, and Sheila rearranged the lilies of the valley. Sheila then put her hand on Karl's arm. "We'd better leave Nancy and Jody to enjoy their food while it's still hot," she said.

Bess winked as she, George, and Ben took off. The Reismuellers and Dave excused themselves, leaving Nancy and Jody to eat their dinners. Nancy took another spoonful of soup. The thick crust of cheese was disturbed only in one spot, so the soup had been kept warm. It was now a perfect temperature.

"Gosh, it was almost like we had a Tall Pines staff meeting," Jody said with a grin, and she speared a shrimp.

"It was crowded all of a sudden," Nancy agreed.

After she took another spoonful of soup Nancy heard Jody's voice as if from a distance. "Are you all right, Nancy?" the girl was saying.

Nancy felt her face grow hot. A wave of dizziness passed over her. "I'm fine," she managed to say. "It's awfully hot in here, though, don't you think?"

Jody was staring at her as if she was concerned. "Not really. Are you sure you're okay?"

Nancy was about to answer her when she felt a sharp stabbing sensation grip her stomach.

It hurt so much, she doubled over from the pain.

"Nancy!" Jody cried, leaning toward her. "What's wrong?"

She tried to force out an answer, but the pain was too intense. The last thing she remembered was tumbling to the floor. Then everything went black.

Chapter
Eight

NANCY OPENED HER EYES. Where was she? Her head was killing her, and her stomach was tied in knots. Looking up at tablecloths and chairs, she realized that she was lying on her back on the floor of the Edelweiss. Jody was kneeling next to her. Nancy pulled herself up slowly, wincing at the pain.

"What happened?" Nancy asked.

"I don't know." Jody's pale face and worried expression told Nancy something terrible had happened. "One second we were talking, and the next you just keeled over and passed out. I called a doctor. Thank goodness there's always one on call for ski accidents."

Though her legs were still shaky, with Jody and the maître d's help Nancy was able to walk to the small employees' lounge off the kitchen. "You'd better lie down," Jody advised, pointing to a couch.

Nancy closed her eyes again, hoping the pain in her stomach would go away—fast. A few minutes later she heard the door open.

"I'm Dr. Gorman," a gray-haired man said, slipping a stethoscope around his neck. "What happened?"

Nancy shook her head. "I'm not sure. I passed out. But right before I did, I had terrible pains. It still hurts," she added, holding her hands to her stomach.

"It must be food poisoning," Jody said.

The doctor asked Jody to leave while he examined Nancy. "What did you eat?" he asked as he took her blood pressure.

"Just French onion soup. It tasted fine."

"Hmm." Dr. Gorman slid a thermometer under Nancy's tongue and checked her pulse. "I don't think it's food poisoning," he told her. "Usually you don't see symptoms of that until three to four hours after eating."

He was silent for a moment as he filled a needle with a clear serum. "Your pulse is still quite slow," he said, giving her an injection.

"If it's not food poisoning . . ." Nancy began, looking expectantly at Dr. Gorman.

The doctor hesitated a moment, then finished packing up his kit. "It could be several things, including a virus. Just to be sure, I'm sending your soup to a lab to be tested. When I get the results I'll let you know. You should be fine now, but you must go straight to bed. Do you need help getting to your room?"

Jody came in and said she'd help Nancy, and the doctor left. "You'll be okay?" Jody asked when they got to Nancy's front door.

Nancy assured Jody that she was fine. "I'll go straight to bed," she said. "My stomach needs all the rest it can get."

Jody laughed a little, then her sparkling green eyes grew serious. "I'm going to tell Mr. Reismueller about this. I tried to find him and his wife when the doctor got there, but they'd left. I'll call him right now, though. He should know. The negative publicity—"

Nancy stopped her short. "My meal at the Edelweiss last night was perfect and earned a rave review. The doctor wasn't convinced I had food poisoning anyway. You heard him. When you get Karl, ask him to tell Sheila I'm not up to skiing tonight."

"You're being very understanding, Nancy," Jody said, and she laughed. "Thank you."

Nancy said good night to Jody and let herself into her condo. Checking her watch, Nancy saw it was only eight-fifteen. She had almost two hours before Bess and George would show up.

"Maybe I will lie down," she said half out loud. Nancy lay on top of the goose-down comforter on her bed and immediately felt herself drift off to sleep.

* * *

Nancy woke up to the sound of the phone ringing and sunlight streaming in through her windows.

"Hello?" she mumbled, shaking her head to try to clear it. She couldn't believe how sick she still felt.

"Nancy?" Bess's voice cried. "Are you all right? We were told you got a bad case of food poisoning at the restaurant, and we decided not to disturb you last night."

Nancy explained that the doctor didn't think it was food poisoning. Bess's reaction was one of shock. "What was it, then?"

"I don't know," Nancy said. "I'll have to wait for the test results, I guess. Until I solve these cases, though, I'll have to be very careful."

"You think there's something else going on at Tall Pines besides the theft?" Bess asked.

"I'm sure of it." Nancy paused. "Someone locked us in that sauna. Someone switched the signs on the ski trail. I got dosed last night with something that made me very sick. Someone's after me, Bess. I'm sure of it."

"You think someone knows you're a detective and wants you out of here?" Bess asked in a low, breathless voice. "But who?"

"I don't know. Someone's found out. Or—"

"Or what?" Bess asked.

"Or someone simply wants to sabotage Tall Pines, and I've been the accidental victim each time," Nancy offered.

"Someone like Rob Watson, you mean," Bess said.

"Exactly."

After a short pause Bess asked, "What can George and I do to help?"

Nancy thought for a moment and then asked her friends to go to Jody's apartment, sneak in, and do a search of the girl's belongings. All three times that Nancy had been hurt Jody either had been there or had known where she was going to be. This made her highly suspicious. Could she have stolen the money and found out that Nancy was a detective? It was worth checking out.

"What are we looking for?" Bess asked.

"The rest of the fifty thousand dollars or some sign that Jody's made large deposits in her bank accounts recently," Nancy said. "Check to see if she really did go home yesterday between ten fifteen and ten forty-five," she added, remembering Jody's alibi.

"There's one problem," Bess told her. "I don't know how to break into an apartment."

Nancy had already thought of that. "Her mom should be at work, so try this: Tell the landlady you're planning a surprise party for Jody," she suggested. "Take some balloons. She'll probably let you in to decorate."

Bess giggled. "It just might work."

"Of course it will," Nancy promised.

Nancy lay down for a bit because she still felt awfully woozy, and she worked on a plan to check out Ben Wrobley. Slowly she got dressed and made her way to the building where the employees lived. She knew Ben taught at nine. It was five past now, so that gave her plenty of time to search his place. At the employees' complex Nancy found a directory out front.

Ben's apartment turned out to be at the far end of the building. The door was locked, but the lock was only a simple one, not a deadbolt. She pulled a credit card from her pocket and slid it along the doorjamb. A second later she was inside.

The apartment was just one room, she saw. Although small, it was well organized. A daybed with bolsters served as a couch, and cabinets over the desk provided additional storage. The back wall had a compact kitchenette and a door leading to a bath. Large skiing posters hung on the other three walls.

Nancy went to the desk first because it was the most logical place for Ben to hide whatever it was he'd taken from the office. She opened the top drawer. Nothing there but pens and pencils and a blank pad of paper. She leafed through the papers in the file drawer, but there were only copies of skiing articles from magazines.

She went over to search the storage bolsters above the bed, finding only blankets and pillows.

There was one hiding place left. Nancy walked across the room to the dresser. The first three drawers were filled with Ben's clothes. The last drawer held four hand-knit ski sweaters. Nancy slid her hand between each of the sweaters and then under the bottom one. Her fingers skidded on something smooth and flat.

A rush of excitement coursed through her as

she pulled the object out. She'd found a file folder—taken from Dave Kendall's office, no doubt.

Nancy checked the tab. "Inge Gustafson" was printed on it in neat black letters. Ben had stolen Inge's personnel file.

Sitting on the daybed, Nancy spread the folder open. As she started to read the letters and Inge's contract her eyes widened. No wonder Ben was so angry!

The Inge Gustafson Ski School was a sham. Karl had paid Inge a lump sum to use her name, but according to their agreement she had no further obligations—she didn't even have to give a single lesson!

Meanwhile Ben was doing all her work. He must have found out she was never going to show and taken this file as proof of his suspicions, Nancy figured. What was he going to do with the evidence, though?

As Nancy's thoughts spun through the possibilities she heard the rasp of a key in the lock. She searched frantically for a hiding spot, but before she could move, the door swung open. It was too late.

Nancy was caught!

Chapter

Nine

WHAT ARE YOU DOING in my room?" Ben demanded, outraged.

Nancy knew that whatever she did, she couldn't blow her cover. "I saw you take something from Dave's office," she said. "I wanted to find out what it was."

Ben grabbed the folder from Nancy's hands. "You're not reviewing Tall Pines for a ski magazine, are you?" The look Ben gave Nancy was extremely skeptical.

Nancy decided that if her cover had to be blown, she might as well invent a better one—that of investigative reporter.

"Well, no, not exactly," she confessed, playing up her new role. "I'll tell you the truth—if you promise to keep it just between us."

Ben was obviously skeptical. "Okay."

"I heard about the theft a week ago, and I wanted to see if there was something going on at Tall Pines that the readers of *Tracks* should know about," she bluffed.

"So you're doing an exposé," Ben guessed.

"Exactly," Nancy told him. "But if anyone here finds out, I won't be able to learn a thing, and then"—she snapped her fingers—"end of story, right?"

Ben ran his hands through his jet black hair. "I see your point, but I still don't get why you searched my room. I didn't steal the money. Rebecca Montgomery did."

"I've interviewed her. She denies it, and I believe her," Nancy said, her hands on her hips.

Ben unzipped his parka and tossed it on the bed. "Then someone else took it."

Nancy gestured to the file lying beside Ben's jacket. "We both know that the Inge Gustafson Ski School is a sham. Maybe you wanted to get back at Karl for treating you so badly."

Ben's eyes blazed with anger. "Maybe I do want to get back at him, but I wouldn't steal from him. I'm not stupid." He paused. "You can get your story however you want," he went on angrily. "And when you do, you'll find out I'm innocent. Now I think you'd better go." With that Ben walked to the door and opened it. "Don't worry, though," he said quietly. "Your secret's safe with me."

Nancy smiled at the ski instructor. "Thank you," she said softly. She didn't know if Ben was telling her the truth—either about his not being the thief or about how he wouldn't tell anyone that she was "investigating" the theft at Tall Pines. Could she really believe him?

"Of course I understood," Sheila said when Nancy went to call on her at her condo. "Come in. Karl and I felt just awful when we heard what happened last night. Are you all right now?" she asked, her crystal blue eyes showing her concern.

Nancy's smile was brave, and Sheila wouldn't have guessed how queasy she still felt. "I'm fine, really," she fibbed gracefully. "I'd like to interview Karl if I could," she said after she and Sheila were seated on the couch. "Do you know when he'll be back?"

"I'm not sure," Sheila said. "He had some kind of problem to handle this morning." She tapped her fingers nervously on the arm of the couch. "My husband's too trusting. I mean, who else would hire a person with a criminal record?" she blurted out.

Sheila must have realized what she had let slip because her mouth instantly clamped shut. Before Nancy could question her further the phone rang, and at the same time there was a knock at the door.

"Would you get the phone?" Sheila asked Nancy as she hurried toward the door.

Nancy picked up the receiver that was on an end table beside the couch.

"I've got what you want," a man announced before Nancy could identify herself. "Meet me at that unfinished building tonight at ten." Without waiting for a response the man hung up. Nancy put the receiver down, completely puzzled by what she had just heard. Who was the man, and what did he have? What unfinished building was he talking about?

As she thought over the man's words Nancy remembered seeing Sheila the day before with the man in the black fedora by the new pond. There was an unfinished building there—the snack bar. Maybe the caller was the same man.

"Aren't these gorgeous?" Sheila came back into the room, her arms filled with flowers. "Karl sent them." She sniffed deeply.

"They're beautiful," Nancy agreed.

Sheila placed the floral arrangement in the middle of the coffee table and touched one of the petals. "This is a very rare iris," Sheila told Nancy as she sat down again. "Who was on the phone?" she asked, curious.

Nancy told her about the man's call, careful to watch the woman's reaction. "He didn't leave his name," she said.

Sheila flushed. She fingered the iris petal again, and Nancy could see her hand trembling. "He must have the anniversary gift I want for Karl." Sheila's words were spoken hesitantly, and her eyes never once met Nancy's.

Nancy had a strong suspicion Sheila was lying and decided to ask her about the day before. "Didn't I see you near the skating rink yesterday?" she asked. "I wanted to try it out but didn't know it wasn't finished yet."

The older woman's eyes narrowed. "No, it's

not done yet. You must have seen me there with the, uh, contractor. Karl asked me to meet him." With that she got up off the couch, picked up the flower arrangement, and nervously paced the room. "Now where should I put these?" she asked absently.

It was obvious to Nancy that the woman was hiding something. But what?

Sheila set the bouquet down on a nearby table and checked her watch. "Oh, Nancy, I'm so sorry," she said. "I just remembered I have an appointment in ten minutes, and I haven't even finished getting ready. Would you excuse me?" she asked, giving her a tense smile.

Nancy nodded and stood up. "Sure. Tell Karl I'll be in touch with him for that interview."

"Of course." As she held the door open for Nancy, Sheila smiled again. "Now, you take care of yourself," she said in a motherly tone.

Nancy smiled back and took off for her condo. She wanted to see if the doctor had left a message about what had caused her to pass out the night before.

When Nancy let herself into her condo the phone was ringing. She rushed to pick it up and heard Dr. Gorman identify himself on the other end. "I have the results of the tests," he said.

"And?" Nancy asked.

She heard Dr. Gorman clear his throat. "Nancy, I'm afraid your soup was poisoned."

"Poisoned!" Nancy closed her eyes and began to think. First the sauna, then the trail signs—those could have been pranks aimed at the resort, not her. But poison? It was obvious now that someone was after her. Why, though?

"Nancy?" Dr. Gorman asked.

"Oh—I'm sorry," she said, then she paused. "Dr. Gorman, what kind of poison was it?"

"Convallatoxin," the doctor explained. "It's similar to digitalis, which is used to treat cardiac patients. That's why your heartbeat was so slow. What I can't tell you is how it was administered."

"Is it a powder?" Nancy asked, trying to imagine how someone had gotten the poison into her soup.

"No. The original source is a plant, but the lab didn't find any evidence of flower parts. They think the poison was a liquid."

Nancy thought for a moment. "There were flowers on the table," she said. "Someone accidentally nudged the table, and the vase tipped over."

"Some of the water might have splashed into your bowl," Dr. Gorman concluded. "What kind of flowers were they?"

"Lilies of the valley."

Nancy heard him turning the pages of a book.

"That's it!" the doctor cried. "Lilies of the valley are highly poisonous. Even the water they've been standing in can cause serious illness."

"Are you sure?" Nancy asked.

"Yes," he said. "But that's good news. The poisoning must have been accidental."

It was a comforting theory, but Nancy had a strong feeling that it was wrong. The poisoning had been no accident. The vase of flowers had been in the center of the table, too far from her bowl for an accidental spill to reach her soup.

Nancy thanked the doctor and hung up, her mind reeling. There was no doubt about it. Someone had deliberately poisoned her, someone who knew about flowers.

Still, after all her investigating, Nancy had been unable to narrow her list of suspects. Now Dr. Gorman's diagnosis had made the case even more complex.

Nancy had a new suspect: Sheila Reismueller.

Chapter
Ten

THE CASE NOW HAD a new angle. Not many people at Tall Pines knew enough about flowers to know that lilies of the valley could be poisonous. But Sheila Reismueller would have that kind of knowledge. She had also picked up the flowers and rearranged them when they were knocked over.

But why would Sheila want to poison her?

If the resort owner's wife knew Nancy was a detective investigating the theft, and if Sheila was hiding something about the theft, that would give her a reason to poison Nancy.

But that was a lot of ifs. Maybe there wasn't any connection at all between the theft and the poisoning.

Sheila's nervousness around Nancy *was* suspicious, though. Nancy didn't believe Sheila's explanation about the phone call, either. But what was she hiding? It made no sense.

With a sigh Nancy picked up the phone. One thing she could do was check on the Tall Pines employees. She wanted to find out who at the resort had a record. Sheila had said someone did. There was a chance that that person had slipped and committed another crime.

Within a few minutes Nancy was connected to Chief McGinnis of the River Heights Police Department. With a little convincing Nancy was able to get him to run a trace on her main suspects: Ben Wrobley, Jody Ashton, and—just to be on the safe side—Sheila Reismueller. The chief agreed to contact her as soon as he found out anything.

Almost as soon as Nancy hung up the phone she heard a knock on the door. Bess and George were back.

"You were right!" Bess exclaimed, grinning. Obviously they were pleased with their investigation. "When we told Jody's landlady we were planning a surprise party for her, she let us into the apartment." Bess chuckled. "Those balloons were worth their weight in gold."

"So what did you learn?"

Bess's smile faded as she and George entered the condo. "Not much. We couldn't find the money anywhere. We searched everything."

"How about bankbooks? Did you find them?"

"There was only one savings book," George said, "and that didn't have any big deposits.

Jody's been putting in small, regular amounts every payday."

"That seems to back up Jody's story that she's saving money for college," Nancy said, thinking out loud.

"The only strange transaction was one Jody made—a big withdrawal," Bess said, tossing back her long blond hair.

That *was* strange. "How much?" Nancy asked.

"Two thousand dollars," George answered. She sank into the sofa and let out a long sigh. "It doesn't seem like we're getting anywhere on this case," she said, shaking her head. "Rebecca's been calling me to find out how we're doing. What can I tell her, Nan?"

"You can't tell her much, but I guess you can say my cover's blown, and that someone tried to poison me last night," Nancy said.

"Nancy!" Bess cried. "Are you joking?"

George's eyes became round. "Poison?"

Nancy nodded and quickly told her friends about the lab results. "So the culprit has to know something about flowers. Any sign that Jody does?"

George looked at Bess, and they both shook their heads. "Ben doesn't, either," George said.

"That leaves Sheila. . . ." A thought nagged at Nancy. Who else at Tall Pines knew about flowers? Then it hit her. "And Dave Kendall!"

It was ten-fifty, and Nancy had almost forgotten her eleven o'clock appointment with Dave. She grabbed her jacket and headed for the door.

"See you at the snack bar for lunch?" she asked. "Twelve?"

"Sure," George said, confused. "Anything else we can do?"

"Nope!" With that Nancy waved goodbye and was on her way to Dave Kendall's office. Since she'd arranged to interview him anyway, she thought, this would be a great opportunity to find out exactly how much he knew about flowers.

When Nancy entered Dave's office the general manager was standing in front of a filing cabinet.

"Hi," Nancy said as she entered the office. "Ready for our interview?"

Dave turned around, and Nancy saw that he was holding a small trowel. Light streamed through the windows onto the masses of orchids. "Just give me a second to finish potting this, and I'll be with you."

Dave brushed off his hands and sat down behind his desk. "Now what can I do for you?" he asked. "I hope you're enjoying your stay here."

"I am." Nancy glanced at the orchids. "Those flowers are beautiful," she said. "Do you grow anything else?"

Dave leaned back in his chair and smiled. "I've tried, but my green thumb seems limited to orchids. Strange, because most people find that they're the hardest to grow."

"It is strange," Nancy agreed, turning back to him. She cleared her throat and took out her notepad. "It seems that your prankster has struck again," she said. Then she went on to explain the details of her poisoning the night before. "I know my editor is going to want some reassurance that things are under control at Tall Pines before we print any review. Do you have a comment?"

Dave was silent for a moment, giving Nancy the impression he was carefully weighing his words. "From what you say, it sounds like an accident—an unfortunate one, to be sure, but still an accident. The vase overturned, and obviously water splashed into your soup." He paused. "You have my personal assurance that everything here at Tall Pines is in order. Any other questions?"

Nancy tapped her pencil on her notebook. Dave's explanation didn't take into account what had happened in the sauna or on the ski trail. His manner was professional, but he could easily be hiding something.

She spent a few more minutes posing questions that she thought a reporter for *Tracks* might ask. Dave easily answered her questions about their expansion plans and advertising campaign, showing little nervousness or concern that she might be anything more than a reporter. If he suspected she was a detective, he didn't show it.

Nancy realized she wasn't going to get much more out of Dave Kendall and finished up the interview. "Thanks for your time," she said, standing to leave.

"No problem," Dave said. He gave her a polite smile and a firm handshake. "You must be almost done with your story."

Nancy packed her notebook and pencil and headed for the door. "Almost," she told him.

"That's good," he said, holding the door for her. "And don't worry about these accidents. In my experience, when a resort first opens there are always a few wrinkles to iron out."

Nancy thanked him and left, thinking that what was happening at Tall Pines was a lot more serious than a "few wrinkles." She made her way to the snack bar to meet Bess and George and wondered along the way why Dave Kendall was so reluctant to take the accidents seriously. Was it simply his wanting to reassure her because she was a reporter, or was the man trying to cover something up?

Just as Nancy was coming up to the ski shop she saw an expensive-looking green sports car pull into the main parking lot. From the spotless shine and the temporary plates Nancy could tell that it was brand-new.

She admired the sleek lines of the car as the driver steered it into an empty space, stopped, and got out.

Nancy's mouth fell open in amazement. The person getting out of the brand-new sports car was none other than Jody Ashton!

Chapter

Eleven

JODY PATTED THE FENDER of the car before carefully locking the door. As she turned she saw Nancy.

"Isn't it the best?" she asked, tossing her keys in the air. "I just picked it up. I can't believe it's mine—finally. Wow!" she said under her breath, gazing at the car one last time.

"It's gorgeous," Nancy agreed. She ran her eyes over the car and calculated to herself what it must have cost. Even if Jody had had enough for a down payment from her savings account, how could she possibly afford the monthly payments if she was saving for college? Unless she'd just come into some money—like fifty thousand dollars from the Tall Pines payroll, for example.

"There's a sleigh ride at dusk today," Jody was saying. "Are you going?"

Nancy's thoughts were still on Jody's brand-new car. She nodded absently. "I wouldn't miss it."

"Well, I'd better get back to the shop," Jody said. "See you later!" She waved and walked off toward the main building.

Nancy made her way to the snack bar, mulling over this latest development. What if Jody had taken the money and found out Nancy was investigating the theft? The girl would have a good reason for trying to get her off the case. Jody had known she was going to the sauna and that Nancy and Bess were going to ski Aerie. Only her theory didn't account for the fact that, as far as she knew, Jody didn't know enough about flowers to poison her. Sheila was still her number-one suspect for the poisoning.

Nancy glanced around the snack shop for Bess and George. The room was filled with guests, but there was no sign of Nancy's friends. She decided to check out the gift shop and ski school.

As she opened the door to the ski school Nancy immediately saw George standing in front of the counter talking to Ben. There was no sign of Bess.

After Ben and George finished their conversation Ben went over to his locker. Nancy shot George a warning look and asked casually, "How are the trails this morning?"

"Great," Ben said. "The fresh snow last night really helped— That's odd," he said, interrupting himself.

"Is something wrong, Ben?" George asked.

Ben was standing next to his locker, a puzzled

expression on his face, holding a bunch of white flowers. Nancy raced over to Ben. "Can I see those?" she asked, reaching for the flowers.

It was a bouquet of wilted lilies of the valley!

Ben just stared at Nancy, his confusion obvious. Finally he handed her the flowers.

"Do you know what these are?" Nancy asked.

Ben shrugged his shoulders. "They look like dead white flowers." He sounded genuinely puzzled.

"They're lilies of the valley," Nancy said, watching Ben's face.

"So?" Once again Ben's voice was casual. He seemed to have no idea of the flowers' significance.

"What's wrong?" George asked innocently. Nancy could see in her friend's eyes that George was as surprised as she was to see the flowers.

"Last night someone tried to poison me with lilies of the valley," Nancy explained.

George gasped. "You're kidding," she said, pretending to be surprised to protect Nancy's cover. "You're the reporter, aren't you?" When Nancy nodded, George asked, "Why would someone try to poison you?"

Ben grew pale. "Don't look at me!" he cried.

"These *were* in your locker," Nancy said, holding out the flowers. "They didn't get in there by magic."

Ben pointed at his locker. "Check it out," he said. "It wouldn't take Houdini to pick this lock. Anyone could have put those flowers in there."

"But why?" George asked, wrinkling her nose.

"This is totally strange. How would anyone know other people would be around when you opened your locker? It makes no sense that anyone, including you, would stash those flowers in your locker. Why not just throw them out?"

"Maybe someone wanted to frame me," Ben suggested. "Or at least make it look like I could be guilty."

Nancy was quickly assessing the situation. Ben's actions weren't those of a guilty person. He'd seemed honestly confused by the flowers. She was beginning to think the ski instructor was telling her the truth about them. Also, Ben was right—anyone could have broken into his locker and planted the lilies. But why? Why would anyone do something like that?

Ben grabbed his jacket from the locker and slipped into it. "I've got a lesson," he explained. "Sorry I can't stick around. See you later this afternoon, George?" he asked with a raised eyebrow. "Say, three o'clock?"

"Perfect," George said, beaming at him as he left.

"Ski lesson?" Nancy asked. George's smile indicated that there might be something more than skiing going on between the two of them.

George started to blush. "Something like that. Come on," she said. "I'm starving!"

At around seven that night Nancy and Bess joined the crowd that had gathered in front of the lodge for the sleigh ride.

"Look at all these furs," Bess said, wrinkling

her nose at the coats many people had on. "Think of all those poor animals—" She shuddered and didn't finish the thought.

George came up to Nancy and Bess just then. "Good day on the trails?" Nancy asked with a wink.

"Perfect!" George said as the sound of bells filled the air. The crowd became silent and turned to watch the sleighs approach.

"This is going to be fun," Bess said excitedly, clapping her hands together as the sleighs drew closer. There were seven of them, all painted black. Two horses harnessed to each sleigh pulled them up to the crowd of guests. Tall Pines drivers held the horses in check with forest green harnesses.

"Let's ride with Ben," George suggested when she saw him driving the lead sleigh, but the girls were too late. Other guests piled into the first six sleighs, leaving Nancy, Bess, and George to climb into the last one.

The girls wrapped their legs in woolen blankets, and each draped another one around her shoulders. Their driver, a thin blond woman with her hair pulled back in a ponytail, smiled at them. "Ready?" she asked.

Bess beamed at her. "You bet!"

"Heeyah!" the woman said, snapping the reins. With that they skimmed along on the snow and entered the woods. The sleighs in front of them were barely visible through the thick pines, and the only sounds were the steady beats of horses' hooves, the jingle of sleigh bells, and the lulling whoosh of sleigh runners over the hard-packed snow.

A clump of snow fell into their sleigh from one of the overhanging pine boughs. Bess shivered and pulled her blanket tighter around her. "This is a little spooky, huh?"

"I think it's beautiful," George said, lifting her eyes to the darkening night sky.

They rode without speaking for a few minutes, then George broke the silence and pointed to an area just ahead of them. "That's a great trail for night skiing." She turned to Nancy. "Let's try it tomorrow."

"You two go right ahead." Bess snuggled deeper into her blankets. "This is my idea of a terrific winter sport."

The sleigh took a path that ran beside a trail. Nancy saw two men on the trail skiing in parallel tracks, moving quickly and gracefully.

"Good, aren't they?" Nancy asked, pointing the skiers out to George.

Her friend followed Nancy's gaze and nodded. "Almost professional," she said.

As the sleigh drew closer Nancy studied the skiers' backs. Moonlight filtered in through the trees and shone brightly on the shorter of the two men. Nancy knew she'd seen him before. There was no mistaking that head of white hair. It was Rob Watson.

What was Watson doing skiing on Tall Pines's trails? Checking out the competition, or had he come back to cause more trouble?

Nancy felt adrenaline rush through her. The

man Rob was with had on a Tall Pines jacket. Who could he be?

She strained her eyes, trying to get a better look at Rob's companion.

Finally the taller man turned his face toward their sleigh, and Nancy gasped at who it was.

It was Dave Kendall!

Chapter

Twelve

NANCY WHISPERED, pointing at the two skiers, "It's Rob Watson and Dave Kendall."

"Rob Watson and Dave Kendall!" George practically shouted. "What are those two doing hanging out together?"

Nancy's thoughts quickly went back to when she'd caught Watson entering the Tall Pines offices. What if Rob had had an appointment to see Dave and hadn't been breaking in? He might have taken off because Nancy saw him and not because he was afraid Dave would catch him. Dave's acting angry at Rob could have just been a bluff to throw Nancy off his track.

"Maybe Dave's giving him a tour of the trails," Bess suggested.

George's eyes narrowed. "At night? Somehow I don't think so," she said. "Nancy, are you thinking what I'm thinking?" she asked.

Nancy nodded. "There aren't many reasons for the general manager of Tall Pines to be meeting a competitor unless they're working together," she said. Nancy quickly explained how she'd seen Watson in Dave's office.

"Watson's renovations!" George said. "What if Dave stole the money and split it with Rob?"

"But why?" Bess asked.

George leaned forward to get the attention of the woman driving the sleigh. "Would you mind stopping?" she asked. "I'd like to take a walk in the woods."

"A walk?" Nancy and Bess asked as their driver reined in the horses and the sleigh came to a halt.

George hopped out of the sleigh. "I'm going to follow Rob and Dave."

"That's crazy," Nancy said. "We can't possibly catch up to them on foot. Or do you have a plan?"

George's grin told her all she had to know. "Coming, Bess?"

Bess shook her head and tucked the blanket in tight around her. "You guys go ahead. I'll meet you back at the condo, okay?"

Nancy and George waved a quick goodbye as the sleigh started to move again. "This way." George motioned to Nancy to follow her as she started to run alongside the ski tracks. Rob and Dave were skiing at a good pace and were almost out of sight.

"I still don't think we have a chance," Nancy said, falling to her knees in a deep snowdrift.

"They're on skis. How can we possibly catch them?"

She searched down the trail and could just make out Rob and Dave as they made their way around a far bend.

"There's a way, Nan. I promise you. I've skied this trail before. It bends to the right and goes deeper into the woods. Then it bends back," she told Nancy. "If we cut straight through this meadow here, we should be able to cut them off."

"George, you're a genius!" Nancy said. "Let's go!"

They left the trail and rushed across the meadow. The snow had a thick crust that kept them from sinking in. Soon they'd crossed the meadow and were back in the woods. George pulled Nancy behind a tree next to the trail, and both girls held their breath, waiting for Dave and Rob to reappear.

George studied the tracks. "They haven't come yet," she said, pointing to the light dusting of snow in the tracks. "The snow would be packed if someone had skied on it."

Nancy kept her eyes on the trail, but Dave and Rob were nowhere in sight. The minutes ticked by, and still they didn't show. "They should be here by now," George said, checking her watch.

"Let's wait a little longer," Nancy said. But fifteen minutes passed, and Dave and Rob still hadn't skied past them. Nancy tried to control her disappointment. "They must have turned off the trail," she said. She stomped her foot in frustration. "Another dead end!"

"Maybe they went back to Dave's office," George suggested. "Let's head over there and see."

"George, you're full of great ideas tonight!" Nancy hugged her friend and stepped out of the woods onto the trail. "Even if Dave isn't there, we can check out his office. The last time I searched, the receptionist interrupted me before I could finish."

When they reached the administration building they saw that all the lights were off. "Looks like they didn't come back here," George said, biting her lower lip.

"That's okay," Nancy said. Her frustration had melted away. Being able to search Dave's office was something, at least. She reached into the belt pack she wore around her waist. She pulled out her lock-pick kit and a pocket flashlight. Within a minute she'd opened the front door. The door to Dave's office was easy enough to unlock, and within another minute she had that open, too.

Nancy switched on the flashlight and closed the door behind them.

"What first?" George asked.

"The personnel files," Nancy said. "Sheila told me Karl had hired someone with a record. Chief McGinnis is searching, but he hasn't called yet. Maybe we'll find the evidence we need here in one of the files."

Nancy moved to the first of the cabinets and opened the drawer. George went to the other and started checking. Thumbing through the hanging folders, Nancy quickly found the section with the personnel files.

"Ashton, Jody," Nancy read on the first file. Inside she found letters of recommendation and Jody's employment application. Nancy flipped through it and discovered that the last page of the application was missing. Strange. Nancy checked another employee file. Sure enough, Jody's application was missing a list of previous employers and a signed statement that she had never been convicted of a criminal offense.

"Find something?" George asked.

"I'm not sure." Nancy handed George Jody's file and pointed out what was missing. While George flipped through it, Nancy reached for Dave's folder. She leafed through the recommendations and pulled out his application, which was complete, unlike Jody's. Nancy turned to the back page and glanced at his previous job experience. Nothing unusual, except there was a two-year gap right before he'd joined Tall Pines.

George was back at the other cabinet. "One of these files is empty," George said.

"What kind?" Nancy asked.

"It's a bank file," George told her. "Monroe Savings and Loan."

"Maybe it's misfiled. The folder could be with the other bank records," Nancy suggested. "Keep looking."

Nancy went back to checking the employee files but didn't turn up anything new. George was still flipping through the other file cabinet.

"Something is definitely wrong here, Nancy,"

George said. "This bank folder is the only one, and it's empty. There aren't any other bank records here at all, even though this is where all the rest of the accounting stuff is."

Nancy peered over George's shoulder. "Karl's office?" she wondered.

"Let's check it out," George agreed.

Within a minute Nancy and George were inside Karl Reismueller's office. Nancy ran the flashlight over the dim interior.

"This looks more like someone's living room than an office," George said in an astonished tone.

With its plush carpet, long leather couch, and mahogany desk and credenza the office was quite elegant. Nancy went toward Karl's desk while George made for the credenza.

"Nothing here," George announced a few minutes later. She sounded discouraged.

"Nothing in the desk, either." Nancy was thoughtful. "How can you run a ski resort without any bank records?" she wondered aloud.

"It's not that there aren't any," George said. "The empty folder proves that. It's just that we can't find them."

Nancy scanned the room one last time, her gaze landing on a mahogany wall unit that matched Karl's sleek, modern desk. She went to it and pulled open the doors, revealing a personal computer.

"Maybe this is our answer." Nancy switched on the computer and pulled a chair over. The machine made a soft whirring noise for a few seconds, then it flashed a message.

" 'Please enter password,' " George read over Nancy's shoulder. "If this is like most systems, we've got only three chances. After that it'll lock up."

Nancy thought for a moment. "Most people pick a password they won't have trouble remembering. What about 'Pines'?"

She typed in the word and pressed the Enter key. "Invalid password. Please try again," the system responded.

They had two more chances.

"How about 'Karl'?" George suggested. "It is his name—chances are, he wouldn't forget it."

Nancy laughed and typed in the name. " 'Invalid password. Please try again,' " came the reply.

Neither George nor Nancy spoke, but they both knew they had only one more chance. Nancy closed her eyes and tried to think. "What's the most important thing in Karl Reismueller's life?"

George thought for a moment. "His wife!"

Nancy smiled and typed in "Sheila." The computer began to whir.

"We did it!" George crowed as a menu appeared on the monitor.

"Let's try the general ledger system," Nancy said, entering the code from the menu. Another menu appeared, asking her which company records she wanted to see.

"Wow! Karl owns a lot of companies." George started to read the list of names. "All-State Printing, Toys-for-All, Well-Heeled Cobbler. Is there any business he's not in?"

Nancy selected Tall Pines and began reviewing the financial information. "There are a lot of loans," she told George as they studied the screen. "Actually, I'm not surprised. That's pretty normal for the first year in business."

"What about the other companies?"

Nancy returned to the menu and asked for information about Karl's printing company. She stared at the screen for a minute, then inquired about the chain of toy stores. The answer was the same for each.

"Every one of these companies has borrowed money to the limit," she said. "I don't understand. If he's doing well, he shouldn't have so many loans. Where's Karl's Midas touch that everyone talks about?"

"Do you think he's in financial trouble?" George asked.

"It sure seems like it." Nancy flipped to another screen. "More debt. Opening Tall Pines must have strained Karl's finances to the breaking point. Hey"—Nancy looked up at George—"I just remembered. The other night at dinner Sheila was about to say something about money problems when Karl cut her off."

George nodded her understanding. "No wonder Karl was so upset by the theft. He couldn't afford to lose fifty thousand dollars."

"That was covered by insurance," Nancy reminded her. "But the rest of Karl's businesses don't seem to be doing well, either."

"I wish we could find the bank records," George said. "They might explain a lot."

"We still don't know why they're missing," Nancy agreed. "Or who took them." She scrolled through several screens but couldn't find a single menu directing her to Tall Pines' bank records.

George leaned over her shoulder and watched while Nancy worked. "So what does this all mean?" she asked.

"Reismueller has financial problems," Nancy said, leaning back in her chair. "Someone's got the bank records. That someone could be Dave."

"I don't follow," George said. "You're way ahead of me."

"What if Dave is working with Watson, and they stole the money to cause Karl trouble?" Nancy suggested. She was piecing together her theory as she spoke.

"But you just said he got the money back from the insurance company, so I think that whoever stole the money really needed it. I don't think that person was just causing Karl trouble," George said.

"That's true," Nancy agreed. "But Dave and Watson could still be working together. The money for renovations, and the sabotage to drive people away from Tall Pines."

"But how's that connected to the records?" George asked.

Nancy thought for a moment. "Dave could be holding the records as a way of blackmailing

Karl. Maybe Karl found out about the theft and threatened to turn Dave in."

"I guess that makes sense," George said. She bit on a fingernail. "Still, it doesn't really explain why someone tried to poison you specifically and why all the attacks have been made against you."

George had a point. So far Nancy didn't have any proof that Dave was capable of poisoning her. The only person who had the knowledge to do that was—

"Sheila!" Nancy cried. "I completely forgot." She rushed to turn off the computer and pick up her flashlight. "Come on, George."

"You completely forgot what?" George asked, following Nancy out of Karl's office.

Nancy told George about Sheila's appointment with the strange man who'd called earlier that day at the Reismuellers' condo. "It's almost ten now. We've got to get to the skating pond."

"What does it mean?" George asked.

Outside the administrative offices a light snow had begun to fall, and it was pitch-black. "I don't know," Nancy answered, "but I'm going to be there to find out." She started walking in the direction of the pond.

"I'm coming with you," George announced.

"I don't think that's such a good idea," Nancy said. "Bess is probably worried about us."

George ran her hands through her dark curls. "I don't know, Nancy. You might be in danger."

"It won't be the first time," Nancy said with a laugh.

"Okay." George took a deep breath. "Just promise me you'll be careful."

"Aren't I always?" Nancy said. With that she said goodbye to George, arranging to meet back at George and Bess's room at the main lodge.

In a few minutes Nancy had reached the skating pond. The whole area between the pond and the snack bar was dark, lit only by the moon and stars. As Nancy approached the unfinished snack bar she checked carefully in all directions. No sign of either Sheila or the man. She sprinted the last few yards and stood outside the door of the building, listening carefully. There was no sound, and the building seemed empty. Carefully she eased open the door and slipped inside.

Nancy looked around, searching for a place to hide. Her eyes lit on a pile of wood paneling stacked along one wall. Perfect! If she hid behind it, she'd be able to hear the conversation without being seen.

She moved toward the paneling. As she did she heard a sound coming from behind her. Someone else was in the snack bar!

Nancy turned, but it was too late. She saw a tall, dark figure, a raised arm. Before she could move there was an instant of blinding pain, then darkness.

Chapter

Thirteen

NANCY MOANED SOFTLY as she came to in the cold and dark, not sure where she was. Then memory rushed back. She had come to the snack bar to find Sheila and the stranger. Instead, someone had found her.

Sitting up, Nancy held her head in her hands, trying to fight the wave of dizziness and nausea that came from the throbbing pain at the back of her head. That must have been where she was hit. The dizziness passed, and Nancy took in her surroundings. The building appeared to be empty. There was no sign of Sheila or the man, nothing to indicate that anyone else had been there except the faint scent of perfume.

Nancy took a deep whiff and frowned. The fragrance was unmistakable. As far as she knew, only one person at Tall Pines wore that spicy mixture of roses and lilies: Sheila Reismueller.

It had happened so quickly that Nancy hadn't recognized the person who hit her. She didn't even know if her assailant had been a man or a woman. It could have been Sheila, the man she was meeting, or anyone else, though Nancy doubted the third possibility. All she knew for sure was that someone didn't want her nosing around at Tall Pines.

As Nancy stood up her foot kicked a hard object, and she bent down to pick it up. It was a flashlight. She was pretty sure it hadn't been there when she'd come into the snack bar. It must be what she had been struck with, Nancy thought, slipping the flashlight into her belt pack.

She made her way out of the building, on the watch for Sheila or the man she'd been meeting. Nancy figured they were both long gone—she wasn't sure how much time had passed—but she needed to be sure. The question was, which of them had knocked her out, and why?

"How'd it go?" George asked when Nancy appeared at their door.

Nancy took off her coat and sat cross-legged on one of the beds. "To make a bad pun," she said with a smile, "it was a stunning experience."

After Nancy explained what had happened, Bess was truly alarmed. "Nancy, I'm worried. There's a criminal running around, and he's determined to hurt you. First the poison, now this."

"I think 'he' is a 'she,'" Nancy told her friends. "Sheila knows enough about flowers to have poured the water in my soup, and that was definitely her perfume I smelled. But I still don't understand what Sheila doesn't want me to know. It didn't make sense that she would be involved in stealing from her husband's resort. The success of Tall Pines seemed so important to Sheila."

"Maybe the meeting between her and the stranger had to do with Karl's shaky finances," George suggested. At Bess's perplexed expression George told her cousin what she and Nancy had found out in their search through Karl's computer earlier.

"Wow!" Bess said. Then her expression changed. "I don't get it, though. What could Sheila possibly have to do with the missing bank records or the theft?"

Nancy explained her theory about Dave's blackmailing Karl with the bank records. "Maybe Sheila was meeting with someone who was going to take care of the Reismuellers' problem with Dave," she suggested.

"You don't mean . . ." George asked, her voice trailing off.

"Getting rid of him and Rob . . ." Nancy shook her head to clear her thoughts. "The only way to find out is to confront Sheila or trick her into revealing what's going on." She pulled the flashlight out of her belt pack. "I found this on the ground next to me. I think she or the man she was meeting used it to knock me out."

"You're not going to show it to her, are you?" George asked, deadly serious. "If you're right about your suspicions, it could be dangerous to confront her."

"George is right, Nancy." Bess got up from the couch and paced the room. "Sheila could be trouble. Besides, if you're going to confront anyone, it should be Dave Kendall. If your theory is right, Dave's the one behind all the attacks."

Nancy thought for a moment. Bess and George had a point—if Dave really was the thief. She still hadn't ruled Jody out as a suspect, though. That brand-new car didn't fit with her saving for college. Thinking about it, she realized she didn't have enough clues to confront anyone.

She let out a long sigh. "I guess you're right," she admitted. "Besides, it's too late to do anything."

"What can we help with tomorrow?" George asked eagerly.

"I want you to check out Jody," Nancy said. She told her friends about Jody's new car. "Call around and try to find out whether or not she paid cash. I'll check out Dave."

Bess put her arm around Nancy. "Don't worry," she said as if she sensed Nancy's frustration. "We still have a couple of days to get to the bottom of this."

When Nancy woke up the next morning she saw that the message light on her phone was lit. She dialed the operator, who told her that George and Bess had had to make an emergency trip home. Apparently something had happened to

Bess's parents, and the cousins had left first thing that morning.

Nancy showered and got dressed. She tried calling the Marvins' house, but there was no answer. As she left her condo she found herself hoping that everything was okay with Bess and George. She realized, though, that there was nothing she could do to help them. She had her hands full trying to help herself.

Nancy decided to start with Jody since Bess and George couldn't. She was heading past the ski shop on her way to the main building when she heard a familiar voice.

"Just the person I wanted to see," Ben called. "Come on into the ski school."

Nancy followed him inside and over to the ski school counter. He pulled a pair of skis and poles from behind the counter. "Look what I've got for you." He handed Nancy the set, along with boots and a folded sheet of paper.

"It's from Jody," Nancy said as she read the typewritten note dated the day before. "She said the equipment's from the latest shipment." Looking at Ben, Nancy asked, "Do you know where Jody is? I want to thank her." She also wanted to question Jody, but she didn't want to tell Ben that.

"It's her day off," Ben answered. "Sometimes she comes here and skis, but I think I heard her say something about staying home today."

Nancy tried to hide her disappointment. She'd have to find Dave first now. She thanked Ben and asked if he could keep her new equipment there for her. "I have a few things to do. Maybe I'll be back later to ski."

"No problem," Ben said, putting the equipment against the wall behind the counter. "Let me know if you want another lesson."

Nancy excused herself and went to the administration building to find Dave. But when she reached the office, both his door and Karl's were closed and locked.

"I think Dave's out skiing this morning," the receptionist said in response to Nancy's question. "If you want to see him, you might try the Cascades trail. It's one of his favorites."

Nancy hustled back to the ski school to pick up her equipment. Outside she tightened her boots into the ski bindings and slid her hands into the pole straps, then skied gracefully to the trail head.

For a few minutes Nancy just concentrated on skiing. The new skis were shorter and the poles longer than the ones she had used before. Ben had told her it would be the perfect equipment for skating, but it took Nancy a few minutes to feel comfortable with it. Soon, though, she was gliding along the trail, pushing off with her left ski and gliding on the right as Ben had taught her. There was no doubt about it. The new equipment was terrific, and she was soon skiing at a fast clip.

The beginning of the trail was easy, and her arms and legs were moving in a tight, comfortable rhythm. Nancy kept her eyes peeled for

Dave, and as soon as Aerie split off she took Cascades. After only a few minutes on the trail Nancy spotted a man with a Tall Pines jacket in the distance. She put on the speed, sure that it must be Dave Kendall. When there was only twenty feet between them Nancy called out his name.

"Dave! Wait for me!"

The man turned—it was Dave. Instead of slowing his stride, though, Dave quickened it, shooting farther away from her.

Nancy wasn't going to let him get away that easily. She slid both skis into the tracks and resumed a diagonal stride. She stretched her right arm out, gaining the maximum distance she could with her pole. As she pushed off with all her might, pulling the pole behind her, her other arm swung forward.

The distance between Nancy and Dave shortened. She reached forward again, putting more power into her poling. It was the only way she knew to gain real speed. If she could just keep going, she'd catch him.

With a final burst of energy Nancy began to double-pole. She reached forward with both poles at the same time, pushing off with every ounce of energy she could muster. The trail dived down into a deep forest. Dave was closer. In a few more strokes she'd be down the slope next to him. She reached forward and dug her poles into the snow.

Then suddenly, without warning, Nancy felt herself fall forward. One minute she was skiing—the next, the binding on her right ski had snapped open.

Nancy tried to control herself, but it was no use. She fell to the ground, head over heels—and started rolling and tumbling downhill, headed straight for a huge tree.

Chapter

Fourteen

NANCY CONTINUED to hurtle through the air. Moving instinctively, she tucked her body into a ball and shifted her weight to the right.

It worked! Nancy rolled in the snow and slid to a stop just inches from the tree.

"Are you okay?" Dave Kendall's skis sprayed snow as he stopped next to Nancy.

She took a moment to catch her breath, then stood up carefully. "I'm fine," she answered, brushing the snow off.

Before she could say anything more Dave headed back up the trail. When he returned a minute later he was carrying Nancy's skis under one arm. "These must be yours," he said as he handed them to her.

Nancy took the skis and checked them out. There didn't seem to be anything wrong with the binding that had snapped open, no reason why it should have failed. But as Nancy looked more closely she saw that the front screw, the one that held the binding to the ski, was missing. It must have been loose when she started up the trail, and the extra force she put on the skis racing downhill toward Dave had caused it to come out.

"You could have been seriously hurt," Dave said when Nancy showed him the binding.

Nancy gave Dave a long look before she spoke. "I've been involved in an awful lot of 'accidents' since I came to Tall Pines," she said. "A jammed sauna door, mysteriously switched trail signs, poisoned soup, and now a broken binding. I'm beginning to wonder why someone's trying to hurt me."

"I guess you never thought being a reporter could be such a dangerous profession," Dave said, raising his eyebrow. "Or that a ski resort could be such a treacherous place."

With that, Dave turned around in the trail and started to ski off, leaving Nancy to walk back by herself. Nancy instantly weighed the consequences of dropping her cover. It was something she had to do if she was going to get anywhere with him and her questioning.

"I'm not a reporter, Dave," she called to him evenly.

He turned around to face her, his nervousness and anxiety apparent. "You're not?" he asked.

Nancy let her ski drop to the ground. "No. I'm a detective."

"A detective!" Dave let loose a peal of laughter. "A detective!"

This was hardly the response Nancy had expected. "What's so funny?" she asked, studying him curiously.

"This whole time I thought you were a reporter." He paused. "Aren't you awfully young to be a detective?" he asked.

"Not really," Nancy told him, crossing her arms. "You still haven't explained what's so funny."

Suddenly Dave got serious. "Nothing."

Nancy paused. "It wouldn't have anything to do with that missing bank file, would it?" she asked.

Before Dave could answer, two skiers came down the trail, and Dave stepped out of their way. As soon as they had passed, Nancy asked him again about the file that was missing from his office. "Where is it, Dave?" she asked. "What's in it that made you take the file? Does Rob Watson have it?" she bluffed.

At Watson's name Dave shot Nancy an angry look. "What do you know about Watson?"

"Only that I saw you skiing with him last night," Nancy told him. "And that I suspect the two of you are behind my 'accidents.'"

"What makes you say that?" Dave asked. He leaned on his ski poles and narrowed his eyes. "What if I told you I was just giving Rob a friendly tour of our state-of-the-art trails?"

"That doesn't explain what he was doing in the administration building the other night," Nancy said, meeting his glance. "Or why you've always been near whenever I've almost been injured."

Nancy ticked off the evidence on her fingers. "Fact: You knew I was going to take a sauna. Fact: You came by my table the night I was poisoned. I'd say it's probably even a fact that you and Rob stole the money from Tall Pines and framed Rebecca for it—"

"That's enough!" Dave stopped her. He held up a gloved hand and shook his head slowly. "I'll tell you the truth. I did block that sauna door, and I even switched the trail signs. I came by the ski shop right after you and that girl went up on the trails. Ben told me you were skiing Aerie. I came up Cascades and switched the signs."

"But why?" Nancy asked. "Lots of people could have gotten hurt, not just Bess."

Dave hung his head for a moment, then finally looked at Nancy. "I believed that you were a reporter," he said, giving Nancy a weak smile, "not a detective. I wanted you to give Tall Pines a rotten write-up. The best way to guarantee that was to cause trouble for you. But I never meant for anything serious to happen—you have to believe me."

"The poisoning wasn't serious?" Nancy emphasized the last word. "You could have killed me!"

"I dribbled only a couple of drops of the water in your soup when I stood the vase up," Dave explained. "It was enough to make you sick but not seriously harm you. And I knew someone would come along when you were locked in the sauna. As far as the trails are concerned, I didn't know your friend was a novice skier."

"What about these?" Nancy asked, pointing to the bindings on her skis. "Was this another one of your planned 'accidents'?"

"Nope," Dave said, holding up his hands. He shook his head and leaned forward on his poles to look at the bindings. "I didn't have anything to do with that."

Nancy narrowed her eyes. "Were you anywhere near the skating pond last night?" she asked.

"Nope," Dave repeated. "Why?"

"Someone knocked me cold, and since you've admitted to the other accidents, I thought maybe you were responsible for that one, too," she said.

"I wasn't near the place." Dave actually smiled now. "Looks like I'm not the only one who wants to give you a hard time, eh?"

Nancy didn't think he was funny. She wasn't sure he was telling the truth. But if he was, there was still another criminal to catch. She kicked at the snow and thought out loud. "You wanted me to give Tall Pines a bad write-up. Why? Was your stealing the payroll cash part of your plan to cause trouble at Tall Pines, too?"

"I didn't have anything to do with the theft," Dave said, suddenly very serious again. "As far as I know, Rebecca Montgomery took the money."

"Rebecca denies it, and I believe her." Nancy told him that Rebecca was the reason she was at Tall Pines. "I honestly believe she's innocent. In fact, I still think Rob masterminded the theft and you were his accomplice."

"What?" Dave's face reflected his shock. "You've got to be kidding."

"No, I'm not. It's hardly a secret that Rob is making major improvements at his camp. How's he paying for them?" Nancy looked at Dave for a moment before she said, "I saw the file you have on Rob in your office, and I know how little money he makes. I think you and Rob decided that an extra fifty thousand dollars would help him nicely."

"Look, Nancy, I had nothing to do with that robbery, and neither did Rob." Dave's voice was low and insistent. "I admit I engineered those accidents, but I didn't steal anything."

"Where did Rob get the money for the construction?" Nancy asked.

"The same place most people do—the bank. He took out a huge construction loan. I thought he was crazy to start a big project, but sometimes you can't talk sense to Rob."

Nancy watched as a clump of snow slid down a pine bough and landed on the ground. "What's between you and Rob, anyway? When did you get to be such good friends? I doubt Karl Reismueller will be happy to hear about your friendship," she concluded.

Dave was hesitant but finally spoke up. "No, Karl wouldn't be too happy, especially if he found out I work for Rob Watson," he said.

"You work for Watson?" Nancy asked, stunned by the news.

"Yep." Dave pressed his lips together. "I know it sounds a little sleazy, and I guess it is. When Rob heard about Karl's plan to open Tall Pines, he asked me to get a job here and do what I could to sabotage the place. Then, when I told him a reporter was coming to review Tall Pines, he thought it was the perfect opportunity. He told me to make sure you gave Tall Pines a bad write-up. What better way than to make you miserable while you were here?"

Shaking her head in disgust, Nancy said, "That's pretty low."

"The resort business is competitive, but as in any other business, people don't always compete honestly," Dave said with a shrug. "But I didn't steal that money, and I don't know a thing about your bindings, or who knocked you out cold, or that missing file you keep talking about. That's the truth." He laughed a little. "I know you don't have any reason to believe me, but I am leveling with you."

With that Dave picked up Nancy's broken ski and studied the binding. "I think I can fix this good enough to get you down the trail," he said, pulling out a pocket knife. As Nancy watched, Dave moved another screw to the front of the binding.

"You'll have to go slowly," he told her, "but it will sure beat walking."

Nancy hooked her boots into the bindings and tried to glide. Though she felt a slight wobbling, the skis seemed reasonably secure.

"I think it'll be okay," she told Dave. "Thanks."

He stepped into his own bindings and slid his hands into the pole straps. "I'm not proud of my part in this," he said as he skied in the tracks next to Nancy. "When I get back I promise I'll tell Karl I quit. I hope you can keep it quiet about your 'accidents.' I really can assure you that I never meant to harm you."

"I'm glad to hear you say that," Nancy said. "Because if you weren't quitting, I would have to press charges against you. I'd suggest you clear out as soon as you can."

When they reached the bottom of the trail Nancy returned her skis to the shop, her mind fully occupied. The fact that Dave Kendall was only partially responsible for what had been happening at Tall Pines was frustrating news. It meant that Nancy still had to discover who had knocked her out, sabotaged her skis, and stolen the payroll money. It also failed to explain who Sheila's mystery man was or who had taken the missing bank file.

Nancy was about to find Jody Ashton's home address when her name was paged over the intercom. She picked up a house telephone on the ski school counter and told the operator she was ready for the call. In a second Chief McGinnis's voice came through.

"You were right, Nancy," the police chief told her. "One of those people does have a record. She was picked up for grand theft auto."

Theft. It was what Nancy had expected, the repetition of a crime pattern.

"Who was it?" she asked. "Sheila Reismueller?"

"No, Nancy. Sheila's clean. Your car thief is Jody Ashton."

124

Chapter

Fifteen

NANCY HUNG UP the phone, her mind whirling. Jody had left her the skis with the faulty bindings. Part of Jody's employment application was missing from the files—probably in order to hide her criminal past. Although she claimed to be saving for college, Jody had just bought a brand-new car.

"Nancy?" It was Dave Kendall. He had just come in and was standing next to her, a concerned expression on his face. "Is everything okay?"

After letting out a deep breath, Nancy nodded and took out her notebook from her belt pack. "I'm fine. Look—I need a favor."

"Anything. I owe you at least one." He leaned toward Nancy and whispered, "Thanks for being so understanding about what I did," he said.

"It's between you and Karl when you leave," Nancy said. She grabbed a pencil from her belt pack and said, "I need to know Jody Ashton's address."

Dave picked up the house phone and waited for the operator to answer. Within a few minutes he'd gotten Jody's address and phone number for Nancy.

Nancy thanked him and headed out of the ski shop and toward her condo. Once she got there she tried calling Jody's house, but there was no answer. She also called the Marvins' again, but no one was home there, either. Sighing, Nancy picked up the flashlight and stashed it in her purse. The flashlight might prove useful if she needed to get a confession out of Jody. Nancy was sure she'd smelled Sheila's perfume in the building, but there was a chance—however slim—that Jody had been the one to knock her out.

When Nancy reached Monroe ten minutes later it was just noon. She drove through the main shopping area and stopped at a gas station to ask for directions to Jody's street. The brand-new green sports car was parked in front of the building, so Nancy knew that the girl was home.

Nancy parked her Mustang and found Jody's apartment listed on the directory.

"Hi, Nancy." Jody gave her a friendly if confused smile. "What brings you here?"

"Can I come in?" Nancy asked. As she stepped inside Nancy found herself surprised by Jody's reaction. If Jody had loosened the ski bindings,

she should have been startled—even shocked—
to see her.

"Those were some skis you left me," Nancy
said casually, her hands in her jacket pockets.

"What skis?" Jody seemed to be puzzled.

"The ones with the new bindings."

Jody frowned. "I know I promised you new
skis, but the shipment didn't come in before I left
yesterday. I'm hoping it'll be there when I go
back tomorrow."

Nancy wondered if Jody could be as innocent
as she was acting. If she was, Nancy was obviously on the wrong track. "Jody, Ben gave me new
skis with a note from you," she said.

This time Jody made no attempt to hide her
confusion. "But I didn't write any note—I don't
know what you're talking about."

Nancy felt for the note in her jacket pocket,
took it out, and handed it to Jody. "That's not
your signature?" she asked.

"No," Jody said, slowly reading over the note.
She grabbed her purse from the coffee table,
pulled out a pen, and scrawled her name on the
note. Sure enough, the looping script was not at
all similar to the angular signature on the typed
note.

"I wasn't even at Tall Pines today," Jody went
on. "How could I have left you those skis? Why
are you asking all these questions anyway?"

Nancy took the note back from Jody and went
to sit on a cream love seat in the middle of the
living room.

"Someone loosened the bindings on one of the

skis I thought you'd left me," Nancy told her. "I was out on the trails and nearly had a very serious accident."

Jody blanched. "You think *I* did it?" There was a note of outrage in her voice.

"I think you could have," Nancy answered.

"But why would I?"

Nancy decided to make her answer completely straightforward. "To keep me from finding out that you stole the payroll money."

"What?" Jody began to pace her living room, her green eyes alive with anger. "I didn't steal any money! Rebecca did that."

"Rebecca was framed," Nancy said evenly. "You're my number-one suspect."

Jody stopped pacing and was silent for a long minute. When she spoke her face was pale. "What makes you say that?" she asked in a low voice that had a slight quaver.

"First of all, there's the unexplained money," Nancy said. She leaned forward on the couch, resting her forearms on her knees. "You told me how much you needed money for college, then you showed up in a new sports car. One explanation is that you used money you stole from Tall Pines for your car."

Two red spots appeared on Jody's cheeks. "I didn't take the money," she declared.

"Jody," Nancy said slowly, "I know about your car theft conviction."

When Jody spoke her voice was seething with anger. "That's over!" she cried. "I paid for that, and believe me I learned my lesson."

"What happened exactly?" Nancy asked.

Jody sat down in an armchair across from Nancy. When she spoke it was so quietly that Nancy had to strain to hear her words. "A friend and I took her father's car for a joyride one night. We got into an accident and did some damage to the car. I don't know why, but he pressed criminal charges against me. It was booked as grand theft auto, and since I was driving when we got caught, I took the whole rap." Jody shuddered as she recounted her experience. "I got a light sentence, but even so, it was not pleasant. I'll *never* steal again."

There was no doubting Jody's sincerity. Nancy remembered how violently Jody had reacted when she'd first mentioned the theft, and how Jody had declared that Rebecca deserved what she'd gotten. Now that Nancy knew Jody's background she could understand the outburst. She'd paid for her crime. If Rebecca was the thief, Jody felt that she should do the same.

"What about the Corvette?" Nancy asked. "Where'd you get the money for that?"

"The car was a mistake," Jody admitted, grimacing. "I thought I wanted it more than anything else, so I decided to use my college money for the down payment. Now that I've got it, I've realized that college is more important than any car. Luckily the dealer gave it to me on a two-day trial. I'm taking it back this afternoon."

Nancy flashed Jody a reassuring smile. "I think that's a good decision." She paused. There was just one more thing Nancy had to be sure of before she completely ruled Jody out as a suspect. She pulled the flashlight from her purse. "Ever see this before?" she asked.

"Looks like an ordinary flashlight to me," Jody said with a shrug. Then she leaned closer to get a better look. "Wait a minute." Taking the flashlight from Nancy, Jody touched the cracked lens. "This is Karl's," she said. "How did you get it?"

"Karl's!" Nancy exclaimed. "Karl Reismueller's? Are you sure?"

"Of course I'm sure." Jody leaned back in the chair, a smile on her lips. "I've seen him use it. I even kidded him about it once. He said he was too busy to get it fixed." She made a wry smile. "If I had as much money as Karl does, I think I'd just throw it away and get a new one."

So it was Karl Reismueller who'd knocked her out—or someone using Karl's flashlight. All Nancy's reasons to suspect Jody were now gone. All, that is, except for the missing bank file.

"Jody, I have just one more question," Nancy said.

"Shoot," said Jody.

"Did you have any reason to take a file of bank records from Dave Kendall's office?" she asked.

Jody squinted, obviously thinking about Nancy's question. "No." She shrugged. "But if there's something you need to know, I'm good friends with Alyssa Shelly, one of the managers at Monroe Savings and Loan."

Nancy practically hugged the girl. "Perfect. Do me a favor and tell her I'm coming down to ask her a few questions." Nancy waited while Jody made the call. When the girl finished, Nancy said, "I'm sorry I had to ask you so many embarrassing questions. I hope you understand why I thought what I did."

"Don't worry," Jody said. She tossed her auburn curls and smiled. "It's not the first time that stupid mistake has haunted me."

Jody walked outside with Nancy. "I want to return this car before anything happens to it," she said, sighing as they came up to it. "It's beautiful, but to tell you the truth, driving such an expensive car makes me nervous."

Nancy waved goodbye and drove off in the direction of the bank. Along the way she spotted a public phone and decided to try calling the Marvins' one more time.

"I don't understand this whole thing," Bess's mother said when she answered the phone. "Mr. Marvin and I got a phone call this morning telling us to go to the hospital. We hurried over there to find Bess. At the same time Bess was here looking for us."

Nancy frowned.

"Are George and Bess there now?" she asked.

"No," Mrs. Marvin answered. "They drove back up to Tall Pines. Bess said they wanted to help you with your investigation."

As she got back into the Mustang Nancy was relieved that everything was okay, but also worried. The same person had obviously called both Bess and her parents and given them conflicting messages. Was that person Sheila Reismueller? If so, why had she wanted Bess and George out of the way?

The traffic light was red. While she waited for it to turn green Nancy glanced at the stores around her. A short man in a black and white houndstooth suit and a black fedora stopped in front of one of the stores. Reaching into his pocket, he drew out a key and unlocked the door. Nancy stared at him and knew there was no doubt. He was the same man she'd seen with Sheila!

When the light turned green Nancy found a parking spot, got out of her car, and hurried over to the shop. Sam's Pawnshop, the sign said.

The thought of the Reismuellers' financial problems stuck in Nancy's mind as she went in and scanned the shop. Every imaginable item from household appliances to ice skates was arranged on shelves that stretched from floor to ceiling. Were the Reismuellers' problems so bad that Sheila had to pawn something of hers— something valuable?

"Can I help you, miss?" the man in the houndstooth suit asked. Without his fedora he didn't look half so distinguished. His hair was greased back, his eyes were bloodshot, and his hands were long, thin, and bony. "What are you looking for?"

"Do you have any diamond pins?" she asked, knowing it was a shot in the dark.

The man unlocked a drawer behind the counter and pulled out two pins on a velvet-covered tray. "The starburst is nice," he said, "but this other one is one of a kind."

Nancy drew in a deep breath as the man handed her the very same diamond horseshoe pin that had once been Sheila Reismueller's favorite.

"This is beautiful," she said as she held the horseshoe, "but I think you must be mistaken. I'm sure I've seen another one like it."

"No, miss," the man said quickly. "The owner had it made specially for her. I know. I bought it from her myself."

"And how long ago was that?" Nancy asked, turning the pin over in her hands. On the back the initials *SR* were engraved. It had to be Sheila's!

"Just a couple of days ago. I have some more jewelry from the same woman—if you'd care to see it." Nancy shook her head as the man took the pin from her. "Will you be wanting to buy this, then?"

Nancy tried to hide her smile of satisfaction. The pawnbroker had just confirmed her suspicions. "I'll think about it," she said.

The man nodded, putting the pin back on its velvet tray. "Come back and see me when you've made up your mind."

Nancy thanked him and left. As she closed the pawnshop door behind her she felt her excitement building. Sheila had obviously met the man at least twice. Now the question was, did Sheila steal the payroll to help Karl, or was that all Karl's doing?

Two blocks later Nancy pulled her car up in front of the Monroe Savings and Loan. After a few minutes she was sitting at Alyssa Shelly's desk and explaining to the manager who she was.

"I realize this may be confidential information," Nancy said, meeting the woman's soft brown eyes. "But there are a few things I need to know about the resort's finances."

Alyssa Shelly clasped her hands on her desk. "What kind of information?"

"Is Tall Pines sound financially?" Nancy asked. "I mean, would an investor, say, have any reason to doubt she'd put her money in a solid venture?"

Alyssa gave Nancy an apologetic smile. "I'm sorry, but I really can't give out that kind of information."

Nancy thought for a moment. "Can you at least tell me whether Karl Reismueller has any outstanding loans with your bank?"

After a moment Alyssa nodded. "Yes, he does."

Leaning forward in her chair, Nancy said, "Just tell me if I'm right about something. I have a feeling Karl has been late with his payments lately, but that suddenly—say, just about three and a half weeks ago—he made a payment of forty-eight thousand dollars." Studying Alyssa closely, she asked, "Do your records back that up?"

Alyssa glanced through the papers in the file on

her desk. "I'd say those are pretty good guesses," she said with a smile. She hastened to add, "I can't confirm that officially, though."

Grinning, Nancy thanked Alyssa for her help. That was all the proof she needed. Karl Reismueller was definitely her man.

Chapter

Sixteen

KARL DID IT, Nancy thought as she drove back
to Tall Pines. As strange as it seemed, he had
stolen money from his own company to make the
loan payments. From the files she'd seen on the
computer, Nancy knew that the expense of opening Tall Pines had drained him of cash. Now she
knew he'd been in danger of losing the resort.
Karl was obviously willing to do anything to keep
the resort running.

Nancy parked her car next to her condo and
raced inside. She wanted to call Bess and George
to tell them what she knew. When she placed the
call she found out the cousins weren't back yet.
As soon as she hung up the phone, it rang. The
operator came on the line and told her Karl had
left a message asking her to find him on the
Cascades trail. Nancy thanked her and hung up.

Great, Nancy thought. That saved her the trouble of looking for him. Before leaving to meet Karl Nancy called and left a message for Bess and George telling them where she'd be.

With that Nancy picked up her old skis and headed to the trail head. Karl hadn't said where on the trail he would meet her, but she ran into Ben as he was coming out of the ski shop.

"Karl told me to meet him on the Cascades trail," she told him. "Do you have any idea where on the trail I should try?"

Ben shrugged. "That's odd. I know he does like the view near the hut where Cascades and Aerie meet. He might have gone there."

"Thanks." Nancy flashed Ben a quick smile, put on her bindings, and headed up Aerie, which she knew would be the fastest way to get to the small hut. As she skied she felt a chill and wondered why she was going off alone to meet Karl. It seemed strange that he wanted her to find him on the trail. Given what she knew about Karl and his deceptions, she knew she shouldn't trust the man. Still, she wanted to confront him with what she knew, and the sooner she did that, the better.

The sun was beginning to set. If Nancy hadn't been so worried about finding Karl, she would have enjoyed the view. The fiery red ball of a sun appeared to be suspended among the pines, and the growing darkness cast a mysterious pink glow over the trail.

Nancy had no time to admire it, though. Her

arms and legs were moving in a smooth and steady rhythm as she forced each stride to take her farther and faster.

When she first saw Karl he was only a speck in the distance. For a few minutes she wasn't even sure it was him. Then he turned slightly, and she recognized his profile. The man was definitely Karl Reismueller.

He was skiing more slowly than Nancy. As she drew closer Karl stopped. It took only a few more glides for Nancy to reach the man's side.

"We've got to talk." Her words came out in short bursts as she tried to catch her breath.

In a movement so swift she had no way of anticipating it, Karl grabbed Nancy's arm.

"I don't think there's anything to talk about," he snarled. "You've meddled once too often. This time you're not going to get away with it."

Nancy jerked her arm, trying to break loose from Karl, but she had no success.

"You're going to have an unfortunate accident." Karl laughed, and the sound sent shivers up Nancy's spine. There was no mirth in his laughter, only evil pleasure.

Suddenly he released her arm. "Stay next to me," he ordered. "Don't even think about getting away."

Nancy took a deep breath, trying to quell her fear. She leaned forward on her poles and pushed off. In that split second she had the advantage of surprise. When Karl had grabbed her arm he had dropped his poles, leaving them hanging by the straps around his wrists. It took him a few precious seconds to grip the poles and begin to ski. Those seconds were all Nancy needed.

She skied off the trail and into the forest. On the Aerie trail, with its double set of tracks, she'd have no chance of escaping Karl. Here she'd have the protection of the trees. Their trunks were so close together that only one skier could move comfortably between them. It would be more difficult for Karl to catch her.

Nancy kept her poles close to her side, bending over slightly to gain more power. Her arms and legs moved rhythmically, and her skis glided smoothly over the packed snow.

"You can't escape!" Karl's voice came from a distance.

Nancy refused to turn around. It would break her stride, costing her valuable seconds. She forced her arms to stretch even farther, propelling her skis forward.

"Give up, Nancy! You can't win." This time Karl's voice sounded closer.

Nancy shifted her weight to her right ski, turning sharply around a large pine tree. She needed a plan of escape. Her eyes moved quickly across the horizon. The forest thinned, and she could see a clearing. Was that dark spot a building?

"You'll never outski me," Karl taunted. There was no doubt that he was gaining on her. This time his voice sounded as though he was only a few yards behind her.

Nancy strained as she tried to identify the dark spot. It *was* a building! She recognized the small

139

hut where the trails divided. The building could be a safe haven. She had to reach it before Karl.

"Give up, Nancy! You have no chance."

The hut was in sight. Though every muscle in her arms and legs burned from exertion, Nancy forced them to move even more quickly. She was almost there.

"You fool!" Nancy could hear the swish of Karl's skis. He was close now, dangerously close.

She turned for the first time. He was only ten feet behind her, grinning as though he had no doubt he'd win.

Now! It had to be now!

Nancy gripped both poles. With a quick twist of her wrists she planted the poles on her binding release buttons. Then, before Karl realized what was happening, she stepped out of her skis.

"Stop!" he yelled.

He was too late. Nancy ran into the hut and slammed the door behind her.

She reached to slide the bolt shut, but her hand hit the flat wooden surface of the door. There was no bolt! With a cry of frustration Nancy realized she was trapped. With no way to lock the door, it would be only seconds before Karl broke in.

"That was very stupid, Nancy Drew." Karl shoved the door open and stood in the doorway. He reached into his pocket and drew out a gun.

Nancy stared at the gun and felt cold fear in the pit of her stomach. "You won't get away with it," she said, trying to keep her voice low and steady.

Karl took another step into the room and slammed the door behind him. "Who's going to stop me once you're gone?" he asked. The light of the fading sun streamed through the one window, and Nancy could see Karl's grin. "It's a shame your little accident this morning didn't finish you off."

She had to keep him talking. That would give her time to think of a plan. "So you were the one who fixed my bindings," Nancy said. "That was clever. If I had been hurt or killed, it would have looked like an accident."

Karl shrugged and trained the gun on her. "If it didn't, Jody would have taken the blame." He gave Nancy a long, appraising look. "I kept another copy of the note I wrote, just in case you threw the first one away. I had the story all planned. It's even better than the one you were supposed to be writing for *Tracks*. Want to hear my story?" Karl asked. "Jody found out you were a detective. She didn't want anyone to know about her stealing the money, so she arranged a little skiing accident."

Unfortunately, Nancy knew Karl had a story someone—even the police—might believe.

"Very nice," Nancy said. "I still don't know how you found out I was a detective."

"You're not the only one who knows how to investigate," Karl told her. "Your name sounded familiar, so I did some checking with people I knew in River Heights. They told me who you were. A quick call to *Tracks* confirmed it all. That's when I put two and two together about you and your friends. You were quite a trio. Isn't it a shame you won't see them again?"

For the first time Nancy felt real fear. "What did you do to George and Bess?" she demanded.

Karl laughed. "Don't worry. It was nothing permanent. Without you, they're no threat. I just got them out of the way today." He paused, cocked his eyebrow at her, and glanced at the gun he was holding. "I told you I planned everything. The only thing I didn't plan was that you'd walk away from your little skiing accident this morning."

Karl took another step toward Nancy. "When Sheila told me you were asking a lot of questions I started worrying. Then I happened to be passing by the administration building last night and saw you and your friend come out. That was when I knew I had to get rid of you."

"That wasn't very smart, leaving your flashlight in the snack bar," Nancy told him.

Karl made no attempt to deny Nancy's accusation. "I didn't plan to leave it," he said, "but I heard Sheila coming, and I didn't want her to know I was there. I slipped out before she saw me."

Nancy had to keep him talking while her mind raced for a plan. The door behind Karl was swinging in the wind. If she could just get past him, she might be able to escape.

"And you're willing to risk a murder rap just to cover up a theft?" Nancy asked, pointing at the gun in Karl's hand.

"You don't understand, do you, Nancy Drew?" Karl's voice was low and angry. "I was the man with the Midas touch. Everyone considered me a genius. People were always calling and asking for my opinion. Then things started to fall apart. Tall Pines cost a lot more than I'd planned, and we had a bad season at the toy stores. Suddenly the famous Karl Reismueller money machine wasn't making money anymore."

Karl's voice grew harsh. "I couldn't let anyone know. It would destroy my reputation."

"So you stole money from your own company."

Karl laughed. "I told you I was brilliant, didn't I? It was easy. The insurance company covered most of the loss, so I walked away with almost fifty thousand dollars."

Karl glanced at his watch. "We've wasted too much time," he said matter-of-factly.

With that, Karl cocked the gun.

"Nancy Drew, you've got to die."

Chapter
Seventeen

NANCY DREW IN a sharp breath. The sound of the gun's cocking echoed in her ears. Karl was truly serious. He *was* going to kill her!

"How will you explain a gunshot wound?" she asked, swallowing hard and trying to hide her fear. "No one will believe it was an accident."

Karl laughed. "Of course they won't! I'm smarter than that. The gun's only to make sure you ski over the cliff." He shook his head sadly. "It will be such an unfortunate accident. I may even close the trail for the rest of the season so that none of the other guests will be in danger." Karl's low chuckle made Nancy's skin crawl.

"People know I'm a good skier," Nancy said. To her own ears her voice sounded quite desperate. She hoped Karl couldn't tell. "No one will believe I skied off a cliff."

Karl wasn't interested in conversation. "Stop

stalling," he ordered. His empty hand pointed toward the door. "Out! It's time for you to take a little fall."

Nancy stepped toward the door. Karl was waiting for her to go out ahead of him. Just as she was passing him Nancy seized her only opportunity. She shot her leg out in the quick reflexive kick she'd been taught in her martial arts classes.

It worked! The gun went spinning out of Karl's hand and landed on the floor. Nancy lunged, tackling Karl with all her might. Though he was a big man, he wasn't prepared for the sudden attack. Surprise and skill were on Nancy's side, and he fell easily to the ground.

The gun lay on the floor two feet from Karl's outstretched hand. Nancy moved quickly, reaching for it. But her luck ran out. The older man was too swift. He grabbed Nancy's ankle and yanked her off balance.

"I'm going to kill you!" he cried as he wrestled with Nancy, trying to pin her to the floor. Although Karl far outweighed Nancy, she had the advantage of agility and cunning. She struggled against him, trying to keep him away from the gun. She twisted—hard—out of his grasp and rolled away from him. At that very moment the door swung open, and George and Ben burst into the room.

"Need a little help?" Ben asked.

For an instant Karl was so surprised that he didn't move. It was the break Nancy needed. She launched herself at Karl, forcing him back down on the floor.

George moved quickly to the side of the room. "I've got the gun," she announced, and she pointed it at Karl.

"Thanks, guys," Nancy said as she jumped to her feet. "Your timing was perfect."

"Are you sure they're all coming?" Sheila's voice quavered with emotion, and she drummed her fingers on the arm of the wingback chair. Though she was once again at home in her condo, it was obvious that she was still reliving the events of the previous evening.

"They'll be here," Nancy assured her.

Nancy had driven Sheila to the police station the night before and stayed with her while Karl was booked on charges of defrauding the insurance company, theft, and attempted murder.

"I still can't believe Karl did all that," Sheila said. "Of course, he never really confided in me about his business. Whenever I asked he told me it was complicated, and I wouldn't understand."

"But you did pawn your diamonds, Sheila. You must have known Tall Pines needed money."

"Karl told me we had minor cash-flow problems," Sheila explained. "I thought the quick money I'd get from selling my jewelry would help. But I had no idea he was in so deep or that he'd consider stealing." She hid her face in her hands. "Oh, Karl," Sheila said. When she looked up at Nancy there were tears in her crystal blue eyes. "It's a terrible thing when your husband's ambition turns him into a criminal."

Nancy felt bad for the woman. She obviously

had no idea of the awful things Karl was capable of. "I'm just glad George and Bess got back in time to save me," she said.

"You were very lucky," Sheila agreed. "How can I ever apologize to you for what has happened here?"

A brisk knock on the door prevented Nancy from answering. Sheila hesitated, then rose to her feet and opened it. "Come in," she said.

George and Bess were followed by Rebecca, Ben, and Jody. When everyone was seated Sheila leaned forward in her chair. Her blue eyes were serious, and her lips trembled as she began to speak.

"I asked you all to come here," she said, "because I wanted to apologize for everything that's happened. Even though I didn't take part in the things that Karl did, I do feel responsible. You see, Tall Pines was my dream. If it hadn't been for me, Karl would never have built the resort."

"It was a wonderful dream," Bess said. "This is the best resort I've ever seen."

Sheila managed a small smile. Then she turned to Rebecca. "I'm so sorry for what we put you through. I hope you'll take your job back."

Rebecca's grin was the only answer anyone needed. "I'll be back at work first thing tomorrow," she announced.

George shot Rebecca a conspiratorial look. "See," she said. "I told you Nancy would help."

There was one more question Nancy wanted answered. "Were you by any chance responsible for a page being missing from Jody's personnel file?" she asked Ben.

He flushed. "I was afraid you'd find out about Jody's conviction and put it in your article, so I destroyed that page."

The last pieces fit into the puzzle.

"You've been a great manager," Sheila told Jody. "The gift shop is booming, and so is the ski shop. I think you have the qualities I need in a general manager. Do you think you could handle the job?"

"You bet I could!" Jody exclaimed, her eyes widening.

"Then it's settled." Looking at Ben, Sheila added, "I'm going to hire a painter."

"A painter? Why do you need a painter?" he asked.

This time Sheila chuckled. "To letter the new sign. You know, the one that will say the Ben Wrobley Ski School."

Before Ben could react George cried, "That's great! It sounds so much better than the Inge Gustafson School."

"I'm glad you said that," Ben said with a laugh. "It would sound conceited coming from me."

"Of course, there's a pay raise that goes along with the new sign," Sheila pointed out. "You may have to wait a bit until I sell all our other assets, but even with the expense of Karl's defense I think I'll be able to manage raises."

A broad grin creased Ben's face. "That sounds even better than the sign." He leaned forward and smiled at Nancy. "And to make up for what you've been through, Nancy, I'll be glad to give you a season's free skiing lessons."

Nancy glanced at Sheila, Rebecca, George, and Bess before she answered Ben. "No, thanks," she said with a grin. "I think I'll try a less dangerous sport—something like hang gliding."

NOBODY'S
BUSINESS

Chapter

One

"WOULD YOU take a look at this place?" Bess Marvin exclaimed. "It's so romantic!"

Nancy Drew steered her blue Mustang into the parking lot of the Lakeside Inn and parked. "You think everything's romantic," she teased, turning to grin at her best friend. "Inns, movies, can openers, rutabagas . . ."

Giggling, Bess zipped up her fuchsia jacket and pulled her matching hat down over her long blond hair. "In this case you have to admit I'm right," she insisted, getting out of the car.

Nancy climbed out of the driver's side and stretched her long legs, which were stiff from the hour-long drive from the girls' hometown of

1

River Heights, in the Midwest. The cold January wind whipped through Nancy's reddish blond hair and numbed her cheeks and hands.

"The inn *is* beautiful," she agreed, her blue eyes gazing at the rambling old stone building nestled in a dense thicket of trees at the edge of a lake.

Two stories tall, the Lakeside Inn had turrets and gables and chimneys poking up from the sloping red clay roof, and stone terraces outside each window. To the right of the inn Nancy spotted a gazebo, a boathouse, and a pier that extended into the frozen silver lake.

"I can't wait to see the inside," Bess said. "Ned told you Andrew has already totally gutted it, right?"

Just hearing the name of her longtime boyfriend, Ned Nickerson, made Nancy want to see him. She'd seen him only once since he'd been home on winter break from Emerson College. Ned had been spending most of his time helping to renovate the Lakeside Inn. Andrew Lockwood, a friend of Ned's who had recently graduated from Emerson, was doing the renovation for his father, who owned the inn.

"I'm glad you suggested we pitch in and help with the renovation," Nancy told Bess, pulling up the hood of her kelly green parka. "This way Andrew gets two extra pairs of hands, I get to spend three whole weeks with Ned . . ."

"And I get to meet Andrew," Bess finished.

"George is going to be sorry she missed out."
George Fayne, Bess's cousin and Nancy's friend,
was on a ski trip in Colorado with her parents.

Laughing, Nancy locked the car, and the two
girls walked across the lot toward the inn. There
were only a few cars besides Nancy's, as well as a
beat-up red school bus with "TeenWorks"
painted along the side. Up ahead a semicircular
driveway led to the inn's front entrance, which
consisted of broad granite steps and a pair of
fifteen-foot-high wooden doors.

"There you are!" a deep, familiar male voice
called a moment later. "What took you so long?"

Despite the cold, Nancy felt warm all over as
she looked up to see her tall boyfriend, wearing
jeans and a flannel shirt, standing in the inn's
doorway. With his brown eyes and wavy brown
hair, he looked more handsome than ever. Nancy
broke into a run, her long legs speeding her up
the curved driveway and into Ned's outstretched
arms.

"I missed you," she whispered into his ear as
he held her close. Then she tilted back her head,
and their lips met in a lingering kiss.

"That was definitely a greeting worth waiting
for," Ned said, his brown eyes sparkling down at
her. "Hi, Bess," he added, giving her a kiss on the
cheek. "Come on in and meet Andrew, you guys.
He's been dying to meet my girlfriend, the world-
famous detective."

Nancy blushed slightly. She had solved dozens

of cases, but she was still embarrassed by the attention she sometimes received. "For the next few days don't think of me as a detective," she said quickly. "Think of me as a pair of helping hands. You're not the only one on break, Ned."

"Sorry we're late," Bess added. "I had to run some errands for my mother."

Nancy and Bess followed Ned into the large high-ceilinged lobby. The floor was covered with sawdust, but Nancy could still see how elegant the decor had once been. On either side of the lobby an elegant staircase with a mahogany banister curved gracefully up to the second floor. An open doorway framed by marble columns led to a long hallway that ran from left to right.

Ned showed Nancy and Bess a metal rack in the lobby where they could leave their jackets. "I'll give you a complete tour later," he told them. "Basically all the rooms facing the front are offices, and the rooms facing the lake are for guests. There's going to be a kitchen, a dining room, a ballroom, and a library, too."

"Sounds pretty grand," Nancy said, feeling her nose start to itch from all the sawdust. She searched in her jeans pocket for a tissue and found one just before she had to sneeze.

Bess nodded toward the curved stairways and asked, "What's upstairs?"

"Twenty bedrooms, each with a private bathroom," Ned told her.

"Sounds like a lot of work," Nancy commented.

Ned let out a long breath. "Tell me about it. The framework for the walls is already up, though, and we're almost finished with the electrical work," he explained. "We've just started the plumbing. Then we plasterboard the walls."

With a worried look at Ned, Bess said, "I hope you don't expect me to know exactly what I'm doing."

"Andrew's got a great foreman," Ned told her. "He'll tell you exactly what to do. Come on, let's go meet him. Andrew and some of the others are in the ballroom."

He led them through the marble columns and made a left down the hall, which was lit only by work lights hanging from overhead beams. The corridor ran the length of the inn. Its walls were made of stone, Nancy saw, with wooden framework built against them. Electrical cables were laced through the framework.

"Wow, this place is huge," Bess said, pausing as they went through a wide doorway. Nancy stopped next to her and looked around.

The ballroom was fifty feet long and had a vaulted ceiling that stretched the full height of the inn's two stories. An old chandelier still hung from the ceiling, but it didn't seem to be working. The room was lit by freestanding work lights. A large overhanging balcony jutted out of the left wall, about fifteen feet up. The ballroom floor was covered with large drop cloths, but a folded corner revealed a marble floor underneath. Loud, funky music blasted from somewhere overhead.

Half a dozen teenagers on ladders were scattered around the room, attaching electrical cable to wooden frameworks like the ones Nancy had seen in the hall. A few other teens sawed copper pipes over wooden sawhorses. Several more people stood in the middle of the room, talking and looking at an unscrolled blueprint set up on a table made of two wooden sawhorses and a few sheets of plywood.

"Andrew!" Ned called over the music. "Nancy and Bess are here."

A tall young man stepped away from the group around the blueprint and walked toward Nancy, Ned, and Bess. His straight black hair hung over his high forehead, and his hazel eyes were magnified by a pair of round, wire-rimmed glasses. He wore jeans and a black sweatshirt with white lettering that read Melborne Community Theater.

"Andrew Lockwood, meet my girlfriend, Nancy Drew," Ned said, putting his arm around Nancy. "And this is her friend Bess Marvin."

Andrew gave the girls a warm smile. "It's really nice of you to pitch in with the renovation," he told them. "At the rate we're going, I can use all the help I can get." He sighed, and several worry lines appeared on his forehead.

"What do you mean?" Nancy asked. "Aren't things going well?"

Andrew looked over his shoulder, as if to make sure no one else was near enough to overhear. "These renovations are taking a lot longer than I expected," he confided, frowning. "They're costing a lot more, too."

"I'm sorry to hear that," Nancy told him.

"I wish we'd come earlier," Bess added. "I think working here will be a lot of fun. This inn is definitely going to be great."

From the dazzling smile Bess gave Andrew, Nancy could tell that getting to know Andrew was what Bess was really looking forward to.

Andrew didn't seem to notice her interest, however. He merely shrugged and said, "I hope so. My father will kill me if I don't come through on this within the budget he gave me."

His last words were drowned out as the music switched to a new song with a catchy rhythm.

"Great music," Nancy told Andrew. She nodded toward a teenage girl with waist-length blond hair who moved to the beat as she worked on her ladder. "I see it helps keep your workers going."

"They're so young," Bess added. "They look like they're our age."

Andrew nodded. "They are," he said. "My dad gave me a very limited budget for the renovation, so to save money, I'm using TeenWorks. It's a vocational program for local teens, run by the county. The kids learn skills like plumbing, electrical work, carpentry . . . and they earn money at the same time. Though, of course, they don't earn as much as union workers."

"Don't they go to school?" Bess asked.

"This *is* school, some of the time," Andrew said. "They have classroom training, too, but a lot of their education is on the job."

"And that's where they *really* learn, of course," said a voice from behind Nancy's shoulder.

Turning, Nancy saw an attractive woman who looked to be in her early thirties and had shoulder-length red hair and a light dusting of freckles on her nose. She wore a green silk blouse that brought out the green of her eyes, faded blue jeans that showed her slim figure, and shiny black lizard-skin cowboy boots.

"Nancy, Bess, this is Colleen Morgan," Andrew said. "She's the coordinator for TeenWorks."

Colleen laughed. "What Andrew really means is that I'm a bored housewife looking for a way to kill time," she said, "so I volunteer."

Raising his eyebrows skeptically, Andrew said, "'Bored housewife' is hardly the term I'd use. Colleen is selflessly devoting her time to this project even though she could be jetting around the world," he explained to Nancy and Bess. "You see, she's married to Frederick Morgan— of Morgan Lumber, Morgan Steel, Morgan Financial Services—"

"Enough!" Colleen shushed Andrew, waving a

well-manicured hand that was heavy with rings. "You're giving away my dirty secret. Well, right now I need to be jetting around this building. I want to see how the rest of the gang is doing upstairs." With another wave of her hand, she headed for the archway leading out of the ballroom.

Nancy was impressed that this wealthy woman cared about helping others. She couldn't help thinking it would have made more sense if Colleen wore a sweatshirt and sneakers rather than her expensive outfit. Then again, maybe they *were* her casual clothes.

"Yo, Andrew," a wiry teenage boy spoke up as he entered the ballroom and sauntered toward them. He had razor-cut platinum blond hair and wore a baggy, untucked shirt, black jeans, and a pair of purple hightop sneakers.

"I hate to bother you," the boy said, "but it's sort of important."

"Sure, Blaster," Andrew said. "I want you to meet my friends, anyway."

"Blaster?" Bess asked, looking perplexed. "Is that really your name?"

The boy flashed Bess a cocky grin and said, "It's Master Blaster, the music meister."

"Blaster's our deejay," Andrew explained. "He keeps music playing on his tape player while we're working."

"The hottest mix in town," Master Blaster added, winking at Bess. "I'm wired for sound—

9

when I'm not doing the electrical wiring for the inn."

Bess's cheeks turned pink, and Nancy had to smile. It looked as if Bess had actually met a guy who was even more of a flirt than she was!

"Blaster's the assistant to the master electrician," Andrew informed them. "He graduated from TeenWorks in June, and now he's on staff." Turning back to Blaster, he said, "So what's up? Don't tell me there's another problem."

Blaster looked apologetic. "You told me to come to you if any more tools were missing. Well, now I can't find my soldering iron, and Natalia Diaz told me she's missing her three-eighths drill bit *and* the drill."

Andrew's lips pressed together in a thin line. "I can't believe this," he muttered. "Every day it's something else. Tools keep disappearing, some of the wiring got cut in the dining room, and someone tore up some of the floorboards upstairs."

Nancy didn't know much about construction, but something about these accidents seemed weird. "Where was your soldering iron the last time you saw it?" she asked Master Blaster.

"Upstairs, in one of the bedrooms," he replied. "My boss, Eddie, called me into another room for about two minutes. When I got back, the iron was gone."

"And you didn't see or hear anybody?" Nancy asked.

Blaster shook his head. "I don't know what it is," he said. "I've worked on a lot of jobs before, but I've never seen one where so many things went wrong." He fixed his dark brown eyes on Andrew. "Maybe somebody doesn't like you, man."

Suddenly a mischievous twinkle lit up Blaster's eyes, and he added, "Or maybe it's the Lakeside ghost."

"Ghost?" Bess echoed. She looked as if she didn't know whether to be amused or scared.

Blaster nodded. "Sure. An old place like this is definitely haunted," he said, doing a dance step in time to the beat of the music blasting overhead.

"Don't listen to him," Andrew told Bess, rolling his eyes. "He's just babbling."

"Sorry," Blaster said. "Oops! I think I hear Eddie calling me." With that he bounded out of the room.

Turning to Andrew, Nancy inquired, "So, what about this ghost story?"

"It's not really much of a story," Andrew said, shrugging. "The inn was built over a hundred years ago as a popular society resort. Lots of big business moguls from Chicago would come here and stay all summer."

"I can see why," Bess said, letting her blue eyes gaze around the room. "You can tell how elegant it must have been."

"I hope it will be again, too," Andrew said.

11

"Anyway, two of the families that came here, the Aarons and the Murrays, were bitter rivals because they owned competing oil companies. The families never even spoke to each other until one summer when Lawrence Aaron fell in love with Rosalie Murray."

"Uh-oh," Nancy said. "I can see where this is going."

Andrew grinned at her. "You guessed it. They wanted to get married," he said. "Their parents threatened to disown them, but they went ahead with the plans, anyway. The wedding was scheduled to take place in this very room."

"What happened?" Bess asked.

"The night before the wedding, there was a big fire at the inn," Andrew went on, "and Rosalie disappeared. The inn was nearly destroyed."

"What about Rosalie?" Ned asked. "Did they ever find her?"

"No," Andrew told him. "Some say she died in the fire, brokenhearted, and that her ghost still haunts the inn. But, of course, that's totally ridiculous. Everybody knows there's no such thing as—"

He broke off as the amplified music stopped in the middle of a song. A moment later a chilling, anguished wail echoed in the ballroom.

"Aaaaaaagh!"

The sound made Nancy's skin crawl and sent icy shivers running down her back.

"Aaaaaaagh!" The wailing continued, even

louder now, and Nancy jumped as it was echoed by a frightened scream from Bess. Up on their ladders and down on the floor, the teenage workers looked around anxiously.

"Oh, no!" Bess shrieked. "The ghost is right here in this room!"

13

Chapter

Two

LET'S GET OUT of here!" Bess shouted over the eerie shrieking. Her cry was echoed by some of the teen workers.

With a hand on Bess's arm Nancy looked quickly around the ballroom. "Calm down," she told everyone. "I'm sure there's an explanation."

"Maybe this place really *is* haunted," the blond girl on the ladder suggested.

The wails stopped as abruptly as they'd started, leaving a ringing echo in the huge room.

"It's haunted all right," Andrew said grimly. "By a practical joker with a bad sense of humor."

Nancy had been thinking exactly the same thing. Pointing up to the balcony, she said, "The music seemed to be coming from there, and it

14

stopped right before the wailing started. My guess is that someone's been playing with your stereo, Andrew. Can we go up there and check it out?"

"Good idea," Andrew said, heading for a door set in the wall beneath the balcony.

He led Nancy, Ned, and Bess through the door and up a dimly lit staircase. It smelled damp and musty, and cobwebs dangled from the ceiling. The group's footsteps echoed noisily as they climbed.

When they reached the top, Andrew led them through an open doorway and onto the balcony. A compact stereo system sat on the floor, its components stacked on top of each other and connected by wires to two large speakers.

Kneeling down in front of the stereo, Nancy placed a hand on top of the tape deck. It was still warm, even though it was turned off. Only one of the two cassette decks had a tape in it. Nancy pushed the Eject button and found a cassette hand-labeled Master Blaster's Super Mix. When she popped it back into the cassette deck and pressed the Play button, the same dance music that had been playing when they'd come in blasted from the speakers.

"Did you find anything, Nan?" Bess asked.

Nancy tapped the empty second cassette player. "It's what I didn't find that's got me wondering," she said. "Someone could have sneaked up these stairs and put in another tape of the wailing

15

sounds we heard. Then the person could have taken the tape out and sneaked out again."

"Blaster isn't going to be too happy that someone changed his program," Andrew commented, frowning. "In fact, I'm surprised he hasn't come up here, yelling like a maniac. He hates it when anyone else touches his sound system."

Nancy stared at Andrew. "I wonder why he didn't show up," she mused. Unless he was the one responsible, she added to herself. Blaster had left the ballroom a few minutes before the ghostly wails replaced the music. That was long enough for him to have changed the tapes himself.

Then she shook herself. Stop playing detective, she told herself. You're on vacation, remember?

Nancy looked up as Andrew let out a groan. "Every time there's a delay like this, it costs me money," he said, taking off his glasses and wearily rubbing his eyes. "My father's going to kill me if I go over budget."

"Don't worry about him," Ned said, clapping Andrew on the back.

As Ned spoke consolingly to Andrew, Nancy wandered toward the shadowy stairway. Just before the entrance to the balcony, she noticed an alcove she hadn't seen before. A metal plate was attached to the wall there, with several black dials on it and some holes with bare wires sticking out. It looked like a master light switch.

Before she could take a closer look, Nancy heard a sound on the stairs below her. She froze and listened. Were those retreating footsteps? Maybe the intruder was still nearby.

"Where are you going?" Bess asked as Nancy ran from the balcony.

"I'll be right back," Nancy called over her shoulder. She rushed down the stairs two at a time, trying to make out a figure in the darkness.

When Nancy got to the bottom, she realized that there was a hallway that led from the ballroom. The footsteps sounded far away, but Nancy ran blindly down the hallway toward them. Suddenly she saw a rectangle of daylight appear in the distance and a silhouetted figure pass through it before the hall went dark again. It was a door leading outside.

Picking up her pace, Nancy barreled the rest of the way down the hall, flung open the door, and felt a cold rush of winter air slap her in the face. She was standing a few yards from the rocky shore of Moon Lake.

Hearing a snapping, crackling sound to her right, Nancy turned and saw a slender girl with dark curly hair running toward a grove of trees. Though the girl was far away, Nancy could also see that she had a single streak of coppery red in the middle of her curls.

Nancy took off after the girl, but she kept losing sight of her among the dense evergreen trees. Then the girl disappeared altogether. Nancy stopped to listen, but the woods were still except for the sound of her own heavy breathing.

With a sigh of frustration, she trudged back to the inn. The sun was already setting over the lake, bathing the stone building in an orange glow.

The back door was ajar. As Nancy approached it from the rear, she pulled it open—then stopped short. "Blaster, what are you doing here?" she asked in surprise.

The wiry teenager looked just as surprised to see her. "Just, uh, getting some air," he mumbled. Then, turning his back to Nancy, he headed down the dark hallway toward the ballroom.

It was clear Blaster was covering something up. Could he have had something to do with the eerie music, or with the girl who'd just run off?

Nancy hurried to catch up with him. "Did you see anyone just now?" she asked. "A girl with curly dark hair?"

"I didn't see anybody," Blaster said, striding the last few steps to the door and throwing it open. "Like I said, I was just getting some air." Hands in his pockets, he walked past the other teenagers and left the ballroom.

"What happened to you, Nancy?" Bess asked as she, Ned, and Andrew hurried over to her. "You're sweating!"

Quickly Nancy described what she'd seen, adding Blaster's strange behavior. "Does that girl sound like anyone working here?" Nancy asked Andrew.

Andrew glanced uneasily at Nancy. "Not that I know of," he replied after a moment.

"Wait a minute," Ned said, turning to Andrew. "That sounds exactly like Jul—"

Andrew cut off Ned with an angry glare.

"Sorry," Ned said, backing off. "I know you don't like to talk about her."

"Talk about who?" Nancy asked. "If you have any idea who she might be, you should tell us. She could be the one causing the problems here."

Ignoring Nancy, Andrew said gruffly, "It's five o'clock—quitting time. Why don't you guys go home and meet me back here tomorrow morning at eight?"

Nancy studied Andrew's tensely set jaw and the troubled look in his hazel eyes. What had come over him all of a sudden?

"You know, Andrew," Bess said, laying a hand on his arm, "I feel so embarrassed at the way I freaked out over the ghost. I hope you won't hold it against me."

Andrew looked right over the top of Bess's head at two teenage boys pretending to duel with strips of wood, banging them together with loud clacks. "Hey!" Andrew shouted, striding away from Nancy and her friends. "Stop messing around!"

"Oh, well," Bess whispered to Nancy. "I guess I didn't make much of an impression on Andrew."

"Don't let it get you down, Bess," Ned said. "You wouldn't have had a chance with him no matter what."

"Oh, great," Bess said, rolling her eyes. "That's comforting."

"No, that's not what I meant." He shot Andrew a quick look, then said, "Let's go get some dinner. I'll explain then. There's a great Mexican restaurant right up the road."

"Thanks for driving me, by the way," Ned said. "I can't believe my car's in the shop—again."

"No problem," Nancy said, slipping her arm around his waist. "The more time we spend together, the better I like it. Consider me your personal chauffeur for the next three weeks."

After waving goodbye to Andrew, the three of them got their jackets in the lobby, then went out to Nancy's Mustang. Ned directed Nancy to a narrow road that curved around the lake. In a few minutes they saw a cluster of small buildings, among them a crafts boutique called A Show of Hands, a post office, a bank, a small grocery store, and a Mexican restaurant, Paquito's.

Nancy parked, then she and her friends entered the tiny restaurant. A half dozen wooden booths filled the room, and the stone walls were draped with colorfully striped blankets.

"So tell me," Nancy said, sliding into a wooden booth beside Ned. "What's the story with Andrew? What's he hiding about this J person?"

"He's not hiding anything, exactly," Ned began. "It just hurts him to talk about it. A few weeks ago his fiancée, Julie Ross, broke up with him. He's been really devastated ever since. I don't think he could even look at another girl."

"And you think that girl I saw was Julie?" Nancy asked.

Ned nodded. "She fits the description perfectly. How many girls have brown hair with a red streak running through it? And she works right next door here, at A Show of Hands. It's just a short walk from the inn."

"Why did Julie break up with him?" Bess asked. "He seems like a nice guy."

Ned plucked a tortilla chip from a bowl on the table and dipped it in salsa. "She got tired of waiting for Andrew to make up his mind," he explained. "See, Mr. Lockwood doesn't just own the inn. He owns a lot of real estate around here, and he wants to bring Andrew into the business now that he's out of college."

"I get it," Nancy put in. "This renovation project is like a trial run."

"Exactly," Ned told her. "The thing is, Andrew really wanted to be an actor. He planned to marry Julie and move with her to Los Angeles. He was going to start auditioning and taking acting classes. Julie's a sculptor, and she was applying to art school there."

"Sounds romantic," Bess said, her blue eyes shining. "Did Julie go to Emerson, too?"

Ned shook his head. "Actually, Andrew's four years older than Julie—she's nineteen. They met doing community theater in Melborne. That's where they're both from. It's about ten minutes from here. Andrew was acting, and Julie was painting sets. It was love at first sight."

"If they were so in love, then what was the problem?" she asked Ned.

"Andrew was really torn between Julie and his father, and he kept putting off moving. I think he's really afraid to disobey his father. Mr. Lockwood's a real dragon. Finally Julie just ran out of patience. She decided she'd rather break up with Andrew than wait any longer."

"I feel sorry for Andrew and Julie," Bess said, sighing.

"It *is* too bad," Nancy agreed, "but it could explain what's going on at the inn. Julie might still be so resentful that she's causing trouble just to get back at Andrew and his father."

"It's possible," Ned said. "So that's the story, Bess. I hope you're not too disappointed."

"I'll get over it," Bess said cheerfully. "Besides, I happened to notice that Master Blaster's really cute, too."

A waitress came to take their order, and soon the table was filled with steaming, cheesy enchiladas, crisp tacos, and rice and beans.

As they ate, Nancy kept thinking about Andrew's predicament. "No wonder Andrew kept mentioning how angry his father's going to be," she said aloud, nibbling on her taco. "It sounds as though Mr. Lockwood will have a fit if the inn isn't a success."

"You said it," Ned agreed. "Andrew's petrified. He's almost used up all the money his father gave him for the renovation, and there's still a ton of work to be done. Plasterboard, floors, fixtures. If anything else goes wrong, he'll be a nervous wreck."

"Maybe we can help," Nancy offered. "I mean, if we can figure out who's behind the pranks, that will be one less thing for him to worry about."

Ned was about to object, but then he leaned over to kiss Nancy on the cheek. "So much for taking a break from detecting," he joked. "I bet Andrew *would* appreciate your help."

Tapping the table with her fingernail, Nancy said, "Too bad we can't go back for another look right now. It'd be easier to check out the place without everyone else there, but it's probably locked, right?"

Ned pulled a key from his pocket. "Not to me," he announced. "Andrew gave me this. It's for the back door, so I can get in when he's not there."

After dinner Nancy, Ned, and Bess drove back to the inn and let themselves in the back door. It was the same one Julie had escaped through, Nancy realized. The long hallway was even dark-er than it had been earlier, and Nancy couldn't find a light switch. She fumbled in her purse for her penlight but couldn't find it.

"Uh-oh," Bess said as the three of them felt their way down the pitch-black corridor. "This place is even creepier at night than in the daytime."

At last they reached the door to the ballroom. After quietly opening it, they stepped into the cavernous room, which was already glowing from the shafts of moonlight slanting in through the windows. The dark shadows of sawhorses and ladders made irregular shapes on the floor.

"Aha! Here it is," Nancy crowed, finally finding her penlight in her purse. Flicking it on, she said, "Let's start at the front entrance."

Shining the small, powerful beam, she led the way out of the ballroom and down the main hall. As they stepped into the lobby, she shone her penlight over the sawdust-covered floor, then raised it higher.

Nancy tensed as her beam barely caught a strange swinging movement over their heads.

"What's that?" Bess asked nervously as a faint, creaking noise sounded.

Nancy swept the beam of light toward the ceiling—and her mouth fell open in silent horror.

Hanging from the rafters in a noose was a limp, lifeless body!

Chapter

Three

BESS GAVE A piercing scream. "He's dead!"

Nancy felt stiff with fear, but she forced herself to shine the penlight over the hanging form, from the bottom up.

The person wore no shoes, just white sweat socks and a pair of old, baggy jeans tied tightly around the waist with a rope. Aiming the beam higher, Nancy saw that the torso was covered by a plain gray sweatshirt tucked into the jeans.

Taking a deep breath, she aimed the light at the person's face.

"It's a dummy!" Ned exclaimed as the penlight illuminated a cloth bag filled with soft stuffing.

Nancy felt her whole body slump with relief. "Somebody find a light switch," she said.

A few seconds later some bare bulbs in an overhead fixture went on, casting eerie shadows against the walls. Ned stood by a light switch at the foot of one of the sweeping staircases. Near him Bess was leaning against a ladder, staring in horror at the life-size hanging dummy.

"That beam's too high for someone to reach without a ladder," Nancy pointed out. "Bess, don't move or touch the ladder with your hands. I want to check for fingerprints."

Bess carefully lifted her elbow off the ladder, and Nancy took a closer look. "Hmm, it looks like someone wiped it clean," Nancy said. "There's not a speck on it, but everything else is covered with sawdust."

She cast her eyes downward. "All these footprints are too scuffed to see clearly," she added, frowning. "Whoever hung the dummy went to extra trouble not to leave fingerprints or footprints."

"I don't get it," Ned commented, coming over to the ladder. "If there is a practical joker working here, why would they do something like this? It's not funny at all."

Nancy thought for a moment. "I don't think the person is trying to be funny," she said. "I think they're trying to scare us, or Andrew, or someone else."

"But why?" Bess wondered aloud. "What could they possibly gain by it?"

"Good question," Nancy said. "Let's search the rest of the inn to see if we can figure out an answer."

"What are we looking for?" Bess asked.

"Just keep an eye out for any tools or anything that looks strange," Nancy told her. "But first let's cut this thing down so it won't scare anybody else."

After the dummy had been laid to rest on the dusty floor, Nancy, Ned, and Bess examined the front and back doors. "No sign of forced entry," Nancy observed. "The intruder had to have a key."

Next the three teens searched the downstairs rooms, offices, and hallways. They didn't see anything unusual, or find any of the missing tools, but it was hard to see much in the dim light of the few work lights. A search of the upstairs bedrooms proved equally fruitless.

"The only place we haven't checked is the basement," Nancy said when they returned to the lobby.

"I think it's still locked," Ned told her, "and Andrew has the only key. He doesn't want anyone going down there unsupervised because the stairs are rickety and it's too filled with junk to walk around in."

"Let's try it, anyway," Nancy suggested. "I want to be sure."

Pulling back one of the white drop cloths

hanging beneath the left staircase, Ned revealed a solid oak door with a rusted knob. He turned the knob and pulled, but it wouldn't budge.

"Oh, well," Nancy said. "We can check again tomorrow, as soon as it's light."

"Good idea," Bess agreed. "Now let's get out of this spooky place before we run into Rosalie Murray's ghost!"

"And that's when we found this," Nancy told Andrew early the next morning, holding up the dummy in the noose to show him. She, Ned, and Bess had arrived before eight so they could talk to Andrew before the TeenWorks crew arrived.

"It was hanging from the rafter up there," Ned added, pointing.

"We thought it was a person," Bess said, putting her hands in the pockets of her pastel pink overalls, which she wore over a matching long-sleeved T-shirt.

Andrew tucked the dummy under his arm and looked anxiously around the empty lobby. "Please don't mention this to anyone else," he said. "If word of this gets out, my work crew might panic, and I can't afford any more delays. I'm going to throw this thing out before anybody sees it."

Nancy followed as Andrew walked to the front door, flung it open, and went outside. The day was so cloudy and overcast that everything seemed to melt into a monotonous dark gray.

"Do you have any idea who might have put the dummy there?" Nancy asked.

Andrew shrugged, then tossed the dummy into a large green Dumpster just outside the entrance. He covered the dummy with some large plastic garbage bags that had been lying on top of the other debris.

"Andrew," Nancy said gently, "I know about Julie. If you think she's out to get you, I wish you'd tell me. The only way I can help you is if you're honest with me."

"It's not Julie," Andrew said, staring at the trees beyond the inn. "I know her. She'd never do something like this."

Nancy couldn't tell if Andrew really believed what he was saying or if he was covering up for Julie. Maybe he still loved her and didn't want her to get in trouble. After all, Andrew hadn't been the one who wanted to break off their engagement.

"Look," he said, turning to face Nancy. His hazel eyes were troubled behind his wire-rimmed glasses. "I appreciate the fact that you're looking into these pranks for me. But lay off Julie, okay?"

"I know you still care about her," Nancy sympathized, "but I can't ignore the facts. Julie was in the inn yesterday, and she ran away from me right after the wailing music was played."

Honk! Honk!

Nancy turned toward the parking lot and saw a

small caravan of cars pull in, followed by the red TeenWorks bus.

Andrew put on a cheerful smile and waved at the teenagers who were piling out of the bus. "Let's just try to forget about all this stuff, okay?" he said to Nancy. "We've got a lot of work to do."

"Hi, Andrew!" Colleen called, stepping out of the bus in a full-length sheepskin coat and striding up the path in brown lizard-skin cowboy boots similar to the black ones she'd worn the day before.

"What's on the agenda for today?" Colleen asked as several of the teenagers gathered around her. Most of them wore jeans, sweatshirts, and sneakers.

"Don't tell me," said Natalia Diaz. "We have to climb on more ladders and do more wiring."

A tall, skinny guy with cornrow braids turned to Andrew. "I guess Natalia never told you that she's afraid of heights."

"Ivan!" Natalia laughed, giving him a playful poke in the ribs.

"We'll be finishing up the wiring today," Andrew said without laughing. "Also, cutting and threading pipes for the bathrooms and the kitchen. Electrical people, talk to Eddie Garcia in the ballroom. Plumbing people, work with Dan Nichols in the dining room. Colleen, Ned, Bess, and Nancy, I'd like to show you guys the basement."

As everyone headed into the lobby, Colleen

remarked, "I thought we'd never see the mysterious basement. Did you finally get a hauler to come pick up all the junk down there, Andrew?"

"Yes, believe it or not," Andrew told her, rolling his eyes. "He'll be here the day after tomorrow, so I want to get everything out and ready for him before then. Anyway, Dan Nichols, our foreman, wants to pour a cement floor Friday, so the area has to be clear."

"Sounds like a tall order. It's already Tuesday," Colleen said as Andrew pulled aside the drop cloth covering the basement door. "We might have to pull some of the kids from their other jobs."

"I hope not," Andrew told her, frowning. "This job's going too slowly as it is." He reached for the key ring that was attached by a metal chain to one of his belt loops and sifted through until he found the key he wanted. Then he unlocked the basement door and pushed it open. A musty, burnt smell wafted upstairs, mixing in with the smell of sawdust.

"Smells like no one's been down there in a long time," Nancy said.

Andrew nodded. "I went down early this morning to connect some work lights," he said, "but I'm the only one who's been in the basement since the fire fifty years ago, not including some inspectors and the architect who measured it for the renovation." Shaking his head, he added, "It's a real mess down there. Most of the stuff is left over from the fire, and half of it's so burned up you can't even tell what it is."

After grabbing a rolled-up blueprint that was leaning against the wall next to the door, Andrew started down the stairs, followed by the others.

"Wow!" Bess exclaimed when they'd gotten halfway down the stairs. "When you said this was a mess, you weren't kidding."

Broken lamps were piled on top of charred wooden beams. Damp, moldy mattresses with the springs sticking out were stacked unevenly, some piles reaching almost to the low ceiling. And there were stacks and stacks of yellowed newspapers and magazines everywhere.

Peering over the mess, Nancy saw that the room stretched for dozens of yards in front of them and to the right and left of the stairs. It seemed to be the same size as the whole first floor. At her feet were the remnants of a wooden floor, but most of it had burned away, leaving bare earth.

"No wonder the inn almost burned down," Colleen commented, picking up a newspaper and glancing at it briefly. "This place is a firetrap. We should get rid of all these newspapers immediately."

"I want to get rid of everything," Andrew said as they all found a place to stand at the foot of the stairs.

Peering out into the basement, Ned said, "So this is going to be a recreation room?"

Andrew unrolled the blueprint he carried and held it out so the others could see. "It's going to be more than that," he said. "There's going to be a dance club, a snack bar, video game room, pool table, and a full-length bowling lane."

Nancy looked over Andrew's shoulder at the neatly drawn blue lines. "Pretty impressive," she told him. "Where do we start?"

"I want to get an inventory of what's down here, see if there's anything salvageable we should keep, and then figure out the best way to get this stuff up the stairs. Some of it's pretty big."

"I think I see a piano," Bess said. "We'll never get that up the stairs."

"We can break up anything that's too heavy," Andrew said. He bent down to pick up a hatchet from beneath the staircase. "I brought a half a dozen of these down for that earlier."

Nancy took a winding path through the broken furniture and other debris. The basement seemed to go on and on, and the damp air still carried the burned-carbon smell of the long-ago fire.

After about twenty steps Nancy found that she couldn't go any farther. Her way was blocked by what looked like a makeshift wall of scraps of lumber, several dressers, and an old metal filing cabinet.

"That's strange," she murmured, veering around the wall. It extended for three sides, with the permanent stone wall closing off the fourth.

"Hey, Andrew!" Nancy called. "Come look at this."

He was still carrying the hatchet when he reached her, followed by Ned, Bess, and Colleen.

"I don't think this was part of the original floor plan," Nancy joked, showing him the makeshift wall.

"And it's not part of the new plan, either," Andrew said. "Let's chop it down. Stand back, everybody."

As Andrew hacked away at the barricade, prying nailed boards, Nancy watched curiously. Someone must have erected it on purpose. But why? And when? Andrew had said the basement had been locked for fifty years.

A ragged opening appeared in the wall, and Andrew stopped so that Nancy could climb through it. It was a tiny space, maybe six feet square. A mattress with a crumpled blanket lumped on it lay on the earth floor beneath a transom window in the stone wall. Around the blanket were greasy wrappers from several fast-food restaurants, a pair of ripped jeans, and a few dirty T-shirts.

"The inn's already had a guest!" Nancy called through the opening to her friends. "And pretty recently, from the looks of it. There's not much dust gathered on this stuff."

"But how could anyone have gotten in here?" Andrew asked, peeking in. "I'm the only one who has a key to the basement, and there's no other way in."

Nancy looked up at the transom window, which was tilted open. "Someone could have fit through there," she said.

"They'd have to be pretty thin," Andrew commented, "but I guess it's possible."

"Maybe this is where Rosalie's ghost goes in her spare time," Bess said with a nervous giggle.

"I doubt it," Ned said, peering through the opening in the makeshift wall. "I've never heard of a ghost who eats Buddy Burgers."

Nancy laughed, climbing back through the opening to rejoin her friends. "My guess is that it was a homeless person. Someone probably found his way up to the lake and spent a few nights here, that's all."

"Or maybe he's still here," Andrew put in. "That could be the explanation we've been looking for. Maybe the guy likes his free room and doesn't want us barging in on him."

"It's possible," Nancy admitted. "But if the person's been wandering around the inn, someone would have been sure to see him by now."

Colleen pressed forward to the opening and scrutinized the small room. "Well, whoever he is, he'll be in for a nasty surprise if he comes back," she said fiercely. "He has no right trespassing. I'll personally supervise the cleanup down here."

"And I'll make sure he doesn't come back,"

Andrew added. "I'll have that window nailed closed right away."

"Yo, Andrew!" called a familiar voice. Nancy heard steps on the stairs. A moment later Blaster appeared at the foot of the stairwell.

"What is it?" Andrew asked irritably.

Nancy noticed that Blaster's face didn't look as cocky and confident as it had yesterday. In fact, he looked seriously worried as he raked a hand over his razor-cut platinum hair.

"Uh-oh," Andrew said. "Don't tell me more tools are missing."

Master Blaster shuffled uncomfortably, kicking the toes of his sneakers against the hard-packed earth. "I think it would be better if I showed you," he finally said. "Natalia Diaz has it, upstairs."

Andrew threaded his way through the basement, pushed past Blaster, and ran up the stairs two at a time. Nancy and the others were right behind him.

"What is it?" Andrew asked breathlessly when they'd all reached the lobby. A group of teenagers stood near the basement door, surrounding a girl with shoulder-length black hair and amber skin. The girl clutched something in her hand.

"Show him, Natalia," Blaster said grimly.

The girl's pretty face was anxious, and her hand trembled as she held out a scrap of paper to Andrew. "I found this upstairs," she said in a faint voice.

Nancy gasped as she looked over Andrew's shoulder and saw the paper. It was splattered with blood and had a message scrawled on it in uneven letters:

The warnings are clear. Stay out of my inn. Leave the past alone, or the walls will come tumbling down!

Chapter

Four

ANDREW READ THE NOTE aloud, then crumpled it in his fist. "This can't be happening," he groaned. "My father will kill me if he sees this."

"Let me look at that again," Nancy said, taking the note from Andrew's hand and smoothing it out. There was something odd about the blood, she realized. It was too thick and bright to be real.

"This looks like nail polish," she murmured, chipping at the glossy red streak with her thumbnail. "Where did you find this, Natalia?"

The dark-haired girl nodded toward the stairs. "I was going into one of the rooms upstairs. It was wedged between the floorboards."

"Was it hard to see?" Nancy asked.

Natalia shook her head no. "It was sticking straight up in the middle of the floor."

Nancy exchanged a meaningful look with Ned and Bess. They'd inspected the upstairs rooms thoroughly last night, and none of them had seen any note. Whoever had left it must have returned to the inn after they'd left or come back early this morning. Or maybe the person had never left, Nancy thought, recalling the hidden room downstairs.

"Can I keep the note?" Nancy asked Andrew. "It might help me figure out what's going on."

"Sure," Andrew said with an unhappy shrug. "I don't want it."

"Mrs. Morgan," Natalia said, approaching Colleen, "I hope you won't think I'm a total wimp, but I'm not sure I want to be part of TeenWorks anymore. This job's getting too dangerous."

"I'm with her," said the tall, lanky boy with cornrow braids. "If the walls come tumbling down, I don't want to be here when it happens."

Colleen gave Andrew a concerned look. "I'm responsible for these kids," she said. "I can't allow them to work in an unsafe environment."

"I understand completely," Andrew said. "I'm just as concerned as you are. But look—so far, no one's been hurt. I think the threats are aimed at the inn itself, not at anybody working here. Bear with me a little while longer, okay?"

"I'll have to leave it up to the kids," Colleen

said. "If any of them want to leave, I can't stop them."

Andrew's shoulders tensed. "Do what you want. But anyone who's working, get back to work."

Nancy noticed some of the kids hesitate, but they all returned to their jobs. The renovation was still in business, at least for the moment. Andrew turned and strode through a small doorway to the right of the lobby.

"Andrew," Nancy called, following him. "Can I talk to you for a minute?"

He stood aside so Nancy could go through the door ahead of him. Nancy entered a small, messy office with stone walls and a desk piled high with papers. A circular file and a phone were balanced precariously on top of some of the papers. A large window looked out onto the driveway.

"Welcome to command central," Andrew said glumly, sitting down behind the desk.

Nancy sat down on a folding chair in front of the desk. "I know you're getting tired of bad news," she told Andrew, "but I have to tell you, this looks even worse than I thought yesterday. This is more than mischief. It looks to me like sabotage. Someone doesn't want you here, and they might not let up until you stop the renovation."

Andrew took off his glasses and wearily rested his head in his hands. "The way things are going, I'd be better off if the inn never opened at all," he mumbled. "All these problems are putting me way over budget. My father's going to think I'm a moron. Maybe I *was* a moron for agreeing to do this project in the first place."

"Stop blaming yourself. Someone else is doing this, not you," Nancy said firmly. "Besides Julie, can you think of anyone else who might have some reason to get back at you or hurt you?"

Andrew lifted his head to look at her, his jaw clenched. "I've already said that Julie didn't do it. She's a sweet, gentle person."

"Who must be pretty angry and hurt right now," Nancy prodded gently.

"Sure she is. And I don't blame her one bit. I'm a wimp for not taking a stand with my father. I deserved for her to leave me," Andrew said miserably. "But Julie's not destructive. I know she's not responsible for what's happening here."

Nancy shot him a skeptical glance. "Then what was she doing at the inn?" she pressed.

With a deep sigh Andrew replied, "I wish I knew. And I wish she hadn't run away so I could tell her again how much I care about her."

Nancy sympathized with him, but she knew that wasn't going to solve his problems. "Is there anyone else who might want to hurt you?"

"No one I can think of," he told her.

"At any rate, I've got two more suspects," Nancy said.

A spark of curiosity lit up Andrew's eyes. "The homeless person?" he guessed.

41

"That's one," Nancy said. "If he's still around, that is. I'm going to go through the stuff downstairs and see if there are any clues to the person's identity."

"Who's the other suspect?" Andrew asked.

"Master Blaster."

Andrew looked at Nancy in surprise. "Really? Why would he want to sabotage me?"

"I don't know," Nancy admitted. "But it was weird that he didn't react yesterday when someone turned off his tape. And he seemed really nervous when I caught him in that back hallway." Getting to her feet, she said, "I'm going to start checking out some of these leads."

"Keep me posted," Andrew said, giving her a weary smile.

Leaving the office, Nancy went looking for Bess. She found her in the dining room, next to the ballroom. It, too, was a cavernous room with a high ceiling and a fireplace that was large enough for a person to stand in. On either side of the fireplace, glass doors led out to a stone patio overlooking the lake. Several sets of sawhorses were scattered throughout the dining room, where teenage workers in goggles were cutting through copper pipes with electric saws.

"Nancy, look!" Bess shouted gleefully from behind a sawhorse. Nancy saw that a tall, balding middle-aged man in overalls was standing behind Bess. "This is Dan Nichols, the construction foreman," Bess went on. "He's showing me how to use a power saw."

"Not bad," Nancy said, grinning as Bess sliced neatly through a pipe.

"Good job," Dan complimented her, then moved on to the group at another sawhorse. When he was out of earshot, Nancy gestured to Bess to turn off the saw.

"Do you think you can handle two jobs at once?" she asked Bess in a low voice. "While you're working, keep an eye on Blaster."

Bess's blue eyes lit up as she said, "You think *he's* the troublemaker?"

"I don't know yet," Nancy said truthfully. "But I think we should watch him. He's probably in the ballroom with the electrical people."

Bess nodded solemnly, but there was a sparkle in her eye. "Then I won't let him out of my sight for a minute."

"I knew I could count on you," Nancy said dryly. "Meanwhile, I'm going to pay Julie Ross a visit."

After grabbing her down jacket from the metal rack in the lobby, Nancy left the inn by the back hallway door. She wanted to cut through the woods Julie had run through the day before to see how far away her store was from the inn.

The day was still dark and overcast, and Nancy had trouble finding her way through the trees. Still, she made a rough guess as to which direction Julie had gone, and soon she could see the cluster of stone buildings that made up the tiny town of Moon Lake.

Within minutes she was standing in front of A Show of Hands, the boutique where Ned had said Julie worked. A bell tinkled as Nancy pushed open the door and went inside. The walls of the store were lined with ceramic bowls, beaded earrings, clay sculptures of birds in flight, and other handmade objects.

In the back a slender girl sat in a separate work area, behind a half-formed piece of wet clay on a clay-spattered table. She wore a white smock over blue jeans, and her hands were covered with the reddish brown clay. As soon as Nancy saw the copper streak in the girl's dark curls, she knew this was the same girl she'd seen the day before.

"May I help you?" the girl asked. Her face, though attractive, looked tired, and there were dark circles under her eyes.

"Just looking," Nancy said lightly. She didn't want to give away her purpose for being at the shop right away. If Julie knew that Nancy was the girl who'd chased her through the woods, she would probably clam up.

"I'm Julie," the girl said with a smile. "If there's anything I can do, just ask."

"Thanks," Nancy said, approaching Julie. "Did you do these bird sculptures?" When Julie nodded, Nancy said sincerely, "They're beautiful. It's hard to believe you can find such high-quality work in an out-of-the-way place like this."

"Tell me about it," Julie said, skillfully shaping the wing of a bird with a flat wooden stick. "I'm from Melborne, but that's almost as small as Moon Lake. Stick the two together, and you'd still need a magnifying glass to find them on a map."

Nancy laughed. "Well, I guess you can leave any time you want, right? Not that you'd want to, of course. It's so peaceful here."

"Peaceful and *boring*," Julie put in. "As soon as I get into art school, I'm out of here."

"So there's nothing keeping you here, then?" Nancy asked.

Julie focused on her sculpture for a moment, then looked at Nancy with clear gray eyes. "I try not to get tied down to anybody or anything," she said lightly. "Life's easier that way."

"Uh-huh . . ." Nancy pretended to look at a copper candlestick, but she was actually studying Julie out of the corner of her eye. Julie was doing a good job of covering up her hurt feelings. Then again, she didn't know Nancy, so there was no reason for her to reveal anything personal.

"What brings you to Moon Lake?" Julie asked. "It's not exactly the peak of the summer season."

"I'm, uh, helping out at the inn," Nancy said vaguely. "There's a renovation going on."

Instantly Julie's eyes grew hard. "I know all about it," she snapped. "Boy, I just can't stand hearing about that old place."

"Why not?" Nancy inquired.

Julie stabbed the clay bird with her wooden stick. "Let's put it this way," she said in an ice-cold voice. "I hope that old dump burns to the ground!"

Chapter

Five

JULIE'S GRAY EYES flashed angrily for a moment. Then, as if she were embarrassed at her outburst, she stared down at her sculpture.

"What do you have against the inn?" Nancy asked.

Julie opened her mouth to answer, but she was interrupted by the tinkling of the bell at the door.

An older woman with fluffy white hair entered and asked, "I'm looking for a rag doll for my granddaughter. Could you show me what you have?"

"I've got to help this customer," Julie told Nancy in a quiet voice. She disappeared through a door in the back, then reemerged a minute later

47

with clean hands and went over to the older woman.

Nancy waited to question Julie, but after the older woman left, a young couple came in. Then a plump middle-aged woman emerged from the back of the store, holding out a cardboard box.

"Julie! Beverly Brandt's order finally came in," the plump woman said. "I want you to deliver it for me."

There was no point in sticking around, Nancy realized. She would have to come back later to question Julie further. Nancy decided to take the road this time, but the walk back to the inn still took only a few minutes. There was no question Julie could come and go quickly.

As Nancy headed up the curved driveway, she saw that a long black limousine with tinted windows was parked right in front of the entrance. The license plate read LOCKWD-1. This had to be Andrew's father's car.

The second Nancy entered the inn, she heard a loud, harsh voice fill the lobby.

"You're a disgrace!" the man's voice yelled. "I trusted you with this job, and what do I find when I get here? Utter chaos!"

"We've had some problems. . . ." Andrew's voice was barely audible.

"Don't give me excuses!" the man yelled. "Give me solutions! If you weren't my son, I'd fire you!"

Nancy wished she weren't overhearing the

conversation. As she quickly crossed the lobby, she glanced into Andrew's office and saw a tall, robust man with steel gray hair slicked straight back. He had a strong profile and was dressed in an expensive-looking charcoal gray suit.

"What's that?" Andrew's father demanded as Andrew mumbled something under his breath.

"Nothing," Andrew said.

Not wanting to embarrass Andrew, Nancy stepped quietly over to the hallway that led to the dining room and ballroom. Behind her she could still hear Mr. Lockwood's angry voice.

"Don't think you're getting out of this," he thundered. "I gave you this job to teach you responsibility. How can I trust you with the rest of my properties if you can't get this right?"

"Maybe if I had a little more money . . ."

"Oh, no," Mr. Lockwood said. "You got yourself into this mess. You'll have to figure a way out on your own."

Shaking her head, Nancy hurried away from the voices. Now that she had seen Mr. Lockwood in action, she understood why Andrew was so scared of him. Anyone would be. She couldn't help feeling sorry for Andrew.

Ahead of Nancy loud rock music was once again blaring from the ballroom. When she got there, she saw that Bess had kept her promise. She wasn't just keeping an eye on Blaster, she was dancing with him!

Blaster was holding Bess's hands and demonstrating some complicated moves while Bess tried to follow. Bess glowed as she gazed at Blaster, while Natalia and several other teens stood nearby, shouting encouragement.

Uh-oh, Nancy thought to herself. Bess wasn't going to be a very objective observer of the deejay. And if he was the person behind all the trouble, Bess might even be in danger.

"Hey!" Andrew shouted, appearing behind Nancy in the door to the ballroom. Apparently, his father had left. "What do you think you're doing?"

Bess guiltily dropped Blaster's hands, and the deejay said, "We're just taking a little break."

"Looks like you're goofing off to me," Andrew said. "Aren't you supposed to be helping Eddie?"

"You got that right!" called a voice from up in the balcony. "Get up here, Blaster. I need you to help me test the master light switch."

Nancy looked up and saw a wiry man in coveralls with straight black hair. Ned was also up in the balcony, removing the rickety-looking guardrail. "Don't get too close to the edge, Eddie," Ned warned. "I haven't put up the new railing yet."

"I'll come help you with that, Ned," Andrew said. He followed Blaster toward the door in the wall that led to the back hall and balcony stairs.

Taking Bess aside, Nancy said in a low voice, "Bess, I need to talk to you about Blaster. I know he's cute—"

"Adorable," Bess cut in, grinning.

"But he may also be very dangerous," Nancy went on.

Bess's eyes turned serious. "I hear what you're saying, Nancy, but I honestly don't think Blaster's guilty. I can feel it."

"I'm not putting down your instincts," Nancy said. "I'm just saying we don't have enough information about him yet to come to any conclusions. So be careful around him, okay?"

Bess didn't look convinced, but she nodded.

"Good," Nancy said. "Now, let's go to the basement. I want to check out the stuff the homeless person left behind."

When they got to the bottom of the stairs, Nancy was amazed at how much cleaner the basement looked than it had earlier. Several wide, clean paths had been cleared through the burnt, broken furniture. Colleen Morgan knelt on the bare earth floor, stacking old newspapers in a cardboard box.

"Are you working here all by yourself?" Nancy asked as she and Bess went over to Colleen.

Colleen looked up and brushed a strand of red hair out of her eyes. "Hmm?" she said distractedly. "Oh, no, not really. I've got some of the kids helping me, but I sent them upstairs for a break. They've been hauling all morning."

"But you're still working," Nancy observed. "That's real dedication."

Colleen barely looked up as she kept going

through the yellowing stacks of newspapers. "I'm just happy to help out."

"Wouldn't you rather be doing something more glamorous than cleaning out a dirty basement?" Bess asked. "I know I would if I were you."

Looking up with a smile, Colleen said, "Believe me, there's nowhere I'd rather be than right here. I've had it easy all my life. Nannies, private school, summers in Europe. Not that I'm complaining, but I *like* working with TeenWorks. It feels good to know I'm making a serious contribution to these kids."

The heavy cardboard box was now full of newspapers, and Colleen lifted it, starting for the stairs.

"Let me help you with that," Nancy offered.

"No, thanks," Colleen said brightly, shifting the box in her arms. "I can handle it."

"Well, at least let us help you clean up the basement," Bess said.

"Don't worry about it," Colleen said over her shoulder. "The kids and I will take care of everything."

Bess stared up the stairs at Colleen's retreating cowboy boots. "Wow. I hope I'm as selfless as she is when I'm a fabulously wealthy socialite someday."

Laughing, Nancy walked down a cleared path toward the spot where she'd found the makeshift room that morning. As she neared the stone wall, she recognized the transom window and the mattress, but all else had been cleared away.

"Oh, no!" Nancy cried, rushing forward. "What happened to my evidence?"

"It was just a bunch of hamburger wrappers," Bess consoled her. "I doubt you could have learned anything from it."

Nancy wanted to kick herself for not thinking to ask Andrew to leave this area alone until she'd examined it.

"Maybe the homeless person's stuff is still here somewhere," Bess said, coming over to join Nancy. "The basement's still pretty messy."

"That's true," Nancy said, brightening. She knelt by the mattress and lifted it up so she could look under it. The only thing she saw was hard-packed earth and a crumpled piece of fabric. Kicking the fabric out with her toe, Nancy let the mattress drop. Then she picked up the moldy-smelling fabric and tried to smooth it out on the ground. It was a T-shirt, filthy and wrinkled, with a few faded words on the front.

"'Bentley High Boneheads, Class of Seventy-seven,'" Bess read, kneeling next to Nancy. There was also a picture of a skull wearing a mortarboard.

Turning the T-shirt over, Nancy saw just two letters printed on the back: G.L.

"I don't get it," Bess said. "What does it mean?"

Shrugging, Nancy said, "We don't even know

if the T-shirt belonged to the person who slept down here. But if it did, the letters on the back could be his initials."

"It looks as if G.L., whoever he is, graduated from Bentley High School in 1977," Bess said.

"That's a good guess," Nancy agreed. "Bentley's not too far from here. We could go over to the high school and try looking him up in one of the yearbooks."

"Sounds good to me," Bess said, standing up and brushing the dirt off her pink overalls.

"I think we've learned everything we can from this," Nancy said, holding her nose as she dropped the T-shirt onto a pile of garbage. "It stinks! Meanwhile, I'm hungry. Have you eaten lunch yet?"

Bess gave her an apologetic look. "We all had sandwiches while you were gone. Let me see if I can scout one out for you, though."

"Thanks," Nancy told her. "I'll check with Ned to see if he wants one, too.

While Bess went off to find sandwiches, Nancy returned to the ballroom. Up in the balcony Andrew and Ned were about to fit the new guardrail into place. Blaster's music filled the room, though Nancy didn't see the deejay anywhere. It was midafternoon, but the day was still so gloomy and overcast that almost no light came in through the windows. The room was lit only by a few work lights scattered around the ballroom.

"Hey, Ned, this is just like Romeo and Juliet," Nancy called, coming directly beneath the balcony.

Ned blew her a kiss as he lifted up the new metal rail, with Andrew directing him.

"'What light through yonder window breaks . . .'" Nancy said, quoting from the play.

"I think you've got it backward," Ned said, grinning down at her. "That's Romeo's line."

"Well, you're the one who's up on the balcony," Nancy said with a laugh.

Ned started to say something, but his voice was suddenly cut off as all the lights went out at once. The ballroom was plunged into dark shadows.

Nancy jumped as a heavy metal object clattered to the floor just inches away from her. A second later she heard a much more frightening sound.

It was the bone-cracking thud of a body landing right beside her, followed by an anguished groan.

Chapter

Six

A FEELING OF DREAD washed over Nancy. "Turn on the lights, somebody!" she yelled.

A moment later the work lights in the ballroom flickered back on, and Nancy saw Ned lying on the floor at her feet, clutching his right arm.

"Ned!" she cried, dropping to her knees beside him. His face had gone white and was contorted in pain. "Did you break your arm?"

Grimacing, Ned nodded. "I think so. You might say my arm broke my fall." He tried to laugh, but then he winced.

"Does anything else hurt?" Nancy asked.

"Not really," Ned answered. He gingerly raised himself to a sitting position and looked around at the group of teens that had crowded around him.

Andrew's head appeared over the edge of the balcony. Blaster was right behind him. "I'll call an ambulance!" Andrew shouted.

"No," Nancy said, pulling her car keys from her purse. "We'll make better time if I drive him to the hospital myself."

"For a guy who fell fifteen feet, you were pretty lucky," Bess said to Ned as Nancy pulled out of the Melborne Community Hospital parking lot a few hours later. "A simple fracture's not too bad."

Ned groaned, sinking against the passenger seat. "Tell that to my coach," he said. His right arm was encased in a plaster cast and held in a sling under his leather jacket. "I won't be able to play basketball for five whole weeks—at the peak of the season."

"I'm just glad you'll be able to play at all," Nancy said.

It was after five o'clock, and the sky was pitch black, starless, and gloomy. Just the way I'm feeling, Nancy thought. It was bad enough that someone was sabotaging the inn, but where did that person come off hurting innocent people? Nancy was more resolved than ever to track the culprit down and bring him to justice.

"What happened up there, Ned? Did someone push you?" she asked, glancing at her boyfriend.

Ned stared out the window as they passed a strip of used-car lots. "It all went by so fast. All I know is, I was standing close to the edge when the lights went out. I don't think I felt anyone touch me, but I'm not completely sure. I definitely lost my balance."

"So the real question is, who turned out the lights?" Nancy said. "We know Blaster was working up there on the master light switch."

"Yeah, but Eddie was with him," Ned said. "He couldn't have turned out the lights and come forward to push me with Eddie watching."

"Uh, excuse me," said Bess, "but Eddie *wasn't* with Blaster."

Glancing at Bess in the rearview mirror, Nancy asked, "How do you know?"

"Because when I went to the kitchen to look for a sandwich, Eddie was there," Bess said. "He was at the circuit breaker, talking to Blaster over a walkie-talkie. He was telling Blaster to flip certain switches, and then he'd see if the lights were working."

"So what does that mean?" Ned asked. "That Blaster turned off the lights by accident?"

"Maybe," Nancy said, "or maybe he did it on purpose, since no one was watching him."

Nancy turned the Mustang onto the thruway, heading for Mapleton so she could drive Ned home. It was too late to go back to the inn. They'd already called Andrew from the hospital to let him know what was going on.

"It's possible Julie paid the inn another visit," Nancy added. "Though I'm not sure how she could have turned off the lights with Blaster in the alcove by the switches."

"Anyway, why would she do that?" Ned asked. "She was mad at Andrew, not me."

"That might have been the real accident," Bess put in. "Maybe Julie intended to push Andrew off the balcony but couldn't see in the dark and pushed you instead."

Shaking his head doubtfully, Ned said, "I don't know, Julie's not like that. She's sweet."

"Andrew said the same thing, but she didn't sound so sweet when I talked to her at the crafts store today," Nancy said. She quickly recounted Julie's bitter remarks about the inn.

Ned still didn't look convinced. "There has to be some other explanation for what happened," he said. "Maybe it was the person hiding in the basement. He could still be around somewhere, too."

"Nothing points to him being behind any of these accidents," Nancy told him, "but I do want to get over to Bentley High School and see if I can find out anything about the Boneheads and G.L."

"What are you doing here?" Andrew exclaimed Wednesday morning as Nancy, Ned, and Bess entered the inn's lobby. Andrew was on his way out the door, a ledger under his arm and car keys jangling in his hand. "You should be home taking care of that arm, Ned."

Grinning, Ned said, "I figured even if I can't work, you could use some moral support after everything that's happened."

"That's for sure," Andrew said glumly. "We had another incident last night."

"Oh, no!" Bess said with a gasp. "Was anyone else hurt?"

Andrew shook his head. "Fortunately not. I'm on my way to meet my father at his office, but I guess I can take a minute to show you." He crossed the lobby and went inside his office, reappearing a moment later with a note in his hand. The words *Come back to me* were printed on it, and bloodred paint drippings covered the page.

Taking the other message out of her purse, Nancy compared it to the one Andrew held. The handwriting in both notes looked the same, and so did the red enamel paint.

" 'Come back to me?' " Bess repeated. "I don't get it. Who's 'me'? And who is 'me' talking to?"

Nancy frowned and turned to Andrew. "You're not going to want to hear this," she told him, "but that message could be from Julie. Maybe it's her way of saying she wants to get back together."

For the first time since Nancy had mentioned Julie as a suspect, Andrew didn't object. "It's possible," he admitted quietly. "But I have no idea how she could have gotten inside the inn. All the doors are locked at night, and there's no way she could get a key."

"The message could also be from the ghost that's still haunting the inn, looking for her lover," Bess piped up.

Andrew looked at his watch and groaned. "I don't have time for this now. My father wants me to give him a full accounting of all the work we've done. I'd better leave now or I'll be late."

After Andrew left with his ledger, Nancy, Ned, and Bess headed for the ballroom, where they found Dan Nichols and about ten of the TeenWorkers nailing thick gray slabs of plasterboard to the wooden framework against the walls. The clattering and banging of their hammers was nearly drowned out by loud, fifties-style rock and roll blaring from the stereo on the balcony.

"Ned, would you come up to the balcony with me?" Nancy asked. "I want to try to figure out what happened yesterday."

"Might as well," Ned agreed, with a nod at his cast. "I'm not going to be much use here."

They climbed the back stairs to the balcony, and Nancy shone her penlight into the dimly lit alcove right outside the entrance to the balcony. The master light switch was there, now fully wired with eight black dials.

"This must have been where Blaster was working yesterday," Nancy said. "It's only a few feet from the alcove to the front of the balcony, where you were working. He definitely could have turned off the lights and pushed you."

"I'm still not sure I was pushed," Ned said.

"But we *are* sure someone turned out the lights," Nancy reminded him. She stepped through the open doorway and onto the balcony. There was a second light switch just inside the door.

"This controls the lights downstairs, too," Nancy said after quickly flipping the switch off and on.

She thought for a moment, then said excitedly, "That means Julie *could* have turned off the lights. It's possible that she sneaked up the stairs past the alcove where Blaster was working. She wouldn't have needed to use the master switch. She could have turned the lights out from here."

"Maybe," Ned said. Nancy was glad that he kept a careful distance from the balcony's edge, even though the new railing had been installed.

"Now that I think about it," Nancy went on, "Julie was sent on an errand by her boss yesterday, not long before your accident. It would have been a perfect opportunity for her to come here without her boss wondering where she was."

As Nancy peered at the balcony switch, she noticed a reddish brown muddy substance on the lever. "Hey, Ned," she called. "Look at this."

He came over and picked at the dried, cakey substance with his good hand. "Looks like clay."

"And it matches the color of the clay Julie was working with yesterday," Nancy said excitedly. After searching in her purse for a slip of paper, she chipped off a sample of the reddish brown substance and carefully folded it inside.

"Now I'd really better pay Julie another visit at the store," Nancy said, "so I can check this sample against the clay she uses. I'm almost positive it'll be a match."

Nodding, Ned said, "I think I remember Andrew saying she doesn't work there every day, though. Maybe you can get her home address from Andrew. He has a file of address cards in his office."

"Good idea," Nancy said. "While I'm at it, I'd like to get Blaster's address, too. Do you think Andrew would mind if I looked them up now? I wouldn't disturb anything."

"That should be okay," Ned told her. "It's not top secret information or anything."

Nancy and Ned went back down the balcony stairs, through the ballroom, and down the hallway to Andrew's office, off the lobby. After knocking softly, Nancy pushed open the door. Hearing a jangling sound, she checked behind the door and found two keys hanging from hooks. One was labeled Front Door and the other said Back Door.

"So that's how the intruder got in at night," Nancy murmured, half to herself.

Giving Nancy a perplexed look, Ned asked, "What are you talking about, Nan?"

She showed Ned the keys. "There are plenty of times when Andrew's not in the office," she said. "Anyone could have come in here and borrowed the keys, then made copies and returned the originals before Andrew noticed they were gone."

"That's definitely possible," Ned agreed.

Moving over to the desk, Nancy found a circular file of address cards precariously balanced next to the phone on top a pile of papers. She pulled a notebook from her purse and jotted down Blaster's and Julie's addresses.

"They both live in Melborne," Nancy said. "That will save time if we need to visit them at home. . . . Oops!"

Nancy reached out to steady the circular file, which had started to slide down the stack of papers. She pushed some of the papers aside so she could set the file down on the desk. As she did, a bright red ink stamp on several of the papers caught her eye.

"'Overdue,'" she read aloud, then peered more closely at the papers. "These are bills. Electrical cable, five hundred dollars," she read off one. "Copper pipes, seven *thousand* dollars."

Shuffling through the papers, Nancy saw that every single one of them was a bill, and they were all overdue.

Nancy did some quick mental calculations.

"These run into tens of thousands of dollars!" she exclaimed.

Looking over her shoulder, Ned observed, "Andrew wasn't exaggerating when he said he was in debt."

"And his debt is even worse than we realized," Nancy said. She pressed her lips together, concentrating as an idea began to form in her mind. "Maybe Andrew wasn't joking when he said he'd be better off if the inn never opened," she said slowly.

"What are you saying, Nan?" Ned asked.

Nancy paused, gathering her thoughts. "You've said Andrew's always been afraid to stand up to his father," she said at last. "Maybe Andrew was causing all the problems because he didn't want responsibility for the inn and couldn't figure any other way out."

Ned's mouth fell open. "You mean . . ."

Nancy nodded. "Maybe the person sabotaging the inn is Andrew himself!"

Chapter

Seven

Nancy gasped as she realized something else, so horrible she could hardly even think about it.

"Andrew was the person closest to you when the lights went out," she said softly to Ned. "He would have had the best opportunity to turn off the lights and push you off the balcony."

"No way!" Ned protested vehemently. "Andrew would never do anything to hurt me. Besides, why would he do something like that?" he asked. "Hurting me won't save the inn."

"Maybe he doesn't want to save it," Nancy said. "If he's really desperate to get out of his father's clutches, he might do anything, even hurt you, to stop the renovation. He could have caused all these accidents and written the threat-

66

ening notes so that it would seem like it wasn't his fault that he failed."

Ned shook his head. "That's not like Andrew," he insisted. "He's not the bravest person in the world, but he's not a liar."

"He's not a renovator, either," Nancy reminded him. "He wants to be an actor, right? You admitted that he's only working for his father because he's too scared to say no."

Ned's expression darkened, and he turned away from Nancy, slowly leaving the office.

"I know it's upsetting," Nancy said, following him into the lobby. "But think about it. Most of the damage was done at night. Andrew could have stayed late, after everyone left, and written the notes or rigged up the dummy."

Turning to meet Nancy's gaze, Ned said, "But what about the ghost noises coming from the stereo?" Ned asked. "Andrew was standing in the ballroom with us when that happened."

"He could have used a remote control," Nancy suggested.

"But we didn't find a tape or anything in the stereo with ghost noises on it," Ned said. "Andrew couldn't have removed it because we were with him the whole time."

Ned had a point, Nancy realized. "But if he's working with someone—"

"I'm glad *someone's* working."

Nancy jumped at the sound of Andrew's voice behind her and Ned. Whirling around, she saw that Andrew was just coming in the front entrance, his ledger under his arm.

"Who are we talking about?" Andrew asked.

"Um, my father," Nancy quickly lied. "He's just hired a new partner at his law firm."

Shooting Nancy a hard look, Ned walked quickly over to Andrew and put his left arm around his friend. "How'd it go with your dad?" he asked.

Before Andrew could answer, Colleen appeared between the marble columns framing the front hallway. "Do you guys have a minute?" she asked. "I'm calling a little powwow in the ballroom."

"Right now?" Andrew asked, grimacing. "I don't think we can spare the time. My dad says if we don't pick up the pace, he might have to fire TeenWorks and get a professional contractor."

Colleen drew herself up straighter. "My kids are very professional," she said in a defensive tone. "You'll be lucky if we stay on the job after all that's happened here. That's why I'd like to have a meeting with you, as a matter of fact."

The tension in the room was so thick that Nancy felt she could cut it with a knife. No one said a word as Colleen led the way into the ballroom. About fifteen people, including Bess, sat on the floor, eating sandwiches and drinking cans of soda.

"Well?" Andrew asked, crossing his arms.

"I'm concerned," Colleen began. "There've been too many accidents on this job. I just don't feel comfortable having these kids in danger. We can't risk another fall like the one that happened yesterday." She nodded toward Ned's fractured arm. "That's why I think this renovation should be called off, at least until we figure out who's responsible for all the problems here."

Andrew quickly scanned the teenagers' faces. "I'm concerned about everyone's safety, too," he said. "But I can't afford to stop the renovation. We've lost too much time and money as it is."

"It's too dangerous to continue," Colleen insisted.

Natalia Diaz spoke up from where she was sitting cross-legged on the floor. "It's more than dangerous. It's depressing," she said. "We've worked so hard here, but lots of the stuff just gets undone."

"Hey," Colleen said, going over to hug Natalia. "Your moods are upsetting me even more than all the accidents. Cheer up, guys!"

The teenagers looked at one another. After an uncomfortable silence, Colleen clapped her hands and strode back and forth in front of the group. "I know the perfect thing to get us all out of this slump," she said, her green eyes sparkling. "Let's have a party!"

"Now?" Master Blaster asked hopefully.

Colleen laughed. "I was thinking about after

work hours—like, how about tomorrow night? We can have it at my house. I'll call a caterer, and Blaster can provide the music, of course. If you all show up, it'll be a big bash."

A round of cheers echoed in the ballroom, and Andrew looked expectantly at the teenagers. "So? Does that mean we can get back to work?"

"For now," Colleen said. "But if there's any more trouble, you'll be hearing from me."

"Fine," Andrew said with a resigned sigh. "Meanwhile, lunchtime's over, folks. Everybody back to work."

As the group broke up, Bess got to her feet and came over to Nancy. "I guess I'd better keep an eye on Blaster," she whispered cheerfully, watching the deejay as he headed into the hallway.

"This time I'm coming with you," Nancy said firmly. "I want to find out what he knows about Ned's fall from the balcony."

The two girls followed Blaster into the hall, past the dining room, to the last room on the left. Like the bathrooms upstairs, this room was bare, with pipes sticking out of the framework walls in a few places.

"Can we help, Blaster?" Bess asked, pushing up the sleeves of the yellow sweatshirt she wore over her jeans.

Master Blaster grinned when he saw Bess. "Do you know anything about electricity?" he asked.

"Not really," Bess admitted.

"That's funny," Blaster said, moving a step

closer to Bess. "Because as soon as you walked into the room, I felt a power surge."

Bess's face turned red, and her eyes sparkled with pleasure. Obviously, Nancy was going to have to keep an eye on *both* of them!

"What are you working on?" Nancy asked as the deejay knelt on the floor by a tool chest and pulled out a pair of metal clippers. He deftly sliced through a heavy electrical cable attached to the wooden wall frame and pulled out a black and a white wire.

"I'm wiring some outlets," he said, taking a rectangular metal box from his tool chest. Swiftly and efficiently he ran the wires through a hole in the top of the box and clamped the metal box to the drywall stud.

"Pretty impressive," Nancy said as she watched.

Master Blaster shrugged. "It's a living."

"You don't sound too excited about working here," Nancy said. "Or maybe it's just all the strange things that have been happening."

"It's just that I won't be working here for too long, that's all," Blaster said.

Before Nancy could probe further, Bess said, "It's just until you become a top deejay and record producer." Turning to Nancy, she said, "Blaster's told me all about his music."

"It's very fresh," Blaster said. "Sort of a mix of my own melodies and lyrics over existing music and sound effects. It's hard to explain."

"It sounds really original," Bess said. She seemed to have totally forgotten about the case.

With a stern look at her friend, Nancy said to Master Blaster, "It must have been pretty weird yesterday, up in the balcony, when all the lights went out. What happened? Did you flip the dining room switch by accident?"

Blaster's cocky demeanor vanished instantly. His face reddened, and his hands shook a little. "I swear I didn't do it," he said. "I was running a check on the downstairs lights when it happened. Eddie can back me up."

Master Blaster seemed awfully nervous for someone who claimed to be innocent. "I guess the person who did it must have run right past you, then," Nancy said. "Did you hear or see anything strange while you were working up there?"

Blaster shook his head, then suddenly became very intent on screwing the metal plate into the wall. "I didn't see anything," he said hesitantly. "I had my back to the stairs and my ear to the walkie-talkie."

Nancy felt certain that he was lying. She was about to press him for more information when Andrew poked his head in through the doorway.

"Can you give me a hand, Blaster?" Andrew asked. "I need some help in the ballroom."

"Sure," Blaster said, standing up quickly. He looked relieved to have an excuse to leave.

Shrugging at each other, Nancy and Bess followed the guys back into the ballroom. Andrew went over to stand beside a pulley that was attached by a cable to the old crystal chandelier hanging from the ceiling. Ned, Colleen, and half a dozen other teenagers were gathered nearby.

"It's time to take this baby down," Andrew said. "It's been up since 1913, but it's damaged beyond repair."

"Too bad," Nancy said, admiring the grand chandelier.

Andrew placed both hands on the pulley's winding mechanism. "I need you and Ivan to help me crank this, Blaster," he said.

The deejay stood beside Andrew and the boy with cornrow braids. With all their strength they turned the crank. Nancy saw beads of sweat break out on the three guys' foreheads as they began to slowly lower the chandelier.

"That thing must weigh a ton," she commented.

"It's so sad," Bess said. She moved toward the chandelier and craned her neck so she could see it. "It's kind of like the end of an era."

"Hey, Bess," Nancy began with a worried glance toward where Andrew, Master Blaster, and Ivan strained against the crank. "I don't think it's a good idea to stand—"

The sudden sound of tinkling glass overhead drowned out Nancy's warning. Looking up, she felt her breath catch in her throat. The cable had ripped almost in two, and the chandelier was swinging crazily.

The next thing Nancy knew, there was a ripping noise and the chandelier was hurtling down through the air, straight toward Bess's head!

Chapter

Eight

NANCY LEAPT FORWARD, throwing her weight against Bess and knocking them both out of the way. A split second later the chandelier landed with a deafening crash against the floor.

For a moment the two of them lay motionless, stunned and breathing heavily. Thousands of shards of broken crystal surrounded them. Worried cries rang out in the room, and she and Bess were soon surrounded by Ned, Andrew, and the others.

"Are you okay?" Ned asked, his brown eyes filled with concern.

Nancy sat up gingerly. "I think so," she said. "Bess?"

"S-still in one piece," Bess said in a squeaky voice. With Blaster's help, she rose to her feet. "Thanks, Nancy. That's probably the zillionth time you saved my life, but it means just as much every time."

Looking gravely from Nancy to Bess, Andrew said, "Maybe Colleen's right. This job *is* getting too dangerous. If people's lives are in danger—"

"We're fine," Nancy assured him, taking Ned's hand as he helped her up.

"But who knows what's going to happen next?" Andrew said, shaking his head. "I just increased my insurance coverage, but I don't think it's going to be enough if these accidents keep up."

Hearing Andrew's words, something clicked in Nancy's mind. Insurance! she thought excitedly. That could be the whole key to what was happening.

Maybe Andrew had decided to junk the whole project and collect on his insurance, Nancy thought. He could blame the inn's failure on the saboteur, and he'd be able to get back some of his father's investment. That way he'd be free to go to California and pursue his acting career, and no one would ever have to know that he was the one causing the accidents in the first place.

Nancy was almost sure that foul play was behind this incident, too. She bent over the huge pile of shattered crystal and stared at the broken end of thick cable that was attached to a metal ring at the top of the chandelier.

Hmm, that's strange, she thought. The cable end wasn't torn evenly. Half of it was neatly cut, as if someone had sliced through it on purpose with metal clippers.

Nancy took Andrew aside as Bess, Colleen, and some of the teens found brooms and started sweeping up the crystal shards. "I think someone cut halfway through this cable," Nancy told him, "knowing that the weight of the chandelier would break it the rest of the way."

"But that's impossible," Andrew insisted. "I checked the cable last night, and it was fine."

"You weren't around for a while this morning, though," Nancy countered. "Someone could have sliced it then." If you didn't do it yourself, she added silently.

Andrew shook his head. "I don't see how," he said. "The pulley and cable were locked in a closet in my office all night. I just brought it out myself a few minutes ago."

Speaking in a low voice, Nancy told Andrew her theory that someone might have sneaked into the office and copied the keys when he wasn't there. "It could have been Blaster, or the homeless person," Nancy said. "Or maybe Julie."

Andrew started to object, but Nancy cut him off. "Whoever it is, they might be planning to return tonight to plant more nasty surprises."

Her blue eyes sparkled as she added, "I have an idea, though." Gesturing for Ned and Bess to join them, she said, "Why don't we camp out here tonight? Or maybe I should say camp in. If someone tries to break in, we'll have a better chance of catching them off guard."

"Sounds like fun," Bess said. "But after this narrow escape, I think I'm going to need a big picnic dinner to revive my spirits."

"That can be arranged," Ned said, smiling.

Nancy wondered if Andrew would try to resist the sleepover, but all he said was, "I could bring some sleeping bags. We have tons of camping stuff in our attic at home. My family used to go camping a lot when I was a kid."

"You can stay up all night and tell ghost stories," Master Blaster said from where he was sweeping crystal shards nearby.

Nancy wished she'd been more careful to make sure no one overheard their plans. Colleen seemed to have heard them talking, too, because she walked over to Nancy a moment later.

"I know I'm not responsible for you the way I am for the other kids," Colleen said, "but are you sure staying here's a good idea? You could be dealing with a very dangerous person."

"We'll be fine," Ned assured her. "There are four of us. You know what they say about safety in numbers."

Colleen looked skeptical. "But what if something happens to you? You're miles from the nearest police station."

"Thanks for worrying about us," Nancy said, "but we've been through a lot together. We've gotten pretty good at taking care of ourselves."

With a shrug Colleen said, "Suit yourselves." Stepping away, she called out, "Come on, TeenWorks people! Anyone who's not sweeping, let's get back to the basement. We have to clean out the rest of the stuff by tomorrow night."

As most of the teens followed Colleen out the ballroom door, Nancy turned to Andrew again.

"Would you mind if I borrowed Ned for the rest of the afternoon? I've got a little checking up I want to do," she said. "We can pick up some food for dinner and meet you back here tonight for our camp-out."

"Sure, if it will help you find whoever's doing all this stuff," Andrew said. "See you guys later."

"Where are we going?" Ned asked when they got to the lobby.

Nancy draped his leather jacket over his bad arm, then slipped on her down parka. "I thought this would be the perfect excuse to spend some time alone with you," she said, grinning. "If we have to spend your vacation chasing after suspects, at least we can do it together."

"There's no one I'd rather chase suspects with," Ned said with a warm look that made Nancy tingle all over. "Who's first on our list?"

"I want to find out if the clay sample from the balcony matches the clay Julie works with," Nancy said. "Then I want to go to Blaster's house and see if I can figure out what he's hiding."

She and Ned got in the Mustang, and Nancy headed for the small road that curved around the lake and into the town of Moon Lake. As she approached A Show of Hands, Nancy saw that Julie and the middle-aged woman were just locking up the boutique.

"Hmm," Ned said as Julie got into an old gray car and pulled away from the curb. "I guess you'll have to wait to check out that clay sample."

Nancy slowed down, keeping a discreet distance behind Julie's car. "I'm going to follow her," she decided.

After a short drive down curving, tree-lined roads, Nancy followed Julie's car into a suburban neighborhood.

"This is Melborne," Ned said, reading a sign. "She's probably going home."

A few minutes later Julie turned onto a quiet street and pulled up alongside a small but well-kept white house.

"Not too incriminating so far," Ned said.

"No," Nancy agreed. She parked diagonally across the street and watched as Julie got out of her car and headed up the front walk. After Julie had closed the front door behind her, Nancy said, "I'm going to try to talk to her."

Ned nodded. "I'd better stay here. Julie knows

I'm Andrew's friend. If she sees me with you, she might not be too cooperative."

"Good point," Nancy said, opening her door. "I'll try not to be too long."

After hurrying up the front walk, Nancy rang Julie's doorbell and waited. Half a minute later Julie opened the door. She looked even more tired than the day before, and her brown curly hair looked messy and unkempt. Nancy wondered if Julie had slept well the night before—or if she'd been busy sabotaging the cable at the inn.

Julie looked at Nancy in surprise. "Weren't you in my store yesterday?" she asked.

Nancy nodded, then said, "I know you're probably surprised to see me. I'm Nancy Drew."

"That name sounds familiar for some reason." Julie said, her gray eyes growing hazy.

"Could I talk to you for a minute? I'd like to ask you a couple of questions."

"That's it," Julie said, snapping her fingers. "I've heard Ned Nickerson talk about you. You're a detective, right?"

There was no point denying it. "Yes, but—"

"Did Andrew's father send you here?" Julie asked suspiciously.

"No," Nancy said quickly. "Mr. Lockwood has nothing to do with this."

"I don't believe you," Julie retorted, scowling. "He's already had one private detective tailing me. Isn't that man ever satisfied? He's totally ruined my life."

Julie slammed the door in Nancy's face, and Nancy heard the sound of a deadbolt locking.

"Please, Julie!" Nancy called, knocking on the door. "You've got it all wrong. . . ."

A few seconds later Nancy heard a stereo blasting loud rock music and saw the window shades being yanked down. Julie had made it very clear that she wasn't home—at least not for Nancy.

"What happened?" Ned asked when Nancy got back in the car.

"She wouldn't even talk to me," Nancy said, buckling her seat belt. "She thinks I'm working for Andrew's father."

"So what do we do now?" Ned asked.

"Let's find Blaster's house," Nancy said. She flipped open her notebook to find the address. "I know he lives in Melborne, too. Here it is— Eighteen Rose Avenue. Maybe we could find a gas station."

Ned's eyebrows knit together, and he said, "I thought we passed the street not far back. Why don't we turn around?"

Nancy made a U-turn, then headed the Mustang back the way they had come. After only a few blocks, she saw Rose Avenue off to the right. She turned onto it and drove several blocks until she came upon number eighteen, a two-story brick house.

Together, Nancy and Ned walked up to the front steps, and Nancy tapped on the iron door knocker. A few moments later the door opened a crack, and an elderly woman peeped out at them. She wasn't very tall, but she was heavyset, with short, steel gray hair.

"Yes?" the woman asked.

"Hi, I'm Nancy Drew," Nancy said pleasantly. "And this is Ned Nickerson. We're working with Blaster on the renovation of the Lakeside Inn."

"Has something happened to him?" the old woman asked, her dark eyes fearful. "He said there'd been some accidents the past few days."

"No, no, nothing like that," Nancy said quickly. "Blaster's fine. But we are trying to figure out who's been causing the accidents there, and we were wondering if we could talk to you."

"Me?" the old woman asked, opening the door a little wider. "You don't think my grandson's responsible, do you? He's a good boy."

"Blaster's your grandson?" Ned asked.

The old woman nodded. "He's lived with me since his parents died, ten years ago."

"Oh, I'm very sorry," Nancy said gently. "We don't know for sure who's responsible for what's happening at the inn," she added. "But you might be able to help us rule out Blaster."

The woman peered from Nancy to Ned to Ned's cast. After a long moment she said. "Please, come in. I'm Olivia Deekman."

Mrs. Deekman showed them into a small living room furnished with heavy, dark wooden furniture. A fire crackled in a fireplace against one wall, and dozens of framed photographs rested on the mantel. Nancy and Ned sat down on a green square-backed sofa as Blaster's grandmother settled in an armchair by the fireplace.

"What would you like to know?" Mrs. Deekman asked.

Nancy pulled from her purse the threatening note Natalia Diaz had found and held it out to Mrs. Deekman. "Does this look like Blaster's handwriting?" she asked.

Blaster's grandmother took the note and studied it, then shook her head. When Nancy asked her if she knew whether Blaster had any red enamel paint, the old woman said, "All he's got upstairs is a bunch of electronic equipment."

"What about tools? Have you noticed any new ones in his room, like a soldering iron, drill bits, anything like that?" Ned asked, naming the items that had been taken from the inn.

The old woman shook her head again. "Hubert's got a pretty complete set already. He hasn't bought anything new in—"

"Hubert?" Ned repeated, his mouth falling open. "Is that his real name?"

The old woman lifted a hand to her mouth. "Oh, my. Hub— Blaster's going to be mad at me that I let it slip. He hates for people to find out. He's terribly embarrassed about it. I don't know why. It's a perfectly respectable name. He was named after my father."

"Why did he change it?" Nancy asked, although she thought she knew the answer. The name didn't fit his cool image at all.

Mrs. Deekman sighed and stared into the fire. "In the past year and a half Hubert's changed drastically—and more than just his name. His looks, his personality, everything."

Blaster's grandmother got up from her chair and walked over to the mantel, murmuring, "I think I have an old picture here somewhere." She ran her finger lightly along the tops of the framed photographs until she found what she was looking for. "Here it is," she announced.

Mrs. Deekman handed Nancy a silver-framed color photograph of her grandson, and Nancy stared at it in stunned silence.

"Hubert looked a lot different back then, didn't he?" Mrs. Deekman said.

That was the understatement of the year, Nancy thought. Master Blaster did indeed look different. The photograph showed a scrawny kid with dark brown hair, owlish glasses, and a jacket that looked two sizes too big.

"I think the change started when his old girlfriend broke up with him," Mrs. Deekman went on. "Hubert was devastated. I think he was hoping that if he changed his image, he'd win her back."

Nancy looked curiously at the older woman. "Did the plan work?" she asked.

Mrs. Deekman shook her head no. "Poor Hubert."

"He must really have been in love with her for him to change his whole look and personality," Ned said. "Who was she?"

"Her name was Julie," Mrs. Deekman said. "Julie Ross."

Chapter

Nine

NANCY'S MIND was reeling. Master Blaster's ex-girlfriend was Andrew's former fiancée!

That opened up a whole new realm of possibilities in the case. Could Blaster and Julie be working together to ruin Andrew's inn project? That would explain what Blaster was doing by the back door the day Julie had run off through the woods.

"Tell me about Julie," Nancy said to Mrs. Deekman. "Why did she and Blaster break up?"

Mrs. Deekman replaced the picture on the mantel and sat back down in her armchair. "Hubert and Julie have been friends since they were children," she explained. "They dated in high school, until Julie broke up with him the summer after their junior year."

Ned prodded Nancy in the ribs with his cast, then asked Mrs. Deekman, "What happened? Did she meet someone else?"

Blaster's grandmother nodded sadly. "Julie met an older fellow, a college student," she said. "It was a whirlwind romance, from what I hear. Hubert couldn't accept the fact that Julie didn't love him anymore. He was very jealous."

"And that's when he changed his image?" Nancy guessed.

Mrs. Deekman nodded. "Hubert was always interested in music. When Julie left him, he swore to become a rich and famous recording star, just so she'd regret that she'd walked away from him."

"He certainly seems very ambitious," Nancy said. "I guess that's helped him get over Julie."

"Oh, no," Mrs. Deekman disagreed. "He's never forgotten her. In fact, when she broke up with the college fellow a few weeks ago, Hubert tried to win her back."

"How does Julie feel about Blaster now?" Nancy asked. "Does she want to get back together with him?"

"No. Julie's still pining over her ex-fiancé. Poor Hubert."

Mrs. Deekman probably didn't realize it, but she'd just provided Nancy with a motive linking Blaster to the crimes at the inn: revenge. He might be trying to get back at Andrew for stealing Julie away from him.

Getting to her feet, Nancy said, "Thank you for all your help, Mrs. Deekman." Ned rose, too, and Mrs. Deekman showed them to the door and said goodbye.

Nancy waited until she and Ned were in the car and halfway down the block before she said, "Can you believe it? Blaster and Julie? I never would have guessed it."

"You've got everything you need, now, huh?" Ned said. "Blaster had the motive to get back at Andrew, and he definitely seemed nervous and edgy the past few days. If we can prove he copied the keys or catch him tonight, we'll have it all wrapped up. I told you it wasn't Andrew."

Although it was only five-thirty, it was already dark outside. Nancy peered at the street signs lit up by her headlights, retracing her way back to the inn. "I agree that Blaster is our number-one suspect," she said, "but I think it's a little premature to convict him. There are too many other things we can't explain."

"Like what?" Ned asked.

"Julie's visits to the inn, for one thing," Nancy said. "We know she's been there, but apparently it hasn't been to visit Blaster."

Turning onto the little road that led to Moon Lake, she added, "I can't rule out Andrew, either. He seems to have more reason to want the inn to fail than to succeed. And then there's the uninvited guest in the basement. I still have to follow up on that T-shirt I found down there."

Ned leaned forward to turn up the heat, taking care not to hit his cast against the dashboard. "Well, I'm still convinced it's Master Blaster, but I guess we'll learn more tonight."

Andrew and Bess were in the ballroom unrolling sleeping bags when Ned and Nancy got back to the inn. The big room was dark except for a circle of work lights around the sleeping bags.

"Great, you're back. And you remembered dinner!" Bess called, gesturing to the shopping bag Ned carried.

"We stopped at the store in Moon Lake," he explained, putting the bag down.

Nancy squinted dubiously up at the lights. "We'd better turn those out," she said. "We don't want to scare away the intruder. We should check the front and back doors, too, to make sure they're locked. That way we'll have a little time to hide if we hear the intruder."

"I'll be right back," Andrew said. He jogged across the ballroom toward the main hall, returned after a minute, then disappeared through the door under the balcony.

"We're all set," he said when he came back. He turned out the work lights one by one until the vast ballroom was lit only by silvery moonlight. It took a few minutes for Nancy's eyes to adjust

90

to the darkness, but soon she could make out her friends' faces fairly well.

"So what did you find out?" Bess asked, unloading the grocery bag as Nancy and Ned sat down side by side on a sleeping bag.

Nancy filled them in on how they'd followed Julie and on Mrs. Deekman's revelation about Julie and Blaster.

"Master Blaster and Julie?" Andrew asked, an expression of total shock on his face. "She said she'd had a boyfriend, but I never would have guessed it was him."

"Well, it was. Working here could give him the perfect chance to pay you back for stealing Julie away," Nancy told Andrew.

Even in the darkness Nancy could see the troubled look in Bess's eyes. Nancy decided to let the subject drop for now, but over the next few hours she noticed that Bess was quieter than usual and only nibbled at her roast beef sandwich and potato salad.

"So what's the plan, Nancy?" Ned asked after they'd cleaned up after dinner.

Nancy thought for a moment. "I guess we should stay here," she said. "If someone comes in the back door, they'll have to walk through here, and we're close enough to the front door to hear if someone comes in through the lobby."

"What about sleeping?" Bess asked.

"We can take turns keeping watch," Nancy

said. She planned to stay awake the whole time, though, so she could keep an eye on Andrew. He might try to sneak away during his watch, while the rest of them were asleep.

Bess yawned. "I'm tired already," she said. "What time is it?"

"Almost ten o'clock," Nancy said, checking her watch.

"This is sort of romantic, isn't it?" Ned asked, moving closer to Nancy and putting his left arm around her.

"*Romantic* wasn't the word *I* was thinking of," came Bess's nervous voice.

"You're not still worried about the ghost, are you?" Ned asked her.

Bess smiled sheepishly. "I know it's silly, but in the dark, I feel like Rosalie's ghost could be right here in this room."

Grinning at her friend, Nancy said mischievously, "Maybe her ghost *is* here."

"Yeah, right," Ned said sarcastically. "And maybe I'm—"

He broke off as a sudden, frigid blast of cold air washed over them. A moment later Nancy heard loud, shuffling footsteps echoing somewhere overhead.

"It's Rosalie's ghost," Bess whispered hoarsely, sitting bolt upright.

Nancy craned her neck, looking in the direction the sound was coming from. She tried to stay calm, but she could feel the hairs rise up on the back of her neck.

Suddenly she noticed something white fluttering up in the balcony. Before Nancy could say anything, a high-pitched moan filled the room, and the white shape floated into a shaft of moonlight.

Then, as another moan filled the air, the ghostly form jumped off the balcony toward Nancy and her friends!

Chapter

Ten

I TOLD YOU there was a ghost!" Bess cried. "Let's get out of here!"

Nancy jumped to her feet and ran toward the white form, which fluttered just above the floor a few feet away from the circle of sleeping bags.

"What *is* that thing?" Ned said, behind her.

The white shape lightly touched the floor and flattened out, then went still. Nancy laughed when she realized what it was.

"It's a plain bedsheet, you guys!" she called out. Lifting the sheet, she found some hangers bent in the rough outline of a head and torso. "Someone must have thrown it from the balcony."

"How'd they get up there?" Andrew asked as

he and Bess joined Nancy and Ned by the sheet. "We didn't hear anybody come in."

Nancy was instantly alert, listening. "You guys, the person might still be there," she whispered excitedly, hurrying toward the back door to the dining room. "Wait here. I'm going to check the back door and balcony before the person has a chance to get away."

As Nancy ran down the back hall, she felt another rush of cold air. When she reached the door, it was open. She stuck her head outside and looked at the moonlit lake and at the path running behind the inn, but saw no sign of anyone.

Quickly she closed and bolted the door, then rushed back down the hallway to the ballroom.

"Well?" Ned asked.

Nancy shook her head in frustration. "Whoever it was probably got out the back door."

"Let's check out the rest of the inn, just in case the person's still hiding," Andrew suggested.

Turning on all the lights, Nancy, Ned, Bess, and Andrew scoured the inn, checking all the upstairs rooms, the lobby, the dining room, the kitchen, the library, and the basement. Up in the balcony the stereo was still warm, and the two cassette decks were empty and had been left open. Otherwise, they found no sign of anyone.

One good thing came out of the prank, though, Nancy reflected. Andrew now seemed less guilty than he had before. There was no way he could have rigged the ghost and the sound of shuffling feet himself while he was downstairs sitting on his sleeping bag. It was still possible that Andrew was working with someone, but Nancy doubted his partner was either of her top suspects—Julie or Master Blaster. They both had more reason to hurt him than help him.

"I can't believe the person got away again," Andrew said, frowning, as they all regathered in the ballroom after their search.

Ned gave Andrew a sympathetic smile and said, "At least we stopped him from doing any harm."

"Yeah," Bess agreed, sinking down on her sleeping bag. "I don't know about the rest of you happy campers, but I've had enough excitement. I'm ready to go to sleep."

"We might as well all call it a night," Nancy said. "I think we've seen all the special effects we're going to see. Besides, I want to get up bright and early and go to Bentley High School. It's time to check out that Bentley High Boneheads T-shirt."

"There it is," Ned said early Thursday morning as he and Nancy drove to Bentley, armed with directions from Andrew.

Bentley High School had just appeared over the top of the hill. It was a square, three-story granite building with a tall clock tower.

"I guess school's already in session," Nancy

said as she found a spot in the nearly full parking lot.

"That's what I like about college," Ned said. "We get longer holiday vacations."

They went in the main entrance and found themselves at one end of a long linoleum-floored corridor. Students were gathered by the bright orange lockers lining the walls along either side. After asking some students for directions to the administrative offices, Nancy and Ned went to the end of the long hall and turned right.

"Here we go," Nancy said, seeing an office marked Student Affairs.

Stepping inside, they found themselves in a large room with several tables and chairs and bookshelves lining the wall. The only desk was occupied by a pudgy woman with shoulder-length brown hair and glasses.

"Yearbooks," Ned said, nodding toward a bookshelf filled with identical purple and white books, each marked with a different year.

"May I help you?" the woman asked, looking sternly at Ned.

"Uh, yes," Nancy said. Thinking fast, she pulled her notepad and a pen from her purse and said, "We're reporters, and we're doing a piece called 'Whatever Happened to the Class of Seventy-seven.' It's a series of profiles of the graduates of Bentley High School. We were wondering if we could look at a few yearbooks, just as background."

97

Nancy held her breath, hoping the woman wouldn't ask what paper they worked for. To her relief, the woman simply shrugged and said, "Make sure to put them back when you're done."

With a wink at Ned Nancy walked over to the bookshelf and found the yearbook labeled 1977. Then she sat down at the table farthest from the woman and flipped it open to the table of contents. Ned pulled a chair up next to her.

"Seniors . . . teachers . . . sports . . . clubs . . . " she read, running her finger down the page.

"Try clubs," Ned suggested. "The Boneheads could be some special kind of organization."

Nancy flipped through the pages of black and white portraits, sports teams, and candid shots until she came to the club section.

"There it is!" Ned exclaimed in a hoarse whisper, jabbing a finger at a group photograph.

Nancy's heart jumped as she, too, spotted the Bentley High Boneheads logo. The word *Boneheads* was hand drawn, and each letter was shaped out of white bones, just as it had been on the T-shirt.

"What kind of club was it?" Ned asked softly, looking at the short paragraph under the logo.

Nancy read the paragraph aloud. " 'The Bentley Boneheads are proud of the contribution we've made to our school. We kept our grades low to balance the grade curve. We cut classes so our teachers would have more time for the other students, and we've spent lots of time in the vice principal's office so he wouldn't feel lonely. Party hearty!'"

Breaking into a deep laugh, Ned said, "I guess it wasn't a real club."

The woman at the desk gave them a questioning look, so Nancy punched Ned's arm. "Shh!" Then, turning her attention to the picture, she whispered, "It seems more like a spoof, or a bunch of friends clowning around."

Both the boys and the girls in the photograph had long hair, and most of them wore rock band T-shirts. All in all, there were about a dozen teenagers in two rows, making faces at the camera.

"There are names under the picture," Nancy said, squinting to read the tiny print. "Guy Lewis," she said excitedly, pointing at the third guy from the left in the back row. He was thin, with stringy dark hair and a goatee. "He's the only one with the initials G.L. It has to be him!"

Ned studied the photograph. "I still don't see what his connection to Andrew might be," he commented. "Andrew is years younger than this guy, and they're from different towns."

"Hmm," Nancy said. "It's probably just chance that Guy stayed overnight at the inn, but I'll call Chief McGinnis at the River Heights police station when we get back to the inn. Maybe he has something on this guy."

"Look at that girl Guy Lewis has his arm around," Ned commented, still looking at the photograph. "She looks like somebody, only I can't put my finger on who it is."

The girl was pretty, with hair pulled back into a sleek ponytail. She was slim and wore snugly fitting jeans and cowboy boots. "You're right, she does look familiar."

Once again Nancy scanned the names beneath the picture. When she read the one after Guy Lewis, she nearly fell out of her seat. But another look at the picture confirmed it. "Ned, we know that woman. We've been seeing her every day since Monday," Nancy said.

"Colleen O'Herlihy?" Ned said, reading the name. Then his dark eyes met Nancy's, and his mouth fell open. "You don't mean . . . ?"

Nancy nodded. "The Colleen in the photograph is actually Colleen Morgan!"

Chapter

Eleven

Y OU'RE RIGHT!" Ned exclaimed in a low voice. "It *is* her."

Her pulse racing, Nancy flipped forward in the yearbook to look for the graduation portraits of Guy and Colleen. There was no listing for Colleen O'Herlihy. Guy Lewis, though, was among the seniors. He wore a T-shirt instead of a shirt and tie, and nothing was listed under his picture except his name.

"Maybe Colleen graduated a different year," Ned suggested. He stood up to take out a few more yearbooks but had trouble getting them off the shelf because of his cast.

Nancy jumped up to help him. "Let's split

these up," she suggested. "I'll take seventy-three through seventy-six. You take seventy-eight through eighty-one."

They checked each yearbook thoroughly, but neither of them was able to find any record of Colleen O'Herlihy.

"I don't get it," Nancy said, her brows knitting together. "We know she went to school here. So why isn't she listed with any of the senior classes?"

"Maybe she never graduated," Ned suggested. "Or maybe she transferred to another school."

"That's a good possibility," Nancy said, nodding. "Especially since Colleen said she went to a private school. Maybe she transferred to a private school before graduation."

As Nancy and Ned stood up and began putting away the yearbooks, Ned said, "I wonder if Colleen knew Guy was hanging around the inn."

Nancy thought for a moment. "She didn't act as if she recognized any of the stuff we found in the basement," she said, "though she did seem very eager to clean it out. Maybe she didn't want us to figure out who the homeless person was or that she knew him."

"But what's the connection?" Ned asked. "Why would it matter if Colleen knew him?"

"Good question," Nancy said. "After I talk to Chief McGinnis, I hope I'll be able to answer it."

After thanking the woman at the desk, Nancy and Ned left Bentley High School and got back in

Nancy's Mustang. As Nancy pulled out of the parking lot and started back toward Moon Lake, Ned said, "So you're adding Colleen to your list of suspects?"

"Definitely," Nancy told him. "Not that her knowing Guy Lewis is a crime. For all we know, Guy Lewis just slept at the inn for a few days and moved on. But Colleen sure gave us a false impression of her upbringing. She made it seem as if she has always been rich and privileged, when it looks as if she was just a normal kid who went to public school."

"That's not a crime, either," Ned pointed out.

"If it were, we'd *all* be guilty," Nancy joked. "But my point is that if she hid that, there may be other things she's not telling us."

Ned nodded thoughtfully. "If Guy Lewis is still hanging around the inn, causing trouble, maybe Colleen knows he's there."

"She might not want anybody to know that she's helping him," Nancy added. "After all, she *is* married now. Her husband might not be too understanding if she was spending time with her old boyfriend."

When Nancy pulled into the Lakeside Inn parking lot a short while later, the red TeenWorks bus was already there, as well as some other cars and vans. She and Ned were about to get out of the parked Mustang when Master Blaster came out the inn's front door, wearing a faded denim jacket covered all over with buttons naming famous rock groups. He headed toward a beat-up blue hatchback parked near Nancy and Ned.

"Wait a minute," Nancy said, putting her hand on Ned's arm. "Let's see what he does."

The deejay opened the hatchback, and Nancy could see that it was loaded with shoe boxes. He rummaged in several of the boxes, pulling out half a dozen cassette tapes.

"So that's where he gets his music," Ned said.

At Ned's words a light suddenly blinked on in Nancy's mind. "Why didn't I think of it before?" she exclaimed softly, tapping her forehead with her palm. "Blaster said he uses sound effects when he does his original music. Maybe the ghost noises we heard came from his tapes."

Master Blaster slammed the hatchback shut, but the back door popped open again. After two more tries he finally managed to close it, then headed for the front entrance to the inn.

"Now's our chance," Nancy said as soon as Blaster disappeared inside. She hopped out of the Mustang and hurried over to the hatchback.

"Wow!" Ned exclaimed, coming up next to her and staring through the tinted glass. "Look at all those tapes."

The backseat of the car had been pushed down, leaving a large flat surface that was completely covered by shoe boxes filled with audiocassettes. Nancy estimated that there were at least five hundred tapes.

"It's hard to read the cases through the glass,"

she said, squinting. As she laid her hand against the glass for a closer look, the hatchback popped open a few inches.

Nancy and Ned exchanged a guilty glance. "It's already open," Ned said. "What's a few more inches?"

After opening the hatchback, they took a closer look inside. Most of the tapes were commercial recordings by popular artists, but there were two shoe boxes filled with cassette cases that had been neatly labeled by hand.

Nancy read the titles aloud. "'The Master's Super Mix Part Two' . . . 'High Voltage Party Tape' . . . 'Babies Crying.'"

"'Babies Crying'?" Ned echoed. "What kind of party tape is that?"

"It's not," Nancy replied, growing excited. She peered at the other tapes in the box. "Listen to these. 'Things Breaking'; 'Sneezes and Coughs'; 'Footsteps.'"

"Sound effects!" Ned exclaimed. "Here's 'Thunderstorms' and—"

Nancy didn't hear the rest of what Ned was saying because she'd just found what she was looking for. Right after "Footsteps" was a cassette labeled "Haunted House."

"I think we've hit the jackpot," she said softly, pulling out the cassette and showing it to Ned. "I'll bet you anything this is what we heard inside the inn."

"I *knew* it was Blaster!" Ned said triumphantly. "I just wish I'd brought my tape player so we could listen to it right here."

"We still can," Nancy told him, "on the cassette player in my car."

She quickly slipped the cassettes into the pocket of her parka, while Ned lowered the hatchback roof with his good hand.

After hurrying to the Mustang, Nancy got in behind the steering wheel, and Ned got in beside her. She reached into her jacket pocket and flipped open the "Haunted House" cassette case. Then she turned on the ignition and loaded the cassette into her tape player.

"Hey! What do you think you're doing?" an angry voice growled right outside her window.

Nancy jumped in her seat, then whirled around to see who was talking.

It was Master Blaster. His face was pressed close to Nancy's window, and he was glaring at her with cold, dark eyes.

Chapter

Twelve

A CHILL RAN THROUGH Nancy's entire body as Blaster's furious gaze bored into her.

"Give me back my tape!" Blaster went on angrily. "I saw you steal it."

Nancy unrolled her window slowly, trying to think of what to say. "We didn't steal it," she told him. "We borrowed it."

"We were planning to put it right back," Ned added.

"Yeah, sure," Blaster said, glowering. "You were probably going to make copies of my dance mixes and sell them to some local deejay."

Was he honestly worried about his dance mix? Nancy wondered, trying to read the look in his eyes. Or was that just a cover for what he was really afraid of—that Nancy had caught the person who was trying to scare Andrew off the renovation.

"Actually," Nancy said evenly, "I'm not interested in your dance mixes. I'm more curious about your sound effects."

"Same difference," Blaster said. "I spent a lot of time putting those together. I don't want anybody else to get their hands on them."

Nancy took the "Haunted House" tape out of the player and showed it to Blaster. "We know that someone is trying to scare us away from the place, and twice now we've heard ghostly noises inside the inn," she said. "If these tapes match the sounds we've heard, you're going to look guilty. If they don't, it will help clear you."

"I don't need to be cleared!" Blaster shouted. "I didn't do anything wrong!"

"Then prove it," Ned challenged him. "Let us listen to the tape."

Master Blaster stuffed his hands into the pockets of his jacket. "Fine," he said hotly. "I've got nothing to hide. Go ahead and play it."

Nancy once more loaded the "Haunted House" tape into her player. Her heart started to beat faster as she pressed the Play button.

"*Aaaaaaaaaaagh!*" The tormented cry filled Nancy's car, giving Nancy a creepy feeling. The wails sounded just like the ones they'd all heard the first day at the inn.

108

"Sound familiar, Ned?" Nancy asked.

"Very," he replied, nodding.

Master Blaster's face turned bright red. "You don't know what you're talking about," he said.

Nancy pressed the Stop button and faced the deejay squarely. "Where were you last night, around ten o'clock?" she asked.

"What difference does it make?" Blaster demanded.

"Because that's when we heard some of these sound effects," she answered. "Right before a white sheet came flying off the balcony in the ballroom, rigged to look like a ghost."

Blaster looked from Nancy to Ned, then started to laugh. "Give me a break," he scoffed. "Who'd pull a stupid trick like that?"

"Don't pretend you don't remember," Ned said. "You must have set it up yourself, right after you turned on the stereo."

The deejay held up his hands defensively. "Look, man, I wasn't anywhere near the inn last night!"

"That's funny, because your tapes were," Nancy shot back.

"Well, someone must have borrowed them, like you just tried to," Blaster contended. "They could have made copies and put the originals back when I wasn't looking."

He was putting on a good show of innocence, Nancy had to admit. But that didn't change the fact that he'd acted suspiciously after some of the accidents. Pressing the Eject button, she put the tape in its box and gave it to Blaster.

"Why are you so determined to blame me for something I didn't do?" Blaster demanded, taking the cassette. "I know you've been talking to my grandmother. Well, I'm warning you now. Stay away from her!"

Ned leaned across Nancy to say, "What are you so afraid of, Blaster? That we'll find out the truth about you? Like the fact that you used to go out with Julie Ross?"

Blaster hesitated, then said angrily, "My personal life is none of your business."

"It is when it could explain all the trouble going on here," Nancy said. "Maybe you're jealous of Andrew because he took Julie away from you. Sabotaging his renovation project would be a good way of getting back at him."

Blaster gaped at her. "Why would I want to do that?" he demanded. "Andrew promised me I can be the deejay at the dance club here when the inn opens. It's not big time or anything, but it would be a good start for my career."

Nancy fell silent. He had a good point, and she doubted he was lying—he had to know she could easily check his story with Andrew. Still, that didn't let him off the hook completely.

Giving Master Blaster a hard look, Nancy asked, "Then what were you doing by the back door Monday afternoon, right after we heard the ghost noises? And don't tell me you were just getting some air."

Blaster drew in a deep breath and let it out slowly. After a long silence he admitted, "I was trying to decide what to do about the fact that I'd just seen my ex-girlfriend running away from the inn. Yes, I saw Julie. I saw her the second time, too, right after Ned fell."

Nancy nodded. That explained the clay on the light switch and the wall.

"If you saw her, why didn't you say anything?" Ned asked.

"Even if she's the one causing the trouble, I didn't want to turn her in," Blaster answered with a guilty look. "I still care about her, even after everything she did to me. Oh, why am I even bothering to explain anything to you? I can see you don't believe me."

With a disgusted look at Nancy and Ned, Blaster turned and stalked back to the inn.

"You don't really believe him, do you, Nan?" Ned asked when Blaster had disappeared inside.

"I don't know," Nancy said. "I think he's telling the truth about having seen Julie. That would explain why he was so nervous when I asked him what he saw the day he was up in the alcove."

As she and Ned got out of the Mustang, Ned said, "I guess things don't look good for Julie now, do they?"

Nancy shook her head. "I still want to check

out Guy Lewis and his connection to Colleen Morgan, too," she said. "Come on. Let's go find Andrew. I want to use his phone to call Chief McGinnis."

When they got inside the inn, they didn't see Andrew, or anyone else for that matter, on the first floor. Finally Nancy and Ned found Andrew, Bess, Colleen, and what looked like the entire TeenWorks crew in the basement.

At first it looked as if there was more junk piled up in the basement than there'd been the day before. Then Nancy noticed that only the area near the bottom of the stairs was crowded with old furniture and newspapers. The rest of the basement was nearly empty.

"We've got a good system going," Andrew explained, spotting Nancy and Ned. "It's like a bucket brigade. Once we get everything near the stairs, we're going to pass it up hand to hand. We ought to be finished by the time the haulers get here after lunch. Then we'll be on schedule to pour the concrete floor in the morning."

Nancy was relieved to see that Andrew still seemed dedicated to keeping the renovation going. Maybe she'd been wrong to think he was sabotaging the inn to get the insurance money.

"Listen, I'll come down and help you move stuff in a few minutes," she told Andrew. "Meanwhile, could I use the phone in your office, Andrew? I've got to make a quick call."

"Sure," Andrew said.

Nancy hurried back up the stairs to the lobby, entered Andrew's office, and closed the door behind her. Seconds later she was dialing the number of the River Heights police headquarters.

"Hello, Nancy," Chief McGinnis greeted her warmly when the call was put through to him. "Don't tell me you're on another case."

"It must be fate," Nancy joked. "But listen, I was wondering if you could check somebody out for me. His name's Guy Lewis. He graduated from Bentley High School in 1977."

Nancy explained about the sabotage and pranks at the inn and told the chief about finding evidence that Lewis may have been there recently.

"I'll have to run a check and get back to you," Chief McGinnis told her.

"Could you also check out a woman named Colleen Morgan or Colleen O'Herlihy?" Nancy asked.

There was a long pause before the police chief inquired, "You mean the wife of Frederick Morgan, as in Morgan Lumber, Morgan Steel, Morgan Financial Services . . . ?"

"That's the one. It looks as if she went to high school with Lewis. Not that that necessarily means anything, but if there's any connection between them, I'd like to know what it is."

"I'll put someone on this right away," Chief McGinnis said. "Where do you want me to call you with the information?"

Nancy thought for a moment. "I'll call you," she decided. "Colleen Morgan's working here at the inn. I don't want to risk her overhearing me. Why don't I try you in an hour or two?"

"Good enough," the chief agreed. "We should have something by then."

After thanking him, Nancy hung up. When she returned to the basement, everyone was moving the last of the furniture to the base of the stairs.

Nancy wanted to ask Andrew whether he'd really offered Blaster the deejay job, but Blaster was right next to him, helping him move a dresser. Seeing Bess and Natalia Diaz struggling to carry a fire-blackened mattress from a pile of them at the back of the basement, Nancy went over to help. They dumped it near some others near the stairs, then returned to the back wall for another.

"Phew," Nancy said as she grabbed one end of the mattress. "This thing stinks."

Wrinkling up her nose, Bess added, "From the smell down here, you'd think the fire happened yesterday instead of fifty years ago."

"My eyes are watering," Natalia put in. "The first thing Andrew should do once we clear out this stuff is fumigate the place."

Nancy's eyes were beginning to water, too, and her throat felt dry. There was a choking, bitter smell in the air.

Suddenly she paused and cocked her head.

"Do you smell something?" Nancy asked Bess and Natalia.

Natalia nodded. "It's getting hard to breathe. And it's getting hot in here, too."

"It's the exercise," Bess said, grunting under the weight of the mattress. "All this heavy lifting is making us burn calories faster—"

"I don't think so," Nancy interrupted. She dropped her corner of the mattress, a feeling of dread welling up in the pit of her stomach. A moment later she pointed in horror at the huge pile of broken wooden furniture directly between them and the stairwell.

A thick plume of choking, black smoke rose from the pile, rapidly filling the basement. Already the other teens in the basement were coughing and rubbing their eyes.

As Nancy watched, the huge pile of furniture erupted into flames. Almost instantly everything was awash in a searing orange blaze.

"Let's get out of here!" Nancy cried.

She pulled Bess and Natalia toward the stairs, but their way was blocked by a wall of rapidly spreading flames. The other teens were scrambling around the burning debris, too, looking for an escape route.

Within seconds the fire had completely engulfed the base of the stairs, and Nancy realized the awful truth.

They were trapped in an underground inferno, and there was no way out!

Chapter

Thirteen

W**E'RE GOING TO DIE!**" Bess cried. The other teenagers started screaming, too.

Nancy's eyes and lungs were burning, but she tried to remain calm. "Stay low, everybody!" she yelled. "And keep your nose and mouth covered!"

As the others obeyed, Nancy squinted through the heavy smoke. If she didn't find some way out, they'd all be fried to a crisp in minutes.

"I never should have piled all that stuff in front of the stairs!" Andrew yelled from close by. His black hair was plastered to his sweat-soaked forehead, and his round glasses reflected twin orange flames. "What an idiot I was!"

Coughing, Nancy searched desperately for an

116

escape route. The flames extended all the way around the stairs, but she saw that some parts of the fire burned higher than others. The flames rising from the damp, moldy mattresses were only a foot or so high.

"That's it!" Nancy exclaimed, picking up the mattress she, Bess, and Natalia Diaz had dropped. "We'll make a pathway."

"What are you talking about?" Bess asked.

"We've still got a bunch of mattresses we haven't moved yet," Nancy told her, pointing to the ones piled against the stone wall. "We can drop them over the burning mattresses. That should smother the flames long enough for us to get out of here."

"Good idea," Ned said, then broke into a cough as smoke filled his lungs. "Everybody, grab a mattress!"

Nancy, Bess, and Natalia dumped their mattress on a smoldering pile near the stairs. Then some of the other teens laid their mattresses upright on either side, making a temporary protective wall. When two more mattresses were down, they formed a path to the stairs.

"Now run!" Nancy cried out, urging the others over the lumpy, hot mattresses. When everyone had gone ahead, she and Andrew brought up the rear. Just as she made it to the bottom step, the pile of mattresses burst into flame.

Nancy nearly scorched her hand as it came to rest for a split second against the metal banister.

117

Jerking it away, she scrambled up the stairs and staggered into the lobby.

Gasping for breath, she ran for Andrew's office so she could call the fire department. Before she even got to Andrew's door, however, she heard the wail of approaching sirens outside.

Was the fire department really on its way already? Nancy wondered, pausing. How could that be? The fire had started just a few minutes ago, and everyone at the inn had been stuck in the basement. Who had alerted the fire fighters?

Joining the sweaty, red-faced crowd rushing for the front door, Nancy saw two bright red fire trucks just pulling up the curved driveway.

"I don't believe it!" Andrew cried, standing on the front doorstep of the inn. "How did they know?"

"That's what I was wondering," Nancy said as the fire trucks screeched to a halt and a dozen fire fighters in black raincoats, helmets, and rubber boots jumped out.

"It's in the basement," Andrew directed them as they rushed inside. "Follow me." After instructing the TeenWorks crew to remain outside, he followed the fire fighters inside.

For a few minutes Nancy wandered through the crowd, looking for Ned and Bess. But before she found her friends, Nancy spotted a familiar mass of brown curls with a copper streak.

Julie Ross was rushing through the chaos of fire fighters and distraught teenagers. Tears were streaming down her grief-stricken face. "Andrew!" she called, her voice breaking. "Where are you?"

It seemed obvious that Julie still cared about Andrew. She must have come running from the boutique the second she heard the sirens. But then Nancy remembered Julie's angry words the first time she'd spoken to her at the crafts store: "I hope that old dump burns to the ground."

Nancy frowned, wondering if it could be mere coincidence that Julie was so close to the inn just minutes after a fire started. Even if she'd been at her boutique nearby and had smelled smoke, she couldn't possibly have gotten to the inn so fast. Maybe Julie's display of concern for Andrew was just an act to cover up the fact that she was the one to start the fire.

Just as Nancy was about to follow Julie, someone grabbed her arm. She turned to see Ned standing there, a relieved look on his face.

"The fire's out," he told her.

"Already?" Nancy asked. She checked over her shoulder and saw that Julie was still milling in the crowd outside the inn. Nancy resolved to keep her within eyesight.

Ned nodded. "Fortunately for Andrew, it was contained in that one area and didn't spread," he told her. "The fire fighters were able to douse it pretty quickly."

More sirens echoed through the bare trees, and three Melborne Township police cars pulled up the driveway alongside the fire trucks. Half a dozen officers got out.

A tall female officer and her partner, a beefy red-haired man, got out of the car nearest the inn's entrance. "Andrew Lockwood?" the female officer called.

Andrew appeared in the front entrance of the inn, his sweatshirt sooty and his glasses fogged with smoke. "I'm Andrew Lockwood."

"I'm Lieutenant Oscarson. I'd like to ask you a few questions," the female officer said, taking out a leather-bound notepad. "Are you the owner of this place?"

Andrew walked down the steps and paused a few feet away from Lieutenant Oscarson. "My father is. I'm renovating it for him."

"Yet you've taken out an accident insurance policy on the inn in your name, with yourself as the beneficiary?" the lieutenant inquired.

Andrew took off his glasses and began wiping them nervously on his sweatshirt. "Uh . . . that was my father's idea," he said. "He wants to give me the inn after it's finished. I know how it must look. . . ."

Lieutenant Oscarson fixed Andrew with a stern glare. "About fifteen minutes ago we got an anonymous tip telling us there was a fire at the inn and that the fire was arson," she told him. "We were also told that you'd recently increased your insurance policy. That makes you our prime suspect."

Andrew's eyes grew wide with panic. "That's not true!" he protested. "I mean, I did increase my coverage, but I *didn't* start this fire."

"I can vouch for him," Ned said, looking straight at the police officer. "I was with him every second before the fire started. He didn't do anything except move some old furniture around."

There was something else about the officer's accusation that struck Nancy as odd, too. Stepping forward, she told Lieutenant Oscarson, "There *was* no fire fifteen minutes ago, when the call came. It started less than ten minutes ago, which was *after* you got the tip. Doesn't that seem odd?"

The lieutenant quickly flipped through her notepad. "We haven't yet determined the exact time the fire started."

"The call had to come before the fire started," Nancy insisted. "None of us had a chance to call the fire department after we got out of the basement, yet the fire trucks were here as soon as we got upstairs. I think the person who called is the arsonist. How else could he or she have known in advance that a fire would happen?"

"In that case it doesn't make sense that Andrew would do it," Ned put in. "If he wanted to torch the inn and collect on the insurance, I doubt he would have called the fire department and the police department and given himself away."

Lieutenant Oscarson leaned back against the hood of her police car and studied Nancy and Ned carefully. "You're saying the caller named Andrew to take suspicion off himself?"

"Or herself," Nancy amended. "Do you have any idea who called in the tip? Even knowing whether it was a man or a woman could be helpful."

Making a note in her pad, the officer said, "One of our emergency operators took the call. I'll try to track it down. Meanwhile, I've still got to take Andrew down to the station for questioning." She stood up and opened the back door to her car.

"See you guys later," Andrew said glumly, getting into the backseat.

Ned's brown eyes flashed angrily as he watched the police car roll down the driveway. "I know he didn't do it," he insisted. "We have to do something."

"I'm going to start by calling Chief McGinnis," Nancy assured him, "to see what he turned up on Colleen and Guy Lewis."

Dodging the fire fighters who were leaving the building with their hoses and hatchets, Nancy hurried to Andrew's office.

"Appears we've got something on Lewis," Chief McGinnis said over the line a few moments later.

Nancy's heart started beating faster. "He's got a record?"

The chief whistled. "I'll say he does. He's been convicted of burglary, vagrancy, extortion, and about fifteen years back he belonged to a theft ring that stole audio equipment from warehouses and sold it illegally."

"Wow," Nancy said. "I can see why Colleen wouldn't want anybody to know she knew him. He sounds like bad news."

"It also says here that Lewis was just released from the state prison a few weeks ago," McGinnis added.

Nancy thought quickly. "That could explain what he was doing in the basement," she said. "It looked as if he was here fairly recently. Maybe he thought this place was still abandoned, so he came here to stay when he got out of jail. Unless he had some other purpose. I wonder if there's any link between Lewis and the Lockwood family?"

"Could be," came the chief's voice over the line. "I know some of the guys in the Melborne Police Department. I'll see if they can help out on this."

"Thanks," Nancy told him. "There's something else I don't understand," she went on. "Where's Guy Lewis now? From what I can tell, he's not at the inn anymore. But I think he may be behind what's happened here. Or maybe he's working with Colleen Morgan. Did you find anything on her?"

"Not a thing," Chief McGinnis told Nancy.

"I looked up O'Herlihy and Morgan. She's clean."

Thanking him again, Nancy hung up. She exited through the inn's front entrance just as two officers were sealing the door with yellow tape marked Police Line—Do Not Cross.

Outside, the last of the fire fighters were getting on their trucks and pulling out of the driveway. Nancy spotted Ned and Bess nearby, standing at the edge of the parking lot. The other teens also milled around, as if they weren't sure whether to go back to work or go home.

"I told Bess what we found out about Colleen at Bentley High," Ned said when Nancy joined them. "Did the police find anything on Colleen?"

Nancy shook her head. "Her old friend Guy Lewis has a record, though. And we're not just talking parking tickets."

"Could they have been working together?" Bess wondered. "Colleen could have set the fire, and Lewis could have placed the call."

"It's possible," Nancy agreed.

"What about Blaster?" Ned wanted to know. "He could have set the fire."

Bess started to object, but Nancy said, "He's right, Bess. Blaster was down in the basement with us, but he could have sneaked away at some point to place the call. We were too busy to watch everyone the whole time."

"Julie could have done it, too," Bess argued. "I know I saw her wandering around just now, calling Andrew's name. She's got curly hair with a red streak in it, right?"

Nancy nodded, remembering that she still hadn't had a chance to question Julie. Nancy searched the crowd with her eyes, but Julie had disappeared.

"That's the third time Julie's been at the inn with no explanation," Nancy said. "But she wasn't in the basement when the fire started."

"Do you think she could have sneaked down the stairs and started the fire while we all were working?" Ned asked.

"I doubt she could have done it without someone spotting her," Nancy said.

A loud voice broke into their conversation. "Attention!" shouted a police officer. He stood on the doorstep, holding a megaphone to his mouth. "This area is now off-limits. Please go home and wait for further instructions."

There was a collective groan from the TeenWorks teenagers, who were gathered around Colleen.

"Hey, Ms. Morgan," Blaster said. "Does that mean the party's canceled for tonight?"

"Of course not," Colleen answered at once. "With all the bad things that have happened, we need a party now more than ever. Everybody be at my place at eight o'clock sharp, or else!"

Chapter

Fourteen

As THE TEENAGERS CHEERED, Bess grinned at Nancy and Ned. "I'm glad Colleen has her priorities straight. We could use a party around here."

"Mmm," Nancy murmured distractedly. Seeing that Colleen was about to leave, she hurried over to her, hoping to question her about her relationship with Guy Lewis. "Colleen, could I talk to you a minute?" Nancy asked.

"Sorry," Colleen told her. "I don't have time right now."

"But it's important," Nancy insisted. "I'm trying to locate a man named Guy Lewis. I think he might be responsible for what's going on here."

Colleen's freckled face was blank. "Who?"

"His name is Guy Lewis. I think he's the person who was sleeping in the basement."

Shrugging, Colleen said, "The name doesn't sound familiar. Why are you asking me?"

Nancy's blue eyes bored into Colleen. It seemed unlikely that she wouldn't have the slightest recollection of a guy she'd known in high school. Colleen was definitely hiding something. But whether it was simply the fact that she knew Lewis, or something more, remained to be seen.

"I thought you might remember him from high school," Nancy prodded. *"Bentley* High School . . ."

Nancy saw a flicker of unease in Colleen's green eyes. Colleen glanced quickly at her gold watch, then said, "I'd love to talk to you, but I've got to bring these kids back to the TeenWorks center, and then I have to rush home and prepare for the party. We'll talk tonight, okay?"

Turning away from Nancy, Colleen called out to the TeenWorks kids and started down the driveway to the parking lot. Nancy let out a sigh of frustration as she watched the other woman.

Colleen is definitely hiding something, Nancy thought. And tonight, at the party, I'm going to try to find out exactly what it is.

"This house is incredible," Bess said to Nancy and Ned a few hours later as they entered Colleen

Morgan's mansion. The foyer had polished wooden floors and an enormous crystal chandelier hanging overhead. Intricately patterned Persian rugs were scattered over the floor, and a grand staircase swept upward to the second floor.

After a butler had taken their coats and jackets, a maid led the three teens down a long hallway with oil paintings hanging along the walls and more Persian rugs.

"This is my kind of house," Bess said approvingly.

The thumping bass line of a rock song grew louder as they neared a pair of carved wooden doors at the end of the hall. The maid ushered them through the doors, and Nancy found herself in a living room almost as large as the ballroom at the inn. Groupings of sofas and velvet chairs were spaced around the room, and the walls were paneled with deep red-brown mahogany.

Along one wall several tables were set up, covered with white linen and loaded with food. Uniformed caterers stood behind the tables, serving cold cuts, fruit, and hot dishes in silver warming trays. A makeshift sound system had been set up at the far end of the room and was connected to two six-foot-high speakers.

"Not bad for something Colleen just threw together in a day," Nancy joked, watching the TeenWorks kids, as well as the construction foreman and the master electrician, dancing in a cleared space in the middle of the room.

"I wonder where Andrew is," Ned said, looking around. "Do you think the police would keep him at the station this long?"

"It's hard to say," Nancy told him. "He's had a long day. Maybe he just didn't feel like going to a party."

Nancy turned as Colleen broke through the crowd and came toward them. She wore a royal blue minidress covered entirely in sequins. Her red hair was swept up in a French twist, and she wore diamond and sapphire earrings with a matching necklace. Her hand was nestled in the arm of a distinguished-looking man with graying hair and warm, intelligent eyes.

"Wow!" Bess whispered to Nancy. "I wonder how much that outfit cost."

Looking down at her own purple sweater dress, Nancy said, "I feel like a slob next to her." The dressiest thing she had on was the heart-shaped pendant Ned had given her the year before for Valentine's Day.

"Hi, guys," Colleen greeted them. "I'd like you to meet my husband, Frederick Morgan."

Nancy, Ned, and Bess all shook the hand he offered. "Nice to meet you, Mr. Morgan," Nancy said.

"Please call me Fred," Colleen's husband told them. "And please, start eating right away. I think we ordered way too much food."

"I'll do my best," Bess said cheerfully, heading straight for the catering tables.

"I'm sure you'll find everything you'd like," Frederick Morgan assured Nancy and Ned. "When my wife plans a party, she thinks of everything." He wrapped an arm around Colleen's waist and pulled her close, planting an affectionate kiss on her cheek. "I don't know what I'd do without her."

Colleen looked lovingly into her husband's eyes and stroked the graying hair above his temples. "I don't even want to *think* of what I'd do without you."

"Let's mingle," Ned murmured in Nancy's ear. "I feel like I'm intruding."

With a smile Nancy grabbed Ned's hand and they left the Morgans. Then her smile vanished. "It still doesn't make sense to me," she said in a low voice. "Colleen seems to have everything—looks, money, a wonderful husband . . ."

"Yeah," Ned agreed. "It sort of rules her out as a suspect, doesn't it? I mean, why would she want to make trouble at the inn when her life is going so well?"

"That's the part that doesn't make sense," Nancy said. "If she hasn't done anything wrong, then what's she acting so secretive about? I'm going to try to talk to her one more time."

Nancy waited until she saw Colleen alone, clearing some empty glasses off a coffee table, then strode purposefully toward her. As soon as Colleen spotted her coming, however, she skirted away through the crowd. Before Nancy could reach her, Colleen rejoined her husband, and the two of them wandered out a side door.

"She's avoiding me, I'm sure of it," Nancy said, reappearing at Ned's side. She paused as Blaster's voice boomed out over a microphone.

"Listen up, partiers, it's the music meister," Blaster said. He stood next to the makeshift sound system, wearing a baggy red shirt over faded blue jeans. "You've heard Top Forty tonight, but now it's time for a blast from Master B. You can tell your grandchildren you heard the tune here first—'Bust 'Em Up' by the soon-to-be-famous recording star Master Blaster. I do it louder and faster!

"Yay!" Bess cheered. She was standing just a few feet away from Blaster, looking on encouragingly as he slipped a tape into the stereo and turned it on. First Nancy heard the sounds of cars crashing and glass breaking, followed by a driving beat and catchy riff of synthesized music.

"Not bad," Ned said, tapping his feet.

Nancy automatically started bobbing her head to the beat. "He's talented," she agreed. "But I'm more worried about Bess than the quality of the music." She frowned as Blaster grabbed Bess's hands and led her into a small group of people who were already dancing.

"I'll keep an eye on him," Ned promised.

"You're the best, Nickerson," Nancy said, grinning.

Ned tapped her nose. "It's about time you

noticed," he said warmly. "Uh-oh, you have that look on your face," he added. "What are you planning, Nan?"

"I'm going to look around the house a bit and see if I can learn more about Colleen."

Ned gave her a kiss on the cheek and said, "Good luck. I'll be right here if you need me."

Nancy slipped out the door and followed the hallway back to the foyer. After seeing that none of the servants were around, she raced up the stairs, where she found another hallway. There were so many doors on either side of it that Nancy didn't know where to begin.

She moved quickly and silently, opening the doors one by one. After seeing a workout room with weight-lifting equipment and several bedrooms that didn't look lived in, Nancy opened the door to a room that was larger than the others. It held two dressers, an armchair, and a canopied bed with an embroidered white spread and a dozen white lace pillows. A pair of jeans and a silk blouse lay discarded on the bed.

Jackpot! thought Nancy. This had to be Colleen and Fred's room.

After entering quietly, Nancy closed the door behind her and started opening some of the dresser drawers. All she found were clothes, lingerie, scarves, jewelry, and other accessories. So far it looked as if the only thing Colleen was guilty of was having a fabulous wardrobe.

Then Nancy noticed an interior door, slightly

ajar. Padding softly over the plush white carpet, she opened the door and entered a smaller room with sleek, modern furniture. White shelves lined with books ran around all four walls, with a white laminated counter and drawers beneath. On the counter were a personal computer, laser printer, and fax machine.

Nancy checked over her shoulder to make sure she was still alone, then started going through the drawers beneath the counter. The top drawers held pencils, pens, office supplies, and stationery with Colleen's initials at the top. Lower down Nancy found old invitations from charity balls and several drawers full of photographs of Colleen and her husband.

As Nancy pulled out a deep bottom drawer, her pulse quickened. On top of a jumble of papers were a soldering iron, a drill, and several drill bits—the tools that had been taken from the inn.

Digging beneath the tools, Nancy saw that the drawer was loaded with old programs from school plays and ballet recitals, some dating twenty years back. At last, something from Colleen's past! Now Nancy could see if Colleen really had lied about her background.

Nancy gasped as she recognized a purple and white yearbook dated 1977. It was the same one she and Ned had seen that morning at Bentley High.

After carefully easing the yearbook out so that she wouldn't disturb anything else in the drawer,

Nancy started flipping to the pictures of graduating seniors. The yearbook fell open to the page with Guy Lewis's picture, and Nancy found a white envelope tucked inside.

"Hmm—" she said aloud, picking up the envelope. It was addressed to Colleen and had no return address, but the post office stamp was dated just a few weeks earlier.

Opening the envelope, Nancy saw that it contained several separate letters. And they were all from Guy Lewis!

Nancy skimmed the first one quickly:

Dear Colleen,

Remember old Guy? I bet you'd rather forget—ha-ha. I finally got out of prison after five long years. I need money real bad, and you're just the person to give it to me.

Why should you give old Guy a break? Because if you don't, I'll tell your rich husband that you were part of the theft ring back in high school. That won't sound too good when they write you up in the social register. I'll bet your husband might even divorce you when he finds out you've been keeping dirty secrets.

I'll only keep quiet if you give me fifty thousand dollars, time and place to be arranged. You'll be hearing from me soon.

Guy

Guy was trying to blackmail Colleen! Nancy felt light-headed as she quickly read the other letters.

Guy wrote that he had newspaper clippings detailing Colleen's arrest and the fact that she had served time in a juvenile detention center. He said he'd hidden the clippings in the basement of the Lakeside Inn when he'd passed through there. He also threatened to take them to Colleen's husband if she didn't come up with the money. There was no letter telling Colleen where to meet Guy and drop the money, but Nancy had seen enough.

No wonder Colleen had volunteered to work at the inn. She'd been trying to find the newspaper articles and destroy them before Guy used them to destroy her life.

That explained why she'd spent so much time in the basement with the old newspapers. She probably thought the articles about her were hidden among them. And she'd been trying to scare everyone else away from the inn because she'd been afraid someone else would find the articles before she did.

"What are you doing here?"

Nancy jumped and whirled around to find Colleen standing in the open doorway to the study. Colleen's green eyes flashed as she stared at the letters in Nancy's hand, and there was a tense set to her jaw. Nancy had been caught red-handed!

"Don't even bother trying to think of an excuse," Colleen went on. Her face became an icy mask as she snatched the letters from Nancy's hand, then reached toward a bottom drawer Nancy hadn't yet examined. "I know exactly what you're doing here. You're a real snoop, aren't you?"

Nancy rose slowly to her feet, letting the yearbook slide to the floor. Her eyes darted quickly around as she tried to find a way out of the room. There was a second door in the opposite wall, but Nancy wasn't sure where it led.

"Oh, yes," Colleen said, opening the drawer. "You're leaving, all right. But you're leaving with *me!*"

In one swift motion Colleen pulled a gun out of the drawer and aimed it right at Nancy!

Chapter

Fifteen

NANCY FORCED HERSELF to breathe deeply, fighting the fear that was welling inside her. She didn't want to make any sudden moves that might make Colleen react rashly.

"You're not really going to use that," Nancy said, trying to keep her voice firm.

"Try me," Colleen said, cocking the trigger of the gun.

"How are you going to explain a dead body to your husband?" Nancy prodded. "That's going to be a lot harder than telling him you did time for stealing."

A tiny muscle in Colleen's cheek twitched. "So you read about that, huh? Well, you're going to take that secret to your grave. I'll just tell Fred you were trying to steal my jewelry. I'll say the gun is yours and it went off accidentally. It's unregistered, so Fred will never know I was the one who pulled the trigger."

Nancy shivered at the cool, matter-of-fact way Colleen was talking about murder. So much for the selfless socialite who wanted to make the world a better place.

"You'd do anything to hide the truth from him, wouldn't you?" Nancy challenged.

"You bet I would," Colleen said. "He's the best thing that ever happened to me. Nobody's going to ruin what we have together." She frowned slightly. "But you have a point—a dead body will ruin the carpet. Turn around, slowly, and open the other door."

Stalling for time, Nancy asked, "Where are we going?"

"Never mind where. Just open the door and start walking."

Nancy's mind raced, trying to figure a way out. She had to obey Colleen, but at least she could leave something behind, some sign so her friends would know she'd been here.

Reaching up as if to scratch her neck, Nancy undid the clasp of the pendant Ned had given her for Valentine's Day and let the pendant slip down the front of her sweater to the white carpet. Then, opening the other door of the study, she entered a narrow, dimly lit back stairway. As she made her way down the stairs, she was acutely aware of the hard barrel of Colleen's gun pressed against her back.

"Now, down the hall and out the door," Colleen directed.

Nancy did as she was told and found herself in a four-car garage. The car nearest her was a dark green Jaguar. Colleen gestured for Nancy to get in behind the wheel, while Colleen got in beside her. The car keys were dangling from the ignition.

Pressing a small remote clipped to the sun visor, Colleen opened one of the garage doors. "Drive," she commanded.

"Where are we going?" Nancy asked.

"To the inn. We're going to put an end to this once and for all. You're going to disappear very mysteriously, without a trace, in fact. Even if they question me about it, they'll never be able to pin anything on me."

Nancy gripped the wheel tightly to keep her hands from trembling as she backed the car out of the garage and turned it around.

"You won't get away with this," she said firmly, turning onto the quiet street with its large, stately homes. "The police and my friends already know about your connection to Guy Lewis. If anything happens to me, they'll know you were responsible."

"The fact that I knew Guy in high school

means nothing," Colleen said. "No one else around here knows I was involved in anything illegal, and I don't have a record."

Nancy's curiosity got the better of her fear, and she asked, "Why don't the police know about your involvement with the theft ring?"

"I was only fifteen when I got arrested," Colleen said. "If you're convicted as a minor, they wipe your slate clean when you turn eighteen."

"How convenient for you," Nancy said dryly.

"It was, until Guy came back into my life," Colleen said. The gun in her hand glinted as they passed beneath the streetlights. "Now that you know about it, too, I'll have to take care of both of you."

Glancing at Colleen, Nancy said, "But other people must have known about it, since it was in the papers."

"That was years ago," Colleen said. "It only made the local papers, anyway. When I got out of juvenile hall, my parents moved to another town and put me in a private school where no one knew me. I got a fresh start. I did better in school, and I got into a good college. I turned my life around."

"And look where you are today," Nancy said. "You've moved up to murdering an innocent person."

Colleen shifted uncomfortably in her seat. "Today doesn't count. Once you're out of the picture, I'll go back to my wonderful life with

Fred. He's such a kind, generous man. I can't let him find out about my past. I'm afraid he really would divorce me. Then where would I be?"

Nancy couldn't believe how twisted Colleen was. She actually thought it was worse to lose a rich husband than to kill someone!

Soon Nancy turned onto the winding road leading up to Moon Lake. The road was pitch-black, with no streetlights, so she could only judge where she was going by the double yellow lines illuminated by her headlights.

"I didn't want to hurt anybody," Colleen said after a short silence. "I was just trying to scare people away until I could find the evidence and get rid of it. But everyone was down there in the basement with me, and there was so much stuff. There was no way I could find the articles quickly. I had to create a diversion to buy time."

"You call pushing Ned off the balcony a diversion?" Nancy asked angrily.

"I didn't have anything to do with that," Colleen insisted with a dismissive wave of her gun. "That must have been an accident."

Colleen actually sounded sincere, but considering the situation, Nancy wasn't about to give her the benefit of the doubt.

"What about the chandelier?" Nancy demanded. "I suppose that was an accident, too?"

Colleen's green eyes gleamed with satisfaction. "Nope. I severed the cable the night before, as you so cleverly deduced."

"And you made a copy of Andrew's keys?" Nancy guessed.

"Very good," Colleen complimented her. "Too bad I couldn't get one to the basement, or none of this might have happened. Andrew only has one copy of that key, and he keeps it in his pocket."

"I'll bet you stole Blaster's sound-effects tapes, too," Nancy said.

Colleen bristled. "I didn't steal them, I borrowed them. I put the keys back, and the tapes, too, after I'd made copies."

Nancy didn't bother to mention that Colleen hadn't returned the soldering iron and drill. "And that sheet you rigged up to look like a ghost—that was to scare Andrew off the renovation, wasn't it?"

"I heard Blaster mention ghost stories, so I figured the subject would eventually come up during your little sleepover," Colleen said. "Too bad Andrew didn't take the hint."

"And the dummy we found hanging in the noose?"

"Me again," Colleen said, almost proudly.

"And of course you're the one who wrote the threatening notes and called in the arson tip to the police," Nancy said. "But if you were trying to frame Andrew, it didn't work. I spoke to the officer at the scene and told her the call came *before* the fire."

"So what?" Colleen asked as Nancy pulled into the empty parking lot of the Lakeside Inn. "Other people will look guiltier than me. Blaster, for instance, especially after the business with the tapes. Or maybe, when I finally see Guy again, I'll make it look like he did it."

Nancy shot Colleen a curious glance. "So you don't know where Guy is?" she asked.

"He never said, and I'm in no hurry to see him."

Nancy parked and turned off the ignition. As she and Colleen got out of the car, Nancy cast a longing look at the dark woods bordering the inn. She was too far away to risk running toward the forest, though. Colleen would probably shoot her down before she got there.

"Up the driveway," Colleen directed Nancy, shoving a key in her hand. "Open the front door, then head for the basement."

The front entrance was still sealed with bright yellow tape. Nancy had to peel it off before she could unlock the door. Once the door was open, a burned smell assaulted her nose. The odor grew even stronger as she opened the door to the basement and felt her way down the stairs, with Colleen right behind her.

As Nancy's eyes grew accustomed to the darkness, she was able to make out the distant stone walls and the heaps of charred furniture. Slivers of moonlight crept in through the dusty transom windows.

Nancy looked around for some kind of weapon she could use or an escape route.

"You must have read my mind," Colleen said as Nancy's gaze fell upon several shovels beneath the stairs. "Pick up one of those shovels." When Nancy had obeyed, Colleen directed her to start digging a hole.

Nancy hesitated before plunging the metal blade of the shovel into the hard-packed earth. "What for?" she asked, but the terrible answer came to her before Colleen even opened her mouth.

Nancy was digging her own grave.

"It's the perfect plan," Colleen said proudly. "After you're done digging the hole, you lie down in it and I shoot you. All I'll have to do is throw the dirt back over you, along with Guy's letters and the articles. Then, tomorrow, when the concrete is poured, the evidence will be buried forever."

Nancy shivered. The last thing she intended to do was lie down in the grave and wait for Colleen to shoot her. She'd rather die while trying to run up the stairs. She could only hope that Colleen would make some small slip so she could make a break for it. For now, though, the gun was trained steadily on Nancy, so she dug.

Clink!

Both Nancy and Colleen started at the sound as Nancy's shovel struck something metallic. Scraping away some of the dirt with the edge of her shovel, Nancy saw the corner of a metal box.

"What is it?" Colleen demanded.

"Something's buried here."

"Dig it up," Colleen ordered, an excited look on her face. "Hurry!"

In a few minutes Nancy had unearthed the small metal box, which she handed to Colleen. After opening the box, Colleen removed a few slips of newsprint. "You found it!" she cried triumphantly.

"What is it?" Nancy inquired.

"The articles. Guy buried them! No wonder I couldn't find them. This is my lucky night. I'll be able to get rid of the articles *and* you."

Colleen's expression became deadly serious as she pointed her gun once again at Nancy. "Now, keep digging."

After a while, Nancy had dug a shallow hole about six feet long and three feet wide.

"You know what to do now," Colleen prodded, gesturing with the gun. "Jump in."

Nancy took a deep breath. This was it—her only chance. She moved behind the hole so that it was between Colleen and herself, then started to bend over, as if she were about to put the shovel down. Then, in a sudden, springing motion, Nancy leapt forward, over the hole, toward Colleen, thrusting the blade of the shovel forward like a bayonet.

At the same moment Nancy heard Colleen's gun go off with a deafening explosion.

Chapter

Sixteen

NANCY FROZE, stunned, as the bullet ricocheted off her shovel and whizzed past her head. Then the air was filled with the sound of shattering glass.

As fragments of glass rained down on the floor, Colleen turned for a split second toward the broken transom window above Nancy. That was all the time Nancy needed.

With a powerful thrust she dived for Colleen's arm, knocking the gun out of her hand. As they fell to the floor, Nancy heard Colleen hit with a thud, then her body went limp.

With a feeling of dread Nancy quickly checked Colleen's pulse, then let out a relieved breath.

Colleen was unconscious, but her pulse was strong. She must have hit her head in the fall.

A moment later Nancy heard loud footsteps rumbling across the lobby floor above. "Nancy!" several voices cried out from the top of the stairs. The work lights in the basement blinked on, and Nancy saw Ned, Bess, and Andrew come running down the stairs. She did a double take when she saw who was with them—Julie Ross!—but she'd have to find out about that later. Right now they had to take care of Colleen.

"How did you find me?" Nancy asked as Andrew picked up the discarded gun and stood over Colleen's unconscious form. He took off his jacket and padded it gently beneath Colleen's head.

Nancy slumped against Ned as he placed his good arm around her and pulled her close. "I got worried when you didn't come back downstairs for a long time," he said, answering Nancy's question. "Then I noticed that Colleen wasn't around, either, so I went upstairs and looked for you. That was when I found your pendant in that little room."

"So Ned came downstairs and got me," Bess continued the story. "When we went outside and saw that one of the garage doors was open, we figured Colleen had taken you somewhere, so we called the police. They sent out a couple of squad cars to look for you."

"It's a good thing we guessed she'd come here," Andrew put in. "One of the police cars should be here any minute."

Nancy showed everyone Guy's blackmail letters and the old articles about the theft ring. "Wow," Andrew said, shaking his head. "I never would have guessed."

"I didn't have time to tell you what we learned at Bentley High School," Nancy told Andrew, "what with the fire and the police taking you in for questioning."

"Ned filled me in on the way here," Andrew told her. He glanced down to where Colleen still lay unconscious, her sequined dress wrinkled and dirty. "I still can't believe it."

"Looking back," Nancy went on, "I realize there were things I didn't pick up on—like all the time Colleen spent in the basement and the fact that she got rid of Lewis's stuff so fast. And all those times she tried to talk you into putting off the renovation for a couple of days."

"Yeah," Andrew agreed. "I guess it wasn't for the kids' safety, like she said. It was so she could have more time to find the articles that Guy Lewis left."

Grinning at Nancy, Bess said, "Leave it to Nan to get to the bottom of things," she said proudly. "She always solves the mystery in the end."

"Speaking of mysteries . . ." Nancy said, turning to Andrew. Julie had gone over to him, and the two were holding hands. "Are you two back together?"

Julie smiled up at Andrew, who leaned down and kissed her tenderly on the lips.

"I guess that answers my question," Nancy said.

"After I got out of the police station this afternoon, I realized how much trouble this inn thing has been and how little I cared about it in the first place," Andrew explained. "So when the police released me, I went straight to Julie's and told her I'd made up my mind. I'm going to stand up to my father, once and for all, and tell him I'm moving to California with Julie."

Nancy was glad to see him looking so determined and happy. "We're going to get married," Andrew went on, "and I'm going to try to make it as an actor. Of course, I didn't know if Julie would say yes or not, after everything we've been through."

Julie hugged Andrew tight. "Of course I said yes. I never stopped loving you, even after I broke up with you."

"Is that why you were hanging around the inn?" Nancy asked. The last pieces of the puzzle were falling into place.

Julie nodded, and her face reddened. "I know there's supposed to be a ghost haunting the place. Well, I guess I was the one haunting it, just to keep an eye on Andrew. I was so afraid he'd meet someone else."

"I knew you two would make up," Ned said.

As Julie looked at Ned, a troubled look came into her eyes. "You might not be so happy when you know what I did, Ned," she said nervously.

"What?" Ned asked.

Julie's gray eyes filled with tears. "I'm the reason you fell off the balcony," she said softly.

"*You* pushed him?" Andrew asked, taking a step back to look at Julie.

"No, of course not," Julie said quickly. "But I was hiding up in the balcony that day, spying on you, and you started walking right toward me. I was so afraid you'd see me, I turned out all the lights!"

"So I *did* slip," Ned said, shaking his head. "I didn't think I'd felt anybody push me."

"Can you ever forgive me?" Julie begged. "If I'd known you were going to fall, I would have left the lights on, even if Andrew had found me. I never meant for you to get hurt."

Ned smiled at Julie. "I can't say I'm happy I fell, but I won't hold a grudge. I know you didn't do it on purpose."

For the second time that day Nancy heard the sound of sirens approaching the inn.

"The police are on their way," Bess said with a relieved smile.

"Uhhhh . . ." Colleen groaned. As everyone turned to look at her, Colleen's eyelids fluttered open.

"Perfect timing," Andrew said, as Colleen groggily tried to prop herself up on one elbow.

Colleen's eyes focused on the group of people towering over her, and she let her head drop back to the ground. "Tell me this isn't happening. . . ."

"It's happening," Nancy assured her. "You made it happen."

The tread of heavy footsteps on the stairs announced the arrival of the police. Nancy saw that Lieutenant Oscarson was the first to reach the bottom. Three other officers were behind her. As Andrew handed Oscarson the gun, Nancy stepped over to the police officer and gave her the newspaper articles, briefly explaining the situation.

"I just wish we knew what happened to Guy Lewis," Nancy finished. "Why hasn't he come forward to get the blackmail money?"

As the other officers helped Colleen to her feet, Lieutenant Oscarson asked Nancy, "Are you Nancy Drew?" When Nancy nodded, the officer said, "I got a call from a Chief McGinnis in River Heights. He seems to be a fan of yours."

Bess and Ned both grinned at Nancy.

"He was asking about this same person," Lieutenant Oscarson went on. Then she announced solemnly, "We've just gotten word that Guy Lewis is dead. He was attempting to burglarize a house the other night, and he fell from a second-floor window. Broke his neck."

Colleen let out a gasp. "But . . . why didn't I hear about that?" she demanded. "Why wasn't it in the papers?"

"He didn't have any identification on him," the officer explained. "We had to match his fingerprints to the ones on file, and that took a while."

"So what you're saying . . ." Nancy began as the realization dawned on her.

Oscarson nodded. "Mrs. Morgan went to a lot of trouble for nothing. Her secret would have been safe if she'd just waited it out."

Colleen's whole body shook. "My life is over!" she sobbed as the three officers with Lieutenant Oscarson led her up the stairs. After making arrangements for Nancy and her friends to go to the station to make statements the following morning, Lieutenant Oscarson left.

"Well," Nancy said, turning to her friends, "I don't know about the rest of you, but I'm exhausted."

"Let's go," Ned agreed, taking Nancy's hand. The group left the inn and headed for the parking lot. But before they could get in their cars, they heard the sound of blaring rock music.

"What's that?" Bess asked as the bright headlights of a car appeared from around the bend. A string of headlights followed the first car, and soon the parking lot was nearly full.

"Blaster!" Nancy shouted as the deejay

hopped out of the first car. "What are you doing here?"

Blaster grinned. "When people started leaving, we figured the party was moving, so we packed up our stuff and came, too!"

His eyes widened as he suddenly noticed Julie standing nearby, hand in hand with Andrew. "I guess you guys got back together," he said gruffly. "I hope you'll be happy."

Then he turned quickly and said to the teens who were getting out of the other cars, "As long as the party's here, there's no reason why we can't keep it going. Let's dance!"

Despite the cold, the teens spread out over the parking lot, moving to the catchy beat.

"Do you want to stay for the party?" Ned asked, looking down at Nancy. "If you're tired, maybe we should leave."

Smiling up at her boyfriend, Nancy said, "You know, I think I'm getting my second wind." Her blue eyes sparkled as she added, "This music's a little fast, though. I was hoping for something more romantic."

"That can be arranged," Ned said. He wrapped his arms carefully around Nancy, and she let her head rest against his shoulder. Then, softly, the two of them swayed together in the parking lot to music that only they could hear.

RUNNING
SCARED

Chapter

One

Isn't this fantastic?" Bess Marvin asked, turning to her cousin George Fayne on the balcony of their hotel room. Four stories below, the streets of downtown Chicago were buzzing with activity, and Lake Michigan sparkled under a sunny spring sky. "I can't wait!"

"*You* can't wait?" George arched an eyebrow at her cousin. "I thought *I* was the one running in the marathon on Sunday."

Bess laughed. "Sure, but that's three days away," she said. "Three whole days to explore all the clubs, restaurants, and *stores* here. Chicago is definitely my idea of shoppers' heaven."

"Anywhere you are is shoppers' heaven," Nancy Drew teased, joining her two best friends on the balcony. "What do you say, George—are you ready to go check out the course?"

Nancy and Bess had come with George to Chicago to cheer her on in the Heartland Marathon. Thousands of other women runners would also be competing, including the best female marathoners in the world. The three teenagers had made the drive from their nearby hometown of River Heights a few days early so that George could familiarize herself with the marathon course.

Their hotel, the Woodville, was the headquarters for the marathon. George had been lucky to get a room when the hotel had had a cancellation.

"Um, you guys aren't thinking of running the whole twenty-six-mile marathon course this afternoon, are you?" Bess asked dubiously. She twisted a strand of her long blond hair around one finger as she followed George and Nancy back into their room. "That's at least twenty-five miles over my limit."

Nancy laughed. She knew that the only sports petite, curvy Bess truly enjoyed were shopping and dating. George, on the other hand, with her tall and athletic build, loved physical exercise.

"You're hopeless," George said, rolling her eyes at her cousin. "And there's no way I'd run the whole course right before the marathon." She tossed her clothes on the fold-out cot that had been set up next to the room's two beds, then changed into a red T-shirt and white running shorts.

"Tell you what," George said. "Why don't you

explore Chicago while Nancy and I run? We should be back in an hour or two."

"Sure, I could do that," Bess agreed, letting out an audible sigh of relief. "Of course, if you *want* me to join you . . ."

George shook her head. "Nancy and I will be fine on our own," she assured Bess, tying on a bandanna to keep her short, dark curls off her forehead. "I want to register first, though, if that's okay with you, Nan. The registration room is just downstairs, on the second floor."

"No problem," said Nancy, stretching her long, lean frame. She had changed into yellow shorts and an aqua top that brought out the blue of her eyes and showed off her reddish blond hair.

"I'll come, too, since it's on the way out," Bess offered brightly.

After leaving their room, the girls took the elevator down to the second floor. A stream of people passing through an open door near the elevators told them where to go even before they saw the sign marked Heartland Marathon Registration.

Inside, the room was crowded with runners, officials, coaches, and reporters. Everyone seemed to be talking at once. "This is so exciting!" George said as she, Nancy, and Bess looked around.

Tables had been set up around the room and labeled to divide the runners alphabetically. George, Nancy, and Bess went to the table marked D–G, and George gave her name to the woman sitting behind it.

"Here's race information, a map of the route, and your ID number," the woman said, handing George a manila envelope. "And here," she went on, reaching into a large carton behind her, "is your official Heartland Marathon T-shirt."

"Cool!" Bess exclaimed as George held up the shirt for her and Nancy to see. It was light blue, and on the front was a gold silhouette of a woman runner. On the back Heartland Marathon was spelled out in gold letters.

"Thanks," George told the woman behind the table. She opened the envelope and pulled out the paper with her number, 6592, printed on it.

"Have you run the Heartland before?" the woman asked George.

"First time," George replied.

"One of our sponsors has provided bicycles if you want to explore the course," the woman explained. "You can sign them out and cover the route in about three hours or so. It depends on what the traffic's like."

George caught Nancy's eye. "Let's do it!" Nancy said.

"Great!" George said. "We may not have time to cover the whole course today, but we'll get to cover quite a bit of it."

The woman pointed to the opposite side of the room. "You can get the bikes just past the registration table marked W–Z. They'll tell you where the course begins—it's not far from here."

"Even *I'm* getting excited, George," Bess said as the three girls crossed the room, "and I'm not even running in this—oops!"

Bess stumbled against Nancy as a young man backed into her. "Excuse me," he said in a deep, slightly accented voice. "I must look where I am going." He was about six feet tall and very lean, with blue eyes and a head of curly blond hair.

"You're totally excused," Bess answered, giving the man her warmest grin. "I'm Bess Marvin, by the way."

"It is a pleasure," said the man, smiling back. "I am Jake Haitinck. Are you a runner?"

Bess giggled, then said, "Me? No, but she is." She flicked a thumb at George. "This is my cousin George Fayne and my friend Nancy Drew."

"I am very pleased to meet you," Jake said, shaking hands with the girls.

"Where are you from, Jake?" Bess asked before the other girls could say anything.

"The Netherlands. I am with the International Federation of Racing."

"What do you do, exactly?" Bess inquired.

Nancy exchanged an amused look with George. She didn't think Bess was too interested in the International Federation of Racing, but she seemed *very* interested in Jake Haitinck.

"Well, yesterday I measured the course, to make sure it is the official length," Jake answered. "Today I rode the whole distance on a bicycle and saw that it was all clearly marked. Things like that. This is my first time in Chicago."

"Oh, really?" asked Bess. "Would you like to see a little of the city?"

Jake's eyes lit up. "That would be wonderful!

5

But can you spare the time?" He nodded toward the bicycle table, just ahead. "You were going to take bikes out, weren't you?"

"No," Bess said quickly. "That is, my friends are, but I happen to be free at the moment."

"Then I accept." Jake checked his watch. "I will meet you at the front entrance of the hotel in ten minutes, all right?"

"Perfect," Bess replied, flashing him another smile. "See you then."

As Jake walked away, George shook her head in amazement. "This is a *women's* marathon, and Bess has managed to find the only cute guy around."

Nancy laughed. "At least now we don't have to worry about her getting bored while we're biking!"

"Nancy! See the woman in lavender?" George asked, nodding her head in the direction of a runner.

George and Nancy were riding side by side on a road in Grant Park. They were almost at the halfway point of the marathon course.

Following George's look, Nancy saw a muscular woman with straight brown hair pulled back into a ponytail. She wore lavender running shorts and top and a matching lavender sweatband. Nancy marveled at the way her feet seemed to skim over the pavement.

"She looks good," Nancy commented. "Do you know who she is?"

"That's Renee Clark," George said in an excited whisper. "She's young, but she's on her way to the top. See how relaxed her arms are? No strain. No waste of energy. She has great form."

As Nancy pedaled by, she studied Renee Clark's face. Her expression was serious and intent, but there was no sign that she was laboring. She looked as if she could go on running all day.

"Hey, isn't that a TV crew in that van?" George asked, breaking into Nancy's thoughts.

Looking up the road, Nancy saw a van driving very slowly. A logo on the van's side read ICT, with the words International Cable Television underneath. Through an opening in the roof, a man had a video camera trained on a woman who was running about twenty yards in front of where Nancy, George, and Renee Clark were.

The woman being filmed was tall, with bright red hair, and she wore a black T-shirt and black shorts with silver trim. She carried a stopwatch in her right hand. Next to her, a middle-aged man in a gray sweatsuit rode a bike. He watched the runner carefully and now and then murmured to her.

"Who's that?" Nancy asked George. "She must be someone special, to rate her own TV crew."

George looked, and her brown eyes widened. "She's special, all right. That's Annette Lang, the number-one woman marathoner for the last five years. Black and silver are her trademark colors. She's awesome! I can't believe I'm actually going to be running with athletes like that!"

As Nancy and George caught up to Annette, they slowed their bikes to the runner's pace for a moment.

"I want to watch her from the front," George said, picking up some speed. "She's tall, like me. Maybe I can get some tips by watching her."

Nancy decided to drop back to where the van wouldn't block her view. She slowed down even more and gazed around at the park's trees and greenery, enjoying the beautiful day.

The sudden roar of a car engine startled Nancy. She looked up and saw a black, rust-splotched car speeding out of an intersecting road and heading right toward the van.

Nancy gasped as the van swung sharply away from the car, leaning dangerously on two wheels. She waited for the crash, but at the last second the car turned. Without slowing, it sped down the road on which Nancy was riding.

About fifteen yards ahead of her, Annette and the older man with her quickly stepped to the grassy edge of the drive. Nancy veered her bike closer to the side of the road.

With a sudden chill Nancy realized that the car had also steered to their side of the road—and now it was heading straight for Annette Lang!

Chapter

Two

HER HEART in her throat, Nancy pedaled as fast as she could toward Annette, who seemed frozen in place.

The car engine roared in Nancy's ears as she leaned out and got an arm around Annette. She lunged from her bicycle seat, carrying the runner away from the car's path. A moment later the two of them lay sprawled on the grass by the road, breathless. The car barreled past, just inches from where Nancy and Annette lay.

Nancy whirled her head around. She got only a glimpse before the car vanished, but it was enough to see that the car had no license plate and the windows were tinted.

"What was that maniac doing?" the gray-haired man asked. He was kneeling next to Annette, with his bicycle on the grass next to him. Up close, Nancy saw that he was short and compact, with bristling eyebrows. His light blue eyes were flashing with anger.

"Don't move," he warned Annette as she started to push herself up to a sitting position.

The runner shook her head. "I'm all right, Derek, really. Hardly even bruised." She got up, then brushed dirt and grass from her clothes and hair. A small crowd had gathered, and Nancy noticed Renee Clark among them.

"Thanks to you," the older man said, smiling at Nancy. "Are you all right?" When Nancy assured him that she was, he said, "This is Annette Lang, and I'm Derek Townsend, her trainer. You have fine reflexes, young lady."

Before Nancy could reply, George came rushing up. At the same time the ICT van, which had made a U-turn, screeched to a stop, and three men and a woman piled out.

"Nancy!" George exclaimed. She jumped from her bike, letting it clatter to the ground as she hurried to her friend's side. "That car . . . it looked like a deliberate hit-and-run!"

Nancy nodded grimly. "It seemed that way to me, too," she agreed, getting slowly to her feet.

Derek Townsend frowned. "Deliberate? I don't think— The authorities would have to—"

"Nancy *is* an authority," George insisted. "She happens to be a detective."

The trainer gave Nancy a look of interest. Feeling self-conscious, Nancy smiled and introduced herself and George. She took a step forward to shake Townsend's hand, then winced at a twinge in her left knee.

"Take it easy," a man beside her said. "That knee might be wrenched."

A young man whose knit shirt bore the ICT logo had come over from the TV van and was leaning over Nancy. He was tall, with warm brown eyes, a muscular physique, and wavy light brown hair that had streaks of gold in it.

Nancy flexed her knee and gingerly pressed the area around it with her fingers. "I'm pretty sure it's just bruised."

"If you're sure," the young man said. He held out his hand with a smile. "I'm Kevin Davis."

"Kevin Davis!" George exclaimed before Nancy could introduce herself. "The decathlon champ? From the last Olympics?"

Kevin swung around to face George, and a broad smile spread across his handsome face. "I only took a silver at the Olympics," he told her. "Now I'm retired. What's your name?"

"George Fayne," she answered, returning his smile.

"You look like a runner to me," Kevin commented. "Are you here for the marathon?"

George nodded. "Uh-huh. How about you?"

Kevin gestured to the van. "I'm with ICT. I'm the commentator for their marathon coverage."

"Really? Sounds like fun," George replied. A slight blush colored her cheeks, and her eyes were shining. In fact, it looked as if George and Kevin had forgotten that anyone else was around.

Smiling, Nancy turned away from the two. A few feet away Derek Townsend was watching

11

closely as Annette did some careful stretches. The runner looked up as another member of the TV crew, a young woman with short black hair, came up.

"Ms. Lang, would you mind talking about what just happened for the cameras?" the woman asked.

Annette looked taken aback, then gave the woman a smile. "Uh . . . no, of course not."

Derek Townsend frowned. "I don't think—"

"It's all right, Derek," Lang snapped.

The woman turned to Nancy. "We've got some great footage of you rescuing Annette. Could you give me your name? We'd like to interview you, too."

"Uh, no, thanks," Nancy said quickly. "I'd prefer to remain anonymous."

"Well, it's up to you," the woman said, and turned back to Annette.

"I have to interview Annette," Nancy heard Kevin say to George as the crew was setting up. "Maybe we could talk more later—at dinner?"

George's blush deepened, and she said, "I'd like that. Why don't you join us? My friends and me, I mean."

"Great!" Kevin said. "Where are you staying?"

George told him, and they agreed to meet in the lobby of the hotel at seven.

"Kevin!" A television crew member called from the van, where the camera was set up and Annette Lang stood by. "We're ready to roll."

"See you at seven," Kevin said, and headed toward where Annette was standing.

12

A sound man gave Kevin a hand mike and directed him to the van, on the grass by the road. Annette was already standing in front of the van's ICT logo, with a cameraman facing her, and Kevin took his place beside her.

"Rolling," said the cameraman. Nancy and George moved in closer to watch.

"I'm speaking with Annette Lang, the top woman distance runner, who's just had a serious brush with danger," Kevin said into the mike. "Annette, it appeared to us that someone tried to hit you with a car while you were running. How do you feel? Do you have any idea what it was about?"

"I'm fine, Kevin." Annette threw a dazzling smile at him and the camera. Nancy was impressed by the runner's poise and confidence after her narrow escape. "I can't be certain what this was about. But there are people on the professional running circuit who envy my success and would like me out of the way. If they can't do this by fair means, maybe they're willing to try foul."

Annette straightened her shoulders and faced the camera squarely. "But it won't work," she went on determinedly. "I'll continue to run, and I expect to win on Sunday."

"Have there been other incidents?" Kevin asked. "Do you suspect specific individuals?"

Annette shook her head. "I can't comment on that, Kevin. I'll be happy to talk at length after the Heartland Marathon. Then I hope you'll interview me as the winner—and still the champ!"

She flashed another smile at the camera, then turned to her trainer, who was standing nearby, looking unhappy. "Let's go, Derek," she called.

Derek ran a hand through his gray hair. "I really think we should report this to—"

"*Derek,*" Annette interrupted. "I am going to complete my run. Period. Now, let's get going." She ran off, leaving Derek staring glumly after her.

Kevin turned quickly and held his microphone under Derek Townsend's nose. "Any comments, Mr. Townsend?"

"I . . . no, nothing. Not right now." The trainer looked relieved when the camera stopped rolling and the crew began putting the equipment back in the van. Sighing, Townsend picked up his bicycle.

He was about to pedal off after Annette Lang but hesitated and then beckoned to Nancy. "Miss Drew, are you really a detective?"

Nancy left George, who was talking with Kevin Davis, and went over to the trainer. "Yes," she told him, "but I'm just here to give my friend moral support in the marathon on Sunday."

"I see." Mr. Townsend looked around to make sure that no one could overhear them. "Perhaps your being here is a stroke of luck. Could I consult you this evening?"

"What about?" Nancy asked.

The trainer leaned closer, and his voice dropped to a whisper. "I can rely on your discretion? Nothing of this must get out to the media."

Nancy's curiosity was aroused. "What's this all about, Mr. Townsend?" she asked again.

14

"Call me Derek," the trainer insisted. "The fact is that Annette has received some very nasty anonymous notes, threatening harm unless she withdraws from the marathon. We didn't take them seriously—until now. But in view of what just happened here, I've had a change of heart," the trainer went on. "I think someone wants to kill Annette!"

Chapter

Three

Y<small>OU HAVEN'T TOLD</small> anyone else about these notes?" Nancy asked Derek Townsend.

The trainer shook his head. "As I say, we didn't take them seriously. Annette didn't want her training interrupted, and she didn't want security guards getting in her way. But this hit-and-run business . . . what should I do?"

"I'd like to look at the notes," Nancy said after thinking a moment. "Could I see them tonight? We're staying at the Woodville."

"So are we," Mr. Townsend told her, "like most of the top entrants. I'll drop them by your room tonight." Nancy gave him her room number, and with a wave the trainer rode away.

Looking radiant, George walked over to [ ]
cy. "You don't mind, do you, Nan?" she asked.
"About Kevin having dinner with us, I mean."

"Of course not," Nancy replied, grinning at
George. "I mean, it's not every night we get to
have dinner with a gorgeous sportscaster who's
totally interested in one of my best friends."

"You really think he is?" George asked, blushing. "I mean, he's this famous athlete and TV
guy, and I'm just— You really think so?"

"From the way he looked at you, definitely,"
Nancy assured George. "But listen, something
else is going on, too. I may have a case to work on
while we're here." She quickly told George of
Derek Townsend's concern for Annette.

As George listened, her smile faded. "That's
awful!"

"I'll know more after I look at those notes
later," Nancy went on, picking up her bike. "But
now we might as well check out a little more of
this course."

When Nancy and George finally returned to
their room at the Woodville, Bess was studying
herself in the full-length mirror on the back of the
bathroom door.

"What do you think?" she asked, spinning to
show off the electric blue silk minidress she was
wearing. Its price tag still hung from one sleeve.

"It looks fantastic," George said. "Don't tell
me you already have a date with that guy we met
in the registration room?"

Bess let out a sigh. "Not exactly. Jake has a

really busy schedule until the marathon is over," she explained. "We took a walk and talked awhile. Then he said he had to go, but maybe we'd see each other later. So I went shopping for a dress to celebrate in after the race. How was your ride? Did you check out the course?"

"We biked well over half of it. It's awesome," George said excitedly. "There are going to be a few tough areas, but I think I have a good shot at a new personal best. I'm shooting for three hours and fifty minutes." She peeled off her clothes and disappeared into the bathroom.

While George took a shower, Nancy told Bess about the attempted hit-and-run in the park and the threatening notes Annette Lang was receiving. "Annette's trainer is coming by with the notes tonight," she finished.

Bess flopped down on her bed. "Are you going to investigate it?"

"Maybe," Nancy replied. "We'll see after I talk to Annette's trainer. Oh, I almost forgot," she added. She shot a meaningful look at George, who was emerging from the bathroom in a towel. "George has a date who's having dinner with us."

Bess sat up straight. "A date? How could you almost forget something that important! Who is he, George? How did you meet? I want all the details!"

Bess listened intently while George told her the story. "He sounds great," Bess said when George was finished. "What are you going to wear?"

"I don't know," George said. "What do you think? I wish I'd brought more dressy things."

Bess got up from the bed, went to the closet, and surveyed the clothes they had unpacked earlier.

"How about that dress I brought?" Nancy suggested. She pointed to a cream-colored dress of soft, lightweight wool.

"You'd look gorgeous in that," Bess said, holding the dress up to George. "Kevin will love it!"

"There he is," George whispered nervously as she, Nancy, and Bess entered the lobby at seven that evening. "Here goes." She smoothed the creamy wool of her dress and started toward him.

Kevin Davis was sitting in a chair in a waiting area just beyond the reception desk. He was wearing a navy blazer, striped shirt, and jeans.

When he saw George, Kevin rose from his chair, his eyes sparkling with appreciation. "You look great, George!" he said.

George responded with a smile that lit up her face. "You've already met Nancy, and—"

"Actually I didn't get Nancy's name this afternoon," Kevin said with a laugh. "She preferred to be called 'Anonymous.'"

Nancy laughed, too. "It's good to see you again, Kevin. And this is Bess Marvin, George's cousin."

"It's my pleasure—" Bess broke off as someone spoke up behind her.

"Hello, Bess." Jake Haitinck stood there, wearing a leather jacket over a button-down white shirt and a pair of jeans.

Nancy was about to suggest that Jake join them

19

for dinner, but before she could, a petite young woman with lustrous black hair hurried over to him.

"Jake! I must talk to you!" the young woman said, her dark eyes flashing angrily.

Jake looked embarrassed. "Ah . . . yes, of course. Bess, meet Gina Giraldi. She's a runner from Italy. Gina, this is Bess . . ."

Gina shot Bess a furious glare and turned back to Jake. *"Now,"* she said, crossing her arms.

With an apologetic look at Bess, Jake followed Gina to a separate grouping of chairs.

There was an awkward silence. Then Kevin cleared his throat. "I don't know about you ladies, but I'm starved. Let's eat, shall we?"

They made their way across the carpeted area to the hotel restaurant, called the Great Fire. It was decorated with old-fashioned furniture, gaslight fixtures, and velvet drapes. The menus explained that the historical prints on the walls showed Chicago as it had looked before the famous fire that had destroyed the city, in 1871.

They ordered, and while they waited for their food, Nancy noticed Renee Clark. She was sitting with an older, dark-haired man and a woman in a smartly tailored suit.

"Who's with Renee Clark, do you know?" she asked Kevin. It occurred to her that Renee was someone who would benefit from Annette being forced out of the marathon.

Kevin followed Nancy's gaze. "The guy is her trainer, Charles Mellor," he replied. "The woman is Irene Neff, a public relations rep for TruForm running shoes. Renee has an endorsement contract with TruForm, and Irene is probably trying to psych her up for the race. A win for Renee would be a major coup for the company."

"I didn't realize running was such a big business," said Bess.

"Don't kid yourself," Kevin replied. "There's a lot of money involved here—a twenty-thousand-dollar first prize, plus a car, for the winner. That's just for starters. What with running being so popular, shoe companies hand out a lot for endorsements. Renee gets at least a hundred thousand a year from TruForm. Then there are commercial deals, or the chance of a career in TV sports announcing. Distance *is* big business, especially for the top few runners."

Nancy knew that Renee couldn't have been driving the car that had nearly run down Annette Lang—she had been on the course herself. But perhaps Charles Mellor or Irene Neff had been behind the wheel. Nancy made a mental note to keep her eye on all three.

Just then the waiter appeared with their orders —prime rib for Nancy and Kevin, grilled chicken breast for George, and roast duck for Bess— and Nancy forgot all about the threats to Annette.

While they ate, Kevin kept the girls laughing with stories about his job. Nancy didn't miss the looks he and George kept giving each other. There was no mistaking the signs: a romance was definitely brewing between the two.

Nancy was just scooping up the last of her mashed potatoes when a familiar, grating voice spoke up next to her.

"Well, well, if it isn't Nancy Drew! Is the great detective snooping into something suspicious at the Heartland Marathon?"

Standing there with a smirk on her face was Brenda Carlton. The petite, dark-haired girl was a reporter for *Today's Times,* a River Heights tabloid, but sometimes Nancy thought Brenda's greatest talent was for botching up Nancy's cases. Already Brenda's loud comment had caused several people to turn their way, including Renee Clark, Charles Mellor, and Irene Neff.

"I'm just here to root for George," Nancy said, keeping her tone light.

"Really?" Brenda looked suspicious. "Even though they didn't mention your name, I recognized you on TV, saving Annette Lang from getting run over. Your being here doesn't have anything to do with that, huh?"

Nancy shook her head. "Just a coincidence."

"Annette seems to think someone is out to get her," Brenda persisted. "There may be a story there. Did you get a good look at the car?"

"It happened pretty fast, and all I saw was a battered car with no plates. I can't be more specific than that. Sorry."

Brenda's gaze landed on Kevin for the first time, and her eyes widened in surprise. "Kevin Davis! How do you know these three?"

"We just met today," Kevin explained. "And you are . . . ?"

Brenda smiled smugly and said, "Brenda Carlton, with *Today's Times.* No doubt you've heard of it. We have an impeccable reputation."

"For printing the trashiest stories around, that

is," Bess murmured under her breath, rolling her eyes at George and Nancy.

Ignoring Bess's comment, Brenda asked Kevin, "Did *you* get a good look at the mystery car?"

"Sorry," Kevin said apologetically. "I was watching Annette. Everything else was a blur."

An expression of annoyance flitted across Brenda's face. "I see. Well, I'd better be going, but I'm sure I'll be seeing you around." She walked to a table across the restaurant.

Kevin turned to Nancy, George, and Bess. "She seems a little full of herself," he said. Lowering his voice, he said to Nancy, *"Are* you planning to do any detective work here?"

Nancy hesitated before answering. "I don't know yet. But if it turns out that I am, I hope you'll keep it a secret between us. I work better when I can stay undercover. Which is why I didn't want to be interviewed this afternoon."

"You can count on me," Kevin assured her. "But your pal Brenda may have blown it for you. A lot of people heard her, and they'll spread the word."

Bess looked up from her salad and grimaced. "All this talk about Brenda is ruining my appetite. We need an antidote. I hear they have a rooftop dance club here that's pretty hot. Why not check it out after dinner?"

"Not me," George said. "Until the race I'm not staying up late."

"I'll go with you," Nancy told Bess. "I just want to stop at our room to see if Derek slipped those notes under the door."

Kevin turned to George. "It's still pretty early. How about taking a walk?" he suggested.

"Sure," George replied.

After the group paid the waiter, Kevin and George went out for their walk, and Nancy and Bess returned to their room, just across from the elevators on the fourth floor.

As she opened the door to their room, Nancy glanced at the floor. "No notes," she commented.

"I like Kevin," Bess said. "And I'm really happy for George." She closed the door behind them.

"Me, too," Nancy agreed. "I bet she won't even have to run Sunday's race—she'll be floating!"

Bess laughed, then broke off suddenly at the sounds of angry voices just outside their door.

"Are you threatening me?" a woman's voice demanded.

Nancy's eyes widened in surprise. She was sure that that was the voice of Annette Lang! Exchanging a look of concern, Nancy and Bess tiptoed closer to the door.

"I make no threats, I tell the truth," a second woman replied harshly, in a heavy accent. "Once before you cost me a race, Annette, and I do not forget these things."

Bess clutched Nancy's arm. "I recognize that accent! It's Gina Giraldi," Bess whispered. "She's the one who grabbed Jake when he came over to talk to me in the lobby tonight. She's got a temper that—"

"Ssh!" Nancy whispered, holding up a hand as she put her ear to the door.

"Stay away from me," Annette was saying angrily. "I didn't—"

"I'll get you," Gina interrupted shrilly. "Some time, some place—when you do not expect it and there is no one to protect you—I will get my revenge."

Chapter

Four

THERE WAS SILENCE, and Bess turned to Nancy.
"Do you think Gina had something to do with
that car today?"

"Could be," Nancy said. "She's definitely mad
at Annette. We need to find out why." She
listened intently for a few more moments. "I
don't hear anything. I think they're gone."

Nancy cautiously opened the door and looked
outside. The corridor was empty.

"Gina sounds like someone who could get
violent, if you ask me," Bess said as Nancy closed
the door.

"I wish I knew more about her," Nancy said.

Just then a quiet knock sounded on the door,
and Nancy opened it. It was Derek Townsend,

holding a manila folder. "Here are the notes," he said, handing the folder to Nancy.

Nancy walked over to the room's desk and opened the folder, with Bess looking over her shoulder. There were three sheets of plain white paper, on which letters clipped from newspapers and magazines had been pasted. All the notes were threatening:

This race *will* be hazardous to your health!
You can run but you can't hide!
You're an endangered species!

Bess gasped as she read the notes. "Isn't Annette scared?" she asked Derek. "If it were me, I'd break a speed record running for cover!"

"Annette isn't like that," Townsend replied. "She doesn't scare easily, even when it might be in her best interest."

"One thing about these," said Nancy, her gaze still on the notes. "They were written by someone who's familiar with American slang and usage. So they probably weren't written by Gina Giraldi. Her command of English is good, but it sounds formal, stiff. Not like these notes."

The trainer stared at Nancy. "You suspect Gina? But why would she do something like this?"

"She was having an argument with Annette out in the hall a few minutes ago. We heard it through the door," Nancy told him. "Gina threatened to get even with Annette for something that happened between them. Do you have any idea what it is?"

27

Townsend pressed his lips together. "There's bad feeling between those two," he admitted. "Gina thinks Annette plotted to have her disqualified from the New York Marathon last year —that's one of the biggest on the circuit. And Annette has accused Gina of sabotaging a friend of hers in another race."

"Sabotage?" Nancy echoed. "How?"

The trainer held up his hands in a helpless gesture. "You'll have to ask Annette," he said. "Personally, I think Gina might well be capable of sabotage—or worse. She can be really vicious if she has reason."

"What makes you say that?" Nancy asked.

"I saw her attack a girl who she thought was making a play for Jake. It took two men to pull her away. She has a streak of—"

"Jake?" Bess interrupted. "Jake Haitinck? You mean, he's her boyfriend?"

"He was," Derek Townsend replied. "Jake broke up with her months ago, but Gina hasn't accepted it. As far as she's concerned, he's her property."

Bess sat down on a bed. "Wonderful," she said faintly.

"What's wonderful?" George asked, coming into the room. Seeing Derek Townsend, she said, "Oh, hello." Then she saw the notes on the desk, and her smile faded. "Were those sent to Annette?"

Nancy nodded. "Derek, when and how did Annette get these notes?"

"One of the notes was waiting for us when we checked in here two nights ago. It had been

28

mailed from somewhere in Chicago the day before. Another was stuck into Annette's purse yesterday. The third was slid under her door this morning."

"I need to talk to Annette," said Nancy. "I know she wouldn't go to the police and didn't want guards, but she has to understand that the danger to her could be serious. In order to be any real help, I'll need some more information from her. Will she cooperate with us?"

Townsend sighed. "I'll speak with her. I hope she'll be reasonable, but she *is* headstrong. I'll let you know." He retrieved the folder, then left.

As soon as the trainer was gone, George jumped up, excited to be able to tell her friends what had happened with Kevin. "Kevin and I walked to the lakefront—it's really close. And we talked and talked . . . about running, and athletics in general. I mean, he was such a great athlete, but he's really modest about it. And he was interested in *me,* what I like to do, my family, everything . . ."

George's voice trailed off, and she looked sheepishly at her friends. "Sorry, I guess I'm babbling."

"It's a good thing, too," Bess said, grinning at her cousin. "Otherwise, we would have had to pump you for all this information."

Giving George a hug, Nancy added, "We're really happy for you. Sure you don't want to change your mind and celebrate with us at that club upstairs?"

"What?" George gave Nancy a dazed smile. "Oh, no, I've got to be up early. Kevin has a busy day of work, but we're going to work out together first thing, before he starts. There's a health club that marathon entrants can use right down the block.

"Oh, I almost forgot to tell you!" George went on excitedly. "Kevin got a message at the desk. The networks picked up his story on the car that almost hit Annette. They used his footage on their news shows, even his interview. It could be a big break for him."

As George went into the bathroom to wash before bed, Bess and Nancy applied their make-up. Nancy was grabbing her shoulder bag from her bed when the phone rang.

"Hello?" she said, picking up the receiver.

"This is Derek Townsend."

"Hi, Derek. This is Nancy."

The trainer's voice sounded strained and agitated as he said, "Could you come to Annette's room right now?"

"What's wrong?" Nancy asked him.

There was a slight pause before Derek said, "I—I'd rather you saw for yourself. Please, come right away, it's Room four-twenty-eight, just down the hall from you. Hurry."

"I'll be right there," Nancy assured him, then hung up. She turned to Bess and George, a grave look on her face. "That was Derek Townsend. Something's happened in Annette's room, but he wouldn't say what. He sounded all shaken up, though. I'd better get over there."

"I'll come along," Bess offered immediately.

"Me, too," George chimed in.

The three girls walked to the end of the corridor and knocked on the door marked 428. It was opened immediately by Derek Townsend, who motioned them inside.

Nancy drew her breath in sharply as her gaze swept over the large room. It was a shambles. Shirts and shorts had been torn in half and thrown every which way. Several black-and-silver running suits had been shredded. Running shoes had been cut apart and hung by their laces in the open closet. Two canvas athletic equipment bags had been savagely ripped.

Looking pale and nervous, Annette sat with Derek on the room's couch. "Look on the dresser," Derek Townsend said, breaking the silence that had fallen over the room.

Nancy got a sick feeling in the pit of her stomach when she saw what was on the dresser top. A long, thin-bladed knife had been stuck through a running shoe and a piece of paper.

As Nancy looked at the paper, she heard Bess gasp behind her. On it was a crude drawing in black marking pen of a skull and crossbones. Underneath was another message composed of pasted-on magazine letters:

Your time is running out!

Chapter

Five

"THIS IS AWFUL!" Bess said in a horrified whisper. George shook her head in silent disgust.

After taking one last look at the threatening note, Nancy went over to Annette. The runner stared straight ahead, her jaw muscles clenched.

"Annette, can we talk for a few minutes?" Nancy asked gently. Gesturing to her friends, she added, "You've already met my friend George, and this is Bess Marvin."

Annette nodded to Bess and George, who sat down on the edge of the bed. Looking at Nancy, she said, "Derek says you might be able to figure out what's going on here."

"Possibly," Nancy replied. "How long were you out of your room?"

"I haven't been in here since I changed clothes this afternoon." Annette gave Nancy a weak smile. "After you saved my life. I left at about six to go have dinner at Fritz's Steak House. Then I talked to reporters in the press room. Derek found me there and told me about his talk with you. Then we came up here—and found this."

Nancy caught the look of surprise Bess gave her. "You didn't come in here at all between six and now?" Nancy pressed Annette.

"No, I just told you," the runner answered.

Nancy stood up. "If I'm going to help you, I need your complete honesty."

"What are you talking about? I *am* leveling with you," said Annette.

Squarely facing Annette, Nancy said, "Bess and I heard you arguing with Gina Giraldi in the hall earlier this evening. What were you doing there, if not going to or coming from your room?"

Annette hesitated briefly before answering. "Oh, that. Gina and I don't get along, it's no secret. We ran against each other in Europe, and we argued even then. After dinner I wanted to go to my room to rest, but when I got on the elevator downstairs, Gina jumped in and started yelling the same old stuff. When I got off, she followed me."

Annette shrugged. "I got fed up and told her to leave me alone. We stood there yelling back and forth until another elevator came. It was going up, but I got in anyway, just to get away from her. That was that."

"What happened to Gina?" George asked.

"I have no idea. I just left her standing there."

"Then she could have gotten into your room," Bess suggested.

"I wouldn't put it past her," Derek agreed.

To Nancy's surprise, Annette shook her head. "I don't think so," she said. "Gina's crazy, but this isn't her style. If she wanted to hurt me, she'd do something that would really hurt—trip me or kick me in a pack of runners, where it would look like an accident. She wouldn't give any warning, either. She'd just act."

"Why was she yelling at you?" Nancy asked.

Annette sighed wearily, then explained. "She was disqualified from the New York Marathon last year. A runner claimed that Gina elbowed her so hard she bruised her ribs and couldn't continue. It turned out there was a witness, and Gina was disqualified and fined. The witness testified anonymously, and Gina got it into her head that it was me. It wasn't, but now she swears she'll get even."

Nancy nodded, then said, "Derek mentioned something about Gina sabotaging a friend of yours. Can you tell me about that?"

"It happened earlier this year, in South America," Annette said. "My friend Maria Carlisle had to drop out of a race because of severe pain in her foot. Someone had put a jagged piece of metal under the insole of her shoe, and the pressure of her foot made the edge come through and cut her. *That's* Gina's style," Annette said bitterly.

"You think Gina did it?" Bess wondered aloud.

"Yes, I do. She went around smirking and

dropping little hints when nobody else could hear. 'Too bad about your friend' and 'Better check *your* shoes out next time,'" Annette said, mimicking Gina's voice. "Stuff like that. Of course, nothing could be proved."

Bess moaned, and Annette stared at her. "What's the matter?"

"Bess met Jake Haitinck today," George answered for her cousin. "And tonight Gina gave her an ugly look when Jake was talking to her."

Annette nodded sympathetically. "I'd keep my distance, if I were you," she told Bess. "Poor Jake. Gina won't let him look at another girl."

"Can you think of anyone else who might have it in for you to the point where they'd do all this?" Nancy asked Annette. "There are the notes, the hit-and-run attempt, *and* ruining your things."

Annette shrugged. "I'm number one now, and everyone else wants what I've got. Some of the runners make a personal thing of it and say I'm stuck-up, stuff like that. I admit I'm not Miss Popularity, but nobody's ever done anything this terrible to me before. I have no idea who it is."

"When you were interviewed today, you gave the impression that you could name people if you wanted," Nancy persisted.

"Did I? Well, if I did, I was stretching the point a little." Annette gave Nancy a sly grin. "Give the public what they want, right?"

Annette didn't seem to be taking this very seriously, Nancy thought. "You might also push whoever is responsible for the threats into doing something more extreme," she warned. "I'd cool

35

it on hints like that. Anyway, I'll look into the situation, but please keep it confidential. As far as the rest of the world is concerned, I'm just here to root for George."

"If Brenda hasn't ruined that already," George said quietly.

"Annette, if you don't want to bring the police in," Nancy continued, "that's all right—for now. But a time may come when we have to tell them what's going on."

"Wait a minute—" Annette seemed ready to argue.

"That's not negotiable," Nancy cut her off. "I know you have your priorities here, but your well-being is *my* priority. Do we have a deal?"

Annette looked quickly at Derek Townsend, then replied, "Okay. I guess you know what you're doing." She stood up. "Now, if you don't mind, I'd like to call it a night. It's been a rough day, and I still have to straighten up this room.

Nancy, George, and Bess said good night and went back to their own room.

"It sounds as if anyone could have gotten into Annette's room and done that damage," George commented as she got ready for bed. "Gina could have or Renee Clark or Irene Neff—"

"Irene Neff?" Bess cut in. "Why her?"

"She has a stake in Renee winning the Heartland Marathon," Nancy supplied. "If Renee wins, it's good for TruForm, and that means it's good for Irene. So it's possible that *she* could have broken into Annette's room."

Nancy went over to their own door, opened it, and examined the keyhole. "It doesn't look as if it would be hard—a file or credit card would do the trick."

"You ought to know, after all the locks you've picked on your cases," Bess put in. She glanced at her watch. "Not to change the subject or anything, but it's not even ten, Nan. There's still time to get in a little dancing."

"I'm with you," Nancy said. "Let's . . ." Her voice trailed off as the phone rang.

"Not again," Bess muttered as George picked up and said hello.

"Oh, hi, Kevin," George said, her face brightening. "What? . . . Really? . . . That's great!" Turning away from her friends, she whispered, "I'm glad I met you, too. . . . Okay, see you tomorrow morning. . . . Good night."

She hung up and turned back to Nancy and Bess, her eyes gleaming. "That was Kevin."

"Gee, I never would have guessed," Bess said, grinning.

George didn't even seem to notice her cousin's teasing. "His agent just called to say he's setting up a meeting with a network sports executive," she went on, "about announcing on 'Worldwide Sports.' That's the big time!"

"That's fantastic!" Bess exclaimed. "You must be good luck for Kevin!"

"That's what *he* told me," replied George, turning red. "There's more, too. He and Annette have worked out a deal for exclusive interviews about her trouble here and how she's resisted the pressure to drop out of the Heartland Marathon. That's two big breaks in one day, and it's all because of his story on Annette. Isn't it great?"

As Nancy listened, a very disturbing thought occurred to her. "That's really exciting," she murmured, hoping she sounded more enthusiastic than she felt. "It's a great chance for Kevin—and for Annette. She'll be getting a lot of publicity as well, won't she?"

"But she's already on top," Bess put in. "She's getting about as much coverage as she could, isn't she?"

"Hmm," Nancy said. She didn't like what she was thinking, but she couldn't ignore it.

Kevin Davis seemed like an ambitious sports announcer, and "Worldwide Sports" was the biggest sports show there was. Nancy had assumed it a coincidence that Kevin happened to be on the scene when Annette was nearly hit by that car in the park. Now she realized there was another possibility. Maybe Kevin himself had maneuvered the attacks against Annette in order to *create* the story that would help build up his career. And if that was true, George was falling in love with a criminal!

Chapter

Six

"Nancy, did you hear a word I just said?" Bess's voice brought Nancy back to reality. Blinking, Nancy saw that her two friends were both looking at her expectantly.

"Oh—sorry," Nancy mumbled.

Bess placed her hands on her hips and said, "I was just saying, if we don't hurry, we'll never make it to that club. Let's go!"

"Right," Nancy agreed, shaking herself. She glanced at George, wondering if she should say something about Kevin.

Maybe I'm just blowing this all out of proportion, she thought. She decided to hold off until she found out more about the sports announcer.

Still, she was preoccupied as she and Bess said

39

good night to George and took the elevator up to the fifteenth floor, the rooftop level, where the club was located.

"Mrs. O'Leary's Cow." Bess read the neon sign outside the club's doorway. A small plaque explained that it was named after the cow that was supposed to have started the Great Fire of 1871 by knocking over an oil lamp.

Through the doorway Nancy saw that the walls were patterned with cartoon cows in funky outfits and sunglasses, dancing and sitting at tables. "I'm going to like this place," she said, grinning, as they went inside and looked around.

On the walls of the club were flashing lights, and a purple neon stripe edged the high ceiling. The whole place was alive with dancers, moving to rock music being played by a band set up at the other end of the room. The café tables lining the walls were crowded with people.

Nancy noticed a few women wearing Heartland Marathon T-shirts, though no one she recognized. Like George, the serious contenders would be in training and in their rooms.

"This is fantastic!" Bess said, speaking loudly to make herself heard over the amplified band. "George is really missing out!"

Maybe it was just as well George wasn't there, Nancy reflected. She really needed to talk to Bess about Kevin. "Listen, there's something that's bothering—"

"Hi, Bess! Hi, Nancy!" Jake Haitinck stood before them. "Want to dance, Bess?"

Bess hesitated and looked at Nancy.

"Go ahead," Nancy urged. "We can talk later."

A moment after Bess went with Jake to the dance floor, a guy wearing a T-shirt that said Terminally Hip asked Nancy to dance.

She tried to get into the beat, but her mind kept going back to the situation with Kevin and George. When the song ended, she excused herself. She saw Jake and Bess sitting at a tiny table by the wall and went over to join them.

"I'm sorry for the way Gina acted today," Jake was telling Bess.

Giving Jake a brilliant smile, Bess said, "Don't worry about it. It wasn't your fault."

"Still, I feel bad about it," Jake said. "Gina isn't really so terrible. Her—how do you say it?" He ran a hand through his curly blond hair, trying to think of the words. "Her growl is worse than her bite, you know?"

"Well, I *hope* so," Bess said with a nervous laugh, "but I keep hearing stories about how she's done terrible things to people she didn't like."

Jake waved his hand dismissively. "It is only rumors."

Nancy looked at Jake with fresh interest. As a member of the International Federation of Racing, he might have information that could help her get to the bottom of the attacks on Annette. "Do you know Renee Clark?" Nancy asked him.

Jake tilted his chair back against the wall. "Renee? Sure. She is a sweet girl. And a very good runner. She will be the best one day."

"Sounds as if you like her," Nancy said.

"Everyone likes Renee. She doesn't have an enemy. There is only one thing wrong with her."

"What's that?" Bess asked.

"She doesn't have what you Americans call 'the killer instinct,'" Jake replied. "She lets up when she is ahead. She doesn't like to embarrass another runner. Once she lost a race she should have won because of that. Her trainer, Mellor, and the woman from TruForm are always after her not to do that ever again."

Nancy recalled what Kevin had said about there being big money in distance running. "I guess Renee Clark must be a gold mine for Irene Neff's company," she commented.

Jeff gave her a skeptical look. "She will be, once she starts winning. TruForm Shoes is taking a chance on the future with Renee. Irene Neff got them to sign her to a very big endorsement contract. If Renee doesn't start winning, it could cost Irene her job."

Nancy sat up straighter, and Bess leaned in, suddenly more interested.

"What's Irene like?" Nancy asked Jake.

"Very tough, that one. All business."

Bess had started tapping her foot to the music. Turning to Jake, she asked, "Ready for another dance?"

Jake hesitated. "One more," he decided. "Then I have to go to my room. I shouldn't really be here at all."

As they went back out on the floor, "Terminally Hip" appeared and asked Nancy for another dance. She smiled but said no. She just couldn't enjoy herself when she was worried about George.

When Bess and Jake returned to the table, Jake said good night and left.

"He sure is tough to pin down," Bess said, sighing. "I tried to make a date for tomorrow, but he just said he's got a lot to do for the race and he'll call if he has time. That guy really has marathon on the brain," she finished glumly.

Nancy couldn't help laughing. "The marathon *is* his job, Bess, but I hope he gets done early so you can spend some time with him." Leaning closer to Bess, she asked, "Can we talk where it's quieter?"

Bess's hand flew to her mouth. "I totally forgot about that problem you mentioned! Sorry, Nan." She stood up and gestured to a set of glass double doors on one wall. "It looks as if there's a terrace. Let's go out there."

The two girls went through the glass doors to an outdoor space with some tables and chairs. Some of the dancers were cooling off there. Nancy chose an empty table a little removed from the crowd.

"What's the matter?" Bess asked.

"This has to be just between you and me for now, all right? It's about George."

Bess's blue eyes widened. "A problem with George?"

"Not *with* George exactly. It's about Kevin." Quickly Nancy told Bess of her suspicions about Kevin. While she spoke, Bess twisted a strand of her long blond hair between her fingers.

"I see what you mean," she said slowly. "That *is* a problem."

Feeling relieved that Bess was there to share her worries with, Nancy asked, "So what do you think we should do? I mean, don't you think

43

George should know that Kevin is one of the suspects?"

"Definitely," Bess agreed. "The main thing to remember is that George is our friend. I'm sure she'll understand why you're suspicious of Kevin."

"I hope so," Nancy said, giving Bess a grateful smile. But deep down she wasn't so sure.

"I can't believe George actually got up at six o'clock to go work out with Kevin," Bess said the following morning as she and Nancy were finishing breakfast in the hotel's coffee shop. "You couldn't pay me to do that."

Nancy laughed and flipped over the check the waitress had left on their table. "It's eight-forty now," she said. "George's note said to meet her at the gym at nine. We'd better go."

Glancing toward the glass wall that separated the coffee shop from the hotel lobby, Nancy saw Renee Clark coming in from the street with Charles Mellor and Irene Neff. Irene had a grip on Renee's forearm and was talking very intently to her.

Quickly Nancy got up and left the money for their breakfast on the table. "Come on, Bess. You can pay me back later. There's Renee Clark and her entourage, and I want to talk to them. Follow my lead, okay? We're big fans of hers."

Bess grinned at Nancy. "Whatever you say." She followed as Nancy left the café and approached the trio.

"This is the biggest opportunity of your career," Irene Neff was saying in a low, gravelly voice that seemed to contradict her elegant suit and sleek blond hairdo. "We're a team. Charles and I will do all we can, but you—"

"You're Renee Clark, aren't you," Nancy asked in a breathless, gushy voice. "My friend and I think you're terrific! We hope you win on Sunday, and we'll be cheering for you."

Renee gave them a delighted smile, as though she still found it fun to talk to fans. "Thanks!"

Ignoring Irene Neff's annoyed look, Nancy asked, "How do you feel? You think you can get a personal best?"

"It's possible," Renee answered, "if the weather is right, and I get a fast start." She put down the nylon gym bag she held in one hand and gestured to her companions. "This is Charles Mellor, my trainer," she introduced, "and Irene Neff, who works for TruForm Shoes."

When Nancy and Bess introduced themselves, Charles Mellor gave them a polite nod and a murmur of greeting. He looked very fit, with a dark tan and dark hair.

Irene Neff ignored the girls completely. Placing a hand on Renee's shoulder, Ms. Neff said, "Remember what I told you." She turned on her heel and walked away.

Renee followed the older woman with her eyes for a moment before turning to Nancy and Bess. "Irene's not usually like that," she said apologetically. "She just has a lot on her mind.

"Hey!" she added, staring at Nancy more intently. "You're the one who saved Annette yesterday! I saw the whole thing."

"I was just in the right place at the right time," Nancy said, trying to play down the incident.

"Did I understand that you're a detective?" asked Charles Mellor, regarding Nancy with interest. "I couldn't help hearing that woman in the restaurant last night. . . . "

Thanks a lot, Brenda, Nancy thought. Aloud, she simply said, "That's right, I am."

"Sounds fascinating," Mellor commented. "Would it be asking too much to know what you're investigating right now?"

"Nothing, at the moment," Nancy told him. "We came here to see the marathon."

"Right," chimed in Bess. "And root for—"

"For *you,*" Nancy said quickly, flashing Renee a big smile.

"Well, I hope I can win it," Renee said. "I have to get going now, but it was nice talking to you. Charles, see you at the gym after my workout."

"Right," said Renee's trainer. After nodding to Nancy and Bess, he turned and ran to catch an elevator whose doors were just closing. Renee walked toward the doors leading to the outside.

"Brenda sure messed things up last night," Bess said to Nancy. "Who knows how many people know you're a detective now?"

"That's not going to make my job any easier," Nancy agreed. "Come on. I need to make a quick trip to the ladies' room, then let's go meet George. We're late."

A few minutes later the girls left the hotel. It was a crisp, clear day, and Nancy paused on the sidewalk to draw in a deep breath of spring-scented air.

"Have you decided what to say to George?" Bess asked.

"Not yet," Nancy admitted. "I have to talk to her today, though."

Bess nodded. "Good idea. She should know about Kevin before she gets too—"

Wham!

Nancy jumped back abruptly as a large object came hurtling by them from somewhere above and smashed into the sidewalk!

Chapter

Seven

INSTINCTIVELY, Nancy covered her face with her hands. Dirt and sharp fragments were flying everywhere.

After a few seconds the air was calm again, and Nancy dared to look up. "Bess! Are you okay?"

Bess nodded, her eyes wide with fright. Dirt and leaves speckled her jeans. "What happened?" she asked, looking at the object that had caused the crash.

A few feet in front of where they stood, the shattered fragments of a large ceramic planter lay scattered on the pavement, along with a plant and a pile of earth.

It had to have come from the hotel, Nancy

realized. Whirling around, she stared up at the windows. Her heartbeat quickened as she caught a glimpse of a head ducking inside. Quickly she counted the floors.

"Someone was looking out from the ninth floor," she told Bess, and dragged her back toward the hotel entrance. "Come on!"

A small crowd of people was hurrying over to them. "We're fine," Nancy said, pushing past everyone. She and Bess raced inside and went to the elevators. It seemed to take forever until one finally arrived and they were able to jump in.

By the time they reached the ninth floor, all the other passengers had gotten off. The doors slid open, and Nancy found herself standing face-to-face with Gina Giraldi! Gina gave them a cool glance and stepped inside as Nancy and Bess got out. The doors closed before they could speak to her.

Without pausing, Nancy started down the hallway to the right. "I'm pretty sure the room would have to be in this direction," she told Bess.

When they got to Room 926, Nancy paused. The door was ajar. Ready for anything, she pushed it wide open and went in.

A quick glance told her the person had gone. There were stacks of papers and manila folders on the room's low coffee table. The window was wide open, and when Nancy went to look down, she saw the remains of the planter were directly below.

"Gina was on this floor just now," Bess said, joining Nancy at the window. "She could have pushed that planter out." Her voice trembled as she added, "You don't think she did this because I talked with Jake last night, do you?"

"Maybe," Nancy said grimly. "Or maybe she doesn't want me looking into the attacks on Annette."

She turned around and leaned against the windowsill to think. "Maybe it wasn't Gina at all. Let's take a quick look around up here, then go down to the reception desk and find out which rooms our suspects are staying in. I'll bet one of them is in here."

After leaving Room 926, the two girls looked up and down the hallway but saw no one. Then they took the elevator back to the lobby and went to the front desk. When Nancy said that she was running the marathon and asked for the room numbers of her dear friends Gina Giraldi, Irene Neff, Charles Mellor, and Renee Clark, the young woman cheerfully supplied them.

"Bingo!" Nancy exclaimed after thanking the woman and walking away. "Nine twenty-six is Irene Neff's room! And she left us when we were in the lobby talking to Renee."

"But Gina's also on the ninth floor, in nine-fifteen," Bess put in excitedly. "I bet she got into Irene's room and tried to bean us with that planter. She's got the temper for it. And she was right there."

"That's true," Nancy said thoughtfully, "though it seems unlikely that she'd take the risk of sneaking into Irene's room. On the other hand, Charles Mellor and Renee Clark are even less likely candidates, since their rooms aren't on the ninth floor."

Bess's expression brightened. "There's one person who *definitely* couldn't have done it," she said. "Kevin. He's with George at the gym."

"You're right. But we have to consider the possibility that there's more than one person involved here, so Kevin still isn't off the hook."

Nancy's attention was distracted when she happened to glance at the nearby press room. There was Irene Neff, talking with Brenda Carlton, who had a portable cassette recorder in her lap.

"Well, well, there's our top suspect now," Nancy murmured. "Let's try to talk with her."

As they approached the doorway, Irene was saying, "TruForm makes the finest running shoes ever designed. We wanted the best endorsed by the best, and that's Renee. I'm certain that she's on her way to number one. Not just for one race, either—for all time."

"That's quite a claim," Brenda said. "What about Annette Lang? She's got to be one of the all-time best."

Irene lifted her shoulders in a slight shrug. "Annette's all right. She's had a good career, but now she's going downhill. Renee Clark is the future of distance racing. Ask anyone."

Brenda gave Irene Neff a sly look. "I understand you wanted Annette to endorse TruForm and that she turned you down."

This is news, Nancy thought, although she wasn't sure if it was the truth or a concoction of Brenda's, designed to get a juicy reaction.

"Where did you hear that nonsense?" Irene snapped. "Did Annette tell you that?"

"We journalists have to protect our sources," Brenda said smugly. "I'm not at liberty—"

"Never mind. It's not true. Actually, *Annette* wanted to sign with *us,* but we said no. Renee was the one I wanted."

Nancy had heard enough. "Sorry to interrupt," she said, entering the press room with Bess, "but I need to see Ms. Neff for a minute. It's important."

Brenda glared at Nancy and Bess. "How come you have to interfere with a reporter on the job? I thought *you* were only here on vacation."

"I'll be right back," Ms. Neff assured Brenda, sparing Nancy the need to reply.

The TruForm rep gave Nancy and Bess an appraising look, then followed them to some chairs that were out of hearing range of the press room. "Nancy Drew, right?" the woman said impatiently as she sat down. "Let's make this quick, whatever it is. I've got a million things to do today."

"We thought you should know that we were almost brained a few minutes ago by a large ceramic pot that fell from your room."

Irene Neff's mouth opened, but no sound came out of it. *"My* room?" she finally managed to say. "But that's— Are you certain?"

"We just came from there," Nancy told her. "The door was ajar, the window was wide open, and there wasn't a plant in sight. Did there used to be a large potted plant in your room?"

"Yes," Irene replied. "But when I left my room

52

before breakfast this morning, it was still there. I haven't been back since." Irene wrung her hands, and her eyes darted around. "You mean, someone else . . . ? I don't understand."

"When we met you with Renee Clark this morning, you walked away," Nancy pressed. "You didn't go to your room?"

Irene's hazel eyes narrowed. "What's with all the questions?" she demanded hotly. "What business is it of yours where I went? Look, I'm sorry about what happened, but I had nothing to do with it. Now I'm afraid you'll have to excuse me."

"One last thing," Nancy said as Irene started to walk toward the press room. "If you didn't push the planter out the window, that means someone got into your room. Any ideas on who it is or how they got in?"

"None," Ms. Neff said. She walked away without looking back.

"There's something funny about her," Bess said under her breath.

"She was definitely defensive," Nancy agreed. Then, glancing at her watch, she said, "Whoops, we're already half an hour late to meet George!"

The girls arrived at the nearby Pinnacle Club just a few minutes later. The front area was richly carpeted, with several couches and chairs. Posters of well-known athletes from Chicago's professional sports teams hung on the walls.

"Oh, yes," the blond young man at the desk said when Nancy supplied their names. "Your friend has already taken care of the guest fee. You'll find her through there."

Nancy and Bess were heading toward the gray metal door he indicated when George came through it, dressed in sweatpants and a T-shirt. Sweat-dampened curls stuck to her forehead.

"Kevin just arranged to tape an interview with Annette while she's using some of the exercise machines here," George said excitedly. "The club's giving him exclusive use of the big workout room for an hour. He's going to get some terrific material out of this!"

Nancy stepped aside as the door opened again. This time a group of runners walked out, grumbling among themselves. Gina Giraldi was with them, and she had a ferocious scowl on her face. The runners were obviously angry about having to cut short their workout because of Annette's interview.

Renee Clark was right behind Gina. She was the only one who didn't seem upset. She gave Nancy, Bess, and George a smile as she passed by. "My trainer was supposed to meet me here," Nancy heard her say to one of the runners in the group, "but since our workout ended early, I guess I'll just go back to the hotel and find him."

"Where's Kevin?" Bess asked, drawing Nancy's attention back to her friends.

"Oh, he had to make arrangements for the TV crew to come. He'll be back soon," said George.

Giving George a concerned look, Nancy asked, "When did he leave?"

"A while ago," George replied. "He had to cut his workout short when he got the idea of using the gym as background for the interview."

Nancy felt a rush of anxiety. So Kevin *could* have pushed that planter out the window. He was as much a suspect as ever. She would have to talk to George about this—and soon.

"Is Annette here?" Bess asked.

"She was supposed to be here by now, but I haven't seen her yet." Shrugging, George added, "Oh, well, I'm sure she'll be here in a few minutes. Hey, come take a look at the women's locker room. It's awesome! Steam room, sauna, whirlpool, lounge—you name it!"

She led Nancy and Bess through the gray metal door and past a huge room full of exercycles, stair climbers, weights, and some other equipment Nancy didn't recognize. At the far end was the door to the women's locker room. George pushed it open, and Nancy and Bess followed her in.

"Nice," Nancy said, looking around. The locker room was spacious, with wooden benches and shiny red lockers.

"And you haven't even seen the whirlpool and sauna yet." George grinned. "There's even a—"

"Ssh!" Nancy said suddenly. Cocking her head to one side, she strained to identify the faint noise that had caught her attention.

A thumping noise was coming from the far end of the locker room.

"What is that?" asked Bess.

"The whirlpool and sauna are back there," George said. She led her friends down an aisle of lockers and around a corner.

The thumping grew louder as they approached the sauna door. Then Nancy realized that the noise was actually coming from a door next to the sauna. She tried the door, but it wouldn't open.

"Hello?" she called. "Who's in there? Are you all right?"

There was silence.

Worry ate at Nancy as she reached into her shoulder bag and pulled out the lockpicking kit she always carried. She selected a slender length of flexible steel and inserted it into the keyhole. A moment later there was a click. With George and Bess looking on, she pulled the door open.

Nancy gasped as a body fell limply to the floor at her feet.

It was Annette Lang!

Chapter

Eight

"OH, NO!" Bess exclaimed. "Is she . . . ?"

Nancy's heart was in her throat as she bent over Annette to check her pulse. Just then, Annette stirred, and the three teens let out a collective sigh of relief.

"I'll get help," said George, turning to go.

"No!" Annette's voice, urgent and harsh, stopped George in her tracks. "I don't need help. I'm all right. I just blacked out for a second. That closet was so small and dark. I've been afraid of places like that since I was a kid."

The runner struggled to rise, helped by Nancy and George. Bess grabbed a stool for Annette from in front of a locker. Breathing deeply,

Annette sat down. Her hair was a mess, and her clothes were disheveled, but she didn't seem to be hurt.

"Are you sure you're okay?" Nancy asked, kneeling by Annette's side. "What happened?"

"I'm fine," the runner replied. "I came in here a little while ago to put on my workout clothes. Everyone else was getting dressed to leave. Then, about a minute after everyone left, the lights went out. Someone grabbed me from behind, wrestled me into that closet, and locked the door on me."

"Did whoever it was say anything?"

Annette nodded. "I think it was, 'Get smart and drop out, lady, or next time you'll really get hurt.' It was something like that, anyway."

Nancy had to admire Annette; she didn't appear upset or frightened. It was probably just this grit and strength that had made her a champion.

"Could you tell if the person was a man or a woman?" Nancy asked.

"The voice was kind of a whisper, there was no way to know. Whoever it was was strong," Annette said. "It all happened so fast. . . . "

Nancy frowned. "Maybe you should have a guard until the race," she suggested.

"Look, I can't talk about that now," Annette said. "I've got the interview to get ready for, and I look horrible. Will you excuse me?"

Nancy looked at Bess and George, who just shrugged. "All right," Nancy agreed reluctantly. "We'll be right outside."

Annette went to a sink with a mirror over it and began to work on her hair. As Nancy,

George, and Bess left the room, Nancy saw that the light switches were just inside the locker room door. Anyone could have pushed the door open and flipped off the lights. With no windows the locker room would then be pitch-black.

"Gina Giraldi was here, did you notice?" George said, once they were back in the big exercise room. "Renee Clark, too."

"Renee couldn't have done it," Bess objected. "Everyone says she's so sweet and not competitive enough."

"The thing is, we can't eliminate anyone," Nancy pointed out. Including Kevin, she added silently. She decided that now was the time to talk about Kevin.

"George . . ." she began.

"Hi, there, ladies!" Kevin called, entering the exercise room with his crew. He pointed out a weight machine where he wanted them to set up, then came over to George, Nancy, and Bess.

"Is Annette here yet?" he asked.

When George told him what had happened to Annette, Kevin looked genuinely shocked. Then again, Nancy thought, part of his job was putting on a face for the camera. Maybe he was just acting.

Soon after, Annette appeared from the locker room, looking cheerful and refreshed. Kevin hurried over to the runner and grabbed her hands.

"Nancy told me what happened. Listen, are you sure you want to go through with this right now? I mean, we could postpone it."

"No, let's go ahead," Annette said with a

bright smile. "I'm fine, really. It was just a few minutes in a closet, after all."

"Okay, if you're sure," Kevin told her. "Actually, this is going to be a nice additional bit of drama for us."

Nancy caught Bess's eye and knew Bess was thinking the same thing she was: Maybe Kevin had had someone shove Annette into that closet. He might even have done it himself, to create that "nice additional bit of drama."

"I guess you'll be sticking around to make sure nobody drops a TV light on my head," Annette told Nancy blithely. Then she walked over and joined Kevin.

Nancy was steaming when she joined Bess and George behind the camera. As far as she was concerned, Annette's attitude stank. She wasn't taking this seriously enough at all.

As the interview began, Nancy noted that Annette seemed totally unaffected by what had just happened. She looked great and spoke easily and freely. After discussing her training routine, Kevin brought up the subject of the threats and assault attempts.

"Yes, there have been some threats and attacks on me in the last few days," Annette said, her expression growing serious. "But I won't let my life be controlled by the people who are responsible for this terrorism. I intend to run and win."

"She looks good," Bess whispered.

"Mmm," said George, but her eyes remained focused on Kevin.

When the interview was over, Kevin said, "Great! Now we'll shoot some cutaways."

"Cutaways?" Annette repeated.

"TV slang," Kevin explained with a smile. "We'll shoot you using a stair climber, exercise bike, and so on, without sound. Then we'll use those shots over the dialogue. Otherwise, it'd look too dull."

As they started to film the cutaways, Nancy leaned close to George and said, "Listen, we have to talk about Kevin. I think you should—"

"Can't it wait?" George cut in. "I want to shower now, so I'll have a few minutes with Kevin after this is done." George disappeared into the ladies' locker room before Nancy could reply.

Nancy sighed. Obviously her talk with George would have to wait until Kevin wasn't around. When George emerged from the women's locker room and rejoined Nancy and Bess twenty minutes later, filming was just ending.

"Okay, that's it," Kevin announced. "This is going to look great, Annette, and *you* look fantastic."

Seeing George, he went over to her. "I have to look at the tape and help edit it. If you want, you could watch us do the editing."

"Sure," George agreed. "I've already done my workout here, and I guess my training run can wait until this afternoon."

Kevin gave her a big smile. "Great! Let's see . . . it's eleven. Meet me in the hotel lobby at one, okay?"

George nodded. "Fine. See you then."

"Tell you what," Annette said, coming over to Nancy and her friends a second later. "I need to do some shopping, since all my gear was shredded last night. Do you want to come along?"

Nancy was surprised at the invitation but relieved that she wouldn't have to fight to accompany the runner.

Ten minutes later the foursome was back at the Woodville. They went over to the concierge's desk, and Annette said to the woman there, "We'd like the name of a good sporting goods store."

"Maybe I can help you out," said a gravelly female voice.

Nancy turned to find Irene Neff standing at a nearby message board, where notes were posted for marathon participants.

"Hello, Irene," Annette said coolly. "Know a good place to buy running gear? I suppose your opinions on *that* ought to be reliable."

"I know all the best stores, dear," Irene returned. "That's my job, to know the best—the best shoes, the best stores, the best runners."

Annette simply shrugged, but Nancy was aware of an intense current of hostility vibrating between the runner and Irene Neff.

"Try the Winning Margin," Irene suggested. "It's a new store in the Magnificent Mile district. You can get there quickly by cab, and the store has good-quality things."

"Thanks, Irene," said Annette. "If it's good, I imagine they'll have other brands than TruForm."

Annette turned to leave, but George held her back. "I just want to leave Kevin word about where we're going, in case we're late getting back." She scribbled a hasty note and left it on the message board, then followed the others out.

The Winning Margin was an enormous place full of every brand of sporting equipment and clothes.

"Hey, Bess, come with me while I look at running shoes," George said, pulling her cousin down an aisle toward the footwear area.

Bess grinned at Nancy over her shoulder. "Did you ever think you'd see the day when *George* had to drag *me* to go shopping?"

Nancy laughed, then followed Annette to a section where running clothes were displayed. "I'm surprised that you have to shop for this stuff at all," Nancy commented. "Don't you get free stuff from a lot of companies?"

"Sure," Annette told her, pulling an outfit in green and gold from the rack. "I market my own line, too. You saw those black-and-silver suits— those are my trademark colors. I'll wear one of my designs in the race on Sunday. But I still like to shop for other stuff I like."

Annette selected several items to try on. Nancy decided to try on some tops and a yellow warmup suit with neon blue trim.

At one end of the department there was a hallway leading to a row of dressing rooms. Nancy didn't see a sales clerk, so she took her things to a booth while Annette went to another.

After sliding the curtain closed, Nancy hung her things on the hooks provided. She changed first into the yellow-and-blue outfit, then studied her reflection in the booth's full-length mirror.

63

The fit was perfect, Nancy noted with satisfaction, and the yellow fabric set off the rich reddish blond of her hair. She would definitely buy that one, she decided. She stepped back to grab the matching warmup jacket from another hanger.

Nancy had gotten her arms partway into the sleeves when suddenly someone behind her threw a sweater over her head and face. Then, before she could react, she felt herself being grabbed around the neck, also from behind!

She jerked her arms instinctively upward to dislodge the hands at her throat, but the half-on jacket blocked her movement. The powerful hands applied greater pressure, cutting off her windpipe. She opened her mouth to scream, but no sound came out.

Nancy started to feel faint. She couldn't see anything, and the ironclad grip around her throat continued to tighten. She was powerless to fight!

Chapter

Nine

THINK, DREW, Nancy ordered herself. She forced herself to ignore the pain and suffocating feeling that threatened to overwhelm her. Dropping her hands, she sagged back against her assailant, as though losing consciousness. The hands around her neck relaxed slightly.

That was all Nancy needed. She kicked back with her shoe, feeling a sharp impact as it connected with her opponent's shin. Summoning all her strength, Nancy spun out of the deadly grasp and stumbled forward, tearing at the sweater that was covering her face. She turned, but there was no one in the booth with her. She had to take several heaving breaths before she felt clear-headed enough to step out through the curtain and into the corridor between the booths.

It was empty.

"Annette!" she croaked. Her head ached, and her throat was sore and tender.

"What is it?" the runner called back.

Nancy swallowed to moisten her throat. "Someone just grabbed me through the curtain of my booth. I fought him off, and he ran."

"*What!* Hang on, let me get my clothes on."

A minute later Annette joined Nancy in the corridor. As she hastily zipped up her jacket, Annette asked, "Are you all right?"

"I'm okay, but it was a scary moment," Nancy said. She headed out to the sales floor. "I want to see if anyone noticed anything."

There was now a salesclerk on the floor. She was helping a woman choose a sweatsuit. "Excuse me," Nancy said to them. "Did anybody run out of this corridor just a minute ago?"

The clerk stared at her, and Nancy realized she was still wearing the running clothes she had been trying on. "Run out? Sorry, I didn't notice," the clerk said. "Why? Is something wrong?"

Nancy saw Annette shake her head slightly. "No, it's all right," Nancy said. "Um, I'll just go change out of these, then."

Nancy was conscious that the clerk was watching her as she and Annette walked back toward the dressing rooms. Nancy quickly changed back into her jeans skirt and white blouse.

"I was just thinking," said Annette. "Whoever did that obviously thought you were me."

"Maybe," Nancy agreed. "Or it was someone

who doesn't want me to investigate your case. The question is, who knew we were coming here?"

Annette scowled. "Irene Neff did, for one."

Before Nancy could comment, George and Bess walked up, both carrying plastic shopping bags. "I got some fantastic running shoes," George said.

"And I called Jake at the hotel. Lunch is on!" Bess added excitedly. "I found the best—" She broke off and stared at Nancy. "What's wrong?"

When Nancy explained what had happened, Bess's hand flew to her mouth, and George asked quickly, "You're all right?"

"Fine," Nancy assured her friends, "except for a bruise on my throat."

"Most of the suspects in this case spend all their time in the gym, Nan," Bess said. "They're *all* strong."

"But they didn't all know we'd be here," Nancy pointed out.

"Irene knew," said George.

Nancy nodded and thought, So did Kevin. You left him a note. And anyone could have seen that note—Gina or Renee, anyone at all.

"Well, shall we go back to the hotel?" Annette suggested. "I'd like to get something to eat, and I need to get in a run this afternoon."

Giving the runner a stern look, Nancy said, "I'll join you on that run. I don't think you should go out alone."

"I need a run, too," George said. "I have to meet Kevin at the hotel, but I can meet you later."

Annette shrugged. "Fine. I won't be running long or hard—not with the race two days away. I have to save most of my energy for Sunday."

"Yikes!" George gulped, looking at her watch. "It's almost one o'clock. I have to meet Kevin!"

At the hotel Bess raced up to the room to get ready for her lunch date, and George left for the ICT studio with Kevin. Nancy and Annette checked the message board, then went up to the runner's room. It was undisturbed.

"What now?" asked Annette, closing the door and looking irritated. "Do you plan to stay with me *all* the time? Is that necessary?"

Nancy crossed her arms over her chest. "I just wanted to make sure that your room was safe. You don't seem to understand that you may be in real danger." It wasn't easy making Annette grasp the seriousness of her situation.

"There are several people who stand to gain if you can't run Sunday," Nancy continued. "Renee Clark would be more likely to win, Irene Neff's company would get good publicity, Gina Giraldi would have her revenge. . . . And there may be others. You agreed to cooperate with me."

Annette gave Nancy an apologetic smile. "Sorry, I'm not used to having a bodyguard around. Okay, I'll behave. And I won't go anywhere until we run later this afternoon, all right?"

"Fine," said Nancy, smiling back. "I'll meet you in the lobby at three, then."

Nancy left Annette's room and went down the hall to her room, where she looked up the address of TruForm's Chicago office. It was only a short distance away. Nancy walked to the office, hoping that Irene would be out on business or having a late lunch.

TruForm occupied a suite of offices that were decorated with modern furniture. Nancy asked for Irene Neff and was directed to a corner office. When she got there, a secretary was just putting on her jacket in an outer room.

"Hi," Nancy said brightly. "Irene here?"

"Not at the moment," the secretary told her. "Can I help?"

"But she said she'd be here," Nancy lied, trying to look disappointed.

The secretary shrugged. "She's out of the office for the afternoon, and I'm going to lunch."

Perfect! Nancy thought. Aloud, she said, "I'll try another time, then." Before the secretary could ask her name, Nancy walked away.

She paused at a water fountain just down the hall, then bent to take a drink. She watched from the corner of her eye as the secretary picked up her shoulder bag and passed behind her. The woman didn't even seem to notice Nancy.

Nancy looked up and down the hall. Then she returned to Irene's office and tried the door. To her relief, it swung open. Nancy slipped inside and closed the door behind her.

The office was bright and attractive, with huge windows and modern chrome and steel furniture. Posters from TruForm advertisements hung on the walls. A big advertisement featuring Renee Clark hung behind the desk.

There was a filing cabinet in one corner, and

Nancy went over, opened the top drawer, and flipped through the files. They seemed to be arranged alphabetically, yet Nancy failed to find Renee's folder among the Cs.

Frowning, she moved to the next drawer, where the Ls were. There she found a folder labeled Lang, Annette, and she pulled it out.

A copy of a letter from Irene to Annette was the only thing that caught her eye. In the letter TruForm made a large endorsement offer to the runner. So, Irene had been lying when she said that TruForm had turned down Annette's offer of endorsement!

Of course, Nancy could understand why Irene wouldn't want to admit publicly that TruForm had been turned down by a top runner—it would be bad public relations. Nancy knew she needed better proof than this, though, if she was going to prove Irene was behind the threats.

After replacing the file, Nancy went over to Irene's desk. Her pulse quickened as she spotted a folder with Renee Clark's name on it. Nancy leafed through the contents.

"Mmm. Interesting," she murmured, pulling out a letter. It was addressed to Irene and signed by the chief executive of TruForm Shoes. The letter was dated just two weeks earlier.

The tone of the letter was friendly enough, but the substance was serious: It had been Irene who had gotten the company to gamble big money on the future of Renee Clark, the chief executive stated. Renee's future had better start *now*. If the deal with Renee didn't begin to pay publicity dividends immediately, the letter went on, Irene would find herself out of a job.

Nancy let out a whistle as she restored the letter to the file. In the race for a prime suspect, Irene Neff had become the front runner.

Finding nothing further of interest, Nancy slipped from Irene's office. Luckily, most of the other offices' occupants seemed to be out to lunch. Nancy's growling stomach reminded her that she needed to eat, too. After shooting a smile at the receptionist, she breezed out the office door.

She had a quick lunch of pizza and soda, then returned to the Woodville. She had twenty minutes before she was due to meet Annette and George. Time enough to go up to the room, change clothes, and think about the case. Nancy took the elevator to her floor, then stood in the empty hall, fishing through her purse for the room key.

Just as she found it, a loud angry voice erupted from somewhere nearby. With a shock Nancy realized that the voice was coming from *her* room. It didn't sound like Bess or George, though. She ran the few steps to the closed door.

Her key was in the lock when a terrified scream rang out from inside. This time Nancy recognized the voice. It belonged to Bess!

Chapter

Ten

NANCY FLUNG OPEN the door and rushed inside.

Bess was backed up against the wall next to her bed, her face white as chalk and her eyes wide with fear. Gina Giraldi was standing in front of her. Her face was a mask of rage, and her hands were clenched into fists at her sides.

"Nancy, help!" Bess cried. "She's insane!"

"Leave him alone!" Gina shrieked.

Nancy ran over and quickly stepped between the two girls. "That's enough, Gina," she said. "You're asking for trouble. Now get out of here."

The dark-haired runner spun around to face Nancy. "Aha, the lady detective speaks," she sneered. "What I promise, I will do. Your friend will suffer if she does not do as I tell her."

Nancy took a step toward Gina. "If you do anything to Bess, it'll be the dumbest move you ever made. If we have to call the police, you're out of the marathon."

Gina's sneer remained in place, but she left without a word. As Nancy closed the door, Bess flopped facedown on the bed.

"Are you all right?" Nancy asked.

Bess rolled over onto her back and looked at Nancy. "I'm fine. I was just afraid, that's all. She's the scariest woman I've ever met."

Nancy sat on Bess's bed and put a comforting hand on Bess's arm. "She was threatening you about Jake, wasn't she?"

Bess nodded. "The thing is," she said, sitting up on the bed, "I've already decided he's not my type."

"Not your type?" Nancy gave Bess a puzzled look. "How come?"

"It was our lunch date that did it. All he's interested in is running. He talked about how he likes being with the runners' federation, how he used to run, how great he feels working with runners, blah, blah, blah. I tried to change the subject, ask him what kind of music he liked, or what kind of stores they had in the Netherlands, but he'd just start talking about running again."

Nancy couldn't help laughing. "Sounds like you made the right decision," she said. "I'm sure Gina will lay off you now."

"I sure hope so," said Bess. She lay back down

on the bed and stared up at the ceiling while Nancy changed into sweatpants and an Emerson College T-shirt that her boyfriend, Ned Nickerson, had given her.

"When are you going to talk to George about Kevin?" Bess asked.

"This afternoon," Nancy answered, sighing. "I can't put it off any longer."

Nancy entered the lobby, wheeling the bike she had gotten from the second-floor marathon room. Seeing no sign of Annette or George, she went over to the message board, but there wasn't any message for her there.

Renee Clark was also there, with her trainer and Irene Neff. Nancy had just greeted them when a familiar voice spoke up behind her.

"Hi, Nancy! How's your *vacation* going?"

Wearing a triumphant grin, Brenda Carlton walked over to Nancy.

"Hello, Brenda," said Nancy, stifling a groan. "Get any hot stories lately?"

"Actually, I'm on the trail of something major," Brenda said smugly. "I'm meeting Gina Giraldi later, and she's going to give me the lowdown about who's doing dirty deals."

Pointing a manicured nail at Nancy, she continued, "And I bet I find out who's behind the attacks on Annette before you do. What's that I see in your eyes, a little jealousy?"

Nancy felt like strangling Brenda. Renee, Charles Mellor, and Irene Neff were eagerly drinking in every word Brenda said. Not only that, but Kevin and George had come up while Brenda was talking, and Kevin was listening. Now practically every suspect in her case knew that she was looking into the attacks on Annette!

Speaking through gritted teeth, Nancy said, "Can I see you in private?" Without waiting for an answer, she pulled the reporter away from the group by the message board.

"Hey, cut it out!" Brenda protested. "You're hurting my arm!"

Nancy let go, once they were far enough away to talk without being overheard. "Don't you have any sense?" she snapped before she could stop herself. "You just broadcast it to everyone in the lobby that Gina could make trouble for people. What if Gina is planning to finger one of them? You might have put her in serious danger!"

"You're just worried that I'm going to show you up for the overrated fake you are," Brenda purred. "Sorry, Nancy, but I'm keeping on this story. You'll just have to read about who threatened Annette in *Today's Times.*"

Brenda strutted off, leaving Nancy simmering.

As Nancy rejoined the others, Annette appeared, wearing silver-and-black running shorts and a matching top. "Ready?" she asked Nancy and George.

"George just has to change," said Nancy with a nod toward where Kevin and George were holding hands and talking quietly together.

Tapping her foot impatiently, Annette called, "George, can we get going?"

George looked up, slightly taken aback. "Oh—

sorry. I'll only be a minute," she said. After saying goodbye to Kevin and arranging to meet him after the run, she hurried to the elevators.

"Sorry I can't go with you," Derek, Annette's trainer, told the runner, "but I have to meet with that fellow upstairs in the marathon office. Where are you going to run?"

"In Grant Park, south along Lake Shore Drive," Annette said. "If that's all right with you," she added to Nancy.

Nancy ignored the slight touch of sarcasm in the runner's voice. "Sounds fine," she said.

"Have fun," Kevin told Nancy and Annette. "Well, I'd better go. I'm already late filing the piece I just edited." He waved and headed for the hotel's entrance.

"I'm off, too," Derek added.

After he left, Nancy and Annette drifted over to scan the message board while they waited for George. There were dozens of memos, appointments, questions, and answers. Nancy's eye was caught by an unusual piece of stationery with a red marbled design. Written on it, in a distinctive backhanded scrawl, was "Grant Park, 3:30. Fountain."

Nancy looked up as George reappeared, wearing a cutoff pair of orange sweatpants and a blue T-shirt. "Sorry I kept you waiting," she told Annette. "And thanks for letting me run with you. You don't know what a thrill this is for me!"

"Relax your arms!" Annette told George. "Your fists are clenched, and you're wasting energy. It makes your whole body more tense."

Annette and George were running side by side through the park, with Nancy pedaling alongside. Annette had been giving George pointers as they ran, and George looked as if she were walking on air. Even if Nancy was on a dangerous case, she was glad that it gave George the opportunity to train with the best.

The weather was cool, and there was a slight breeze. Somehow, in the park, the noises and crowds of the city seemed a lot farther away than they actually were.

"You're right," George told Annette after taking several strides. "I can feel the difference already. Thanks."

Nancy smiled at George, but a sober thought kept nagging at her. Every time she had tried to talk to George about Kevin, she had been interrupted by something. It was hard getting George away from Kevin long enough to tell her, but now she would do it. If only she could—

Zing! A high-pitched whining distracted Nancy from her thoughts. A split second later a piece of bark flew from a tree just alongside her.

Huh? Nancy thought. What was—

She jumped as a puff of dust kicked up just in front of Annette.

With a flash of panic Nancy realized what was causing the disturbances: bullets.

Someone was shooting at them—and using a silencer!

Chapter

Eleven

"**A**NNETTE! GEORGE!**" Nancy shouted, stopping her bike with a jerk. "Somebody's shooting at us. Head for cover!"

The other two didn't wait or ask questions but raced for the side of the path.

Her heart pounding, Nancy jumped from the bike and threw herself to the ground on the other side of the path from George and Annette. She was fairly sure this was the side the shots had come from.

With a quick turn of her head, Nancy saw that the other two had taken shelter behind the thick trunks of two old oaks. "Are you guys all right?"

"Fine!" George yelled back.

"I'm okay, too," Annette added.

"I'm going to look around!" Nancy shouted to them. "Stay put until I get back."

"Should you do that?" Annette called. But Nancy was already on the move.

She darted from tree to tree, heading away from the path and up a rise. The sniper would probably choose high ground, she reasoned.

Even though she was behind a tree, Nancy felt exposed and defenseless. She fought back her fear and forced herself to look ahead for a clue to the shooter's position.

Nancy froze as a bullet whined by, chipping the tree just above her head. In the next instant she saw a flash from a thick tangle of bushes.

Racing from tree to tree, Nancy headed toward the bushes where she had seen movement. She was about fifty yards away when a figure in dark clothes and a ski mask bolted from the brush and ran, away from Nancy.

Nancy took off in pursuit. "Stop!" she yelled, but it was useless. The person reached a road that was at a right angle to Lake Shore Drive. He leapt into the driver's side of a light blue car with a big scrape on the right rear fender. The engine roared to life, and the car screamed away as Nancy reached the road.

Breathing deeply, Nancy tried to squelch her frustration. She hadn't gotten a good look at the person at all!

Just before the car disappeared out of sight, however, she noticed something that made her start. The car had an ICT placard in the side window!

"Uh-oh," Nancy said out loud. She hadn't

actually identified Kevin, but there were no two ways about it—she had to talk to George *now*.

Nancy's mood was grim as she walked back to where the sniper had hidden. She spotted a gleam of metal in the bushes, bent down, and picked up an empty bullet cartridge. A fast search uncovered two more, which she pocketed. Then she hurried back to the spot where Annette and George were still pressed against the tree trunks.

"All clear," she announced. "Whoever it was got away."

George's face was pale as she emerged from behind her tree. Annette also seemed a little shaken.

"Hey, look at that!" Nancy exclaimed as her gaze lit on a huge structure nearby.

"That's Buckingham Fountain," Annette said.

Water was pouring down the sides of the multitiered fountain to a pool that surrounded it. Something stirred in the back of Nancy's memory, but she couldn't bring it into focus.

"Did you see the person?" George asked, breaking into Nancy's thoughts.

Nancy braced herself. George wasn't going to like what she had to say. "No, whoever it was wore a mask," she began. "The person jumped in a car and escaped." She took a deep breath before adding, "I did notice one thing. The getaway car had a placard with the ICT logo in the window."

George stared blankly at Nancy for a moment. "ICT? But you don't . . . you *can't* think that Kevin is involved with any of this!"

Nancy took another deep breath. "I hope not. But look at what this story is doing for his career. He could have caused any of the incidents. And now, the ICT placard in that car . . . I have to look at the facts, George."

Nancy saw a brief flash of pain in her friend's eyes. Then George looked down and tugged at the cutoff hem of her sweats. "He just would never do any of those things, Nancy," she said, still looking down. "You have to believe that."

"I want to, George," Nancy said quickly. "But until I know for sure, I have to consider him a suspect."

Finally George met Nancy's gaze. There was a determined glint in her eyes as she said, "Well, fine. I mean, I guess I understand. But *I* already know for sure, and I'm definitely going to keep spending time with him while we're here."

George walked away, kicking some gravel on the path, then leaned down and ran one hand through the water in the pool.

Nancy followed George with her eyes for a moment, then forced herself to deal with the case. Turning to Annette, she said, "Now that you've been shot at, we have to call in the police."

"But you said you wouldn't! I trusted you!" Annette cried angrily.

"I said I'd try not to. But now you've been shot at, and that's where the police come in. Otherwise, we're all in deep trouble."

"But what if they won't let me run?" Annette demanded.

"You'll have to work it out with them," Nancy replied. "Now, you and George wait here while I find a phone."

Nancy trudged up the road. Great, she thought. George is upset, and Annette won't let herself be protected. So much for my fun weekend in Chicago!

Fifteen minutes later a police car drove up to the spot where Nancy had found a phone. Two plainclothes police officers got out.

"Are you Nancy Drew?" asked one officer, a thickset man with jet black hair and long sideburns.

When Nancy nodded, he said, "I'm Sergeant Lew Stokes, and this is my partner, Detective Matt Zandt. Where are the other girls?"

"Waiting for us, back where it happened," Nancy told him. "I'll take you there. In the meantime you'd better take these," Nancy said, pulling the three spent cartridges from her pocket and handing them to the sergeant.

As they drove to the site of the shooting, Nancy told the officers about the other threats and the attempted hit-and-run, as well as about Annette's being locked in the health club closet and her own experience at the Winning Margin.

As she went on, she was aware that Sergeant Stokes was scowling. "We saw that thing with the car on TV," he said at last, "but the rest is all news to us. Just what do you think you're playing at here?"

"We had hoped to clear everything up without a lot of publicity—" Nancy began.

"You amateurs make me sick!" Detective Zandt exploded, speaking for the first time. He was a tall man with a red face and thick, brushed-back blond hair. "People get hurt because of people like you."

There was no point in arguing, Nancy decided, especially since she had been saying basically the same thing to Annette a few minutes earlier.

At her direction the officers parked the car and made their way down to the path where Annette and George waited. The two police officers questioned the three girls about all of the threats and attacks. When Nancy mentioned Kevin as one of her suspects, George opened her mouth as if to object. Then she clamped it shut again and turned away.

At last the questioning was over, and the officers drove the three girls back to the hotel, with Nancy's bicycle loaded into the trunk. No one said anything, and Nancy found her mind wandering.

Suddenly an image of the fountain in the park flashed into Nancy's mind. "The fountain!" she said excitedly. "Buckingham Fountain!"

"Nancy, have you lost your mind?" George asked. "What are you talking about?"

Nancy whirled to face Annette. "There was a message on the board in the hotel lobby today that said, 'Grant Park. Three-thirty. Fountain.' Did you notice it?"

Annette's eyes flitted nervously. "A message? There were a hundred messages on that board. Why would I notice that one?" The runner's cool self-control seemed to be cracking a little—not that Nancy could blame her. She *had* just been shot at.

"We were shot at in Grant Park, at three-thirty, by the Buckingham Fountain," Nancy explained, leaning forward excitedly. "That note was to tell the sniper where we'd be. But who else knew?"

From the front seat Sergeant Stokes asked, "Any chance that the note is still on the board?"

"We'll be at the hotel in a few minutes," his partner spoke up. "We can find out then."

"Derek knew where I'd be," Annette said, answering Nancy's question. "But surely *he's* not . . . Derek wouldn't—"

"I'm not accusing him," Nancy said quickly. "I'm just thinking things through."

She glanced at George, who was looking at her with troubled eyes. "I know what you're thinking," George said. "That Kevin knew, too. Maybe he *was* there when we were talking about where to run, but I still don't think . . ." Her voice trailed off, and she stared straight ahead.

Suddenly Annette snapped her fingers. "Nancy, I just remembered! I stopped off at the marathon office on my way to lunch. Someone asked me about good runs in the neighborhood, and I mentioned Grant Park, that I was going there this afternoon. Irene Neff was there at the time—she must have heard me. So was Gina. Either of them could've waited at the fountain until we came by."

"Does notepaper with a marbled design in red ring a bell?" Nancy asked.

Annette shook her head.

"At least we know that there's more than one person involved here," Nancy went on. "There's the shooter, and the person who wrote the note *to* the shooter. So we've learned something."

But we're not learning enough, Nancy added to herself, or fast enough.

At the hotel everyone piled out of the car. "I want you all to stay close until my partner checks that board," said Sergeant Stokes while his partner disappeared through the hotel's entrance. "We're not done here yet."

The three girls waited silently on the sidewalk next to the hotel's curved entrance drive. Detective Zandt returned a moment later.

"The note is gone," he told his partner.

Annette tapped her foot impatiently. "What now?" she asked.

"We'll need to see those anonymous notes," Sergeant Stokes told her. "Then we'll talk to Derek Townsend and, uh, let's see . . ." He consulted a list. "Renee Clark, Irene Neff, Charles Mellor, Gina Giraldi, and Kevin Davis. That'll do, for now."

"I should hope so," Annette muttered. "By the time we're done, the marathon will be over." She glanced up the hotel's drive. "Well, we can at least get started right away. Here comes one of the suspects now."

A light blue car with an ICT placard in the window pulled to a halt behind the police car. Nancy recognized Kevin's face behind the wheel.

She felt a knot twist inside her stomach as she recognized something else—a large scrape on the car's right rear fender.

Kevin was driving the same car the sniper had escaped in!

Chapter
Twelve

As KEVIN GOT OUT of the car, the two officers approached him. "Kevin Davis?" Sergeant Stokes asked.

"That's me," Kevin said cheerfully. Waving at George, Nancy, and Annette, he said, "Hi! How was your run?"

As the officers identified themselves, Kevin looked puzzled. He gave George a questioning look as the group filed into the hotel and headed for a grouping of chairs and a sofa. George smiled encouragingly at him, but Nancy noticed that her eyes were filled with worry.

"I'll find Derek," Annette offered as the others sat down. "He has those anonymous notes."

87

With a nod Detective Zandt said, "Why don't you wait with him in your room? We'll be up to see you shortly." After giving him her room number, Annette hurried toward the elevators.

"Mind telling us where you've been for the last hour or so?" Sergeant Stokes asked Kevin.

Kevin hesitated before answering. "I was . . . attending to business. Why?"

Why is he being evasive? Nancy wondered.

When the officers told Kevin about the shooting, Kevin looked at George with alarm. "You were there, too! Are you all right?"

George nodded, and Nancy was relieved to note that for once Kevin didn't seem interested in another "little bit of drama" for his big story on Annette. He seemed genuinely concerned for George.

"Mr. Davis, we need to know where you were at the time in question," Detective Zandt went on.

Kevin's mouth fell open. "Am *I* a suspect?"

"Your car matches the one the gunman drove," said Stokes. "The color, the scrape, ICT placard."

"I'd rather not say where I was," Kevin said, suddenly flustered. "But I had nothing to do with any shooting or anything else illegal!"

Detective Zandt hooked his thumbs in the belt loops of his slacks. "How do you explain the car?" he asked Kevin.

"I can't. I only took it fifteen minutes ago. ICT has a pool of cars. You sign a log when you take a car out and when you return it. And you put down the time. Check the log if you want." Kevin pulled a pad and pen from his inside jacket pocket and wrote something down. "Here's the ICT number. Call the office."

"I'll do just that," said Detective Zandt, getting up and heading for the bank of phones near the elevators.

Sergeant Stokes leaned forward in his chair and said to Kevin, "We understand you're covering what's been happening to Annette Lang here. Is it fair to say that the more that happens to her, the better it is for your career?"

"Sure," Kevin replied, shrugging. "We figured that it would be a good thing for both of us."

The sergeant gave Kevin a puzzled look. "And just how would it be good for Annette Lang?"

"Annette wants a shot at a job like mine, in sports broadcasting," Kevin explained. "You see, about a year ago she was given a trial with 'SportsTalk'—that's another cable sports show. But on the first day's taping, she was so nervous that she froze up in front of the camera. The ratings were so bad they never asked her back."

Kevin shook his head ruefully. "It's a pretty cutthroat business. She never got a second chance until now. The ICT brass have been impressed with Annette in the footage we've shot."

Nancy looked at Kevin in surprise. This was news.

"And it looks as if I might be headed to a job with a bigger network show," Kevin went on proudly. "Which means that ICT will be in the market for a track analyst real soon. They'll probably give Annette serious consideration."

Nancy looked up as Detective Zandt returned and sat back down. "I called ICT. Kevin Davis signed the car out at four o'clock, like he says. And he was in the office just before."

"Hmm," said Sergeant Stokes, stroking his long sideburns. "Who had the car before Davis?"

"The log says it was in the garage since eleven this morning. But from what the guy told me, it seems as if security there is pretty lousy. There's just one guy with the cars, and if he leaves, the cars are unattended. The keys just hang there on a numbered board. I got the feeling that it would be easy for someone to take one."

"Let's be reasonable here," Kevin urged. "If I *was* going to commit a crime, would I use a car with an ICT placard?"

Kevin had a point, Nancy had to admit.

The police officers exchanged a look. "All right, Mr. Davis, that's it for now," said Stokes. "But we may want to see you again." He looked at his partner. "Let's find Annette Lang and Derek Townsend."

There was an awkward silence after the officers left. "Uh, excuse me, I have to call my agent," Kevin finally said. He looked at George and squeezed her hand. Then he got up and left the two girls alone.

"George?" Nancy said tentatively. "Nothing would make me happier than if Kevin is innocent. I hope you believe that."

George sat still a moment, then turned toward Nancy. "I know," she said softly. "I guess I couldn't help getting upset about it back in the park. It's just that . . . well, I feel as if there's something really special happening between Kevin and me. And to think that he might have . . ."

Her words trailed off into a huge sigh. "But you're right—a lot of stuff *does* point to him."

"*And* to Irene Neff and to Gina Giraldi," Nancy reminded George. "We don't know for sure that Kevin *did* do it, either."

George smiled weakly. "Right again, Nan." Her smile brightened as Kevin walked back up to them.

"Great news!" he said. "My agent says that 'Worldwide Sports' wants me to announce for them on a trial basis, starting next month! I'm taking you all out to dinner to celebrate—and I won't take no for an answer!"

George's glum mood seemed to melt away as she looked up into Kevin's handsome face. "It's a date!" she told him. "If that's okay with you, Nan," she added quickly.

"Definitely," Nancy agreed. She could see how important this was to George, and she wasn't about to let down her friend.

"So meet me here at seven-thirty," said Kevin. He hesitated, then asked George, "Would you mind if I talk to Nancy alone a minute?"

"Uh, sure," George agreed. "I'll be over by the message board."

"Listen," Kevin told Nancy once George was out of earshot, "I have no hard feelings about you suspecting me. I know I acted suspiciously just now. I didn't want to say where I was this afternoon because . . . well, I bought George a good-luck gift for the race."

91

He glanced over his shoulder to be sure George wasn't looking, then retrieved a small box from his jacket pocket and opened it for Nancy. Inside was a thin silver chain from which dangled a small silver charm in the shape of a running shoe.

"Oh, it's darling!" Nancy exclaimed in a low voice. "George is going to love it."

Kevin held a finger up to his lips. "Don't say anything. It's a surprise."

"Your secret is safe with me," Nancy assured him. Kevin looked sincere, and Nancy wanted to believe him—now more than ever. George's happiness depended on it.

"I shouldn't have had the chocolate soufflé," Bess groaned as she, George, Kevin, and Nancy returned to the hotel after dinner. "I'm going to turn into a total blimp."

"If you are, so am I," Nancy told Bess with a laugh, "since I had it, too."

George grinned at her friends. "One thing I love about being in training is carbo-loading. I mean, I ate a huge plate of pasta with pesto sauce, *plus* soup and salad and chocolate cake." Reaching out for Kevin's hand, she said, "Thanks for taking us."

In response, Kevin gave her a kiss on the cheek. "I guess I'd better head home," he said. "Tomorrow's going to be a busy day, what with interviews and prep work for Sunday's race."

"I can't believe it's the day after tomorrow," George said, her eyes glowing with excitement. "I'd better get to bed."

Bess yawned. "After that dinner I'm ready to

call it a night. Thank you, Kevin. It was fabulous."

"My pleasure," he replied. "Good night, all." He kissed George lightly on the lips, then left the hotel.

There was an elevator waiting, and the girls stepped in. When it stopped at the fourth floor, Nancy said, "You two go on. I'll be back in a few minutes."

"What are you doing?" Bess asked, holding open the elevator door after she and George got out.

"I want to see Irene Neff and Gina."

George raised an eyebrow. "Need some help?"

Shaking her head, Nancy replied. "No, thanks. If there are too many of us, they might get defensive."

As the doors slid closed, Nancy considered how to approach the two women. I might as well be direct, she decided. Brenda's already blown my cover. It was ten-thirty, and Gina was probably in bed. If she was caught unprepared, she might let something slip or leave evidence in view.

After getting out on the ninth floor, Nancy made her way to Room 915, which she remembered was Gina's. When she knocked on the door, there was no answer. She knocked again, more loudly. Still nothing.

Gina's breaking training, Nancy thought. On an impulse she got out her lockpicking kit. Seeing that the hallway was deserted, she went to work. A moment later the lock clicked open.

Nancy pushed the door inward, but it would

93

only go a few inches. The security chain held it closed. Through the narrow opening, Nancy saw that the room was dark.

So she *is* in there, Nancy thought. All I'm finding out is that she's a sound sleeper. As Nancy shut the door, she paused. Was that a noise inside? She froze, listening, but heard nothing else. Probably just my imagination, she decided.

Continuing down the hall, Nancy went to Room 926, Irene Neff's room, and knocked on the door. Irene opened the door and looked surprised to see Nancy.

"What is it? It's late," Irene said coolly.

"We need to talk," Nancy told her. Without giving Irene a chance to say no, Nancy breezed past her and entered the room. There were papers scattered over the table. A coffeepot and a half-full cup sat there as well.

"You know, you're getting to be a pest," Irene snapped. "What do we have to talk about?"

Nancy sat on the couch facing the table. "Did the police see you today?" she asked.

Irene's eyes narrowed. "Yes. I had nothing to tell them—or you."

"These attacks against Annette are getting more intense, and I need to find out a few things," Nancy said, swallowing her irritation.

"From me?" As Neff paced in front of her, Nancy thought she looked more nervous than angry. "Why me? I didn't shoot at her. I've been in meetings all day."

Nancy was about to ask Irene about her day's

schedule when she saw something on the table that made her stop in her tracks.

In the middle of the mess of papers was a distinctive piece of notepaper. It had exactly the same red marbled pattern as the one that had advised the sniper to be at the fountain in Grant Park!

Chapter

Thirteen

NANCY TRIED not to show her excitement as she took a second glance at the paper.

Wait a minute, Nancy thought. The handwriting on the note was different from the writing she had seen on the marbled paper on the message board, Nancy realized. This was more rounded and vertical.

"I have to finish up some work," Irene said suddenly, looking edgy. "Let's cut this short."

"It won't take long," Nancy assured her.

Irene stopped pacing and faced Nancy. "You don't understand, I'm a busy woman," she snapped. "I don't have time to play detective games with you, so you can just find someone else to pester."

Nancy made no move to get up. "All right," she said. "I suppose you've already told the officers on the case how Annette Lang turned down an endorsement deal with TruForm, which gives you a motive for wanting to hurt her—"

"That's not true!" Irene sputtered.

"I happen to know it *is* true," Nancy countered, without saying how she had found out. Fixing Irene with a steady gaze, she went on. "And I imagine you told the police that your job hinges on Renee Clark winning the Heartland Marathon, so I won't have to mention it to them."

Nancy rose from her chair and said smoothly, "Well, good night, Ms. Neff. Sorry to bother you."

"Wait a minute." Irene's voice was urgent. "What are you saying? Do you really suspect me of being connected with the attacks?"

"You have an interest in eliminating Annette from the race," Nancy said, sitting back down. "And you suggested shopping at the Winning Margin this morning. Someone attacked me there."

Irene sank down on the couch next to Nancy. "But this is absurd! I'm no criminal."

"One other thing," Nancy continued. "There was a note on the message board before Annette, George, and I went out to run. It gave the exact time and place where the shots were fired."

Irene stared blankly at Nancy. "Those detectives said something about that, too. You think *I* wrote the note?"

"It was written on very unusual paper—

97

exactly like that piece," Nancy explained, pointing to the red marbled note. "That isn't your notepaper?"

"Of course not!" Irene reached among the papers on the table and grabbed a sheet of ivory paper with Irene Neff printed at the top. "This is mine."

Nancy kept her eyes fixed on the other woman. "Then whose is this other paper?"

"How should I know? I mean . . . there may be dozens of people who have paper like that." Irene fidgeted nervously with the sheet of personal notepaper she still held.

Shooting Irene a skeptical glance, Nancy said, "You don't know who sent you this note?"

There was a long pause. Finally Irene turned to face Nancy, her mouth set in a grim line. "I won't tell you. I can't."

Nancy stood up. "Ms. Neff, somebody shot at Annette. She might have been killed. This is no time for holding anything back. I thought you might prefer to talk with me in private here, rather than being questioned by the police, but it's up to you, naturally."

Irene leaned into one corner of the couch. She looked trapped. "All right, I'll tell you," she said at last. "But you have to promise not to tell the police."

"I could get in major trouble for withholding evidence of a crime," Nancy told her. "But I'll promise not to tell the police if it isn't necessary. That's the best I can do."

Ms. Neff sighed deeply, then said, "The note

was from Renee, but I can't believe she'd do anything criminal. She can hardly bring herself to make a rival runner feel bad by beating her in a race."

This tallied with what Jake Haitinck had told her and Bess about Renee Clark the night before at the dance club. "Is this her regular style of notepaper?" Nancy asked.

"I've gotten one or two other memos from her on it, but I don't know if she has a lot of it or not. I don't know . . . really!"

Nancy took another look at the note. "This is definitely not the handwriting that was on the message board," she said, thinking aloud. "Can you think of someone else who might have persuaded Renee to improve her chances by starting this campaign against Annette? Gina, possibly? Charles Mellor?"

"I cannot imagine Renee having something to do with anything illegal under any circumstances. Period."

Nancy's gut instinct told her that Irene was telling her the truth. She thought for a moment, then asked, "What about Charles Mellor? How did he become Renee's trainer?"

"Her old trainer retired two years ago," Irene explained. "Renee was just another runner then, nothing special. Charles came up after a race and started giving her tips, and she listened. Next thing, he was her trainer, and she was a major contender."

Nancy stood up. "Okay. That's all for now."

Irene clasped her hands nervously together as

she, too, rose from the couch. "You're not going to bother Renee with this now, are you? She needs her sleep."

Nancy paused. "What about Charles Mellor?"

"You can give him a try," Irene said, gesturing to her phone.

Nancy got no answer from Mellor's room. It was now after eleven, so she decided to call it a night.

When she got back to her room, Bess and George were already asleep in their beds. After changing into her nightshirt, Nancy slipped between the sheets of the cot, but she had a hard time falling asleep.

The race was the day after tomorrow, and she didn't feel any closer to finding who was after Annette. If she didn't make some progress—and quickly—the Heartland Marathon might be the last race Annette Lang ever ran.

"Good morning, sleepyhead."

Nancy heard Bess's cheerful voice and rolled over onto her stomach. "Hrmphh," she mumbled sleepily.

"Come on. George is already working out at the gym, and I'm starving. Get up, Drew."

Cracking open one eye, Nancy saw that Bess was perched on the edge of her bed, her arms crossed over the oversize pink cotton sweater she was wearing with white leggings.

"Okay, okay," Nancy said, pushing the covers aside and swinging her feet to the floor. "Just give me a few minutes to get dressed.

Fifteen minutes later Nancy had showered and

was dressed in jeans and a blue pullover. "Ready," she said, grabbing her shoulder bag.

As they got into the elevator, Bess said, "After that dinner last night, I'm definitely on a diet today. I'll have poached eggs, not fried, without bacon. And less toast, with no—well, only a little—butter."

Nancy was chuckling as the elevator doors opened into the lobby. Her smile disappeared, however, when she saw Brenda Carlton standing there, looking annoyed.

"Have you seen Gina Giraldi?" Brenda asked as Nancy and Bess got off the elevator.

"Good morning to you, too, Brenda," said Nancy. "And no, I haven't. Why?"

Brenda frowned. "We were supposed to meet for that interview a half hour ago. Nobody's seen her, and when I tried calling her room, there was no answer."

"Maybe she went somewhere and got delayed," Bess suggested. "Or maybe she forgot about it."

"Forgot about it?" Brenda repeated, glaring at Bess. "Forgot about an interview with a *major* paper? I don't think so."

Nancy rolled her eyes. *Today's Times* was hardly a "major paper." Trust Brenda to exaggerate her own importance.

Still, Brenda's words triggered a slight tingle of concern in Nancy. Gina didn't seem like the kind of person who would miss out on a chance to get newspaper coverage.

"Let's go knock on her door," Nancy suggested.

101

Nancy, Bess, and Brenda took the elevator to the ninth floor and went to Gina's room. Nancy knocked on the door. There was no answer.

"Now what?" asked Bess.

In response Nancy took out her lockpicking kit and began to probe the lock.

"Hmm. I see you've learned a trade from all those criminals you go after," Brenda remarked snidely.

Nancy didn't bother to answer. A moment later there was a click, and Gina's door opened. The shades were drawn, and the room was in shadow.

"Hello?" Nancy called. "Gina?"

There was no answer. Stepping forward, Nancy flipped on the lights. Bess and Brenda were right behind her.

Nancy froze at the sight before her. Behind her, Brenda and Bess both let out horrified cries.

Gina lay stretched out on the floor, unconscious, an ugly, dark bruise on her forehead.

Chapter

Fourteen

NANCY FOUGHT BACK the wave of nausea that swept over her. She hurried over to Gina and quickly checked her pulse. It was there but very weak.

"She's alive. Call the house doctor and an ambulance," she said to Bess and Brenda, who stood stiffly by the door.

Bess nodded and went to the phone. Brenda sat on the bed, looking as if she might faint.

"Don't touch anything in here," Nancy cautioned. Suddenly a chilling thought hit her.

When she had tried to get into Gina's room the night before, the security chain had been on. It could only have been fastened from *inside* the room. For all she knew, the attacker could have been going after Gina at the exact moment that Nancy had been there!

Nancy pushed away the awful thought as Bess hung up the phone and announced, "The doctor and paramedics are on the way." Looking at Gina, she added, "I guess I'd better call the police, too."

She picked up the phone again and dialed. After a brief conversation, Bess hung up and turned to Nancy. "Sergeant Stokes says they'll be here in ten minutes and not to touch anything."

Before long, Gina's room was filled with paramedics, the hotel's doctor, and a crowd of police technicians accompanied by Sergeant Stokes and Detective Zandt.

"Looks like a serious concussion," said the hotel doctor. "We won't know how serious, however, until I run some tests and take X-rays at the hospital."

Nancy, Bess, and Brenda looked on as the paramedics carefully laid Gina on a gurney and wheeled her out. Curious onlookers were urged to move away by a guard at the door.

While Detective Zandt directed the police technicians in dusting for fingerprints and looking for clues, Sergeant Stokes led Nancy, Bess, and Brenda over to a quiet spot near the door. They told him all they remembered about finding Gina.

"Annette Lang has been the main target until this," Sergeant Stokes said. "Any idea why someone would go after Gina Giraldi?"

"Gina planned to give a story to Brenda," Nancy explained, nodding at the reporter. "She

104

was going to expose some crooked dealings by someone connected with the Heartland Marathon."

Stokes scribbled notes and nodded.

"Brenda bragged to me about her scoop yesterday," Nancy went on, "in front of a number of people—Renee Clark, Charles Mellor, Irene Neff, Kevin Davis . . . I don't remember who else. She said specifically that Gina was going to name names."

"Is that so?" Stokes said, giving Brenda a sharp look. "Not too smart, ma'am."

Brenda glared at Nancy but said nothing.

The police sergeant tapped his pad with his pen. "Someone is at large who was desperate enough to try to shut Gina Giraldi's mouth permanently to keep something secret," he said. "He or she might try the same thing on you and your friends. So watch out. You could be in danger."

He looked at Brenda again. "That goes double for you."

"What do you mean?" Brenda asked indignantly.

Nancy answered for the sergeant. "The person who attacked Gina can't be sure that she didn't *already* talk to you. So you might know things you shouldn't. If I were you, I'd watch my back."

"And learn to keep your mouth shut," Sergeant Stokes added. "Otherwise, you can get people into trouble, including yourself."

Brenda nodded, but there was a defiant look in her eyes. She still didn't seem to recognize the seriousness of her slip.

"Now," said Stokes, consulting his notes. "We got preliminary statements yesterday from Irene Neff, Renee Clark, Annette Lang, Charles Mellor, and Kevin Davis. I'm going to need to know their whereabouts for last night, too."

It took some doing, but Sergeant Stokes managed to find everyone. Renee Clark and Charles Mellor were at the gym, but Irene and Kevin both had to be tracked down at their offices. Annette was on a run, so the police officer left a message for her at the front desk, asking her to join them when she returned.

An hour later everyone but Annette and Kevin was assembled in the lobby. George had joined them, too, when she returned to the hotel after her workout.

Sergeant Stokes decided not to delay questioning any longer. Taking Nancy, Bess, and George aside, he said, "I'd like you to be here, too. See if what they say fits with what you know."

As the sergeant led them into the empty press room, Brenda Carlton started in as well.

"Where are you going?" Stokes asked, barring her way.

"I thought I'd sit in," Brenda said with a smile that faded quickly under Stokes's glare.

"You thought wrong. This isn't an open forum for your gossip column. It's police business."

Red-faced, Brenda turned and left the room.

Stokes stood in front of the three suspects, who sat on the room's couch. Nancy, Bess, and George stood off to the side.

"Sometime late last night, Gina Giraldi was attacked by someone. She sustained serious head injuries and is unconscious in the hospital at this very moment."

Nancy studied the suspects' reactions as they heard this news. They all looked shocked.

"You can't think any of us had something to do with this?" Renee asked.

"We'll be talking to a number of people," said the sergeant, avoiding a direct answer. "There may be a link between what happened to Gina and some ugly attacks on Annette Lang lately."

"That car that almost ran Annette over," Renee said softly. "I saw that—it was awful!"

"That and other things," said the sergeant. He paused as Annette entered the room, still dressed in her sliver-and-black running outfit.

Nancy noticed that the runner appeared shaken. Her eyes darted every which way, and her hands were clasped together so tightly that her knuckles were white.

"Please join us, Ms. Lang," Sergeant Stokes said.

"Is it true, what I heard about Gina?" Annette asked in a shaky voice, sitting down on an upholstered chair.

The police officer nodded. "It's true."

"So what do you want with me?" Annette asked.

"Give me a break!" Irene burst out. " 'What do you want with me?' " she mimicked. "As if everyone didn't know you hate Gina. You're what's called a *suspect,* Annette."

"I'm a suspect?" Anger replaced the worry in Annette's face. "If there's a logical suspect around here, you're it. If Gina was planning to

expose any dirty linen, yours would be at the top of the bag."

"What is that supposed to mean?" Irene demanded, standing up.

Nancy saw Sergeant Stokes listening quietly. Questioning suspects this way might be unorthodox, but Nancy now realized that the sergeant had probably done it intentionally. Things might be blurted out in anger that wouldn't be said otherwise.

"It means that you're the most likely one to have organized a conspiracy against me," Annette shot back. She turned to Stokes and explained. "She's had it in for me ever since I turned down an endorsement contract for TruForm, and she'll do anything to improve Renee's chances of winning."

"That's a lie!" Irene took a step forward, but Sergeant Stokes stopped her with a gesture.

At that moment Kevin walked into the room. He seemed taken aback by the tension and hostility and said nothing as he took a seat across from Annette.

Irene picked up where she had left off. "It's true, I did talk to Annette about endorsing TruForm, but I'm *glad* she turned us down. Renee is the runner we want. We don't need to sabotage you, Annette. Renee will beat you fair and square!"

"Why are you making these accusations against Irene?" Renee suddenly jumped into the argument and faced Annette. "You have no proof —you're just doing it to hurt her. I used to admire you, Annette, but now I think you're just selfish and malicious. I'm going to *enjoy* beating you tomorrow."

Annette smiled. "Talk is cheap, Renee. You're going to eat those words."

"All right, that'll do," the sergeant interrupted, raising both hands to stop the flow of accusations. "This is all very interesting, but I have some questions to ask everyone before you can go. I want you all to tell me where you were between nine last night and eight this morning. Let's start with you, Ms. Neff."

"I was in my room, working until one-thirty. Then I went to sleep. I came down for breakfast with Renee and Charles at seven-thirty."

Renee had gone to sleep early. She was up at six-thirty, did some light exercise in her room, and met Irene and her trainer in the lobby at seven-thirty. Kevin had gone home after having dinner with George and her friends, and Mellor and Annette stated that they had been in their rooms the whole night. No one had any witnesses.

Sergeant Stokes sighed. "This certainly hasn't gotten us anywhere. I'm giving you all my phone number. If any of you wants to tell me something in confidence, just call. For the moment that'll be all. Ms. Drew, stick around a second."

"We'll wait outside," Bess whispered as she and George filed out with the others. When the press room was empty, Sergeant Stokes turned to Nancy.

"I called the River Heights police and spoke to the chief there—McGinnis, I think it was," Stokes said. "He tells me you're not just a meddling busybody, that I can trust you. So I will. Do you have *anything* to add about what's going on here?"

"Nothing," Nancy answered. "Are you doing background checks on the suspects?"

The sergeant nodded. "They're in progress. I should have results today. I'll keep you informed, and I assume you'll do the same."

"You can count on it," Nancy assured him.

As soon as she rejoined her friends outside the press room, Bess grabbed her arm. "There's something we have to do right away," she said.

"What?" Nancy asked.

"We need to have breakfast—before I starve to death!"

"How was your run, George?" Bess asked that afternoon when George returned.

"Short but great," George replied. Nancy and Bess were sitting on the terrace, and George had gone out to join them. "I just wanted to run enough to keep limber, and I met up with a group of runners like me who're doing their first marathon. We're getting together later for a big carbo-loading dinner. Any news on Gina?"

Nancy shook her head. She had called the Good Samaritan Hospital, where Gina had been taken, a few times. All they could tell her was that Gina was still unconscious.

The phone rang just then, and Nancy went into the room to get it. "Are you busy?" Annette asked. "There's something I need to talk to you about."

"Sure," Nancy said. "Is something wrong?"

There was a slight pause. "Could you come downstairs and meet me in the lobby?"

Nancy agreed, but she was frowning as she hung up the phone. "Annette wants to talk to me downstairs," she told Bess and George. "She wouldn't say what it's about, but I have a feeling it's not good news."

"Maybe Bess and I should come, in case there's some kind of trouble," George suggested.

"Definitely," Bess agreed.

In the lobby Annette greeted them with a nervous smile. "Let's go outside, where we won't be overheard."

Nancy looked around. The lobby wasn't very crowded, and nobody was paying them any particular attention. But Annette appeared to be on edge, so Nancy decided to humor her. The runner was under a lot of strain, after all.

"Is something wrong?" Nancy asked as Annette led her, Bess, and George out of the Woodville and down the hotel's curved drive.

Annette nodded and said, "It's about what's been happening the last few days."

"What?" Nancy asked. Her concern grew as she noticed Annette's pale face and red-rimmed eyes.

Suddenly a squeal of tires made Nancy spin around.

A beat-up car had swung its nose toward the sidewalk just behind them. Nancy realized with a start that it was the same car that had tried to run down Annette in the park!

The passenger door flew open, and a man clothed entirely in black jumped out. His face was covered by a ski mask.

Before Nancy, her friends, or passersby on the busy street could react, the man sprinted up behind Annette and grabbed her around the throat with his left arm. With his right he twisted her arm sharply behind her back and dragged her toward the waiting car!

Chapter

Fifteen

Annette let out a scream of terror that spurred Nancy into action.

She leapt forward as the struggling pair neared the car and kicked sharply at the side of the attacker's knee. There was a muffled cry of pain from behind the ski mask, and the man dropped Annette's arm to clutch his leg.

Nancy lunged for the mask, but the assailant jumped back out of her reach. As he did so, Annette was pulled off-balance, and she fell to the ground, out of the assailant's grasp.

The masked person dived headfirst into the front seat and slammed the car door shut. Several passersby were spurred into action and headed toward the car. Before they or Nancy could get to it, the car took off down the drive and swung out into the busy downtown traffic. Even through the tinted glass, Nancy could see that the assailant was at the wheel. Then the car was gone, leaving an angry blare of horns behind it.

"That's the same car that the person who shot at us was driving," Nancy said.

"And that was definitely a man," George said.

"Yes, it was," Nancy said.

A few feet away several people were helping Annette to her feet. "How are you?" Nancy asked, going over to the runner. "Are you all right?"

"Fine, thanks to you," Annette replied. "I owe you again, Nancy."

"No problem," Nancy told her with a smile. "All part of the service."

The crowd that had formed dispersed. Suddenly Nancy noticed that Brenda Carlton was standing outside the hotel's entrance. An expensive-looking camera was hanging from the reporter's neck, and she was talking into a portable tape recorder in her hand.

"Boy, Brenda doesn't lose any time getting a story—" Nancy muttered. Then she broke off as another thought occurred to her.

"Don't go anywhere," she told Annette. "I'll be right back."

Nancy hurried over to Brenda and asked, "Did you see what just happened?"

"Naturally," Brenda said, giving Nancy a satisfied smile. "And I got great pictures, too. My editor is going to love this."

Something about the reporter's timely appearance seemed very fishy to Nancy. "Why were you out here, Brenda?" she asked.

Brenda attempted a casual shrug, but it didn't look convincing. "I just happened to be outside."

"Just happened?" Nancy repeated, crossing her arms over her chest. "Come on, Brenda, try again."

"I don't know what you're talking about," Brenda said indignantly.

"You never carry a camera—you're not a photographer. Come on, Brenda, let's have it."

Glaring at Nancy, Brenda said, "Well, so what if someone called me? I don't see what difference that makes."

Nancy resisted the urge to shake the reporter. "Tell me all about it."

"There's not much to tell," Brenda said airily. "I was in my room, and the phone rang and someone said that if I wanted a good item, I should be in front of the hotel with a camera in five minutes."

So someone *had* warned Brenda. But who? The attacker seemed like the logical person—no one else would know what was going to happen. But why would the person *want* to get publicity and risk being identified? It didn't make sense.

"The caller didn't give a name?" Nancy asked.

"Of course not," Brenda answered. "Reporters get anonymous tips like that all the time."

Ignoring Brenda's snooty attitude, Nancy asked, "You couldn't tell if it was a man or a woman?"

Brenda held up her hands. "Funny, now that I think about it, I can't say. The voice sounded whispery."

Stifling her disappointment, Nancy thanked Brenda and walked back to Annette, George, and Bess. They were still waiting on the sidewalk where the attacker had let go of Annette.

"Where's Kevin?" Annette was asking George. "I want to tell him what just happened and get it on tape fast, while it's still fresh in my mind."

At the runner's words Nancy stopped dead in her tracks. Annette didn't seem at all shaken up anymore. She actually seemed excited.

Thinking back, Nancy remembered the calm way Annette had handled just about all the threats and attacks. Suddenly things were starting to make sense.

"Kevin can wait a minute," Nancy told Annette. "Now, what was it you wanted to tell me?"

Annette stared blankly at Nancy. "Tell you?"

"That's right," Nancy said patiently. "You called me because you had something to tell me. Then you insisted we go out front where we wouldn't be overheard. Remember?"

"Oh, right—of course." Annette seemed flustered. "I guess nearly getting snatched like that scrambled my brains a little. I'm not thinking straight."

"Take your time," Nancy urged. "You said that you wanted to tell me something about what's been happening to you for the last few days."

Annette's eyes were on Nancy, but they weren't

focused. "Yes, I did. I think Renee and Irene are working together to force me out of the race."

This was nothing new—certainly nothing to drag Nancy outside for. "I see. Is there something that makes them the most likely candidates?"

"Well, yes." Annette swung around to include Bess and George in the conversation. "When those policemen were questioning us this morning, did you notice how Renee jumped up and said that she was going to *enjoy* beating me tomorrow?"

"Yes, I heard her," Nancy replied. "What about it?"

"Don't you see?" Annette fixed Nancy and her friends with an almost pleading look. "She *has* to be part of the conspiracy. She dropped that Goody Two-shoes front she likes to put on and let the *real* Renee show through."

"And that's what you couldn't say inside because someone might overhear it?" Nancy asked.

"Yes," Annette replied. She smiled triumphantly, as if she had just solved the whole case.

Actually, Annette *had* provided Nancy with an important clue, but it had nothing to do with Renee Clark. "I'll keep that in mind," Nancy told the runner. "Let's go back inside."

"What are you getting at?" George whispered to Nancy as they entered the hotel.

"Not now," Nancy whispered back. "You'll find out in a minute."

When the girls were halfway across the lobby, Derek Townsend emerged from the elevator. He hurried over to Annette, his face gray with tension. "Annette," he said, grasping both her hands. "That reporter, Brenda something, just told me what happened. This is terrible!"

"I'm fine, Derek, really I am." Annette disengaged her hands from his and smiled at him.

"Maybe you *should* withdraw from this race," the trainer said. "It's not worth your life to compete, is it?"

"That's out of the question, Derek," Annette insisted, her eyes flashing. "No conspiracy is going to force me out, and that's final. Now I'm going up to change, and then we'll go to the gym for a light workout."

Derek Townsend opened his mouth to object, but Annette had already walked away and was stepping into an open elevator.

"I don't know what to do anymore," he said, turning to Nancy, Bess, and George.

His haggard expression made Nancy realize the toll these last few days had taken on him. She felt sorry for him. She had a feeling the questions she needed to ask weren't going to help his mood any, either.

"Let's sit down and talk for a minute," Nancy suggested. She led Annette's trainer to a nook with two couches facing each other. Nancy sat next to him on one, while George and Bess settled in opposite.

"Mr. Townsend," Nancy began, "give me your honest assessment of Annette's condition. How does she stand up against the best of her rivals? This is just between us, you understand."

The trainer seemed puzzled and hesitated

slightly before answering. "I would say she is certainly still among the best there is, but a number of excellent runners have come up lately. As a result, Annette is no longer in a class by herself, which she was until recently. Renee Clark and a few others are on a par with her."

"So there's no certainty that Annette would win tomorrow, even without these distractions?" George spoke up.

Mr. Townsend shook his head. "No, not at all. It might end up being simply a question of who wants it the most."

Nancy drummed her fingers against the couch arm. "Annette must be thinking about what's next—after she stops running, I mean," she said, "we've heard she'd like to get into sports broadcasting."

Derek chuckled and shook his head. "She did want to, but I'm afraid a fiasco with 'SportsTalk' ruined her chances there."

Obviously, Annette's trainer wasn't aware that the runner might have a second chance at sportscasting.

"I suppose Annette would do about anything for a job like Kevin Davis's," Nancy went on.

"I'll say. Why—" He broke off and gave Nancy a bewildered look. "What's the point of all this?"

Leaning forward, Nancy said, "Mr. Townsend, I'm going to put your mind at ease about the danger to Annette. But I must insist that you keep what I tell you completely to yourself for now."

"Very well," he agreed.

"I'm almost certain that Annette can run tomorrow without fear of being attacked."

"Why?" he demanded. Bess and George were equally mystified.

"Because the conspiracy against Annette was organized by Annette herself!"

Chapter

Sixteen

THE TRAINER gaped at Nancy. "No!" he exclaimed. "It's simply not possible."

"That's totally bizarre," Bess whispered.

"But it *is* possible," Nancy insisted. "In fact, it should have been clear to me all along. No one has a stronger motive for harassing Annette Lang than Annette herself.

"Mr. Townsend, Annette is already finding it crowded at the top. These so-called attacks have been getting her a big dose of media exposure. Kevin says that she pressed him to put in a good word for her with the ICT execs. This is just the break she needs, only she maneuvered it herself."

The man frowned but said nothing.

"I had suspected Kevin Davis of using Annette

121

for career advancement, but it's actually the other way around." Nancy caught George's triumphant look and smiled back.

"Annette could have prepared the anonymous notes, ripped up her own gear, even attacked me in the changing booth," Nancy went on. "I thought it was odd when she asked me to join her on her trip to the store, since she'd been resisting my attempts to protect her. Now I know why she wanted me along."

"But what about Gina Giraldi?" Derek protested. "Surely Annette wouldn't let someone be seriously hurt, or even killed, for the sake of a career. She's not as cold-blooded as that!"

Nancy had been wondering about that herself. "Well, we know she's not doing all this by herself," she said, thinking out loud. "The note on the message board means she's got an accomplice. I guess it's possible that that person has gotten out of control."

"That's right," Bess put in. "Annette really *did* seem upset after finding out about Gina. That was about the only time she ever lost her cool."

Nancy nodded. "Except for when I went after that sniper," she remembered. "I thought she was worried about *me,* but what she was really worried about was that I might catch her accomplice."

"Gee," George said, shaking her head. "Who do you think the accomplice is?"

"I wish I knew, because whoever it is is a very dangerous person," Nancy replied. "I don't think it's Renee or Irene anymore. One, Annette is trying too hard to implicate them. Two, the person who 'attacked' Annette today was definitely a man."

Turning to Mr. Townsend, Nancy asked, "By the way, do you have a sample of Annette's handwriting?"

"I have a note here, actually," he replied, pulling a piece of paper from his pocket and passing it to Nancy. It was a note setting the time of that afternoon's gym workout.

Nancy looked at it and frowned. The script didn't resemble the backhanded writing of the note she had seen on the message board.

"Hey, Nan," Bess spoke up. "How did you figure out about Annette?"

"She didn't set up this so-called abduction attempt very well. She drags us outside as witnesses and calls Brenda's room to ensure press coverage. But when I ask her what she wants to tell me, she has nothing new to say."

"Astonishing," the trainer said quietly. "I'd never have thought it, but listening to you, it all fits."

"Now what?" Bess wanted to know. "Do we go to Annette and make her say who she's working with?"

"I don't think so," Nancy said. "The accomplice is already dangerous. Knowing we're on the trail might make things even more dangerous. I'd like to check a few more things first, before confronting Annette."

"Such as?" George asked.

"Let's call the hospital and check on Gina again," Nancy answered. "If she can talk, she might identify her attacker. Mr. Townsend, I know this is hard for you since you're Annette's trainer. But can you behave toward Annette as if you don't know anything of what we've been talking about?"

The man nodded. "I'll do my best."

Leaving the trainer, Nancy, George, and Bess headed across the lobby toward the phones near the elevators.

"Ms. Drew?" A clerk at the desk motioned to Nancy as the girls passed by. "A call came in for you a few minutes ago. Here's the message."

He handed her a slip of paper that said, "Call Sergeant Stokes." A number was listed beneath.

Nancy hurried over to the bank of phones, and her friends followed. She dialed the number but was told that Stokes was out. She then called the hospital. A nurse informed her that Gina was drifting in and out of consciousness and had said a few words.

Nancy relayed the news to Bess and George. "I think it's worth a shot at trying to talk to Gina."

"I'm willing," said Bess. "Let's go."

George held back. "Would you guys mind if I don't go?" she asked. "There's that early carbo-loading dinner in the restaurant tonight, and then Kevin said he has something special to give me." George's voice lowered as she said the last part, and she gave Nancy and Bess an embarrassed smile.

"No problem," Nancy told George. "Have fun!"

George offered to let them use her car, which was parked in the hotel garage, but Nancy and Bess decided to take a cab to the hospital. They got Gina's room number from the reception desk. On the third floor a nurse directed them to Gina's room.

"She might not make much sense," the nurse warned them. "It's mostly just babble."

The two girls paused just inside the door of the room. Gina's head was wrapped in bandages, and underneath her eyes were huge, ugly bruises.

Bess shook her head angrily. "Whoever did this deserves to—" She broke off as the runner's eyes fluttered open and her lips moved.

Nancy and Bess hurried over to Gina's bedside and bent over to listen.

"Monk . . ." came a faint whisper. "I know him. . . . It was monk . . ." Then she closed her eyes.

"Monk?" repeated Bess, looking at Nancy. "That nurse was right—she *is* just babbling."

"Maybe," Nancy admitted. "Anyway, it looks as if Gina is out again for now. We might as well go back to the hotel. I'll try Sergeant Stokes again. Maybe 'monk' will mean something to him."

"Not there?" Bess guessed an hour and a half later, when Nancy hung up the phone in their room.

Nancy nodded. It was the third time since returning from the hospital that she had tried to contact Sergeant Stokes. Each time she had been told he was out and couldn't be reached. "My stomach's growling," she said. "Let's go eat dinner."

Just then the door opened, and George walked

in. "Look at this!" she exclaimed, holding up the silver running shoe charm Kevin had shown Nancy the day before.

"How cute!" Bess exclaimed, examining it.

"Kevin gave it to me as a good-luck charm for the race tomorrow. *That's* why he didn't want to say where he was yesterday. He wanted to surprise me. Isn't he wonderful?"

Nancy smiled at George. "He really is," she agreed. "Hey, it's only seven-thirty. How come you're not still out with Mr. Wonderful?"

"I have to be up by six-thirty tomorrow morning," George told her. "The race starts at nine, and I should be there by seven-thirty or eight. So tonight I'm not doing anything but sleeping."

After saying good night to George, Nancy and Bess left the room and went to the Great Fire for dinner.

"I never thought I'd feel sorry for Gina," Bess said, taking a bite of her chicken crepes, "but now I do. What a terrible thing to happen."

Nancy frowned and speared a lettuce leaf with her fork. "I just hope we can make sure the same thing doesn't happen to anybody else," she said. Looking up, she noticed a familiar, curly blond head a few tables away.

"Oh, there's Jake," she said. "He doesn't seem too happy." The runner's association official was staring down at his dessert and coffee without touching them.

"Poor Jake. He's probably upset about Gina," Bess said sympathetically. "I'm going to ask him to join us."

She got up and went over to his table. A

moment later Bess returned with Jake, who was carrying his cup of espresso and his dessert plate.

"I am happy for company," he told them. "It saves me from thinking about Gina's terrible ordeal."

Nancy and Bess told him about their visit, trying to make Gina's condition sound as hopeful as possible. They didn't say anything about her mention of "monk."

Jake seemed grateful when Bess launched into a humorous story about George's many failed attempts to get her to take up running. By the end of the meal he was even laughing. When they left the restaurant and said good night, Nancy felt good about the friendship that had begun between them.

She and Bess were headed for the phones to call Sergeant Stokes again when Nancy heard Renee Clark calling her name.

"Nancy! Over here!" Renee was standing by the message board.

Nancy raised her eyebrows at Bess, and the two girls crossed the lobby to the runner.

"All set for tomorrow?" Nancy asked Renee.

"More or less," Renee said distractedly. Nancy noticed that her usual cheery attitude was gone. Actually, Renee appeared very worried.

"Have you seen Charles around anywhere? My trainer?" the runner asked.

Nancy shook her head. "Not since this morning," she answered.

Renee frowned. "We were supposed to have dinner together tonight and go over my strategy for tomorrow. But he's not anywhere around. I called his room several times, but there's no answer, and nobody has seen him since early in the day."

"Maybe he was delayed somewhere," Bess suggested.

"Well, there *was* a note from him on the board," Renee went on, "and in it he said he might be late. But it's so strange that he wouldn't have dinner with me tonight, when I have such an important race tomorrow." She pulled a folded piece of paper from her pocket.

Nancy stared at the note, stunned. It was the red-marbled notepaper!

"Can I see that for a second?" she asked.

"Sure," said Renee, handing it over.

Her pulse racing, Nancy read the brief message: "I may be a little late tonight. If I am, don't wait for me. C."

There was no mistaking that distinctive back-slanted scrawl. It was definitely the same as the handwriting in the note giving the details of the sniper shooting.

And that meant that Charles Mellor was Annette's accomplice—and that *he* had staged where the shooting should take place!

Chapter
Seventeen

RENEE, is this Mellor's regular notepaper?" Nancy asked.

Renee nodded. "It's from somewhere in Europe. Charles lived there for years, and he still has this stuff imported."

"And this is his handwriting?" Nancy pressed.

"Definitely," Renee replied without hesitation. "It's pretty distinctive, isn't it, that backward tilt? He writes left-handed, so—".

"Excuse me," Nancy said, cutting off Renee. "Bess and I have an important phone call to make."

As soon as they left Renee, Nancy told Bess what she had just discovered. "You're sure it's him?" Bess asked, her eyes wide.

129

Nancy nodded firmly. She reached for the nearest receiver when they got to the bank of telephones in the lobby. This time she got through to Sergeant Stokes.

"I have important news," said the sergeant.

"I do, too, and I suspect it fits in with yours," Nancy said over the line. "Let's hear yours first."

"Okay. The only one on your list of suspects who didn't check out squeaky clean was Charles Mellor. His fingerprints rang bells in our computers. According to Interpol, he has a criminal record under another name, Calvin Munk—M-u-n-k."

"'Monk!' Of course!" Nancy exclaimed. "Let me guess," she went on excitedly. "I'll bet Calvin Munk's criminal record has to do with professional track or distance running in Europe."

"Right you are," Stokes answered, sounding surprised. "He was banned from racing in Europe for doctoring some runner's food before a race. He knew his chemistry—he added some poisonous mushrooms to the chicken in wine sauce the guy had ordered. Made the guy sick as a dog. It was supposed to look like food poisoning."

"There's something else, too," Nancy said. She told the detective about Gina saying "Munk" at the hospital. "And Renee Clark just identified the handwriting on the note that had the time and place of the shooting in the park. Charles Munk wrote it."

Stokes made a low whistle.

"Gina and Annette have both been around for a while, and they both have run on the European circuit," Nancy went on. "Gina must have recognized Mellor as Munk from back then."

"That makes sense," the sergeant agreed. "If he thought she was going to talk to Brenda Carlton about some scandal involving him, he might have figured he had to stop her."

"That's another thing," Nancy said. "Munk is half of the conspiracy responsible for all the incidents we've been investigating."

There was a pause before Stokes said, "And I suppose you've worked out who the other half is?"

"It's Annette herself," Nancy told him. She went on to explain her theory that the whole thing was to build up Annette's TV exposure so that she would be hired as a sportscaster.

"And that's who Monk left the note for. He was telling her where to run so that he could set up the shooting. Originally I thought that the note was *for* the sniper, but it was *from* Munk to Annette."

"It *does* fit," Sergeant Stokes said slowly. "Between them they had the means, the motive, and the opportunity for everything. Munk must have been driving the car that was used in the apparent hit-and-run and the so-called abduction attempt."

"And he 'borrowed' ICT cars in all three instances, probably to throw suspicion on Kevin in case he was seen."

"The question is, what was his motive?" Stokes wondered aloud. "What did Munk gain?"

Nancy paused for a moment, thinking. "My hunch is that Annette blackmailed him into helping her. Like Gina, she must have recognized him. She would have known what he had done in Europe and she probably threatened to expose him. The problem is, he's vanished."

After a short silence, Sergeant Stokes said, "Stay put. My partner and I are on the way."

Nancy felt a sinking feeling in the pit of her stomach when the hotel's concierge let her, Bess, Sergeant Stokes, and Detective Zandt into Calvin Munk's room ten minutes later.

"He's already gotten away, hasn't he," Bess said, leaning against the wall next to the door. Empty drawers stuck out of the dresser, and the closet held nothing but some hangers.

"Looks that way," said Sergeant Stokes.

"Take a look at this," Detective Zandt called to his partner as he peered inside the top dresser drawer. He held up two brass rifle cartridges.

Sergeant Stokes examined them. "The same kind the sniper used in the park," he said. Then he went back to searching the area near the bed.

"Well, well." Sergeant Stokes pulled a pad of the marbled notepaper from the bedside table. He held it close to the bedside lamp. "Indentations on the top sheet," he observed. "Munk wrote something down and tore off the sheet."

Nancy went over and watched while he did a pencil rubbing. "A phone number," she said.

The sergeant nodded. "We'll get out an all-points bulletin on Munk," he said, "and we'll check on this number."

"He could still be planning more attacks,"

Detective Zandt said. "If Munk wants to bury his past, he'll go after Annette. That reporter—"

"Brenda Carlton," Nancy supplied.

"Right. She's another possible target. We can keep watch on her, but I don't see how we can keep an eye on Annette along the whole marathon route. We should just put her into custody right now and be done with it."

Nancy held up a hand. "The problem is that Annette's arrest will make news. When Munk hears of it, he'll go into hiding."

"But if she isn't arrested, Munk is bound to be somewhere on that marathon course tomorrow, waiting for her," Bess put in, picking up on Nancy's reasoning.

"Right," the sergeant said. "And we can't possibly cover over twenty-six miles. It would take an army."

"Munk has dropped out of sight and changed identities once before," Nancy pointed out. "If he runs for it, he may be able to do it again."

Sergeant Stokes sighed and scratched his head. "We might be able to arrange to have a police scooter trail Annette along the course. I'll check with the racing association. I'll make my final decision in the morning."

"For now we'll put a discreet guard on Annette's and Brenda's rooms," Detective Zandt added.

Checking her watch, Nancy saw that it was after ten. "Let's tell George what's been happening," she said to Bess.

They said good night to Stokes and Zandt, then

went down a flight to their room. When they opened the door, the room was dark, but Nancy saw George stir in her bed.

"I was just drifting off," George said groggily, sitting up and turning on the bedside light. "Are you guys going to sleep already?"

Bess went over and sat on the edge of her cousin's bed. "We know who Annette's accomplice is," she told George in a rush. "Charles Mellor, except his name is really Calvin Munk."

"Slow down," George urged, holding up both palms. "Charles Mellor is the other half of Annette's conspiracy? You mean, Renee Clark's trainer? What did you say his real name is?"

Nancy quickly told George about the history of Calvin Munk and that he had written the note on the message board. "Now Munk has disappeared, and the police are afraid he might try to hide the truth about his past by killing Annette tomorrow."

"In the race?" George sat bolt upright, now fully awake. "But how? Where? There'll be thousands of people watching, and television crews and everything. Annette is going to be in front of a TV camera for most of the race. He'd be crazy to try anything."

"Maybe he *is* crazy," Bess suggested.

Nancy nodded thoughtfully. "One thing's for sure. He's getting more and more out of control. What he did to Gina shows that he's no longer going to worry about hurting people."

George's eyes widened. "How can we help?"

"Right now the police are taking care of everything," Nancy assured her. "The best thing for us to do is get some sleep. One way or another, tomorrow is going to be a full day."

The phone rang before seven the next morning, rousing Nancy from an uneasy sleep. As she got up from her cot, she became aware of the shower running and saw that George's bed was empty. Bess was still sound asleep.

Nancy stumbled to the phone and picked it up. "Hello?"

"Nancy? This is Sergeant Stokes."

"What's up?" Nancy asked, instantly alert.

"No sign of Munk. That phone number in his room was a gardening supply place. A man with Munk's description bought a supply of a powerful pesticide. The active ingredient is nicotine."

"Nicotine? You mean like in tobacco?"

"Right. It's a colorless liquid alkaloid. A minute amount in a glass of water can be fatal. Munk obviously studied chemistry. The lab guys say you can distill the stuff out without sophisticated equipment."

"Oh, no," Nancy said, feeling a sense of foreboding. "Is it tasteless, too?"

"Actually, according to the lab people, it's very bitter and unpleasant."

"I can't see how he'd sneak it into anyone's food or drink, then," Nancy mused aloud.

"Me, neither. Have you come up with any brilliant ideas on how we can grab Munk?"

"I'm afraid not," Nancy said glumly.

Sergeant Stokes was silent for a moment. "Neither have we," he said. "We're going to let Annette run. Our only hope is to draw him out that way."

"What's the plan?" Nancy asked.

"Zandt and I are going to be just behind the starting area by eight. That's where to find us, if you need us. We've got all the officers we can to work the marathon. They'll be strung along the course, in radio contact with us. And we've got a guy on a scooter, but I'm not sure how much good he'll be able to do. We've got strict orders from the runners association not to interfere with the top runners' progress."

After thanking the sergeant, Nancy hung up. She quickly dressed in jeans and a shirt.

"Breakfast time," George announced brightly, emerging from the bathroom. She was wrapped in one of the hotel's huge, fluffy bath towels and was drying her hair with another.

Nancy gave her Stokes's news. "I don't get it. What will Munk do with nicotine?" George asked.

Nancy shrugged. "Maybe try to poison Annette with it, though I have no idea how," she admitted.

"Ugh!" said George, shivering. "I'm glad the cops are going to be protecting her." Patting her stomach, she said, "I'm going to burn a lot of fuel today. I need breakfast. I can be ready in five minutes. What about you guys?"

"I'll be ready," Nancy said. "But I don't know about Bess." As Nancy headed into the bathroom, she called loudly, "Bess! Wake up!"

"Mmmph," muttered Bess, opening one eye.

"I heard, I heard. I'll meet you in the coffee shop in about twenty minutes, okay?"

"Okay, but get a move on," said George, who was putting on silky blue shorts and her Heartland Marathon T-shirt with her race number, 6592, pinned to it.

A few minutes later George and Nancy were sitting in the coffee shop. They ordered, and as soon as their breakfast was served, George dug into her huge plate of pancakes with gusto.

"You need carbohydrates when you're going to be burning energy at the rate I will be today."

"I know, I know," Nancy said, laughing. "You've told us often enough." Nancy did not feel hungry, though, and barely touched her bacon and eggs. Through the coffee shop's glass wall, she watched the buzzing activity in the lobby.

"Who are all those people?" she asked George, pointing to a large group, all of whom were wearing orange Day-Glo vests with H_2O marked on the backs in big block letters.

"They're the volunteers who'll be manning the water stations," George explained. "The stations are at intervals along the course. The volunteers hand out water and sports drinks as we go by. You get pretty dehydrated, you know."

"I'll bet," Nancy said. "Running twenty-six miles must—" She broke off and stared into the lobby. "George, look."

A middle-aged man had just staggered in through the front door, bleeding from a gash on his forehead. He was quickly helped to a chair by a couple of the volunteers.

"Come on," Nancy said, getting up from the table. "I want to see what this is about."

"He just sprang at me," the man was saying when Nancy and George reached him. "Hit me with a tire iron, yanked off my vest, and ran."

"You mean the H_2O vest?" Nancy asked.

The man nodded just as the hotel's doctor arrived. Nancy stepped back to give the doctor room.

"George, that's it!" Nancy said excitedly, grabbing George's arm. "Munk is going to be at one of those stations with his own supply of doctored water. That's how he'll try to poison Annette!"

George stared at her in horror.

"The worst thing is," Nancy went on grimly, "there are dozens of stations. We don't have a clue as to which one he'll be at!"

Chapter

Eighteen

"THIS IS AWFUL!" George exclaimed. "What can we do?"

"I'm not sure," said Nancy. "Let's finish breakfast and talk."

Back at the table George stared glumly down at her stack of cold pancakes.

"How do the water stations work?" Nancy asked.

"They have cups on a table, and the volunteers fill them from big containers. Then they hold the cups out to runners as they go by." George shot Nancy a worried glance. "You think Munk will try to slip Annette a cup of bad water?"

"Probably," Nancy replied. "She'll be concentrating on the race. There's a good chance she'll grab the water without looking at him."

"Hi, guys!" Bess said brightly. She sat down at the table and opened a menu. "Any news on Munk?" When Nancy explained about the nicotine, Bess looked appalled.

"I was wondering how anyone would drink the stuff if it tastes so bad," Nancy went on. "But when you're dehydrated, you'd gulp it down before you realized what it was. By then it's too late."

George jumped up from the table. "We'd better tell the police what's going on, right now!"

The starting area at Daley Plaza was total bedlam when the charter bus from the hotel let off Nancy, Bess, George, and dozens of other runners. Runners swarmed all over, doing stretches, jogging in place, and finding their starting positions behind the red ribbon strung across a street bordering the plaza.

"The top runners have their own starting point a few blocks away," George explained. "That way their start isn't hampered by the pack—that's regular runners like me."

"I hope the police already have a man with Annette," Nancy said. "Oh—there they are." She pointed to a patrol car parked about fifty yards away. Sergeant Stokes and Detective Zandt were standing next to it.

"I'd better join the runners," George said, bouncing up and down on the balls of her feet. Nancy could see that despite the danger, George was really excited about this marathon.

"Good luck," she said, hugging George. "I know you'll do great. And look at the volunteers before you drink any water—and take just a tiny taste first. Then spit it out if it tastes bad!"

"I will. I hope you find Munk before anyone else gets hurt," George said.

Bess suddenly grinned, pointing over George's shoulder. "Look who's here!" she said.

Kevin Davis, wearing a maroon ICT blazer, was making his way through the crowd toward them. Behind him, near the starting line, Nancy saw an ICT van with a cameraman perched on top, getting shots of the vast sea of runners.

George's eyes sparkled as she turned and saw Kevin. "Hi!" she said.

"I can't stay," Kevin said, fingering the silver charm around George's neck. "See you at the finish line, George," he said, gently squeezing her shoulder. "Good luck."

As George went off to join the growing mob of entrants, an idea suddenly occurred to Nancy. Turning to Kevin, she said, "I need your help."

"Now? I'm pretty busy, Nancy. Can't it wait?"

"This is a matter of life and death," Nancy replied. "I mean that literally."

Kevin frowned, but he let Nancy lead him over to Sergeant Stokes and Detective Zandt.

"We found out something that might help find him," Nancy said. She told the officers about the man they suspected was Munk stealing a Day-Glo vest from a water volunteer.

Detective Zandt listened while leaning against the door of the police car. "Let's have the men pay special attention to those water stations," he told his partner.

Sergeant Stokes nodded and gave orders on the squad car radio.

"How can *I* help?" Kevin asked.

"You'll be following the lead runners, right?" Nancy asked. When he nodded, she said, "I want to ride with your van, along with Sergeant Stokes or Detective Zandt. That way we can grab Munk when he makes his move."

Kevin looked dubious. "I don't know. We're crowded as it is," he explained. "There's the cameraman, a sound man, and the driver and me, plus racks of gear . . ."

His voice trailed off as he saw the determined expression on Nancy's face. "Oh, all right," he relented. "I guess I can fit you in."

"Good," Stokes said. "I'll stay here, since this is our central communications base. Zandt, you and Nancy and her friend go with the ICT van. Take a radio and stay in touch."

"Let's go," the detective said.

Nancy, Bess, and the detective followed as Kevin sprinted toward his van, dodging through the crowd. Within five minutes they were all set up. Kevin and his crew manned the van's rooftop camera, and Zandt, Nancy, and Bess sat below. At the detective's request the van's rear doors were tied open, so they would have the clearest view possible of the runners and the water stations.

"I don't think Munk will make a move until the middle of the race," said Nancy as they drove to the other starting line. "He'd want to catch

Annette when she's likely to be tired and dehydrated and really in need of that drink."

The detective nodded, his eyes on the runners. "I hope we'll be able to keep track of Annette in this crowd."

Following his gaze, Nancy spotted Annette and Renee in the prime spots at the starting line. Dozens of runners stood crowded together behind them. "They won't stay all jammed together for long," Nancy said. "They'll thin out."

A voice over a loudspeaker said, "The Heartland Marathon will begin in one minute."

There was electricity in the air. Runners and technicians stood waiting. "Take your marks," said the amplified voice. "Get set . . ."

The sound of the starter's gun made Nancy jump. The next thing she knew, the top runners were setting off. The van moved forward at roughly the runners' pace, and Nancy, Bess, and Detective Zandt craned their necks to keep Annette in view. Above them the cameraman was getting panoramic shots of the runners as they jockeyed for position. Kevin was speaking into a microphone.

As Nancy had predicted, it wasn't long before some runners moved ahead. Annette established herself as the front runner, slightly ahead of Renee. The crowds lining the route cheered the runners as they passed.

As the van reached the first water station, Nancy tried to focus on each volunteer in turn. There was no sign of Munk. At each succeeding station she felt more tense, wondering, Could this be the one?

At the twelve-mile mark they hadn't seen Munk yet. They passed the halfway mark at just over thirteen miles. Still nothing.

"We've been at this for over an hour," Bess said, her eyes scouring the crowds lining the course.

"Water station up ahead on our right," Detective Zandt called.

Nancy watched closely. The large folding table held many cups and was manned by a dozen or so volunteers. The van was ten yards ahead of Annette when Nancy saw a volunteer with longish dark hair edge forward with two paper cups in his hand. She stared to make absolutely certain . . .

"It's him!" she said, keeping her voice down so that Munk wouldn't hear. "In front of the table!"

At a word from Detective Zandt the van slowed to a crawl, and he, Nancy, and Bess jumped out. "Stokes? We have him spotted," Detective Zandt said into his radio as he went. He quickly gave the location.

Nancy hit the ground running and dashed toward Munk. She was ten yards away when he saw her. For an instant his eyes locked with hers. Then he whirled and started to sprint away.

Nancy was on him before he could get up any speed. She launched herself forward, slamming her shoulder into his legs, and he crumpled forward. Before he could get up, Detective Zandt had pinioned Munk's hands behind his back and put handcuffs on him. He jerked the man roughly to his feet.

"Are you crazy?" Munk shouted. "I'm a volunteer here!"

"It's all over," Nancy told him. "We know everything . . . Mr. Munk. When Gina Giraldi recovers, she'll be able to put you away for a long time."

Calvin Munk paled, and his jaw muscles clenched. "I should have killed her when I had the chance!" he spat out. "And Annette—she deserves to die! She ruined my life! She remembered me . . . the scandal. She threatened to go public—"

"Don't worry," Bess cut in. "Annette will pay for what she did, too."

While the detective read Munk his rights, two squad cars pulled up on a side road, sirens wailing.

"Why did you attack Gina Giraldi?" Nancy asked as two uniformed officers came to take Calvin Munk away. "Did she recognize you, too?"

The man nodded. "I think so. I recognized *her,* from Europe. When I heard that reporter say that Gina would expose someone connected with the marathon, I couldn't take the chance that it was me. I had to shut her up first."

"You were the one who tried to drop that huge pot on our heads!" Bess accused.

Munk glared at her. "You were stupid not to get the message and back off." He was still ranting angrily when the patrolmen led him to their car.

"Come on," Detective Zandt said, heading for the other squad car.

"Where are we going?" Nancy asked.

"To the finish line," he replied. "You want to

145

be there when we collar Annette Lang, don't you?"

The finish line was in Grant Park, under a decorative archway. A digital clock on top of the arch ticked off the time elapsed since the start of the race. It read 2:18. Reporters, photographers, and fans were waiting for the lead runners to appear.

Nancy noticed Irene Neff pacing nervously near the red tape. She went over to the woman and told her about Calvin Munk. Irene's jaw dropped in amazement.

"Renee will be upset," she said. "Charles helped to make her what she is."

Nancy returned to where Bess, Detective Zandt, and Sergeant Stokes were standing, just beyond the reporters at the finish line.

"The lead runners will be here in about fifteen minutes," Sergeant Stokes informed them. "Last we heard, Renee Clark and Annette Lang were neck and neck."

"I wonder how George is doing?" said Bess.

"She won't finish for at least an hour after the winner," Nancy said.

Soon she heard a burst of cheering and applause, then more cheering, even closer. As the cheering grew still louder, she saw Renee Clark sprint to the tape. She looked tired and winded, but her face was lit up in a winner's smile. Behind her by a hundred yards was Annette Lang, running as hard as she could.

Irene Neff rushed up to Renee, and the two

hugged. Nancy heard Renee ask, "Where's Charles?"

"He couldn't be here," said Irene. "I'll explain after you meet the press." Renee's beaming grin faded to a look of puzzled concern, but she let herself be led to the circle of reporters.

As Annette crossed the finish line, cameras flashed, and there was more cheering. The detectives waited until she had caught her breath, then approached her.

"We'd like to talk to you, Ms. Lang," said Sergeant Stokes.

"Now? Why?" Annette asked, taken aback. "It'll have to wait—I'll be with the press for a while."

"Do you want your arrest filmed for the evening news?" Stokes asked.

Annette gave a short, sharp laugh. "My *arrest?* I'm the victim here, remember?"

"Annette, I found out who was responsible for the threats against you," Nancy said, meeting Annette's glare. "I found out that it was you."

"Calvin Munk is under arrest," Sergeant Stokes added. "He's talking to my men now."

When Annette didn't say anything, Nancy said, "That's a nasty bruise on your shin. That must be from when I kicked you, after you attacked me at the Winning Margin."

Annette gave a long sigh, "You could never understand," she said. "After all this time in the spotlight, I couldn't see myself becoming a has-been, tomorrow's trivia. I figured if I could get a shot at TV work, I'd still be a somebody."

"How did you connect Munk and Mellor?" Nancy wanted to know.

"His handwriting," Annette said. "He looks a lot different now from the way he did then—new hair color, clean-shaven, thinner—everything. But once I saw his writing, I saw through the rest. I knew it was him."

Annette smiled, as if she were proud of her treachery. "He once sent me a note of congratulations for a race I won in France. The day we got here, I saw him pin a note to Renee on the message board, and I recognized the writing— it's very distinctive. I already had the plan, but I needed someone to help me, and I put the pressure on him. But I had nothing to do with Gina!" she exclaimed. "That was his doing!"

"You still have plenty to answer for," Sergeant Stokes said, leading her to a police car. He stopped and turned to Nancy.

"I have to hand it to you. You'd make a fine police officer."

Nancy blushed and murmured her thanks. The police drove away with Annette, but Nancy and Bess waited for George near the huge digital clock. Kevin joined them a while later.

More and more runners were coming across the finish line. A few collapsed and were helped up by volunteers and taken to first-aid stations.

"There she is!" Bess screamed, pointing down the course. It was George, looking more elated than tired. At the finish line she looked up at the clock, and her face lit up.

Bess rushed over and flung her arms around her. "Three hours, forty-seven minutes! A personal record!" George gasped, returning Bess's hug and then doing the same with Nancy. "Munk," she said, "is he—"

"In custody. Annette, too," Nancy assured her.

"Hi," said Kevin, giving George a big hug. "Good work. I was thinking of making a trip to River Heights—maybe in a week," Kevin went on. "How does that sound?"

"It sounds perfect," George told him, grinning. "I can't wait!"

Kevin turned to Bess. "Listen, I have a friend I think you'd like to meet. Want me to call him tonight? We can all go out to dinner together."

Bess's blue eyes shone for a second. Then she got a suspicious look on her face.

"What does he do?"

"He's a runner, middle-distance events—"

"No, thanks," Bess said, cutting him off. "I'll pass."

"But why?" Kevin asked, perplexed.

"I've sworn off runners," she said. "They all have one-track minds—and the only thing on them is track!"